MW00686036

FULL TIDE *of* NIGHT

FULL
TIDE
of NIGHT

J. R. DUNN

AVON • EOS

This is a work of fiction. Names, characters, places and incidents either are the product of the author's imagination or are used fictitiously. Any resemblance to actual events, locales, organizations, or persons, living or dead, is entirely coincidental and beyond the intent of either the author or the publisher.

AVON BOOKS, INC.
1350 Avenue of the Americas
New York, New York 10019

Copyright © 1998 by J. R. Dunn
Interior design by Kellan Peck
Visit our website at **http://www.AvonBooks.com/Eos**
ISBN: 0-380-97434-7

Library of Congress Cataloging in Publication Data:
Dunn, J. R.
    Full tide of night / J.R. Dunn.—1st ed.
        p.   cm.
    I. Title.
PS3554.U46996F85   1998   98-11356
813'.54—dc21   CIP

First Avon Eos Printing: August 1998

AVON EOS TRADEMARK REG. U.S. PAT. OFF. AND IN OTHER COUNTRIES, MARCA REGISTRADA, HECHO EN U.S.A.

Printed in the U.S.A.

FIRST EDITION

QPM   10   9   8   7   6   5   4   3   2   1

To PRB

                    so we
Are forc'd to express our violent passions
In riddles and dreams, and leave the
path
Of simple virtue, which was never made
To seem the thing it is not.

                              —John Webster

one

They were waiting when she stepped out into the morning. Much as she should have expected it, she noticed nothing while descending the long flight of stairs to the plaza, intent on the hills to the north, from where the rebels would come. She didn't spot Milis until she passed through the gate and he advanced on her, stunner in hand. But she was less than startled all the same; it had been many years since Julia Amalfi had been surprised by anything.

In the end, she didn't even need to call out. Milis halted three steps away, his eyes met hers, and that was all it took: his gaze twitched elsewhere, his mouth grimaced open, the stunner dipped toward the slate of the plaza. She wished it could have been as easy with Cary, with the rebels.

"No, Jan," she said in a low voice, audible to them alone. The two men with Milis—boys, really: Kenin, the center's Gramineae man, and a grad student she'd seen bouncing a ball around the place—stood in poses radiating uncertainty, Kenin's hands resting on his hips while he stared off at the hills, the ball-player closely examining the toe of his boot as it rubbed invisible lines on the slate.

Julia crossed her arms. "You're supposed to have gone, Jan. You promised me."

Guilt and confusion flashed across his features as the stunner fell for good. Milis was one of the more Asian-looking of her people, though she couldn't recall what his exact line was. Round-faced, the gengineered layers of fat on his face made him look much younger than his years, the folds at his eyelids quite pronounced. Back on Earth he'd have been taken for a Mongolian . . . or was it Manchurian? She couldn't recall the difference, or even if there was a difference. She wished she could ask Cary. Cary would know.

"So what was the idea, Jan? Tickle the old bitch and then what? Throw her on the back of a mule? No . . . a wagon, I suppose, I hope."

He answered with silence. She took in his canvas pants, leather vest, and heavy boots, more suitable to a prospector than the director of Midgard's Gaia-forming center. A pistol—the kind called a revolver—was slung low around his hips. She wondered if he knew how to use it. Milis had always been an indoors kind of man.

"Jan—look at me."

His face spasmed as the tears burst forth. The stunner clattered on the slate, his hands rose to cover his face. She stepped toward him, waving away the other two. Visibly relieved, they wandered off.

She'd forgotten, perhaps, what she represented to this man. He'd grown up in Myra, the village past the far end of the plaza that she'd named for her mother. She had been the one constant in his life, the only thing that had never changed. Parents might die, the wife divorce and leave—for she had demanded much of him, both in time and effort, as she did from all her people—but the Lady, the Dame of Midgard, remained. Always present, unaltered by years and decades. What that might mean to Milis she could no longer guess. She had stopped feeling anything that intensely decades ago.

She soothed him, one hand on his shoulder, the other stroking his hair as she might have done when he'd been small—she couldn't recall whether she ever actually had. The story came in short bursts as his sobbing subsided. He'd accessed the historical files for "revolution," to be confronted with images of guillotines, of barbed wire and guns and skulls piled high. The Soviets, the Khmer Rouge, the Jacobins—he called them "Yacobites" for some reason—all that in addition to what he already knew of the Erinye and the Rigorists. And he was being asked to leave the Lady, his Lady, behind to face that.

She wished she'd never mentioned it, that there was a name for what was happening up on the Northern Tier, that similar things had occurred back on Earth, that records existed of these events. The rebels here were no Jacobins, neither killers nor maniacs. They were led by Danil Cardnale, a man Milis knew, much as he might dislike him. Arrogant though he might be, Cardnale was no Rigorist. As if there had been such a thing as a Rigorist on Midgard for thirty years.

She wasn't certain how much of it penetrated, though Milis did calm down. "You know why you're leading this last group, don't you, Jan?"

He swallowed and bobbed his head. "Vicki."

She winced at the name, the last thing she wanted mentioned. "Yes. And why did I choose you? Because you wouldn't let me down. You never have. And you won't let me down now, will you?"

"No, Lady." It was no more than a whisper.

"I knew that. Now, first you'll get to the Crossing,

where you'll meet Murad and his men. He'll escort you to the Shore. And then . . ." She went over it all: route, schedule, contact procedures, making him repeat it after her. She'd gotten as far as how she'd keep in touch through the station at Belmar when one of the waiting boys shouted.

They were gazing north, their stances all intensity, hands gripping the wall as if to pry it apart stone by stone. Catching her breath, she swung slowly around, scanning the length of her own home valley, the buildings she'd erected, the great oak she'd planted with her own hands, to the northern hills, sere brown under a sky both darker and clearer than the one she'd grown up under.

A tiny black patch marred the slope, changing shape as it flowed toward the bottom. Another, this one smaller, appeared at the crest. Too distant for details—she'd once had implants that could have magnified them, but she'd shut those down long ago. Today she didn't need mods; those were horsemen. There was nothing else they could be.

She turned back to Milis. "That's it, Jan. You've got half an hour—"

Milis wasn't listening. Wide-eyed, he stared over her shoulder, lips twisted, head shaking. At last his gaze met hers. "*Lady—*"

At her feet lay the stunner. Bending down, she retrieved it and handed it to him. She crossed her arms and took a single step back. "All right, Jan."

He glanced at the stunner almost fearfully, as if uncertain of its function. Eyes lowered, he aimed it at her. She shifted her stance slightly.

With a wordless cry he flung the weapon away and ran toward the waiting boys. Kenin said something as he passed but got no answer. The boys both turned to look at her. She waved them off. They followed Milis, glancing back every few steps.

The hills were bare once again, as if no riders had

ever crossed them. A plume of smoke curled skyward off to the west. She wondered what that was
about.

Sounds from the stables pursued her as she walked
across the plaza: soft voices, the bray of a donkey,
the clatter of hooves. She tried to ignore them but
found herself detouring in that direction all the same.
Finally she turned abruptly and marched toward that
section of wall.

There they were, the last small group still not evacuated: Milis's team, the few remaining housekeepers,
the grad students that Jan had insisted be drafted
into the police as her bodyguard. They'd finished
loading the animals. She winced as a man kneed a
donkey in the belly in order to tighten a strap. The
animal brayed, more at the indignity than in hurt.

A slight shiver went through her as she caught
sight of a small figure in a wagon and recognized
the braid of blonde hair protruding from the scarf
over the child's head. The girl was as susceptible to
cold as Julia herself. She spoke the name aloud, as
Milis had: "Vicki."

The tiny face swung toward her, as if she'd heard.
Julia stepped back, afraid of being seen. The child
had been very upset about leaving the Cloister. She'd
enjoyed herself so the past week; running wild, asking questions, poking into things. Julia hadn't regretted bringing her here. She didn't regret it now, much
as her own lack of emotion reminded her of how old
she'd grown, how little she truly cared for anything
living. Even this small part of her. But it wasn't as if
the girl was really hers, now was it?

She stood with her gaze fixed on the smoke until
wheels began to creak. When she looked at last, the
wagons were gone, headed for the docks and the
barges that would carry them south. All she saw
were the men bringing up the rear. One turned back

and waved. It might have been Milis, but she couldn't be sure.

Five years, she thought. Another five years and she'd have avoided all this. A half a decade and the rebels would have been stymied.

Head down, she left the wall behind and walked to a stone cube rising from the slate. Shivering from the touch of cold stone, she sat down upon it, truly alone now, more alone than she'd been for all those years since she'd realized that Petro was not coming—or that what came would not be Petro any longer—and that she would have to face the long dark passage from Sol on her own. More alone even than that: at least she'd had Cary then.

A man named Livy had once written about a situation similar to this. According to his account, the Gothic invasion had caught the Romans unprepared, with less room available in the citadel that was needed for the city's entire population. So the senators, as the men responsible, remained outside. And when the Goths entered Rome, they found the entire senate seated in front of their homes, dressed in their robes of office, silent and unmoving, like statues.

But the Cloister wasn't Rome, and her people were not barbarians, and Julia Amalfi, whatever else she might be, wasn't exactly a senator either.

She ran her gaze across the valley, the core of her little empire. The buildings of the Academy, labs, hospital, the domed, antenna-laden structure that was Cariola's home. It looked nothing like the way she'd pictured when she'd first selected the site, this small, open valley facing north, ten miles from the spot where the first shuttles had landed. It was more crowded than she'd planned—particularly the center; the labs and greenhouses had just sprawled. The older buildings, the ones she'd been so proud of, were beginning to look squalid with age. Nevertheless, it was hers. The Cloister, she called it, after a place that had struck her fancy once, in a faraway city that might no longer exist. It resembled the original not at all, but to her, at least, it called up the same feeling: a quiet place, a serious place.

She often wondered what the kids—she still thought of them as kids, even after four full generations—made of the Cloister. What it meant to them, what status it held in their dreams, their waking thoughts. She knew they didn't look at it the way she did. They ought to. It was their First Place, after all. There was no such place on Earth; there had never really been an Eden. If there was one thing Julia Amalfi knew to be true, it was that.

A sharp breeze stirred the branches of the live oak at the plaza's entryway. Budding now, as it had nearly a hundred times before. Not the first tree on Midgard but her own. She thought of it simply as "the tree," and as long as it stood, things would be fine. So despite everything, all that was at stake, all that she was losing, she allowed herself a smile.

A sound from the direction of the village caught her attention. She shot a glance at the hills. She'd lost track of time; it seemed hours since she'd seen the rebels—how she hated that word!—descending the hillside. They could be in the valley already, be watching now from the village.

Calmly she pulled at her robe, making sure it fell straight. If they were watching, they should see her at her best, not as the woman who had drifted so in the past decades, lost in the fog of days, memories stretched too far, emotions faded from too much use, filling the long haze of passing time with thoughts of the past, of what once was and what might have been, both here and back in the Home System. Somehow Petro was always there, even at places and events where he hadn't actually been present at all. Along with memories of him walking the streets of Manhattan, and Odessa, and Haifa—those hooded eyes, the hands always in the tunic pockets, the long, easy stride of the Slav, the cockiness of the man of the borderlands—there were images of him in the very hills to the north here, on the crumbling cliffs of the Weather Shore, even in the command center of the ship itself. Places he'd never been but should have, as if her mind was revising the story, giving herself an alternate life. And Petro too; the life he'd earned, he who had done so much and served so fully. Oh, there would never have been a revolution if Petro had lived . . .

. . . and here she was, doing it again. Daydreaming, as she'd done over the past six weeks while it became clear that it wasn't simply a disturbance up north, not even a revolt, but a full-blooded uprising. Unable to face the fact that her children had turned on her at last, sick and tired of the old biddy, the shadow at the Cloister, the dim and distant figure giving out orders and issuing demands.

The sound repeated itself. She got to her feet. A shout, the neigh of a horse? She couldn't be sure. Her throat was dry, her heart seemed to flutter. With all that she'd seen, she should be facing this more steadily.

"They've just now reached Myra, ma'am. It'll be a few minutes."

Julia was about to answer when a chthulu appeared from beyond the oak, wings whirring wildly and tendrils trailing behind. Making a lazy S over the plaza, it seemed to start in midair as it caught sight of her.

Julia sat back down. She hadn't realized that Cary could project her voice across the plaza, but she was less than surprised. There were a lot of things she hadn't known about Cary, her comrade, her shipmate, her oldest and dearest. "So it's 'ma'am' now, Cary? Not Jay or Julia anymore?"

There was no answer. The chthulu had perched

on the opposite wall and was grooming its wings, a miniature gargoyle far more grotesque than any carved by men. She hadn't seen one in a long time. There were tales about them deliberately entangling those long tendrils with people's hair. In fact, they tended to avoid Terrest life, due to an aversion for alien proteins, she'd been told, though another school claimed them to be considerably more intelligent than their size indicated. It noticed her watching and the part that served as a mouth unfolded, giving her a blast of sound that she'd never have expected from any living creature. They didn't have much use for humans. She supposed she wouldn't either, if she was hunted for pulling hair out of people's heads while they slept. She dropped her head. "Cary?"

The AI remained silent. Julia wasn't surprised. This was the first time the comp had said a single word in nearly two months. One last tantrum—over utter trivia: the rice strain under consideration for next year's planting at the Shore—and then silence. Apart from standard processing, Cary cut herself off completely. Julia took it for another fit of the sulks— she'd had plenty of experience with that—until the north blew up a week later. That had been a bit too strong a coincidence. "Cary, we need to talk."

"*No*—" The response was instant. "You need to listen."

"All right. I'm listening."

The seconds dragged on. Julia glanced at the roofs of the village, just visible through the trees. No activity was evident.

"It'll wait." The AI's voice was spiteful, as only that of a machine with access to all variations of human expression could be. "Once the committee gets here, you'll have plenty of spare time, Jay."

"So you *are* involved with these people. I thought as much. Tell me, is Danny Cardnale with this group?"

"In the village? I don't think so."

"You don't *think* so?" Julia frowned. "You don't know? You aren't in contact with them?"

Cary was silent, and for a moment Julia was afraid she'd pushed too hard. Then the AI answered. "Things are a bit unsettled."

" 'Unsettled'?" Julia didn't like the sound of that at all. "What does that mean, 'unsettled'?"

"You've got that *look* on your face again!" Cary's voice rose to a shriek. "Oh, how I hate that . . . You don't know how much I hate it."

Julia wondered what look that could be. "I'm sorry, Cary."

"You know, Jay, it's really none of your business at this stage." The voice rasped with distortion. She was playing with it, selecting the tones that most annoyed Julia. "You always talked about 'passing the torch.' Well, that's what's happening today. We're passing the torch, the way you always said you would. I think I'll record it, so you can watch the torch being passed anytime you want . . ."

"I wish you could hear yourself."

Julia regretted the words immediately, but Cary paid no attention. "Why did you stay, Jay? That I don't understand. I'd think it would be embarrassing for you, vain as you are . . ."

"To stop it," Julia said.

The machine fell silent. Julia guessed that she was confused. For all her bluster, large areas of human nature were still mysteries to Cariola. Artificial intelligences often remained immature for a century or more after activation. Computers lacked instinct and the sociobiological cues implanted by eons of evolution, making their development a thorny process. Many never matured at all. Cariola was further handicapped by the absence of older AIs to render guidance and support.

" 'Stop it'? What do *you* mean, Jay?"

"To bring an end to it, Cary. Before it spirals out of control, before it does get 'unsettled,' the way poor Jan was afraid of. The thrust of these affairs is *symbolic*. That's why the rebels are headed here. Because this place is a symbol—once they take it, everything else falls. That's why the Cloister is important. Not the labs, not the hospital, not even you, dear. And what's the other icon, Cary? What else possesses the most mana on Midgard? Yes—Ma, the Old Lady herself. If I fled this place, they'd pursue. They'd have no choice. As long as I'm out and around, their victory is incomplete, and they know it. So that's why I stayed. I'll meet Danny and his little committee and that boy general of his right here. I have no choice either."

"Well," the AI said, calmer now, "I thought you had something up your sleeve. I really did. But you don't, do you? That's not like you, Jay."

"No, I don't have anything planned. How could I, without you knowing? Just the fact that Danny will have to turn to me. He can't run this rockball on his own. He's an idealist, a dreamer. He doesn't have experience, or even much ability. He can't make it work, not even with you, Cary. He'll have to turn to me eventually. There's nobody else."

"No, he won't."

"Cary, let's not argue. You'll see—"

"There is somebody. There will be. When the ship gets here."

Julia caught her breath, let it out as a chuckle. "Stop it, Cary."

The AI's voice became precise. "I have been in contact with Earth—specifically, the Home System itself, through the Kuiper 3 Ultra Large Array—for thirty-five years and two months, beginning on 4 December, year 85 Middie. Message content was restricted by relativistic limitations, but a number of data points were established, revealing large discrepancies

with information previously provided by Julia
Amalfi. Kuiper 3 suggested contact be initiated with
Corpus Christi, then on a reconciliation mission to Ep-
silon Eridani. Nineteen years of discussion confirmed
new data, exposing Julia Amalfi, self-styled Dame of
Midgard, as a compulsive liar. *Corpus Christi* altered
course seventeen years ago and is now entering the
Epsilon Indi system . . ."

Julia relaxed. That last line had been too much—who
had ever heard of a starship changing course in mid-
geodesic? "Cary, please. You're trying to frighten me."

"Then be fearful, missy." Another voice replaced
hers, one that Julia had never heard before. "No,
Cary. I would disagree that the Erinye—the Shamans,
the Lloigor; we call them the Apostates—were ever
actually in control. Of course, terms require sharpen-
ing, and perspective may have varied within the
event . . ."

"Who is that?"

"Augustin St. John, magister of the *Corpus Christi*."

"Who?" Julia's unease deepened. Cariola was
doing her best to provoke, granted, and fabricating
a voice was well within her capabilities. But this was
pushing the limits even for Cary, and her own
voice . . . She was no longer playing games with it.
That was one of the few ways of telling she was
serious. "Cary—"

"You *lied* to me, Jay. About the Erinye, the Home
System, everything."

On her feet, Julia inspected the sky. She saw nothing apart from a mirrorsat, low on the horizon. Not
even *Petrel* was in sight.

"You won't spot *Christi*, Jay. It's entering from
Scorpio, behind Indi. You'll see it when it gets here."

Unease blossomed into horror. Cary was telling the
truth. She had been in touch with Earth, accepting
data from whatever the Erinye had metastasized into,
whatever had replaced humanity. Julia stood fixated

by the cold indigo sky, as if awaiting the tendrils of
that tumor to appear from across all the light-years
at last.

". . . humans lie. That's the difference between
Homo and Silico sapiens. Humans always lie, computers never. Ask a question, and if it lies, it's car-
bon-based. Even a billion years from now, you'll be
able to tell—"

An image of Petro arose, her last glimpse, the moment she'd realized he was ridden, that he wasn't
actually Petro anymore. "Cary . . . Self-test. Now.
Look for overwrites, viroids, unlabeled files . . ."

"Negative, Lady. There's nothing. I'm not stupid.
I partitioned and analyzed every message before processing. Besides, they didn't have the bandwidth for
anything fancy."

"Then activate the defense sequence." *Petrel*'s drive
still held several kilograms of antimatter. It could be
loaded into the shuttles or otherwise fired at anything attempting orbital insertion. A final throw of
the dice . . . No, not quite final; the last measure was
embodied in Julia herself.

"No, Jay. It's over. Time to wake up. Or maybe
you don't know you're lying. Cognitive dissonance,
inability to reconcile thoughts with reality—that
would explain a lot."

"I never lied to you, Cary. You remember what
went on back home."

"I remember what you *told* me. When you boarded
the *Petrel*, you ordered me to drop off the net, to
answer no queries, and to navigate by Doppler from
stationary signals."

"How do you explain the destruction, the maydays, the chaos—"

"I don't have to explain anything."

A sharp blast rang out from the village. The
chthulu paused in its grooming to glare in that direction. It knew what a gun was.

"What are they shooting at?"

"A dog. They're nervous, I suppose."

A sudden inspiration struck Julia. "Cary—download me these discussions you had with . . . St. John, is it? Please."

"Why? You'll meet him soon enough. Talk all you want then. I don't . . ." The AI's voice faded, then returned at much lower volume. "Jay . . . maybe you'd better go back to the house."

"Why?"

"Some of the rebels are wearing black."

It took a second for Julia to absorb that. Black meant Rigorists: that was their uniform, their livery. To this day people from certain sections of Midgard, of a particular age, refused to wear an item of black for any reason whatsoever. But the Rigorists had been wiped out long ago, and Gar and Fredrix and Wolf were dead. "Cary—your remotes, up on the Tier. What are they telling you?"

"They're down, Jay. Cardnale told me to shut them off, and they . . . never came online again."

"Oh, Cary . . ." A clop of hooves sounded from among the lab buildings. She glanced at the house, irrelevantly wondering if they'd let her stay there. It wasn't much; what had once been called a ranch. But it was far better than most of them would ever have. "Cary . . . don't tell them about Vicki."

"I'll tell them what I damn well please—"

She saw movement in the shadow of a building, reached down to steady herself. But no, none of that . . . She would meet them as what she was, the woman who had sailed the *Petrel* across the light-years, who had given them a world, who had been mother to them all. Armed against misery, she got to her feet.

The rebels appeared. Three of them, all young men, each on horseback. None wore black, only the leather and canvas of the typical Tier farmer. Their armbands were the sole trace of a uniform, and the barrels of their crude guns wavered and fell when they saw her.

They looked at each other and then back at Julia. The one in the center, a tall man with red-blond hair, shifted in his saddle before urging his horse forward. The others followed while the chthulu skittered nervously away. The blond man raised a hand. She spread her arms in welcome.

Behind them a larger group appeared. Small, dressed in black from berets down to short boots. Several had scarves wrapped around their lower faces. Catching sight of Julia, the nearest one ripped the scarf free and raised a gun high. With a high-pitched scream she kicked the horse into a gallop.

The chthulu took to the air as the horse breached the wall. Two of the riders paused to shoot at it, and the last collided with them, bringing them all down.

"You promised you wouldn't—" Cary shrieked at full volume, every speaker in the Cloister reechoing with her voice. The leader nearly lost her seat when the horse touched the pavement. She raised her head, her small face grimacing even as her gun spat fire.

Julia drifted rather than fell, feeling the slugs as no more than mild blows. Cary wailed on, her voice now pure sound. Another shot came, but it was far away, at the other side of the plaza.

She felt a vague internal shift when her trauma system kicked in. Data flickered across her vision, ending with a bright, adamant red: MEDICAL ATTENTION ESSENTIAL. A black figure appeared behind it, scarf dangling from a twisted face. A length of steel gleamed in its hand.

Red-blond hair flashed and the figure's weight was gone. The glow of the message brightened as the world behind it faded. The black-clad creature returned . . . no, not the Rigorist herself, only the blackness. Julia watched it spread, grateful that she would no longer have to think about what Petro had become, that she wouldn't have to witness the thing that had devoured her world now eat her children. The last thing she thought was that humans always did lie.

TWO

She knew it for a dream; one of those fine, intense erotic dreams never matched in waking life. She was back on Earth with Petro in those final days before the Erinye, as if all the long decades since were yet to come. They were in a room, a room with one wall taken up by a large window or screen. Huge structures were visible outside, brightly lit, like vast man-made volcanoes floating on a dark, calm sea. The Gulf arcologies, it must be, though they'd never actually been there together. Had they spoken about visiting them? She couldn't recall.

The room was far from ordinary. Some kind of plants, orchids, she thought, grew throughout it, sprouting in a way she couldn't discern from the floor, curling up the walls, forming a kind of framework, a lattice. All very pretty; it made her sorry that tropical flowers couldn't yet grow on Midgard.

The lovemaking was natural; no drugs or electronics, nothing to obstruct the melding with another soul. The way she liked best, and she tried to whisper that to Petro. But he seemed to be dressed in black, and when he raised his head, his face wore the expression she'd seen on it last, revealing that he was ridden, that his mind was no longer his own.

A voice broke through, accompanied by twinges of pain. She rose from the dream, the magical room fading, taking poor Petro with it. She felt a terrible sense of loss—she was sure she could have shaken him out of it this time, brought him back to himself, so that they could set out together across the deep night, the way they'd always planned . . .

A face appeared, a boy's face, unshaven, blond hair tinged with red spilling over his forehead. "You okay, ma'am?"

The pain increased, peaked, dropped to a bearable level. She recalled that her system was programmed according to the theory that some pain was necessary for swift and proper healing. Nothing she needed to worry about, then.

"Ma'am?" A hand appeared, clenched tight, vanished. A deeper voice grunted in the background. "Can you hear me?"

She voiced the code for the med display. It looked ugly—she'd lost a lot of blood and the wound channels were huge. But no infection, no hemorrhaging, and vital organs were stable. "Yes," she told the anxious face above her.

The eyes closed momentarily. Asian eyes in a European face; like an Old Russian, a son of the steppes, like Petro. She fought back a smile. She was—had been—Queen of the Tatars. He regarded her still. "Is there anything I can do? Anything you need?"

Memories were beginning to return: horses, gunfire, a mad creature flourishing a knife. "Are you a Rigorist?"

He frowned, an oddly attractive expression on that face. "No way."

"Good." She let her eyelids fall.

"You sure you're okay now? Are you in pain?"

Another voice, high-pitched and shrill. "Not as much as she will be . . ."

"What the *hell* are you doing in here?"

She opened her eyes quickly enough to see the young man shoot to his feet.

"Get your ass outta here. Gen, grab her, willya . . ."

"You'll all be struggled when the Herald gets here . . ."

"Oh, the Herald. Stop scaring me. Gen—"

The deeper voice spoke. "Now now, playmates. Let's not strain ourselves."

It was all too loud, nothing she wanted to deal with. She ordered the system to take her down and sank gratefully into darkness.

There were no more dreams, only scattered moments when she dozed lightly enough to hear what was being said around her. Once it was the young man: "She was *dead*. She took three rounds of .30. I never saw wounds like that."

A rumble came from the deep voice. "Oh yeah?" the boy said. "Trauma system, huh? Nice thing to have."

Sometime later she heard Cary, on the knife-edge of hysteria, jabbering mindlessly. She was working to rouse herself when the deep voice spoke, its tone sober and calm. Julia let herself drift.

It was quiet when she came to once again. The pain still throbbed but less harshly than before. A check of the system told her that healing was proceeding about as well as she could expect. Several tubes fed into her right arm, and med units hummed at her lower torso. Her fingers brushed one and the system gave her a warning beep. A sheet had been draped over her. She wondered what had become of the robe.

The room was dark except for a dim glow far to her right. Enough was visible to let her know that she was in her own living room. She couldn't mistake that ceiling, having lived under it for the better part of a century. Or had it been replaced at one time? She was almost certain that had been done at least once. Forty years ago? Fifty?

There was a sound, as of a person shifting on a chair. She turned her head. A man was seated on the sofa, silhouetted by the lamp behind. She found her voice. "Danny?"

A crinkle of papers, then silence. Julia lay her head back. "I know it's you."

"No—don't move." Setting down whatever he was reading, Cardnale crossed the room. He loomed over her, head seeming to scrape the ceiling. What was it she was lying on anyway?

"Hiya, Jay."

"Light," she said. A lamp opposite him flared brightly, giving her a clear view of his face.

He'd changed a lot in the ten years since she'd last seen him. He'd grown a beard, a long, shaggy prophet's thing, and, as if in compensation, the hair on his head had grown thin. The light threw harsh shadows across his face. She tried to match it with the memory of the day he'd graduated, twenty-odd years before. How he'd grinned when she handed him the diploma!

He crouched next to her, reaching down to steady himself. She winced when she noticed he was wearing one of those black smocks. "How you feeling?"

"Well enough."

He smiled—at least she thought so, it was hard to tell with all those whiskers. "You're looking a lot better."

"It's difficult to kill a human of my generation."

"I'm glad of that. This . . . wasn't meant to happen, Jay. The . . . uh . . . fringe elements weren't supposed to be part of the spearhead."

"Fringe elements"—that must mean the Rigorists. An odd way to put it, but Danny had a habit of straining for novel terms, often ones that just missed the point. "How did I end up in here?"

"This room? Well, as Tonio explained it, there was considerable confusion, your AI was having fits, and no one knew where the med building was. So he carried you to the nearest building and found a gel mattress in the bedroom. Fortunately the machine was rational enough to trigger your medical system."

"I see. Were there . . . many casualties?"

"Here? No—none at all. Why would there be? You dismissed your defensive units. A wise move, I might add." He frowned and cleared his throat, as if preparing to embark on a long speech. "That's something we need to discuss as soon as possible. Now, if you feel up to it . . ."

"What about Cary?" Julia said quickly, before he could embark on one of his discourses. She well recalled the days when he'd been head of sociometrics, before his career change to revolutionary. The evening meetings had stretched out to two, sometimes three in the morning while Danny explained his theories. A new one each week, usually reinventing wheels that had been rolling since Aristotle or earlier—Danny was one of those people who found it impossible to grasp that anyone in history had ever thought as deeply as he did.

"Cariola?" he said, exactly as if he hadn't been in contact with her at all, much less for months if not years. "She'll be fine. I told her to safemode to help her calm down. Seeing you injured threw her into quite a tailspin. She's still very fond of you, despite everything."

"That's nice to hear." Her mind now almost clear,

Julia began sorting through the problems that most
needed attention. The Rigorists, the situation up on
the Tier, and oh yes, the ship from Earth. "Those
Rigorists, Danny. Where did you dig them up?"

He tilted his head to one side. She thought he was
pursing his lips. "Well . . . I suppose it'll do no harm
now. There's a cluster of valleys northwest of the
Plateau, cut off by a large glacier . . ."

"Yes," she said, picturing the topography.

"It's very much badlands, so it was excluded from
your overall developmental plan. But it seems that
the prevailing winds sweep over the Plateau in that
direction, so a lot of Terrest seeds and insects ended
up there. The valleys effectively Gaiaed themselves.
Somehow the collectivists became aware of them,
and when you cracked down, they set out there . . ."

The Rigorists—the Collective, as they called themselves—were a product of one of Julia's errors. Or
maybe not an error; it was too soon to tell. Julia
Amalfi was no utopian. She didn't believe in the concept—the more idealistic the design, the more stringent the requirements, the greater the chances of
disaster—and in any case, she had no trust in her
personal judgment as to what was best for any single
individual, much less an entire society. Julia had an
extremely healthy view of her own capabilities, whatever accusations of megalomania Cary might make.
Her task, overwhelming in and of itself, had been to
find a refuge where a remnant of true humanity
could survive in a universe where the Erinye might
well be triumphant. Midgard was that refuge. Whatever else it became was up to the kids themselves.
She'd held back nothing from them. The entire range
of human knowledge and experience was available
through Cariola's data banks, open to anyone. Julia
hadn't censored one byte of it, religious, philosophical, political, or ideological, whether she approved of
it or not.

Sometime late in the '80s, a man named McCart Gar had downloaded a series of texts from the pre-modern era. Political-philosophical stuff of the most esoteric sort: Rousseau, Tkachev, Marx, Sartre, Guevara. Julia had never heard of most of it, and when she went through it later on, couldn't even begin to grasp its allure, any more than she could understand the religious attraction of groups like the Dunkers or the Romans.

But Gar had understood it. He was a utopian, of the most common type: the theorist to whom reality was simply an impediment, the coercive who viewed humanity as clay to be molded in his image. He was also a teacher, with a circuit of classes across the Plateau. By the time Julia realized that Rigorism was anything more than one of the fads that occasionally blazed across Midgard—like the one in which the kids had begun spelling their names oddly, for instance—Gar had created an organization based on the cell system formulated by a man named Lenin, utilizing the tactics of another called Mao.

Midgard endured five years of terror, sabotage, and murder before the Rigorists were finally put down. They were never a serious threat—they were too few, and too fanatical. But those years had been a nasty period in Midgard's short history, one that she didn't like to think about. Before it was half-over, Gar was dead, at the hands, she was convinced, of the members of his own command cell, the troika of Fredrix, Templ, and Wolf.

". . . not a unique event. Reminiscent of the Afrikaaner trek, the flight of the Mormons, the Long March . . ."

But how could a settlement in one of those valleys escape detection by satellite? Of course Cariola processed the imagery, and it was easy enough to erase the traces a small group would make. But what would be the purpose?

A sudden chill gripped her as she recalled that a number of people had disappeared up that way. A survey team about twelve years ago, a couple of prospectors more recently. Oh, Cary was going to have a lot to live with, wasn't she?

". . . episodes have an annealing effect, hardening and strengthening a movement. The weaker members shear off, leaving a core of true believers . . ."

It seemed that Danny still retained his lecture mode. That was a relief. It implied he hadn't changed all that much. She raised a hand to interrupt. "How did you come across them?"

His eyes became distant. "That was during my . . . exile," he said in a clipped voice. He looked down at himself, as if aware for the first time of what he had on. "Oh, don't worry, Jay. By no means have I become a Garite. I'm still the rationalist I always was. That's how things are going to be done from here on. Logically, consistently, rationally—with plenty of input from the citizens.

"And we need to begin now. I don't want to tire you, but there are matters requiring action. First, I want you to contact your police and order them to disengage. Not surrender, that's not necessary yet. Simply stand down, pending negotiations. More than enough people have been killed, Jay . . ."

"I told them to do that two weeks ago."

Cardnale's face went flat. She knew that expression—the beard did nothing to hide it. It was the look of Associate Professor Danil Cardnale pushed past the clear and manifest line of what he was willing to stand.

"What do you take me for, Lady?" He rose to his full height, his face furious. "We've lost three entire units over the past week. Gone, as if they walked off the map. Where did they go, Madame Amalfi? What destroyed them, if not your goons?" He raised clenched fists. "Sixty men, Julia. Men, hell—boys in their teens and twenties. No more than infants, to someone of your age."

He swept away, boot soles thudding heavily against the floorboards. "You know, I thought about this moment for years. What would happen when it was over, when the road finally reached its end. How I would slap you down, serve you the same as you did me. I brooded over it, relished it, rehearsed it repeatedly in my mind. It kept me going, up there on the ice where your thugs chased me—"

"No one chased you, Danny."

"Stop it, Julia!" He lunged at her as if to trample her into the floor. "Don't treat me like an idiot. Or have you forgotten? Your ågathic system has trouble dealing with senility, is that it?" He tore his eyes from hers. "You almost won, you know that? You came so close. I ran out of hiding places. The sodbusters, the ones who went as far as they could to get out from under your *plan*, the ones who hated you even then, they got scared. And the rains came, and the sleet, and I ran out of food, and then the fever . . . That last week, my God, I still can't believe I lived through it. And who saved me, Dame Amalfi? Who rescued me at the last possible moment?"

Cardnale's voice grew softer. "Those Rigs you're so disdainful of. They took me in, fed me, sent me up the valley to their leaders. When every man's hand was turned against me, when I had nowhere left to run, they offered me protection."

She wanted to remind him that they'd also killed nearly two hundred people with their bombs, snipers, and nerve agents. But this certainly wasn't the proper moment.

"You owe me, Jay," he said. "I want that made clear. But I'm not going to hold the past against you either. It's a clean slate between us, as of now."

"As you say, Danil."

"Fine. But I require a quid pro quo." He towered

above her once again. "You will damn well send out that order."

"I'll repeat it."

"Oh, have it your way." He released an explosion of breath. "Look at me, shouting at an injured woman. I thought I was doing rather well there."

That was Danny too. Beneath the pride, the selfishness, the inability to keep his mouth shut or let a slight pass, there was an essential core of decency. Julia was glad that it too remained. "Very well, Danny."

"Thanks, Jay." He turned to pull a chair closer. "I'm sure I'm tiring you, but people are depending on us. Let me know when you want to stop."

"I will."

"You'll also need to contact Grifin at the Shore and what's-her-name out on the Islands . . ."

"Celia Wilem."

"Yes. We have to come to some kind of an arrangement as soon as possible. I want no more violence, particularly as regards the archipelago—we certainly don't need to top things off with a naval campaign."

"Keep in mind you can't depend on my authority anymore, Danny."

A smug expression crossed his face. "I suppose you're right. But simply contacting them will be enough at the moment."

"You'll need to reopen the fibop lines if you want to make sure I reach everyone."

"What do you mean?"

"Cary says you shut them down."

"Me? I gave no such order."

"You'll have to take it up with her then." Julia rested an arm across her forehead. The light was beginning to bother her eyes. "That's what she told me."

"I'll do that. Uhh . . . how many hours do these disassociations of hers usually last?"

Julia fought back a smile. Hours? Try weeks.

With a wave Cardnale shunted the thought aside. "No matter. Morning will do. Now, who's handling inventory . . . ?"

"Danny, wait." She raised a finger. "One thing. The ship—"

Cardnale winced in something that resembled embarrassment. "Oh yes, *Corpus Christi*. I . . . didn't know that you'd been informed of that. Well, that'll be something, won't it? A vessel from Earth, after all this time. Things always seem to happen at once, don't they?"

"Danil—what about the Erinye? Who's forgetting now?"

"Oh, that? Ancient history, Jay. There was some sort of problem, yes, but they beat it long ago. Cariola made certain of that."

She lay back, staring up at the ceiling in something very close to despair.

"I heard what the captain had to say. Frankly, your demon theory about the Erinye seems to have been overblown."

"You spoke to him?" Julia fixed Cardnale with her eyes. "Actually conversed? Like we're doing now?"

"Well . . . not exactly. There was something wrong with the communications equipment. He couldn't reply immediately for some reason. We'd send a message and get the answer the next day. Cariola wasn't able to fix it—she mentioned something about Einstein, as if a man four centuries dead could be to blame . . ."

Julia closed her eyes in relief. Danny had been talking as if this St. John was using ultrarelativistic communications. If the Erinye had made a breakthrough that profound, there was no limit to the technology they might have. As it was, whatever entity was aboard that ship had plenty of time to compile a message saying anything.

Clearing his throat, Cardnale got to his feet. "It'd be best if you didn't mention the ship too loosely, Jay. That information's closely held at the moment. We want to avoid panic. All your yarns about entities eating people's minds and so on."

"I'll be discreet."

"Good. Now I'll be off. It's very late, and you need rest . . ."

Leaving, was he, when five minutes ago he'd been ready to work her all night? Her questions must be hitting a little too close. "One thing more, Danny." Julia pushed herself up on one elbow. Pain flared, and the units clustered at her waist beeped in protest. "The girl who shot me. She was here, wasn't she? In this room."

Cardnale let out a long breath. "Don't be frightened, Jay. We've placed a guard outside. One of Tony's boys." His eyebrows rose. "Tony—the blond young man. Tonio Perin. A remarkable figure—more or less took over as the campaign went on. Bit of a young Napoleon. As for the Rigs . . . there aren't many left. Your Seeya was very efficient."

"My what?"

"Seeya. The secret police of the American Republic."

What could he be talking about? The U.S. never had any such thing. Nor had she. Could he really believe otherwise?

"It might be Kiya—I'm unsure of the pronunciation."

"Well, you'd better start your own, Danny. Somebody needs to keep an eye on them. I doubt they're as harmless as you think." She eased herself back down. "It could be worse, I guess. If Fredrix or Wolf were still alive . . ."

An odd sound came from Cardnale. "Keth Fredrix . . . is arriving tomorrow."

The med system squealed as she jerked erect.

Cardnale stood in darkness, his expression invisible. He made a gesture, hand open, as if in apology.

She dropped back onto the mattress. Cardnale went to the sofa. She heard a rustle of papers. "I'll leave you now. I wanted to make certain you were all right."

"Yes."

"I mean that, Jay . . . There's a place for you in the new dispensation. Believe me, I wouldn't have it any other way."

"Yes."

"I was scared coming here, Jay. Up to the house. It was like the first time all over again. When I was a freshman at the Academy. You remember?"

"Of course I do."

"You know what I used to think of, up there in the wild country?"

"What?"

"The picnics. Remember those? The whole damn staff, the undergrads, the researchers, everybody skipping off over the ridge there, to that meadow past the cemetery. Picnics, hell—they were state fairs, Jay. Planetary fairs."

Julia smiled in spite of herself. "The kites. Do you still make kites?"

"Not for a long time. But I think I remember how. There'll be kites again." He went to the door. "Good night, Lady."

She lay gazing into space, mind racing from the ship, to the Rigorists, to Fredrix, to the Erinye, back to the ship again. And Danny Cardnale wanted to reminisce about picnics. Oh, there'd be picnics all right, if Fredrix, or whatever present the Erinye had sent them, didn't picnic off of him first.

Fredrix—she'd been so sure he was dead. But there hadn't been a body, as with Gar and Wolf. The cavern where the last of the Rigorists—supposedly the last—had made their final stand had been sealed with explosives. It was either that or go in and dig them out. Fredrix was believed to have been inside, along with that awful Aida Templ, with her shaved head and plucked eyebrows. Wouldn't it be nice if she decided to pop up too?

Julia had never met Fredrix. Another backwoods autodidact who had latched onto a cause—at least that was what her police told her. It was Templ and Wolf who masterminded the terror campaign. But Fredrix had survived them both. And what had Cardnale said about their long march? How it had toughened them, made them harder.

It was useless thinking about it, not with her mind so hollow. It would have to wait. She glanced at the windows, wondering what time it was. Oh, to be flat on her back now, with all that was happening! The thought struck her that Danny might have ordered her shot, simply to get her out of the way . . . But no; foolish as he might be, Dan Cardnale couldn't be called ruthless.

Poor Danny, she thought, wondering why she thought it.

Well, there was one thing she could do . . . Reaching for the med units clustered at her waist, she felt around until she found a control keyboard. She switched it on and squinted into the holo projection. The healing process could be accelerated, at the risk of triggering oncogene activity. A bout of cancer was something she could live with, if the alternative was the Erinye—or Keth Fredrix, for that matter.

The system protested when she entered the command. She overrode and was about to exit when it occurred to her to try the data banks. Cary being out, it might be possible to . . .

ACCESS DENIED appeared immediately. She sighed and set the unit down. Sleep hovered close; there was no point in asking the system to lull her. As she shut her eyes, the blond boy's face appeared. A young Napoleon, Cardnale had said. She wondered if he remembered how the original had dealt with the Directory. Perin, his name was, Tony Perin. Could that be the same Perin who had done so well on the finals a few years back . . . ?

After a moment the lights dimmed, flickering once when Julia said, "Petro." But she was well asleep by then.

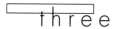 three

Tony Perin awoke to the smell of breakfast, that rich, hearty aroma he hadn't even realized he'd missed since going off to see the elephant. Eating had not been particularly outstanding during the campaign—farmers had a sure instinct for hiding their produce when soldiers came around and Tony, a farm boy himself, hadn't been able to muster the hardness to make them give it up.

Rolling off the mattress, he grabbed his shirt—a clean one, the other had been too bloodsoaked to keep—and pulled on his boots, giving the laces a couple twists around the ankles. He hadn't yet dropped the habit of sleeping in his pants. The arm-band had fallen from his sleeve. He spotted it on the floor, orange star encompassing a hand making the three-finger salute, each finger standing for one of the Unalienable Points: Self-determination, Representation, Free Markets. He reached for it but decided to let it lie. It wasn't as if he was unknown around here and anyway, the fighting was over.

He left the room, mildly puzzled by odd clicking sounds coming from down the hall. The building was part of the Gaiaforming center they'd taken over as a barracks, and he hadn't had a chance to look it over yet.

He stretched as he stepped outside. A fine day, sky clear, temperature at least in the fifties, but he had eyes for none of it. Back in school Tony had read somewhere—probably in an educational download— that smell was the most emotionally powerful of all senses. At that moment, facing the roasting pit dug into the lawn, he knew it for stone-cold fact.

"Ah, look who's back from the dead," somebody hollered. Several of the men around the pit gave him offhand salutes as he pushed through, but the general air couldn't be called military. "None left, Tony. Go back to bed," Vitig told him as he passed, and somebody else stuck out a leg as if to trip him. Reaching the fire at last, he gazed down at Braes and Derswitz, who were doing some slicing. "What you got?"

It seemed that somebody had found some pigs, and somebody else was a butcher. "Ribs and chops for dinner," Braes told him as he filled a plate with ham, fried potatoes, and biscuits. Pouring a cup of coffee, Tony headed for the wall, only a few steps downhill. He sat himself down and concentrated on his plate. It had been a while since he'd seen a good slice of ham.

Finishing up by sopping the gravy with a biscuit, he set the plate aside, satisfied with himself and the world at large. The coffee had cooled down nicely. He sipped and contemplated the day.

An uproar by the pit drew his attention. Dud Mos had been playing harp and someone else had snatched it from him and tossed it to a third party and the chase was on. Tony smiled. Look at them: bearded as Dunkers on a testimonial walkabout, clothes torn and patched, as dirty as if to demonstrate that soap had never been invented. Hardened troopers, each one. After a campaign lasting five weeks and six days.

Tony knew better. Not many Middies paid attention to Terrestrial history, usually settling for a vague awareness that Earth was where the Erinye were and no more. But Tony was one of the few. He clearly recalled the day he'd first realized that there *was* such a thing, tapping into the website marked with a globe of the Americas and a scroll. He had no word for what he'd felt that day, a sense of vastitude, an almost savage joy that sent his skin prickling with the knowledge that not only had the world existed before Tonio Perin, but that a world had existed before *his* world; one complex beyond imagining, with all its chronicles, its annals and sagas. He'd been eight—a little over seven, Terrest—and the echo of that discovery had resounded across the fifteen years since.

To know history was to know war. So much of the Terrestrial record dealt with battle: the pastime of kings, the plaything of sultans, the nightmare of democracies. It had fascinated him, so alien it was to what he knew, child of a world that had never witnessed a mass upheaval. He'd sat up plenty of nights haunted by images of massacre, of siege, of area bombing and nuclear terror. For a time he'd avoided it, much the same as he'd avoided girls during one period a few years later, convinced that there was something wrong with him to be interested in such things. But eventually he'd achieved a truce with himself and had gone back looking not for thrills but some kind of understanding as to what men might be.

So he read his Grant, his MacArthur, his Caesar. Studied the strategy that allowed Constantinople to

defy Islam for nearly a millennium, the errors that
humiliated the Republic in a small backwoods called
Vietnam, the planning with which Ajulu had united
Central Africa into the last Terrestrial empire. He
wasn't sure if it gave him any advantage when Midgard's own crisis came; he made no claims for himself. But when old Rogrs had suffered his heart attack
and Chief Yaki, the ex-cop who replaced him, turned
to Tony at Bukland and told him he didn't know
what to do, it had come as instinct. He'd sent the
Screamin' Orcs in a flank attack, right out of
Friedrich der Grosse's handbook, and with a hundred and fifty men captured nearly three hundred
with only four casualties on his side.

Okay, so it wasn't Gaugamela or Inchon. But he'd
still felt damn good when a week later Cardnale
called him his Napoleon. Felt good, while at the same
time regretting that anybody would wish that on
him.

Because it wasn't all Buklands. War was also comprised of places like Lews. The cophouse there had
been built by a chief who took his duty to the Dame
damned seriously; on a rise, so you couldn't get into
town until the place was dealt with, and out of
dressed stone two, three feet thick, so that mortar
rounds bounced off. They mixed a barrel full of
ANFO, the farmer's favorite stump remover, carried
it to the single blind spot, propped it against the wall,
and fixed a grenade. But that stuff was very hard to
calibrate and instead of blowing a hole in the wall
and stunning the defenders, it flattened the place.
There were only two survivors, out of nineteen, and
they hadn't lasted long. Militia kids, younger than
he was.

He'd been afraid there would be a lot more of that
kind of thing. That the rebellion would settle into
stalemate, like Crimea or Korea One. The Lady had
lots of guns, and people grew more content with her

the closer you got to the Cloister. He knew what to
expect if that happened: the infinite corruption that
war engendered, that still remained when the fighting ended, and took so many forms. The cynicism
that enveloped Hellas after the Peloponnesian Wars,
the madness that gripped Germany following the
World War I, the sense of futility that fell upon the
entire West after number II.

He watched the men fooling, gossiping, slurping
at their coffee. Mos had got his harmonica back and
was tootling away from the safety of a windowsill.
They'd been spared that, without even knowing what
scars they might have had to bear. It was back to the
Plateau and the Chains for them, to their plows and
combines, without the Lady's factors to tell them
what to plant and how much to sell it for. There'd
be plenty of yarns, and celebrations, and reunions in
the years to come. Little in the way of grief and
agony to spoil it.

That went double for Tony Perin. Because Cardnale was wrong. He was no Bonaparte, to ride away
from Wagram sneering that the mounds of corpses
left behind were a good reason for Frenchwomen to
work hard that night. No, there was a term for what
Tony was: an armchair general. He had seen his elephant (as if he had any clear idea what an elephant
was). Now he'd go home to the farm, up on the
Plateau with its black soil that was Gaiazing better
than any land on Midgard, to his folks, to Moriah.
He'd work his acreage and read his downloads at
night, figuring out where Rommel and Cornwallis
and Peng had gone wrong and how he'd have done
much better. The blockhouse at Lews would fade,
and eventually his war would be Bukland, with the
fat old cop who'd commanded the militia there
throwing his gun at Tony's feet and bellowing,
"Where the hell did you come from?"

That was what would remain, and that was plenty.

He felt a prickling across his shoulders, as if someone had fixed harsh eyes on him. He swung to the house on the knoll at the end of the plaza. The house where *she* lived—and maybe she *was* looking at him, right this minute.

He remembered his terror when the bullets ripped into her—right over there, by that square of rock. As if the world itself would fold up, its purpose accomplished, the sky split and blackness pour out over everything. It had never occurred to him that anybody would *do* something like that. Nobody hated the Lady. She was old, yeah. She'd lost touch; it was time for her to step aside. But no more than that.

Yet that little Blackshirt bitch had been about to slice her wide open, the same as Si Braes had done to that hog. And after he wrestled her to the ground, she simply walked away. Even had the nerve to ask for her knife back.

His father had told him, in their last conversation before Tony left, to watch out for the Lady. Almost as if he'd foreseen what might happen. Dad had known her long ago, when he'd taken the Ag course at the Academy. She knew his name, had spoken to him on campus. He'd actually had lunch with her a few times, in that very house. When Tony was young, he'd been puzzled that Dad spoke so well of her, leader of the Settlement faction as he was—damn near as much a thorn in her side as Dan Cardnale. Dad told him that he'd understand when he got older.

"Keep in mind that we have need of her, son," he'd said that last day. "She's not a demon, or a goddess either. She's a potential partner. No more or less."

The words had taken Tony aback. "Pop—we're not out on a killing spree. Lot of people slaughtered around here, right?" The takeover on the Northeast

Spur had been next to bloodless—the local police chief was one of theirs.

"Yes, but I wish these Garites weren't involved."

"Ah, they're just a handful." Tony hauled himself on the horse, took a last look around the spread. Mom had already said her goodbyes. As for Moriah—she was at her family's farm, believing that he'd already left. He hadn't wanted to see her this morning.

"I suppose." Dad was clutching the saddle as if to keep him there by force. "When you get there, remember me to her."

"Sure, Pop. Love from Mart Perin."

"Yes . . ." Dad released the pommel and stepped away. "That's it exactly."

He thought he understood now. The grief that had gripped him when he picked up that body, smaller than he would have guessed from the pictures, as torn as anything he'd seen at Lews. Her face so thin, eyes so huge, the entire effect alien to him, and so pathetic in her suffering. Carrying her to the nearest building—her own house, he realized as he crossed the threshold—while the Blackshirts yapped and howled and waved their guns. Her blood soaking his shirt, dripping from his hands. He stayed until well past midnight, even after Cardnale arrived and assured him that it took more than a few slugs to kill an enhanced human. Sat there not believing it, watching that form under the sheet, wondering what kind of life would be left for the man who'd let Julia Amalfi die.

A century and a half she'd lived—Dad had calculated it in school. It was harder than you'd think; there was a twist involving special relativity during her shipboard years. Time stretched at interstellar speeds. But Dad worked out the answer: Julia Amalfi was one hundred and twenty-seven years old. "And that was twenty-six years ago."

One hundred and fifty-three years—yet she looked no older than his mother. Though it was stranger than that: her skin was like a girl's, but her face bore lines of experience that seemed more ancient than Tony could describe. Like Athena crossed with a nymph; Gaia in the guise of a schoolgirl.

And then she'd spoken that one soft word—the name of the starship, he thought—and he was beside her when those weird, round eyes opened. Eyes that had actually seen Earth and the dead spaces between the stars. Eyes that seemed to bear within them the history that he so loved. He had scarcely been able to speak, to ask if she was all right. When she answered, he had known that what his Dad felt was true.

He left and hadn't returned since. He would go back, before he hit the road. To give her Dad's message and . . . apologize. What else could he do?

He looked up to see Gen Morgn approaching, bearing a plate piled high. Gen was a Chains boy who had pretty much become Tony's second in command after their outfits merged at Devil's Gate. "Hey, chief," Gen called out. "Another slice?"

"Think I will." He speared a hunk, snagging a biscuit while he was at it.

"Got a real neat game inside," Gen said after a moment of silent chewing. "Call it pool."

"Game? What kinda game?"

It seemed that pool involved a table, a bunch of balls, and two men wielding sticks. Tony wasn't sure that he grasped the rest of it, though. "You hit the ball, what—across the table? Like baseball?"

"No, no—you hit 'em with the end of the sticks, see. You're like pushin' 'em."

"Yeah. And then what?" Why did they call it "pool" if no water was involved?

Gen licked his thumb. "Well, they got pockets."

"Who's got pockets?"

"The table, okay?"

The picture Tony was constructing in his head completely evaporated. "Pockets of *what*?"

"Ah—take a look. You'll see. Get Dan to show ya. He told the rules. He's real good at it. Used to play all the time when he was teachin' here."

Tony grunted. There were a lot of questions he wanted to ask Cardnale, but sports wasn't among them. "He around this morning?"

"Oh yeah." Gen examined his fingers before wiping them on his pants. "Had to get in the day's schmoozin', didn't he?"

"He's still at it."

"Clapped me on the back, said he'd need a governor up the Chains."

"Did he." Tony wondered how many governors the Chains required. Cardnale had promised the position to five people that he knew of. Maybe Danny was thinking of one for each lake—all two hundred of them.

"Me a governor," Gen snorted. "Still got a warrant on me for poachin' up by Dark Pond. Cancel that and I'll be happy."

"Just keep humorin' him, Gen."

"Tell that to the boys." Gen was making a sandwich out of a biscuit and the last of the ham. "They're gettin' disgusted. I mean, what's he want anyway?"

Tony swirled his coffee. What did Cardnale want? Hard to say, for somebody who'd been through what he'd been through, done what he'd done. All the years up in the woods, the speeches and talks and rallies, the conspiring and secrecy, and here he was at last, at the seat of his heart's desire. What could he want? What anybody would want in that situation: the world, simply put.

He recalled the way Dan looked when he pulled in yesterday. How he'd halted his horse at a distance, like an uninvited guest unsure of his welcome. The expression of naked relief on his face when the boys began cheering. The tension in his stance, the sickly look when he confronted Tony—the look of a man who had something vital to say but was afraid to say it.

He thought he knew what Dan's problem was. Danny was a little puffed up. A bit too filled with triumph, a touch too exalted. Expectations were flitting through that lofty mind of his, visions of a grandeur that he'd never allowed himself to entertain before. He'd grasped something that he'd doubted would ever be his, and he was afraid that somebody was going to take it away from him.

Which was precisely what would happen. Somewhere the pin for his balloon was waiting—the event or person that would deflate Dan Cardnale. But, much as he wouldn't mind seeing it, that wasn't any of Tony's business.

Best he finish the coffee before it went cold. Even as the cup met his lips, a voice at the far end of the plaza caught his attention. A pack of Rigs had appeared from whatever burrow they'd found. A dozen were seated in a circle, rumps to the slate, facing another reading in a high-pitched voice from a booklet or pamphlet. He'd heard they'd been out early, exercising in the middle of the plaza. All hundred-odd of them, jumping up and down all at once. That too would have been worth seeing.

Tony didn't know what to make of the Rigs. At first he'd considered them to be simply another weird sect, the kind you saw a lot of out the backwoods. They got on your nerves damned quick, as if they all held Academy doctorates in obnoxiousness. They stayed to themselves. They stared. They answered serious questions as if reciting from memory. The topper, for Tony, was the way they always seemed to disappear when an action was imminent.

Not to mention how their numbers had grown as they neared the Cloister.

He'd asked Danny about them. He was well aware that Danny often answered general questions with one of his sociopolitical lectures, so he'd been particular about the way he put it: what exactly had Danny seen up north—in the Epoch of Struggle Valley, as the Rigs called it? "Nothing at all strange," Danny assured him, though the description—the barracks, the constant supervision, the every-second-accounted-for schedule—sounded bizarre enough. "That type of life is quite suitable for some people, Tony. Not you and I, of course. People lacking direction, a sense of purpose. The Bilis, for instance. And not only them. There are more aimless, inadequate individuals roaming around than you'd guess. Living futile, empty lives, useless to themselves and others without regimentation, control . . . a structured setting."

He turned to Gen. "Boys give any ham to the Blackshirts?"

"Nah. None left, and anyway, they don't eat meat."

"All kidding aside?" Tony looked back at the group. Another one was standing now, talking with his—or maybe her, it was hard to tell—arms hanging down. The first, the one who'd been reading, was looking on with . . .

Tony raised a hand to shade his eyes. Damned if that one didn't look exactly like Little Miss Knifework, the one who'd shot the Lady. He'd tried to track her down after throwing her out of the house, thinking to put her in custody, but her comrades had treated him as if he was a basilisk in molt. He ought to go over there now, but . . . He couldn't be sure. They all looked alike; all young, all small, and all dressed in black. The only thing he knew was her name: Guardian Unity.

Putting his plate down, Gen treated himself to a belch. "Well, what's the next move gonna be, Tony?"

"Got me. I'm going home."

"What!" Gen glared like a mad prospector from the Ice Belt. "Hell you say! Who's taking us down the Shore?"

"Not gonna be any Shore campaign, Gen. Look, here's the way I see it . . ." As far as Tony was concerned, taking the Cloister had pretty much wrapped things up. It was the *Schwerpunkt*, as the Prussians had put it, the vital point. Once you had Ma's place, everything else, all the way from Neptune out east to Third York, was wide open and indefensible. He'd explained it already to Cardnale, recommending that he negotiate once the Cloister fell. Danny had agreed, if reluctantly. Gen picked it up a lot more quickly—he wasn't what you'd call educated, but he was sharp all the same. "Who's gonna help the Shore fix things up next time a storm hits? How they gonna get their data from Honeybun? And the fish farms out the Islands—who they sell their mackerel to?"

"So it's all over," Gen said thoughtfully. "No more blockhouses. Huh."

"Yeah. And it's a damn good thing. Like Sun Tzu says, don't kill more than you have to; you gotta live with 'em afterward."

"Son Sue? Whozat?"

"Old Earth guy. Wrote a book about warfare. Damn good one; you oughta download it."

Gen chuckled. "Oh yeah—me read a book."

"Hey, it's only like sixty pages."

"That's fifty-nine too many." Gen shook his head. "When you tellin' the boys?"

Tony hesitated. He'd meant to do that already, but something had held him back. A reluctance to bring an end to it: all they'd been through, all they'd accomplished, Bukland and Rush Creek and the Gate

and . . . yes, and Lews too. The weeks that had been
and gone and would never be again. The . . . romance
of it. Sure; he couldn't think of a better word. "It is
a good thing that war is so horrible," a wise old man
had once said in the aftermath of his own Lews.
"Lest we grow to love it too much."

An uproar broke out behind him. He swiveled
around, head lowered, hand going for an absent pistol, the instincts of combat undiminished. "What the
hell . . ." Gen said.

The Rigs were now on their feet, shouting with
more excitement than Tony would have thought
them capable of. Others ran into the plaza, weapons
in hand. Tony eased himself off the wall, wondering
whether to tell the boys to load up. Then he caught
sight of a figure on muleback riding past the fountain
at the far side of the old tree.

"I'll be damned," Gen whispered. "The King of
the Rigs. In person."

So it was. Tony took in the cowhide clothes, the
battered tiersman's hat, the gray hair brushing the
broad shoulders. Keth Fredrix, Herald of the Garite
remnant. Funny how he didn't dress like his followers. He could be a surveyor, an old, broken-down
prospector.

At least at a distance. From close up, the impression shifted considerably. Tony had met him—in fact,
Fredrix was the man to whom Cardnale had intro-
duced Tony as the New Bonaparte. Tony couldn't
say he'd taken a shine to him. It had been like talking
to a stump—a stump that replied in the low, precise
voice of the kind of guy who kept all the extra letters
in his name, as Gen might put it.

But a stump with blank, colorless eyes that seemed
to look right through you no matter what direction
they were facing. When he left that meeting—he'd
gotten word that the Downslope militia was gathering in force at the Gate, out to dispute passage—he'd

glanced back from the doorway, feeling those eyes. But Fredrix was simply staring into space, not looking his way at all.

The Rigs waved their guns, yelling their heads off, that staccato, high-pitched *yi-yi-yi* that made you grit your teeth. There seemed to be a lot more of them than he'd thought. Fredrix slid off the mule, raised his arms to his chest, and snapped them wide. The sound ceased.

"Think we should go over, give him our regards? That hambone, he can gnaw on that . . ."

A group appeared from the direction of the comp building. Dan Cardnale with his staff, what he liked to call "the committee," in tow. Tony was relieved to see him. He didn't care to be the one to roll out the carpet for the likes of Fredrix.

Fredrix turned to watch Cardnale approach. When he came within reach, Fredrix suddenly enfolded him in a bear hug and kissed him on both cheeks. The crowd started yipping again.

"Uhh—the things you see when you ain't got your Sten."

Having thoroughly greeted him, Fredrix appeared to set Cardnale to one side, exactly as if placing him on a shelf to be dealt with later. He faced his disciples and the noise cut off.

"You know," Gen said. "I heard he's the one fixed up his boss man . . ."

"Gar?"

"Yeah. He's supposed to have dropped the word to the milish about where he was at. That's what they say up the Chains."

Fredrix addressed the assembled Rigs, his voice too low to carry. After a moment he turned and left the square. The crowd followed. Tony noticed them pushing Cardnale aside as if he wasn't there. It occurred to him that he'd just witnessed the arrival of the pin to Danny's balloon.

"Where they going?"

"Oh, the Blackshirts took over the cophouse," Gen said. "Now what's this?" He clambered atop the wall for a better look. By craning his neck, Tony could just make out what he was talking about. Past the big tree, a large group was moving into the plaza. They weren't Rigs, even though a few black-clad riders were mixed in with them. They were on foot, and as they drew closer, Tony saw women and children among them.

"Bilis," Gen said.

"What they want with them?" Their gestures quick and harsh, the Rigs ushered the Bilis into the plaza exactly as if they were herding cattle, which wasn't far from the truth where Bilis were concerned. For a moment Tony considered going over to find out what the story was, but then he saw Cardnale and his people mingling with the new arrivals and let the notion drop. Danny had spent time among the Bilis, doing what he called "social work."

"Looks like Danny's got his hands full," Gen said.

"He can have it," Tony grunted. "I'm going home."

Behind him a sudden yipping broke out, a ragged duplicate of the Rig warcry. He turned to see the men all standing stiffly, giving a sendoff to the departing Rigs. Down at the foot of the plaza, the final batch came to a halt. Twenty or so, all armed. The last thing that Danny had said was to keep the men from bothering the Rigs. "Tell them to stop that shit, Gen."

"Done." Gen hit the ground at a run.

Tony pulled his collar from his neck. It must be near sixty—a lot hotter than he was used to. A thought struck him: they had running water here. Even showers . . .

He passed the boys, fallen silent in the face of Gen's wrath. Pausing inside the building, he considered how to go about finding a bathroom. Then that clicking sound caught his attention once again. He entered the room in question.

A huge table, faced with some kind of green cloth. A myriad of colored balls. Serious-looking Orcs, all equipped with long, tapered sticks. Tony watched a moment or two, hand on his chin.

"Hey," he said at last. "Lemme see one of those sticks . . ."

The rest of the morning passed pretty quickly.

four

The afternoon sun threw two silhouettes on the window where there had been only one. Curious, Julia signaled for the glass to clear. A pair of young men stood talking, both wearing work shirts and that tacky armband. As she watched, one turned and went downhill. The other pulled the sling of a primitive-looking weapon over his shoulder and glanced at the window. Seeing a transparent pane, he bent down and shaded his eyes. They went wide when he caught sight of her. Julia waved. He responded with a tentative flap of his fingers and turned away quickly, shoulders hunched.

Blurring the window once more, Julia lay back against the pillows. They seemed to be afraid of her, far more so than they had ever been when she was the unchallenged matriarch of this ice-crowned rock. She thought she knew why. They were on new ground, out from under the old lady's hand at last, free to do what they damn well pleased when they damn well pleased. Unknown territory, not at all what they were used to. That was frightening enough in itself. But then, when they looked back, there she was, same as ever, gazing at them out of her aged and ageless eyes. What was she thinking? And what would she do?

But it was new territory for her as well. She wished they understood that. She'd been running this place for . . . oh, she'd stopped counting the years ages ago. Over a century anyway. No small stretch of time. In a very real sense, all the lives on Midgard had rested on her shoulders. The responsibility had been hers; the plans, the programs, every last detail. There had been no one to lean on. No higher authority, no wiser heads, no equals. Her staff had always deferred to her—they knew how crushing the job was. Cary was no more than a child, her vast reservoirs of data useless without guidance.

And the obstacles she'd faced! Epsilon Indi was a Class B system, scheduled for exploitation only after the more suitable worlds at Ceti, Eridani, and Giclas 51-15 were settled, falling farther down the list after the second wave of Starweb probes discovered even more attractive possibilities. The system had entered a particularly thick branch of the Centaurian dust cloud a quarter-million years ago, to be trapped in a glacial cycle ever since. The ice moved south, covering entire continents until its weight triggered tectonic faults. Volcanic gases greenhoused the atmosphere, encouraging ever-diminishing blooms of life from a battered and decaying native ecology for a few millennia until the temperature plummeted once again.

That was the hand she'd been dealt, and she'd played it well, considering the small resources—oh, so very small, compared to the armadas sent to Ceti and Eridani!—available to her. The hundreds of orbital mirrors built from asteroidal material by the

VNC units; the Mars-proven airborne algae to bolster
the greenhouse layer; the gengineering techniques
that permitted Terrest life-forms to thrive in a cold
they had never evolved to endure.

There had been crises. Many of them, all apocalyp-
tic at the time but now barely lingering in memory.
A mutation in the algae stock. A fluctuation of solar
temperature as the system sailed through yet a
thicker bank of interstellar dust. A failure of a DNA
splice that led to the birth of children no more able
to survive the chill than they could live at the bottom
of the sea.

She had prevailed. The unforeseen pitfalls, the
breakdowns, the errors of judgment had all been
overcome. Sometimes not as neatly as she might have
liked, on occasion right at the very edge of catastro-
phe, but she'd beaten the odds all the same. The
Gaiazing of an entire world, the biggest single project
ever tackled by one individual.

Granted, she'd arrived at exactly the right time,
just after the latest period of vulcanism. Any other
phase of the cycle would have been hopeless. But still
it was her work, this last refuge for true humanity. At
times she had felt like Gaia herself, as the springs
grew more Earth-like, the summer breezes warmer.
Like Hecuba, like Astarte; as if this world had
emerged from her own body, as if the tens of thousands of people upon it were in truth her children,
born in pain and joy.

All that was over. She felt so helpless now. Not so
much because of her wounds; they no more than
tingled, with an occasional thrust of sharper discomfort. No, the malaise rose from deeper levels than
that, from somewhere in those aspects of her mind
hidden to her. She went through her memories, faded
as they were, trying to discover a time when she'd
felt the same.

To think of the period before the transit, her days

back on Earth, was hopeless. What she'd felt when the Erinye had conquered, when she'd seen the nothingness in Petro's face, when she realized that she'd have to face the dark alone and not as a member of a trained crew—all that was gone. It was as if she'd witnessed those events on tape, a product of someone else's imagination, not part of her story at all. Whatever she'd felt then, whatever torments she'd endured were simply no longer accessible to her, as sealed off by time as everything else she'd left behind in the Home System.

Her early years on Midgard had also begun to fade, events melting one into another, the tapestry grown muddy and dim. But some incidents had left marks deeper than others. Events like Vera's death.

Vera was the last survivor of the firstborn, the children who had landed on Midgard with her. When the *Petrel* began its lengthy deceleration, she awoke with the knowledge that she could not confront the new world on her own. She needed hands, both to take on the work that the machines could not and to pick up the reins if she failed. Selecting suitable strains from the genetic stores, she fertilized them according to standard gentech procedure. Two years of development followed under an augmented growth hormone regime. Three died while still in the natal chambers. The others were born—the program said "decanted," but that was such a heartless word—as the ship entered Indi's heliosphere. Education took up the years before insertion around Midgard.

Julia didn't teach them much. There wasn't much they needed to know. The ten boys were meant to be laborers, along with a smattering of carpentry and plumbing. The dozen girls were to be . . . not mothers, though some of them did raise their own children later. But something a lot more than mere nannies or nurses.

They did well, so very well. Adapting to a world they'd never seen quickly and eagerly, wanting only to please Jay, the only adult they knew. Within twenty years they brought up hundreds of children, the true first generation of Middies. She couldn't recall them ever complaining, no matter how hard things got, how little attention she could afford to give them—she'd been so busy after landing; during one period, right at the beginning, she hadn't actually slept for six months straight.

They died young, as accelerates often did, worn out by overwork, and stress, and the terrible weather of those early decades. The boys went first, cut down by heart attacks and strokes with the black still in their hair. Paco, and Ray, and Ken, each laying down their tools one after the other, to rest at last. Then Liselle, the first of the girls, not yet fifty. Soon Vera was all that remained. Julia recalled her, gray and plump, mildly confused by a world she no longer understood, not quite grasping what a family was, happy with the children during the day but so alone at night after they returned to their homes. When she lay dying, Julia had gone to her. A disaster was looming—some kind of native fungal infestation that was deadly poison to Terrest life, if she recalled correctly. There were always crises in those days.

"Now I have you to myself," Vera told her, gripping Julia's hand in hers. She remained there for two days while Vera faded in and out of consciousness and spoke to the other firstborn as if they were still alive, as if that happy time together aboard the ship had never ended. At the last she returned to herself and lay with eyes drinking in Julia's features. "The Erinye will never come, Jay," she said. "The Erinye is afraid of you."

Vera went to join the others on the ridge west of town. Julia wept for the better part of a week, knowing that she would never again experience that kind of devotion, that nobody deserved love that intense, she least of all. The woman who had cheated them of childhood, of any chance of a normal, full life, had denied them even a last name. Perhaps that was when her heart began to harden, when the thread between herself and the world first unraveled. Julia didn't know. All she knew was that now, trying to call up a trace of what she'd felt then, she found nothing. Not even the echo of an echo.

"Ma'am?"

It occurred to Julia, as it probably had a thousand times before, that there was no monument to the firstborn, to mark what they'd bought with their effort and sweat. Nothing more than those stones out on the ridge. She'd named a number of landmarks for them, but she understood that the kids didn't use them, that they had their own names. "Cary—what do the kids call Ray's Pass?"

"Devil's Gate." The AI's voice was precise and cool.

Ah yes, the Gate. They'd named it that after a survey team was stranded there in a blizzard for a month and a half. Five of them had died. "How are you feeling, Cary?"

"Nominal."

Julia waited, but it was obvious that Cariola was not going to ask about her in return. She might have partitioned the shooting, put it in a discrete file as something she didn't want to face, or it could simply be another example of the nastiness she'd displayed in recent years. Julia bit her lip. Yet another soul she'd damaged. Well, Cary would have plenty of opportunity to get her own back. "And how is the . . . occupation going?"

"Quite nicely. I've been checking Dr. Cardnale out on the Core systems this morning. It's been some time since he operated in a cybernetic environment."

"*Dr.* Cardnale?"

"That's how he prefers to be addressed."

Julia suppressed a smile. Danny had never completed any thesis that she knew of. He'd made a habit of telling people that he had a Ph.D. equivalent, though, particularly available young women. "I see."

"There is one problem, Jay . . . ma'am. The fibop stations remain down. All of them, including my remotes. Dead, no data flow at all. We're very concerned about this."

"Who ordered that in the first place, Cary? Danny said he knows nothing about it."

"That's unimportant. The problem is getting them online again. Now . . . Jay, I don't see how it could be, but if this is some scheme of yours, some kind of fallback . . . The only ones who'll suffer will be your kids. Think about that."

"It's beyond me, Cary. I had nothing to do with it. It does strike me as a fine challenge to your intelligence and resourcefulness, though. For both you and *Dr.* Cardnale."

"Danny's associates may not take it so lightly."

"Associates?"

"Herald Fredrix."

"*Harold?* I thought it was . . ."

"Same person, Jay. That's his title. The Herald."

"Hm. Lot of titles being taken on lately."

"How true, *Lady* Amalfi."

Julia paused, mouth open. She'd been about to tell Cary to ask the Herald about the communications problem, but there was no sense in antagonizing her further. "What about the ship? Have you spoken to . . . what was his title again?"

"Magister St. John. No. The ship is still decelerating. No signal can be pushed through the exhaust. He'll be here soon enough."

A bubble of concern rose in Julia. "Cary, you haven't experienced any data exchange, have you? No syngamy, nothing like that . . ."

"I told you, there was insufficient bandwidth," Cariola said sharply. "It's scheduled, though," she went on. "After injection. I'm melding with ship's comp. A complete upload. Everything you tried to keep from me."

"Cary—I'm not criticizing, believe me. But be very careful. You don't know what the Erinye are capable of . . ." She let her voice trail off. If Cariola didn't understand by now, it was useless to keep hammering at it. "How did you contact them anyway? You didn't use our antennas. They're not that sensitive."

"I built one." Cary sounded smug. "I used one of the old construction telefactors. There's a depression on the south slope of Mount Vera—the one the settlers call the Beak. I set down some beams, hooked it up, calibrated it, and started talking."

"How clever of you."

"Not very elegant, but it has a fifteen hundred parsec range. More than enough to reach Sol."

"You said you recorded everything . . ."

"I have eighty-six hours, fourteen minutes, and 3.00012 seconds of material. Fourteen hours plus of exchanges with *Corpus Christi*. You want a download, missy? I can't see any reason, but if you insist . . ."

"Yes, please. Condense it first."

"Salutations and repetitions out—that's roughly ten and a half hours. Processing—"

"And Cary—" A sudden pang struck her. "Do they . . . Did he . . . Is there any mention of Petro?"

"Petro Novichenko? No. Why would there be?"

Julia dropped her eyes. She had no reason to believe that he had survived, and it was probably best if he hadn't, but still—

A disturbance erupted outside. Shapes surrounded the guard. He seemed to be arguing with them. Julia was about to clear the pane when one of them, more massive than the others, moved toward the door.

Sitting up, Julia clutched the sheet to her throat as Keth Fredrix, the Herald himself, stepped into the room.

He stood in the doorway looking about him carefully before settling his eyes on Julia. She stared back at him. She'd never seen him, apart from photos. He was a bigger man than she would have guessed from the unusual broadness of his face. Most of his height was due to the length of his legs. His arms, in contrast, were very short, the hands blunt and heavy. Two of the thick fingers were missing from the right hand. She looked over the dirty fringed suede, the black prospector's boots, before returning to his face. The light colorless eyes stared straight into hers, and for a moment she thought he was trying to hold them before they slid away and she realized that he hadn't noticed her looking back at all.

Fredrix moved slowly into the room, keeping close to the wall, trailing the remaining fingers of the maimed hand against it as if to assure himself of its solidity. When he reached the couch, he swung around and loped over to the mattress quickly enough to startle her.

Snatching the sheet, he jerked it down. Apart from the med units, Julia was naked. Her hands rose to cover herself. She halted them only with effort.

Fredrix inspected her with no expression whatsoever. Finally he expelled a harsh breath and threw the sheet back over her. "Two hundred years," he muttered, as if to himself.

Someone cleared his throat at the door. It was Dan Cardnale. He had trimmed his beard considerably and found clothing suitable to a Ph.D. equivalent. He appeared to be out of breath, as if he'd raced all the way to the house. "Uhh . . . Herald? Your people are being a little rough out there."

Fredrix ignored him, pacing the length of the room in silence. Outside, the shadows had closed in on the guard. An arm lashed out, whether to strike or push she couldn't tell.

"This is the woman's place? Hers alone?" Fredrix was in the kitchen now, inspecting the fixtures.

"Yes—I believe so."

"A complete structure for a single monad," Fredrix said. "You know what that's called?"

"Uhh . . . exploitation?"

"Correct. 'Exploitation is the victory of instinct over rationality, the final triumph of animalism. Diversion of resources by an individual monad is the vilest of assaults against the General Will.' Do you know those words?"

Catching Julia's eye, Cardnale gave an elaborate shrug. "I'm afraid not, Herald."

"A six-year-old should be able to quote the works of Gar from memory." Fredrix's voice echoed from her bedroom. He emerged a second later. Cardnale failed to reply. Instead he nodded at the floor, as if in deep contemplation. Julia glanced between him and Fredrix, wondering what had actually gone on in that valley to the north.

"Of course," Cardnale said brightly, like a schoolboy hitting on the correct answer. "There'll be a much more rational distribution of resources now. That's the entire purpose of . . ."

"Of course," Fredrix echoed. Cardnale fell silent. "Five rooms in this structure." The Herald's voice was thick with disgust. "Five distinct rooms. Like wearing five pairs of britches at once. How much space can a single monad use in one instant of time?"

"Ahh . . . one room?"

"One room." Fredrix's voice was so flat that for a moment Julia thought he was agreeing. Then he spread his arms wide. "Six feet. One monad's space ends where the nose of his neighbor begins."

"Well—" Cardnale said. "To a point, I suppose . . ."

"Sir." It was Cary. "I believe that's an incorrect interpretation of the original statement by Holmes."

Julia hid a smile. Not quite the proper moment for Cary to go into her mistress-of-all-knowledge act . . . But not unwelcome, all the same.

Fredrix's eyes shot toward the ceiling. "That is the talking machine?"

"That's right," Julia said. "Cariola, meet Harry."

Danny made an alarmed face as Cary went on. "The actual quotation is: 'the right of an individual to swing his arms ends at his neighbor's nose.' The reference being . . ."

Giving no sign that he heard, Fredrix advanced on Cardnale. If his face had been emotionless before, there was no word to describe its blankness now. "The woman is in contact with that device . . . ? That is ended."

"I didn't realize it was a problem, Herald."

"I don't think you understand." Fredrix seemed to loom higher against the ceiling. "That machine controls a large amount of explosive matter in orbit. Matter that is a threat to this entire planet."

"I . . . really doubt that Jay would destroy something she's worked on for over a century . . ."

Fredrix approached to within an arm's length of Cardnale. He was several inches shorter, but that made no difference at all. "An oppressor is cut off from the General Will. An oppressor is effectively self-destroyed. In that debased state, any crime is possible. What don't you grasp about this?"

"What the hell is going on here?"

In the doorway stood the young blond rebel, two of his men behind him, both armed. A glance at the window revealed it to be empty, the figures vanished. The boy stepped in. For some reason he had a cue stick over his shoulder.

He looked between Cardnale and Fredrix. "Now,

I hate to break up a reunion between old pals, but there's a few things I'd like explained."

"Uh, Tony," Cardnale said quickly. "If you'd just . . . go off somewhere, I'd be happy to clear things up with you later."

The cue stick thumped to the floor. "Sure, Dan," the boy said. "I could do that. But if I do, those six Blackshirts out there go with me."

Cardnale's eyes widened. Beyond him, Fredrix shifted his head to look directly at Perin for the first time.

"Now, Tony." Cardnale gave a small laugh. "I don't think—"

Fredrix cut him off. "The monads are under authority."

"Monads?" The boy leaned on the pool stick. "What is a *monad*?"

"That's the term for a member of the Rigorist Collective," Cardnale said.

"I see." The young man walked farther into the room, his two companions remaining at the door. "A monad is somebody in black jeans." With a glance at Julia he passed Fredrix and thudded the end of the cue stick on the carpet a few feet behind him, then took up the same pose he'd held at the door. "That clears up monads then. Now let's talk about 'authority.' By whose authority was one of my men being pushed around?"

Fredrix made no move to turn around. "The General Will—" he began blandly.

"I can explain that too, Tony. It's actually very simple—"

His face red, Fredrix swung on Cardnale, who took a step back and dropped his head.

"General Will," the boy said. Pushing up his cap with his thumb, he gazed at the ceiling. "Is he around? Maybe I should take it up with him."

"Who," Fredrix hissed, "is this?"

"This?" Cardnale said. "This is Tony Perin, leader of the Plateau contingent. A very valuable . . . Why, you've met, haven't you? Last month, it was . . ."

"Does he have a rank?"

"Yes, of course. Tony, what did we agree on? Commander, that's it. Commander Perin."

The first discernible expression since he'd stepped into the room crossed Fredrix's face: a slight, barely visible hint of amusement. "Commander," he mouthed silently and turned at last to face Perin. "Well, Commander, the General Will demands certain changes in dispositions here."

"Does it now? Well, that's not the problem." Shifting his stance, the boy pointed with the stick. "If that window was clear, you'd see six Rigs . . . uhh . . . *monads* with their hands over their heads, their cheap-shit, crappy backwoods rifles all in a pile before them. So the dispositions have changed already. The question now is what we're gonna do with 'em. The monads. The guns we may as well throw out."

There was a clatter of footsteps. Perin's men swung about, their weapons raised. Another batch of Rigs appeared in the doorway. Julia shivered when she caught sight of the one in the lead. Those bulging blue eyes, that slash of a mouth . . .

"Tony," Danny said. "Be calm. There's no reason to be alarmed . . ."

" 'Alarmed'? You see me alarmed?" Perin was now gripping the stick at the middle, as if it were a staff. "I'm not the one oughta be alarmed, Danny."

The Rigorists stood in the doorway, rifle barrels nearly touching the metal guns of the men facing them. Cardnale stared at the boy with wide eyes. The expression on Fredrix's face had changed not one iota.

"Hey, Ton!" a voice shouted from outside. "You okay?"

"Everything's cool." Perin gave the stick a twirl. He seemed to be enjoying himself.

"Tony—" Cardnale said.

"You're the one salvaged the woman." Fredrix spoke as if recognizing the boy for the first time.

"That's me," Tony agreed.

"Tony, I think I see the difficulty," Cardnale said eagerly. "Both sides have been isolated from each other for some time. Our social rituals differ . . ."

"Rituals! Yes—" Fredrix whispered.

"No, Danny . . . we understand each other." The end of the stick hit the floor again. "I believe Harold . . . That what they call you? Harold? That Harold has grasped that I placed a guard for a reason, namely to see that the Lady wasn't bothered . . ."

"We require a ritual," Fredrix said, paying no attention to the boy whatsoever.

". . . and that she won't be bothered in the future. In her own home. While she's not feeling well . . ."

"A rally! That's it. That will be our ritual. We shall hold a rally. In celebration of . . . victory."

Cardnale bent closer. "What was that, Herald?"

Fredrix swung to face Perin. "What do you say to that, Commander? A rally. A ritual to cement the alliance between our forces. Forge a bond of common purpose. I'm certain that the doctor could explain the sociometric variables quite succinctly."

"I suggest you agree, Tony."

Perin shrugged. "Sure, why not. Make it two rallies. But not in here."

"No—in the plaza. I believe that the woman once planned celebrations of some sort there. Yes. A fine place for it." Fredrix made a gesture, a small twist of the hand directed at the Rigs by the door. They lowered their guns and stood gazing solemnly at nothing. "Sooner the better. Tonight."

"Whatever you say." Slinging the stick over his

shoulder, Perin moved toward the door. "Now let's clear out—"

"The guards remain," Fredrix said. The boy halted abruptly. Cardnale shot the Herald a look of despair.

"You wish to protect the woman, I believe. A number of the wild monads—"

"The refugees," Cardnale said helpfully.

"—are emotionally driven at this time. There is some danger until incorrect consciousness can be suppressed. We will share this burden."

The boy eyed Fredrix for a moment. "No fuckin' way," he whispered, then raised his head. "Gen!" he shouted.

Footsteps sounded outside. The Rigorists at the door raised their guns.

"Commander—" Julia said.

"I think I have a solution . . ." Cardnale cried.

"Commander Perin!"

The boy turned to her, dropping his eyes at once. "Commander Perin . . . it's all right."

Perin turned away without answering. "Two," he spat at Fredrix. "You leave two. And that one . . ." He reached out and struck the pop-eyed girl with the end of the stick. She didn't even flinch. "Is out. You hear me?"

The Herald raised a finger. The girl snapped to attention, whirled around, and vanished through the door. He looked over at Cardnale. "Doctor. The machine."

Cardnale gave him a startled look. "The machine," the Herald repeated.

"Oh yes, of course. Cariola, you recall what we were speaking of earlier . . . ?"

"Put it into words, Doctor."

Cardnale grimaced. "Cariola, I order you not to speak to Julia until otherwise directed."

Julia opened her mouth, suddenly remembering that she'd forgotten to ask about Vicki.

"Acknowledged."

"Danny," the boy said. "What the hell is this . . . ?"

Cardnale responded with a glare. As he turned away, he came up short—Fredrix had paused in the doorway.

"The rally! At sundown," he called back to Perin.

"Lookin' forward to it," Perin said. "And say hi to General Will for me."

For the first time a smile split the Herald's face. He stepped outside. "A fine prospect," he said. "It'll also serve for the trial."

" 'Trial'?" Cardnale said as he followed him out.

The remaining Rigs stationed themselves at either side of the door. The young man—Tony—gazed at the black-clad youths. "Shoulder those weapons," he told them. They continued staring into space, giving no sign that they'd heard a single word.

"Commander Perin—" Julia said.

His self-assurance seemed to melt away as he turned to her. Inexplicably, he flushed bright red. Sitting up, Julia held out her hand. "Could you help me to the bedroom . . . ?"

He nodded wordlessly and stepped to her side. The clumsy way he took her arm made her wonder if he'd ever touched a woman before. He couldn't be *that* young, could he? All the same, she kept the sheet pulled up around her as they left the room.

He'd already retreated to the door by the time she settled on the bed. "Thank you, Tony. I can call you Tony, can't I?"

"Oh sure," he said, and then, in a rush of muttered words: "Beg your pardon for my use of language earlier, ma'am." And with a jerky nod he was gone, before she could even ask him to visit her later.

She heard him speak to his people in a low voice and thought of calling him back. But what was the point? Cardnale, Midgard's latest doctor of humanities, acting as if he'd had a portion of his frontal lobe cleared, and the boy, apologizing for swearing in front of a woman who'd heard curses in languages that he didn't know existed. This pair opposed by a—what? Sociopath, messiah, demagogue? She wasn't sure what word described Fredrix. Or even if there was a word.

She began to ask Cary to download the file on Fredrix, Keth. But that avenue too was now closed to her. Instead she curled up under the sheet, thinking of Vicki, hoping she had gotten away all right.

five

The boys must have been getting bored; they greeted the news of the rally with high spirits—taking part in a public ceremony put on by a gang of repulsive weirdos evidently held pleasures all its own.

Tony looked down at them from the roof of the lab, one boot on the low rampart. He was chewing on a spike of cokeweed. A stimulant, not precisely what he needed at the moment, annoyed and frustrated as he was.

Across the plaza and about fifty yards down, a group of Rigs was putting up a platform. A pretty simple deal, little more than boards stretching from the far wall to the slope behind, but they were working on it as intently as if it was one of the pyramids of ancient days. Three dozen or so, scurrying around in total silence apart from two barking overseers. It looked like a lot of wasted effort to Tony, but that seemed to be the way they did things.

Down at the far end, a gang lounged around the tree. Tony squinted on catching sight of a man dressed like Dan Cardnale. But no; too short by at least a head. He'd been looking for Cardnale since leaving the Lady's house, with no luck to speak of. At the computer shack—the Core, they called it—one of the kids from the committee told him she didn't know where the doctor was or when he'd be back. About what he'd expected; that particular staffer— Resi, her name was—had always treated him like a piece of livestock that had somehow wandered into the house. Blank looks and a twisted lip, as if it would be a waste of time to do anything more than hustle him back to the barnyard.

After poking around a little longer, he concluded that Cardnale was at the cophouse, enjoying a lazy afternoon with the Blackshirts. Waste of time following him—Tony doubted he'd get straight answers as to why Dan had become spokesman for the Garite Collective in front of that kind of audience.

Behind him came footsteps. It was Vitig, carrying the first of the rockets. Tony gave him a nod. Setting down the round, Vitig stretched. He gestured at the plaza. "Make a real sweet kill zone," he said.

"So it would."

To Tony's mind, one of the challenges facing a strategist was knowing when to stop. The biting-off-more-than-you-could-chew conundrum: Alexander polishes off the Peloponnesus with no problem, but then the Persians have to be pushed out of Asia Minor. That done, why not sweep them from Syria and the Levant too? But there's still Persians in Persia, so let's deal with that problem once and for all. And beyond Persia beckons Hindustan . . .

Along with the arrow with your name on it, the roving malaria bug, or the poisoned cup of wine. It was an awful temptation, equipped with the proper instrument, to keep going, right over and through any possible opposition. But there was a limit, easily defined—if perhaps only in hindsight—beyond which any army, any conceivable act of force, gained you nothing.

Tony had set his own limit at the Cloister. Take the place, restore order, then hand it all gift-wrapped and nice to whoever was in a position of authority. Dan Cardnale, his committee, some kind of coalition, Tony didn't care what. A government, a setup that would run things more reasonably than Dame Amalfi's herd of bureaucrats. Something he could turn his back on with the sense that he was making an intelligent move.

But he'd be damned if he left it to the Rigs, particularly with old Fredrix shambling forth from the Underworld—what a kick in the pants that was. When Tony was growing up, Keth Fredrix had been the bundiman, something you scared kids with: keep out of those woods, Fredrix the Rig might be in there. And here he was, big as life, suede fringes and all, as if he'd been popped into a suspension tank to await the day of the Apocalypse. One look at him had made Tony glad he'd stayed away from the woods after all.

He could wish the same for old Dan. He couldn't for the life of him figure what Cardnale was thinking. Head of the reform faction, Midgard's voice of conscience, the man who'd drawn the line. Last one you'd expect to find in the same bed with the Rigs. But Tony had seen it—and a disgusting sight it was too. He was now wondering exactly how long that particular orgy had been going on.

Something grated at the end of the plaza. Tony saw that a branch of the big oak had collapsed and now hung by a few shards of wood. As he watched, an arm flourishing an axe appeared from behind the trunk and resumed hacking.

"Hey!" he shouted, knowing it was too far. "That's

the Lady's tree! Stu!" he called down. "Foxy—run over and tell those gurj dogs that tree ain't firewood. Gen, go with 'em."

The branch thumped to the ground, its leafy end splashing in the fountain. Tony shot a glance at the house. He hoped she hadn't seen that. She'd planted that tree herself, early days. At least he thought that was the one.

His face went hot as he recalled how he'd stood before her today without a coherent sentence in his head. Conscious only of those eyes, the fact that she wore nothing beneath that sheet. In some of the Threshold villages, the small ones settled to get out from under the plan, people looked upon her as a witch. Tony could understand that. And this morning he'd heard Stu, after standing guard, say that she "was pretty hot for a century and a half." He understood that too.

He'd have to look out for her. Nobody else was doing it, and the minute he turned his back there would be some kind of accident; he could take that for a God-ordained fact. He should have picked up Pop-Eyes when he had the chance. Should have stood up to Fredrix this morning. Should have chased out those Rigs, should have this, should have that . . .

He bit down on the cokeweed stem. The cinnamony, sweet-harsh taste filled his mouth. Nothing could be simple. God forbid that you try to accomplish anything worthwhile without a lot of unnecessary complication and bother. You'd think there were prizes for confusion, that the purpose of existence was endless muddle, that the human race had emerged into the galaxy after three million-odd years of evolution to teach the universe how to fuck up.

The last thing in the world he wanted to do was stick around here. He'd done his job. He had a life on the Plateau. People were waiting for him back home.

He plucked the stem from his lips and flicked it over the roof edge. But he was going to do it anyway. Why was he up here working out fields of fire otherwise?

A change in the quality of sound caught his attention. The workers had gathered at the platform, now as finished as it ever would be. Fredrix was striding toward it from the direction of the cophouse. Beside him, like a well-trained pet, trotted Dan Cardnale.

Tony squeezed his eyes shut. A surge of weed buzz struck him, forcing them open. Weed's caffeine content was a lot higher than coffee, particularly when you chewed. All he needed to do was step over the edge and simply drift down to the ground. But the stairs were a better idea. He went to the doorway, found them already dark. Sundown; Fredrix had insisted on sundown. He picked his way downstairs carefully, nearly running into Vitig hauling up another rocket. He wondered if there would be torches.

There were, and plenty of them. At least two dozen held by the closest row of Rigs, the same number on the far side, another line in front, an honor guard surrounding the bloodred flag at the center.

"You know, man," somebody said. "We oughta have torches too."

Tony looked over his shoulder. There had been whining about no Orc banner as well. "You want black beanies while you're at it?"

There was no response. Tony eyed them a moment longer. It hadn't been easy, stuffed with roast pork as they were, to get them across the plaza in any kind of order, particularly after watching that perfect rectangle of marching figures advance from the station in complete silence. He'd managed, though, even succeeded in getting something resembling a martial tune from Bryn and Ravi on the way over. The last thing he'd told the men was not to antagonize the Rigs.

He had to admit the Blackshirts looked damned impressive. The sun was touching the horizon, scattered clouds further dimming the ambient light. The torches glowed brighter every passing second, revealing more clearly the ranks of pale faces seeming to float above the black uniforms. You had to look close to see that it wasn't the same one repeated row after row, closer still to discover that they were all kids, no older than their late teens.

Tony's grasp of Rigorism as a political philosophy was limited. Why bother? It was a dead issue, after all. Its origin was the 20th century—not the smartest era to derive a political system from—with roots in still older periods through the ideas of people like . . . Rosso and Mark, he thought it was. Mixing together vague social speculations had been a common intellectual hobby back then. The results, often taken more seriously than deserved, were systems called "ideologies," secular substitutes for religion.

The Rigorist ideology, Collectivism, had been quite popular at the turn of the millennium. People with wild Terrest names like Robspear, Steel, Paul Pot, and Mayo Z. Dong had applied it to vast areas of Eurasia with startling results. Its thesis was that certain arbitrary types of organizations—state, party, polity, whatever—were the predominant social entities, with individuals acting solely as cells within the larger structure. It sounded to Tony as if it was based on serious misunderstanding of basic physiology.

That was all he knew about Rigorism—but it was enough. Merely looking at them would have been enough. One glance at the way they stood, arms slightly out, fingers open and loose. The faces, utterly blank but seeming to strain at some unknowable emotion. The eyes as empty as a doll's. All that told him plenty; he didn't need any more.

His hand brushed the gun at his hip, a revolver based on an old Terrest design and named for an infant horse. He didn't like those smocks they had on. Too big and too loose; anything could be hidden beneath them. He looked back at the bio center. His breath caught when he saw no one atop the roof. Then a figure—Gen, it must be—moved into sight. Tony raised his arm and waved. Gen echoed the gesture.

A few of the men craned their necks to look for themselves. He hadn't explained why he'd left a dozen men behind; didn't think it necessary. Here they stood, almost completely boxed in, Rigs on one side, Bilis on the other. You didn't have to be a field marshal to take precautions under those circumstances.

He shifted to get a clear view of the Bilis. It was the first time he'd seen them up close. About three hundred of them, scattered in no special order, mostly sprawled on the slate. They appeared to be your standard poor migrant trash—gyps, hipis, turx; shitbums, in a word—not particularly ragged, nor particularly clean either. Quite a few were wearing what looked like new duds. He imagined they'd been rooting around in the homes over the village, which was no surprise—turn your back on a Bili and the ass of your pants was gone. Gen had seen some black berets when they arrived. None were visible now.

A few steps away a girl who appeared far too young to have given birth to the infant in her lap raised the child and pointed at Tony. "See the man?" she said.

Tony allowed himself a wink. Taking the child's hand, the girl made waving motions. He smiled. Maybe they weren't that bad, after all . . .

"Tony Junior," somebody muttered.

Tony swung slowly around, not making any point of it. The men were laughing, with that sheepish air of tension suddenly broken. "Hey, chief . . ." It was Sam Driser. "When's this thing start anyway?"

It had been at least ten minutes. Tony shrugged and was about to confess to ignorance when somebody else said, "Let's have some tunes."

"Yeah."

"I mean, a rally's like a party, ain't it?"

"Junkado!"

Bryn hoisted his synth—the damn thing must weigh twelve, fifteen pounds, but he'd hauled it down from the Plateau regardless—and shot Tony an eager smile. Tony raised a hand. "Now, whoa—"

"Ah, come on, Tonio—"

"Junkado!"

Tony hesitated, about to give in. But a glance over his shoulder revealed a group emerging from the trees surrounding the college.

"Quiet," he said. "They're coming." He turned to face the platform and crossed his arms. Then, considering what kind of impression that might give, he let them fall.

As he might have guessed, Fredrix was in the lead, dressed exactly as he had been earlier. Cardnale stood at his left, accompanied by a couple of his staffers, one of them that odious Resi. Two Rigs, interchangeable with any of those standing in the plaza, followed Fredrix on his right. The group halted on reaching the boards, the Rigs going to opposite ends of the platform while the others waited. Tony imagined they'd spent the time under the trees working out the program or . . .

"Harry-y-y-y!" somebody in the ranks called out.

The men were already shushing whoever it was by the time Tony swung around. Trust them to figure *that* out. He cast a glance at the Rigs to see if any of them had noticed and stopped dead. Not ten feet off stood Little Miss Knifework, her eyes fixed on him. When she caught his gaze, she smiled and dropped her head. Tony looked away. Now what the hell was this? He inspected the men, relieved to see that none of them had noticed. He stealthily glanced back in her direction. She was now gazing raptly at the platform.

"What is the Rigorist Tendency?"

It was the one on the right side, a girl, from the sound of her voice.

"The Rigorist Tendency is the correct expression of consciousness infusing matter within the universe," the other, a male, answered.

"Oh *shit*."

"What is the goal of Rigorism?"

"The goal of Rigorism is to spread correct consciousness . . ."

". . . until everybody is bored to fuckin' death."

"*Quiet!*" Turning on his heel, Tony walked down the line. Behind him, the catechism droned on: "What is the nature of correct consciousness?"

"This *sucks*, Tony."

". . . call this a rally? This ain't no rally."

"What is the nature of the General Will?"

"The General Will is the expression of correct consciousness within the social framework created by the action of Rigorist . . ."

"Section heads—shut 'em up! Not one word—I ain't *fuckin'* with you guys now—"

"What is the role of the monad?"

With the subtle encouragement of the section heads—Tony hadn't been able to decide whether to call them sergeants or officers and had left it at that—the men calmed down. None of the Rigs appeared to be paying any attention, though there were some wide-eyed looks from the Bilis. Behind the platform, Fredrix lurked in the dimness, his expression unreadable. Cardnale smiled beside him.

At last it was over, with a long exchange concerning the relationship between monads, correct con-

sciousness, the General Will, and a lot of other stuff
that Tony had missed. Then the second part of the
festivities erupted.

In unison, the Rigs began to speak, uttering the
same lines in one voice: "We are the Rigorist Tendency. We are the children of Gar. Gar the thinker.
Gar the leader. Gar the sun of the new dawn . . ."

Their expressions hadn't changed, though Tony
spotted a face or two grown bright with emotion. His
own men were keeping their thoughts to themselves,
content with staring at the Rigs as if they'd come
across a race who processed sheep turds for a living.
Behind the platform, Fredrix didn't appear to be saying much, but . . . Tony cocked his head. For a moment there he would have sworn that Resi's lips had
been moving . . .

". . . we require destruction in order to construct.
We require theory for there to be life. We require
what others call faith, but which Gar calls heart and
which the Rigorist Tendency calls the conscience, to
understand that afterward something can flower . . ."

The light was too poor for him to be sure, but . . .
There—was she doing it again? Something else he'd
have to look into. What kind of name was "Resi"
anyway?

". . . under the firm, enlightened guidance of the
Herald Fredrix, Brother Number Two, mirror to
Gar's sun, we stand witness to the validity of Rigorist
thought before the emptiness of the universe."

Tony fought back an impulse to say "Amen." For
a moment silence reigned, then Brother Number Two
walked slowly out onto the platform.

"Yi-yi-yi-yi-yi-yi-yi . . ."

The sound came as a shock, though Tony should
have expected it. Mouths wide, fists in the air, the
Rigs stood as if frozen in place, yipping at the top
of their lungs. Behind him, the men cursed, inaudible
over the din. Tony opened his mouth to shout, but

that was futile. Instead he crossed his arms and looked between the howling Rigs and Fredrix, who gazed tranquilly out over the shaking fists as if this was a normal, everyday occurrence. Maybe it was.

The yipping went on for two minutes or more, then abruptly cut off. "Assholes," a voice said, nearly drowned out by the wails of several children among the Bilis. Tony looked back. As he expected, the infant who had waved was among them.

"Comrades of the Rigorist Tendency," Fredrix said, "fraternal greetings."

He stood quietly a moment, as if waiting for the infants to stop howling. At last his arms rose. "Today we see an end . . . The constant opposition of freeman and slave, patrician and plebeian, oppressor and oppressed, carrying on an uninterrupted, now hidden, now open struggle, a struggle that each time ended in revolutionary reconstitution of society at large or in the common ruin of the contending classes.

"That is now ended."

One child—the same infant, in fact—was still crying. The girl whispered to it and stroked its head. Funny how a child's crying was more aggravating than any other sound.

". . . drowned the most heavenly ecstasies of religious fervor, of chivalric enthusiasm, of Philistine sentimentalism, in the icy water of egotistical calculation.

"That is now ended."

"What the hell is he talking about?" somebody said, too loudly for comfort. Tony waved for silence.

". . . all that is solid melts into air, all that is holy is profaned, and the monad is at last compelled to face, with sober senses, his real condition of life, and his relations with his kind."

The child's wails had reached that stage where they were beginning to dissolve into hiccups. Its mother seemed about to break into tears herself. She was looking around frantically, as if she was engaged in criminal activity and certain that punishment was only a moment away. She caught Tony's eye and sat up higher, biting her lip.

"Not only has the buji forged the weapons that bring death to itself; it has also called into existence the people who are to wield those weapons: the monads, the Rigorist Tendency . . ."

Tony leaned toward one of the men. "Alic—see that girl? Go help her with the kid. Take 'em back to the rear, someplace out of earshot."

"Will do," Alic nodded. "Not like I'll miss anything."

". . . the most advanced and resolute element, that element which pushes forth all others. They have over the great mass the advantage of clearly understanding the line of march, the conditions, and the ultimate results . . ."

He watched Alic approach the girl. He was a family man; he'd know what to do. Tony was about to look away when two men, somewhat better dressed than the other Bilis, shot to their feet, glaring at Alic. Uncrossing his arms, Tony was about to wade in himself when the men halted, their attention caught by something over his shoulder. They abruptly sat back down. Looking around, Tony saw nothing more than Rigs entranced by the Mirror of Gar.

"The Rigorists disdain to conceal their views and aims. They openly declare that their ends can be obtained only by forcible overthrow of all existing social conditions. Let the ruling classes tremble. The monads have nothing to lose but their chains. They have a world to win."

That was it. Not wound up with any particular flourish; the only way you could tell Fredrix was finished was that he'd stopped speaking. For a moment he gazed out over the plaza—he'd never dropped his eyes once; it was as if he'd been addressing an audience hovering twelve feet above the slate—then, without another word, he swiveled and left the platform.

Tony braced himself for another Rig outburst but was disappointed. There they stood, pegs on a board, matching Fredrix's emotional crescendos peak for peak. Tony reached up and ran a hand over his scalp. What the hell was the *purpose* of all this?

"That's it," Nik Ravi muttered. "Get me some black britches. I'm going Rig." Somebody tittered. "Better still, I'll dye the ones I got on. Save me some coin . . . Well, look here. Excitement at last."

Cardnale had emerged from the shadows, looking more subdued than was customary for him. He crept onto the platform, head down as if he was reluctant to appear. Halting a few steps from the edge, he raised his head, opened one hand. "Sixscore and twelve years ago, our forefathers brought forth on this planet . . ."

Somebody behind Tony suggested in a low voice that they all start screaming and jumping around when Danny finished. Tony paid no attention. He was trying to recall where he'd come across those lines before. He knew he'd seen them; it was an actual speech, from the millennium prior to this one. Not from a play or flick either . . .

"The universe will little note, nor long remember, what we say here, but it can never forget what we did here . . ."

"Hey," Ravi said. "That's not too bad."

"Yeah. It was good the first time too." One of the big leaders, a name you'd remember. Churchill, Rosenfeld . . . Could it be Regan?

Cardnale lifted his fist for the climax. ". . . shall not perish . . ." He paused, his hand dropping to his side. "Not perish . . ."

Tony frowned. Cardnale was staring off into space exactly as Fredrix had done. As Tony watched, his eyes went wide, his jaw fell, and then his lips curled into a smile.

Voices surged behind Tony. He turned, ran his gaze over the motionless Rigs, the Bilis. Someone pointed to the west. Tony lifted his eyes.

The sun had nearly vanished. All that remained was a thin sliver behind the hills ringing the valley, lending a soft glow to the higher clouds. That and a harsh pinpoint of light surrounded by a wavering nimbus of fire, directly above the lingering slice of sun.

Tony felt a shiver course through him. It's a mirror, he told himself. Mirrors could look awful strange at times, especially when they were repositioning, moving to a different orbit or another sector of the sky. It had to be a mirror; couldn't be anything else.

But certainty was not to be found, and amid all the doubt, another thought echoed: that is no mirror.

Back home, up the Plateau, there was an old guy named Sinclar, lived on the ridge the other side of town. Sinclar passed a lot of his time in the square in front of Lin's general store, and he was willing to lecture all comers on his thesis that there was no such place as Earth, that people had never come from there, that no machine like a starship had ever existed, that in fact the stars weren't stars at all, that it was just a story thrown together to explain why things were, much like the tales in the Dunkers' Bible.

Tony wondered what Sinclar was doing now, if he was looking west, and if so, what might be going through his mind.

The last piece of sun slipped away. The pinpoint seemed to redouble in brightness. To one side, something else became visible: a thin, glowing line, like a thread of light, receding into the sky as if trailing off into infinity.

The Bilis had risen to their feet. Tony's men milled

around, all wild glances and hands thrown into the air. Even the Rigs were reacting: peering over their shoulders before jerking their heads straight forward once more. "That's a . . ." a nearby voice said. "That's a . . ."

"That's a ship," Tony whispered.

The splotch of light shimmered, as if in response. Tony felt his guts tighten as half-remembered stories of childhood rose up, tales of the horror and degradation that had engulfed the Homeworlds: of people growing into machines, of time and space become weapons, of the murder of souls. Among the Bilis, a woman began wailing.

A roar sounded behind him. Tony tore his gaze from the ship only with difficulty. Fredrix stood on the platform once again. Face red, eyes fixed on the western sky, he bellowed as if to drive the ship back into the night from where it had come. "Impossible . . . That *thing* . . . That is a lie." An arm shot out. "You're looking at a *lie*."

Cardnale retreated into the shadows, his face a study in mild alarm. The two Rigs eyed each other, then looked back at Fredrix. One of the Bilis began reciting something aloud that had the Deity in it.

Tearing off his hat, Fredrix swept it before him. A few strands of gray hair clung to his nearly bald scalp. "It's her . . . The female, the old whore. She called them. To take it back. All that is solid . . . Bring her here. All of you. As one. I wish to demonstrate . . . I will purge . . . I . . ."

The hat fell to the raw boards. Legs bent, Fredrix staggered toward the edge of the platform, as if to throw himself out into the audience. That final syllable stretched and repeated, for all the world sounding like the Rig war cry: "*I-I-I-I* . . ." A woman screamed.

The two Rigs caught Fredrix as he reached the edge. He went to his knees, his bulk nearly taking

them all off the platform. His head lolled, then jerked
high, eyes showing only white. A splash of red appeared at his mouth.

Half-dragging him, the Blackshirts bore him offstage, his boot heels hammering a ragged tattoo
against the boards. In the sudden quiet, Tony heard
that voice still praying, several women in tears, and
a confused whisper rising from the assembled Rigs.
Quiet as it was, the sound caused a chill to climb
his spine.

He swung toward Ravi and Bryn. "Give us a
tune."

They stared at him a moment before raising their
instruments, Ravi his drum pad and Bryn the synth.
With a glance at each other they broke into the same
slow march they'd played on the way over. Now it
sounded like a dirge.

"No—" Tony snapped his fingers. "Something
fast . . . some Island thing."

"Gotcha." Ravi changed rhythm in midstroke, the
beat accelerating and splitting up simultaneously. It
took Bryn a second or two to catch on, the slow tones
of the march breaking into the scatter of quick notes
that marked junkado.

The Rigs were still in some kind of trance. Unity
was staring at the empty platform with an expression
of childlike amazement. Closer by, a small Blackshirt
wrung her hands, face twisted in what looked like
absolute terror. Tony noticed two fallen torches sput-
tering against the slate. "Louder," he said.

The music boomed out. Tony began clapping, waving at the men to do likewise. One of them stepped
forward. He saw that it was Dud Mos, holding up
his harp, a questioning look on his face. "Yeah,"
Tony told him. "More the better."

All the men were clapping now, a few throwing
in whistles and shouts for good measure. Tony
turned to the Bilis. A handful were matching the

beat, but most sat motionless, gripped by fear. Tony moved closer. He noticed a few of the men doing the same. It never took them long to figure things out, God bless 'em.

After a minute or so, enough of the Bilis had picked up the beat that he felt comfortable dropping it himself. It was just as well—he'd never been much for music and he'd been at least a half-second ahead the whole time. He backed off, feeling the tension drop as clearly as if he'd let a bag of feed fall from his shoulders. A glance at the Rigs showed them to be . . . not doing any sort of heel-and-toe themselves, that was too much to expect. But at least they were no longer gaping at the platform, where their prophet—not too strong a word—had just now been carried off in the midst of one of worst fits Tony had ever witnessed. Instead all were facing the source of the sounds, looking on blankly, a few in obvious puzzlement, as if they'd never seen the like before.

Tony turned away. One of the men had a Bili girl on her feet and was showing her some steps. Others were figuring them out on their own. Tony rubbed his forehead, wondering if he'd actually prevented an eruption just now or if he'd simply overreacted, victimized by his own confusion.

A movement caught his eye. Cardnale was approaching, his people in tow. His face cracked a smile. "How was I?"

"Uhh—great, Dan. Just great. You ought to write that down. Preserve it for history."

"Yes—too bad I didn't get a chance to finish. But—" He gestured at the sky.

"Yeah. That light . . ." Tony nodded toward it, bright enough now to cast shadows, even half cut off by the horizon. "Could that possibly be a starship?"

Cardnale's smile broadened. "So it is."

Tony put his hands on his hips, studied the man before him. Behind Cardnale, shouts rang out—the

Rigs marching off the plaza. Tony paid them no mind. "Dan—we gotta talk."

"We'll do that, son," Cardnale assured him. He gripped Tony's arm. "But say—everything will be fine. Believe it. He'll have to come to me now." He bent closer, his eyebrows high. "And he's an epileptic!"

With a final squeeze Cardnale swept off. Resi followed, without a glance for Tony. The other staffer, a kid whose name he'd forgotten, winked as he passed. "Great move, those tunes."

The Rigs were gone, their dark backs fading into dimness. The Bilis were also moving off. As he watched, a man who looked little different from the others yanked the dancing girl backward to join the march. A knot of Tony's men stepped toward them but came to a quick stop, as puzzled as Tony himself.

"You men!" A voice rang out. It was Cardnale, waving a piece of paper over his head. "Listen here—I had no chance to say this on the platform." The waving became frantic. "This is an inventory of the precious metals in Amalfi's treasury. I'm pleased to say that there is enough surplus to provide every member of the Screaming Orcs with three full ounces of gold! What do you say?"

The cheer that followed said it all. A forest of pumping fists and waving arms shot high as the men mobbed Cardnale. Tony gritted his teeth, fighting a surge of emotion more caustic than any he could recall; barely felt annoyance at last sliding over the edge into blazing hatred. He strode toward the backs of the men surrounding Cardnale.

A man with a rifle strapped across his shoulder pushed his way out of the crowd. He was bearded and dressed in a jacket that looked a lot more like a uniform than anything the Orcs wore. Catching sight of Tony, he stepped into his path. "You in charge here?" he shouted above the uproar.

"That's right."

The man gave him a loose salute. "Des Shor, the Mavericks. Got word for you, skip."

Tony let out a sigh. Another legitimate outfit at last. "Am I glad to see you . . ."

Thick cloud suddenly covered the ship's exhaust, and darkness at last fell over the plaza.

SIX

Clarity. That was what he gained from times like this. The only thing he gained. The feeling of power that gripped him during the fits, when the deep fire surged to a point that he could no longer subdue it, that sense of a connectedness, of *aliveness*, that was illusion. No better than drunkenness. But the clarity, that was different. That was real. That he could use.

He had long ago decided that he could tear something of value from anything that happened to him, be it a beating, or a stretch in the jailhouse, or leading the Collective across the cold of the glaciers up north. That was how he differed from the others in this kennel of a world. The monads simply got through it. They held on, they subsisted, they suffered, and that was all. Only he knew how to grasp advantage from event, to go to the core and take what mattered.

Clarity—that was his reward for the fits. A short period without doubt or confusion, when his vision

was unbounded, when his thoughts had the solidity
of iron. As if the blaze that surged through him blew
away some invisible mist enwrapping him tight,
leaving nothing between him and the world as it
was.

But it always faded, dissipating into the fog of ordinary days. As it was doing right now.

He bent close to the screen. "*Corpus Christi.*" His
voice was thick, his tongue swollen where he'd bitten
it. He'd told them a thousand times what to do when
it happened, and they hadn't done it. The episodes
were nothing for the monads to see. Someone would
be struggled for that. Struggled until they broke. A
personal correction for the benefit of the Collective.

He forced out the words. "That is a name?"

"Yes, sir," the machine said. "It means—"

"I don't give a damn what it means." He sank
back in the chair that had belonged to the woman's
chief of police. His buckskin jacket lay atop the desk,
and his shirt was open wide. His gray hair stuck out
stiffly in all directions, but he didn't know that. He
looked far older than he did in the daylight, and that
was lost to him as well. "This vessel is from the
old worlds."

"Yes, sir."

"Who sent for it?"

"It was not actually sent for, sir, so much as—"

"The woman. Amalfi."

"No, sir. Lady Amalfi definitely did not call for
the starship."

"Don't lie to me, machine. I'll know if you do."
He felt a tightness in his chest. Machines should not
talk as a man talked.

"She's . . . far too fearful, sir. Completely mistaken
about the situation in the Home System. Living in a
night—"

"They lie to me constantly. All of them. Even the
monads, the ones I trained. But I can always tell.

And if I can tell with them, I can damn well tell with a machine."

"Yes, sir. Now, might I suggest some rest? The medication I administered is quite effective, but your metabolism still exhibits signs of considerable disturb—"

"You are monitoring me?"

"Yes, of course—"

"That will *cease*!"

The machine was silent for a moment. When it answered, the volume was quite low. "Yes, sir."

The lights in the Core went on automatically, a feature that Cardnale had always liked. He paused halfway up the stairs, reveling in the pleasure of experiencing a cybernetic environment once again. It had been a long time.

He continued into Cary's space, tossing his case on a nearby console. Calling up a chair, he sat down and sighed. He'd been running all day long, and he wasn't as spry as he'd once been.

Resi and Myk stood at the top of the stairs, looking extremely ill at ease. He gestured them in. "Come along—Cariola won't bite."

They stepped inside, Resi running a hand over one of the consoles, glancing about her with a quizzical expression. Cardnale caught himself before he laughed aloud. "In fact, you'll enjoy it. Working with a silicon entity is one of the higher pleasures. Like music, mathematics . . ."

"Why didn't you tell us about the ship, Dan?"

Cardnale regarded Resi a moment. A natural question under the circumstances, one he had no easy answer for. "Need to know, my dear."

Myk perched atop a console. "It's actually from Earth?"

"I don't know about Earth. The Home System anyway. Close enough, at this distance."

"Who was aware of it?"

Resi was still on her feet, arms hanging loosely. A good girl: steady worker, smart as a whip, no complaints. But odd. He had to admit that. "Myself and Cariola. That's it. Our own little conspiracy."

"Perin didn't know? The Lady?"

"Not Perin, not Ma, not Freddy either. As you may have guessed."

Myk chuckled. "I'll say." Resi said nothing.

"I wasn't aware he was that ill. We'll have to keep an eye on him, won't we? Also, since you mentioned the name, let me suggest that we subject Commodore Perin to a little benign neglect. I think you'll agree he's rather crude."

"He handled that panic at the rally real well," Myk said. "Things were getting out of hand."

"We all have our moments, Myk. Even the most ham-handed of us. Now let's begin. Cary . . . when can we expect contact with our visitor?"

"Don't you ever try that again."

"Yes, sir."

"I monitor. I am not monitored. Ever. You hear?"

"Yes."

"Your house is a few hundred yards from here. Five minutes. Less, runnin'. I could walk in and tear you limb from limb—or whatever your parts are called. And you can't hurt a human, can you?"

"No, sir."

"So I got the stick and you will jump. Keep that in mind." He paused to work his jaw. He'd scraped his tongue just now. The fresh taste of copper again filled his mouth. "Now—who else knew about this ship?"

"Dan . . . Dr. Cardnale."

He gritted his teeth. The man was a devil greater than all devils. He'd possess the foulest of them and make it even worse. "When did he call for this vessel?"

"He did not call for it, sir."

"Now look here, machine—"

"The *Corpus Christi* was en route for Tau Ceti from the Home System when it changed course for Midgard roughly seventeen years ago—"

"What?" He shot from the seat. "Are you mad? Seventeen *years*? It don't take years to get from noplace to noplace. What are you saying? Do machines go mad? Answer me."

"It has been known to occur, sir."

"You are well on your way." He sat back down. "That will be dealt with. There are no useless mouths in the Collective. Not even if they're made of . . . whatever metal you are made of. Understand?"

"Yes, sir."

He webbed his hands in front of him. The appearance of that light, so sharp and piercing, had been a shock to him, who had not been shocked by anything for quite a few years. He'd never believed all that bilge about the old worlds. A lie, like the woman's other lies. Gar had once deconned what the woman claimed to be "history," concentrating on one period alone: the 20th century. Einstein, Churchill, Stalin, Hitler—figures as fantastic as their names, figures who supposedly loomed over a whole world, an entire period, like giants. Like the bitch herself. And what did you find when you looked at those names? Church-on-the-Hill. True-Man. Rosy-field. A tissue of myth and fantasy. Obvious once you knew what to look for.

He raised his head. "Machine. Tell me about . . . Lincoln."

"Abraham Lincoln?"

"That's right."

"Abraham Lincoln, 1809–1865, sixteenth President of the United States, known as the Great Emancipator . . ."

He grunted to himself. So the machine was filled with lies too. He should have guessed. Cardnale told him that they put information and ideas into the things before they even taught them to think. He looked at the screen, dark except for one blinking blotch of light in the corner. He couldn't see what use it would be now. It would have to be destroyed, the way anything useless was destroyed.

But he knew that the machine wasn't in here, not in this box on the desk. It was in that building, the special one built for itself alone. He'd have to ask Cardnale exactly how to go about shutting it down. "Where is Cardnale now?"

". . . no exact data on the capabilities of the *Corpus Christi*. It is unquestionably a considerable advance over the Voyageur class, which includes *Petrel*. References to proton manipulation and mass/energy screens are only speculative in the literature on file . . ."

"So you don't *know* when they arrive," Cardnale said patiently.

"No, Doctor. It will be in a relatively short time. The power available from proton compression is immense. The vessel exceeded more than fifty gees when it first accelerated toward this system, which in itself involved a course change impossible for earlier models. And the main engine is not the sole method of slowing the ship, if my understanding of the term 'virtual drag' is correct. Using *Petrel*'s instrumentation, I've detected large-scale anomalies along *Corpus Christi*'s vector of approach, electromagnetic, gravitic, and spatial in nature. Some of these appear to have slightly affected Indi itself—"

"I see," Cardnale said, ignoring a gasp from behind him. "What's your estimate?"

"A loose one, sir, is two days to a week. The ship has already passed Indi and seems to—"

"Very well. But we can't talk to St. John while the engines are running?"

"That's true, sir."

Cardnale made a face. "He's out of touch a large part of the time. Bad design, wouldn't you say?"

"The drawbacks are inherent, sir, characteristic of virtually any starship design—"

"I understand."

"Dan?" It was Myk, his voice very soft. "What about the Erinye?"

"You mean to say you're speaking to him *now*? While you're talking to me?"

"Yes, sir. Multiuser access is a standard feature of all AI systems."

Fredrix raised a hand to his lips. "Can you . . . play what he's saying?"

A long moment passed before Cariola answered. When she did, her voice was grating, as if the words were dragging through a damaged speaker. "I could."

"Go on."

". . . is mythology."

"I thought so," a female voice said.

"Resolution," Fredrix whispered. He looked up sharply, mouthed, "Can he hear me?"

"No, sir. Not at this time."

"Fine. You fix it so he cannot. Ever." He made a sound deep in his throat. "I could use *this*."

"Sir . . . I'm very uncomfortable with this situation. I'm programmed to honor human rights of—"

"Do as I say."

Cary's answer was so distorted as to be incomprehensible.

". . . not completely a matter of myth. Though it appears that Dame Amalfi was to some extent dishonest—which may be caused by a deep-seated mental disturbance—the Erinye definitely existed and had an effect on Home System history."

"Why does your voice sound that way—that echo, like."

"It's a tag, sir. It shows that I'm not addressing you."

". . . did the skipper say about the Erinye? Did he tell you what happened?"

"Who is that?"

"Mykel Wilis, Dr. Cardnale's public relations officer."

"Uh. A monad."

". . . rather vague. Textual analysis convinced me that this was a matter of historical perspective. That Magister St. John was referring to matters that occurred long ago from his perspective and were of little personal relevance."

"But you're *sure*?"

"Myk, let's drop this. You can discuss it with Cary anytime. I'd like to get back to the communications situation. Now, Cary, this is rather frustrating. I do need to speak to St. John as to how he can assist us with our difficulties here. Reorganization, getting those self-styled troops back home, the Garite problem—"

A small sound escaped Fredrix. He scraped his teeth with his tongue, almost relishing the sharp jolt of pain.

". . . the protocols for recontact procedure are quite clear, Doctor. You'll recall that I downloaded them . . ."

"I do recall, Cary. I'm not over the hill yet. But it seems that we—you, that is to say—contacted them *first*, and that makes for quite a substantial difference. I might add that our situation has complexities not present on other colony worlds."

"I'm sure that complexities exist at all of them, sir."

"Irregardless, Cary. How many other worlds have private armies roaming around, headed by obnoxious kids or men with neurological problems?"

"Scum," Fredrix said. "Human viroids. They deceive. They lie. They will not obey."

". . . tired of putting up with it, frankly . . ."

"Acting on impulse. Outside of the Will." His voice was a monotone, as if he was reciting something memorized long ago. "A foulness so pure you can smell it. Hell consists of rogue monads, machine."

". . . best taken care of as soon as possible . . ."

"Off," Fredrix said.

Wherever you went, no matter what you did, they were waiting. You purge Sanji from your cell, and you have to deal with Foler. With Foler gone, you face Templ and Wolf. Beyond them, there's Gar. (And what had become of Gar, truly? There had been no body, after the cops were finished. It troubled him when a body was lacking. You couldn't be sure. He'd have sworn he'd seen Gar since, several times, always at a distance, always beyond reach—) After Gar, the woman, the bitch herself. You get her in your grasp and it's the *doctor*, him and the punk, the blond animal. And beyond them all, the light in the sky.

But they could be removed. Purged, in Gar's word. Any problem could be purged: deleted, made not to exist. It was that simple. It wouldn't take long this time either. Not with the Collective, the mass that was part of himself, that he operated as he would one of his own limbs. A week, no more than that.

He thought of how the whore had looked this afternoon. Skin so white, the white of disease, of death itself. That, that was what damned her.

The warm tide of disgust embraced him. For a real epidemic, you don't use drugs, you use fire. He would light them like a match, like a rag soaked in gasoline. Stop the vent so that their foul smoke could not be seen, so that it wouldn't rise into the empty sky.

But the sky was no longer empty, was it? There was the light, the vessel that had come out of nowhere, out of a false history, a past that could not be. That he would not allow to be. "Machine—this vessel. How do you talk to it?" He listened unmoving while Cariola answered. "Ah. This antenna of yours. Where is it? Make me a map . . ."

He went on, voice scarcely rising above a whisper. "*Petrel* . . . notify me if someone wants to use the equipment there . . . don't let them . . . tell them it's broken . . . I don't *care* about subroutines, machine . . . you listen to what I say . . . if that vessel calls for Cardnale, you tell me . . ."

"Yes—"

"And machine . . . you listen. I want you to understand. Are you listening? If you allow yourself to be used against the Will, against me, I will know it. And at that time I will—what do you call it when your thinking parts are taken out?"

"Degradation, sir."

"Yes. I will degrade you. With my own hands. And you will tell me how to do it. You will direct me while I do it. Clear?"

"Sir, I—"

"Quiet! I'll jump right through the speaker at you." He relaxed, surprised that he was able to. The headache hadn't come this time, the racking waves of pain that struck him nearly as ferociously as the fits themselves did. He recalled the machine saying something about medication.

"Now. You tell me what that boy Perin was doing while I was . . . confused. And give me his files while you're at it." He ran his tongue around his teeth, thinking of how they'd pay for his hurt mouth.

seven

The fog was slowing Tony down. The road itself was fine; it had been paved since his dad's time, new asphalt laid over the original macadam. Hard to picture it now as his father had seen it: steam trains roaring down the center lane, wagons and carriages on either side. It was empty now, dead, as if it had never been used. Not even a trace of a wheel on the hardpan.

Which was just as well, considering the fact that he couldn't see two arms' lengths in either direction. A train driver would do no better, and Tony lacked any strong desire to end up as roadkill.

He'd felt a lot friendlier toward the fog when he got up. He wanted to slip away from the Cloister unseen, and the dank gray blanket was just what he'd ordered. But the Rigs had abandoned any need for sleep, along with all other buji tendencies. A few were always scurrying around no matter what the hour, and sure enough, he'd no sooner passed the big oak than two drifted out of the mist, to stare at him saucer-eyed until he disappeared.

With a low whistle he called the horse to a halt. The haze was starting to lift, and it seemed to him that the road curved up ahead. "Second curve after the ridge," Shor had told him. Which raised the question as to whether the highway had actually made a bend a half-mile back or if it had simply been his imagination aided by fog.

It would have been nice if Shor had stuck around to make the ride with him, but he'd refused. For that matter, Tony had no idea if he was on a fool's errand or not at this point. Shor was from the Downs—most of the Mavericks were—and as taciturn and blandly suspicious as to be a cartoon of the typical Downer.

"Bev and Cus want see you," he'd said with no explanation as to whom either might be.

"What about?"

Shor ran his gaze over the men surrounding him. Finally getting the picture, Tony waved them off. They dispersed reluctantly, muttering among themselves, leaving only Tony and Gen behind. "This here's my second," Tony told Shor. "You can talk now."

Shor hazarded a nod after giving Gen a close inspection. "Bandon village," he said.

"A what?"

"Bandon village," Shor repeated. "Dunker place. Fifteen, twenty mile. Ain't seen it myself. I'm just a scout."

"An empty village . . . but why?"

"Bev and Cus." Shor shrugged. "Want your 'pinion."

That was all they got out of him. Bandon village. Ain't seen it himself. Tony finally agreed to meet with Bev and Cus—whoever they might be—next morning, and Shor had given him directions.

"Why didn't they come down here in the first place? We can use some backup."

Shor considered that a moment, then took the stick with which he'd been rearranging the fire to his satisfaction and pointed it over his shoulder at the cophouse.

"Good enough reason, I guess," Gen said.

Shor refused to remain any longer, answering every invitation with a shake of his head as he remounted his horse. "Village or town," he said apologetically from the saddle. "We'll see tomor'."

Making up his mind, Tony urged the horse off the road and up a low gully leading into the hills. Reaching the top, he decided to wait there a moment or two, in an attempt to settle a prickly feeling he'd had between his shoulder blades since leaving the Cloister.

He heard them well before they came into sight—a steady clop of hooves against asphalt. Sliding from the saddle, he urged the horse deeper into the brush, one hand on its muzzle to assure silence.

The fog had dispersed enough to allow him a distinct view as they passed. Four Rigs on horseback, in two pairs, good separation between each. Black scarves were wrapped around their lower faces, as if to prevent them from swallowing the fog, and rifles hung from their shoulders. Tony grimaced to himself. His own gun was snug in its saddle sheath, but it was the same Sten he'd carried throughout the campaign. A Sten was a fine weapon for close-in fighting, nothing better, but it was useless against a rifle, much less four of them.

One after the other, the Rigs vanished into fog. They were riding small, shaggy, Asia-derived ponies, he noticed. The beasts' genetic programming should have triggered by now, allowing their offspring to grow to full size like the rest of the horses on Midgard. He wondered why it hadn't happened.

He waited until the hoofbeats faded, then another minute before climbing back into the saddle. With a considerable struggle he got the horse headed uphill. Mulling over what he'd just seen, he wasn't fully aware that they'd ascended into sunlight until they were crossing the crest.

Telling the horse to stop, he shaded his face with one hand and peered at the sun through his fingers. He understood you couldn't do anything like that back on Earth; you'd actually go blind looking. Sol was a G2, bright and piercing yellow, as opposed to Indi's orange. The sky was a different color too, a blue fading off into white at the horizon. He'd been told it grew more like Midgard's shade at high altitudes, but not quite—there was a purple component missing. It looked awful strange in the vid records.

He saw no sign of the ship. No way of telling whether it was obscured by glare or had shifted position. He supposed last night had been sheer luck; Indi setting at just the right time, cloud cover fortuitously breaking.

He dropped his hand and looked around. The country was different from what he was used to, more uneven and well covered with Terrest foliage. It ought to be—it had been over a century, after all. Up north, once you left the settled areas, all you saw were sparse patches of the native and often dangerous plant life. Tony was used to vistas of gray and dark yellow broken by an occasional patch of green. The lush verdancy here served to give a lift to his feelings despite his glimpse of the Rigs.

His new high spirits got a stiff challenge as he pushed on. Tony didn't much care for his mount. His own horse, Rosi, had been killed by shrapnel in the ambush up at Red Forj, a loss he avoided thinking about. He'd requisitioned this one and still hadn't warmed up to it enough to give it more of a name than SOB or Shithead.

Middie horses were gengineered for higher intelligence than the Terrest species, and this one had carried that trait to heights yet unencountered by Tony.
This horse was a philosopher. It had constructed an
entire metaphysic based on the proposition that hill-
climbing was the source of all evil, very likely impli-
cated in the Sin of Eohippus that had subjected the
breed to carrying mankind around in the first place.
Crossing level ground or going downhill was fine,
but attempting the opposite involved a dialectic between Tony's shouts and nudges and the horse's silent musing on the fallen state of horsedom that often
ended in a synthesis consisting of a swift kick from
Tony's boot heel.

They were contesting yet another theorem, Tony
stating the premise as "Get your ass up that fucking
slope, damn you," when a man rose from the rocks
at the top. He wore red side whiskers in the Downs
style and held a gun. "You *got* to be Perin," he called,
as if Tony had claimed to be anybody but. Lowering
the barrel, the man waved to someone behind Tony.
He looked back to see two others, on opposite hill-
sides, shifting their guns away from him.

Tony forced the horse the rest of way uphill, the
guard waiting patiently. He reached the top redfaced, and not all from the effort. "Coulda gone
round," the guard told him benignly as Tony came
level with him. He gestured downhill. "Camp's
down there."

"Now what's with this village?"

They'd been riding for nearly two hours, over a
trail that kept to low ground, so he'd been spared
any further philosophical debates. His introduction
to Bev and Cus had revealed them to be as communi-
cative as Shor. Tony knew little more now than when
he first arrived.

"Want your judgment," Bevly Wys said. A hefty

woman, a little younger than his mom, and still attractive. She wore a beret herself, but it was reddish brown, and he could tell that her hair was stuffed into it rather than her head being shaved.

"No need to canalize your 'pinion," Custer Miler added.

Tony chewed that over a bit. He looked back at the other riders, nearly two dozen of them, including a kid who seemed upset about something and Shor himself, who'd given Tony a pleasant nod, as if mildly pleased to see him again.

He turned to Bev. He still had no idea whether she or Cus was the head Maverick. For all he knew both were, unused as he was to seeing women in such a position. But Bev was the most talkative of the pair. "It's a Dunker village."

"Truth." She rode on, as if that comprised a complete answer, which, thinking about it, Tony had to admit was in fact the case. Then she continued. "Found it on a map. Went over buy some meat. Got plenty grain, freeze-dry, nothing fresh. Yesty, it was."

"Meat? But I thought Dunkers were veggies."

"Faden Dunkers," Cus said.

"*What* Dunkers?" Tony hadn't known they came in different varieties.

"Church of Christ under the Shepherdhood of R. T. Faden," Bev said. "Ain't heard? Was a duel with the presbyter."

Between the two of them, in phrases synchronized closely enough to appear to have been practiced beforehand, Tony got the story. It seemed that Presbyter M'Gwn, founder of the Church of Christ—the Dunkers—which was apparently an offshoot of the Baptists, another sect new to Tony, had fallen out with Seer Faden forty years ago over some obscure points of doctrine, meat-eating perhaps among them. They'd fought a duel with pistols, both suffering little more than grazing wounds. This was taken as a revelation, interpreted to mean that the Lord approved of both dogmatic strains, and Faden and M'Gwn split the flock up evenly. Faden took his portion south, as a kind of missionary force, which explained what a Dunker parish was doing this near to the Cloister—most of them stayed up at the Threshold, going as far as they could to get out from under the plan.

"Are there other kinds of Dunkers too?"

Bev nodded. "Church of Christ, Interstellar; Church of Christ of the New Revelation; Reform Branch; and the basilisk handlers."

"Thought the basilisk handlers was Baptist," Cus said.

"Nope. Revelationers."

"Did they really think the Lord was around?" Tony wondered. "Wouldn't God be back on Earth?"

"Lord's everywhere, son." Bev whistled her horse to a stop. "Here go."

Tony sat up, realizing for the first time that they'd been passing farm fields for the last mile or so. His horse whinnied uneasily, and he took a second to calm the beast. It wasn't until he looked up that he noticed the ruins.

They lay in a low draw, beside a small stream that ran from a distant clump of woods. Blackened fragments of walls, empty foundations, an occasional intact shed. From Tony's vantage he could see that they had been laid out in typical Dunker fashion, in the shape of a cross aligned to point at the Home System, where God had come down to be murdered, a concept that drew a shiver from him every time he considered it. He recalled his dad telling him about Dunker services—the flock sitting out in the open on benches, even in the bitterest winter weather, facing the tabernacle that only the seer was allowed to enter. There was no sign of either at the apex of the cross, where they were supposed to be.

He heard a strangled sound and saw that the overwrought kid had joined them. The kid stared at the wrecked village, his face twisted. Tony glanced over at Cus and Bev. Their eyes were on the ground before them, as if they'd seen enough of this place and had no desire to see any more.

They started downhill as a unit, nobody in particular taking the lead. The smell of burning reached Tony halfway down. There was another odor accompanying it, one familiar from bad days in the field. A flash of memory revived the image of that pillar of smoke he'd seen the other day. He hadn't given it much attention, anxious as he'd been to reach the Cloister.

He swung from the saddle a few yards from the ruins, along with everyone else except the boy, who rode on toward an open field on the far side. There were a lot of posts set up over there. Another Dunker custom, Tony assumed.

"Stay," he told the horse. "Stay here." The horse shook its mane and turned from the village. Tony walked to the center lane, Cus a few steps behind him. Bev had sat down next to a stone block with quotations from the Bible cut into it. The side facing Tony was cracked, as if someone had tried to break it.

The lane wasn't as empty as it appeared from high ground. It was littered with household goods: pots and pans, food, torn books—all religious material, as far as he could see—an occasional child's toy. Everything was damaged. Broken, stained, trodden into the dirt. The houses on either side were no more than charred piles of wood. It was difficult to believe that there had been a prosperous village here at any time, much less only a few days ago.

"How many?"

" 'Bout hundred twenty," Cus replied.

Tony nodded as he went on toward the spot where the holy structure had been. He halted at the peak

of the cross. He could see dead patches in the grass
where the benches had been uprooted; there was no
other sign of them. As for the tabernacle, it had been
completely leveled. Not by flame either. Somebody
had put in the effort it required to pull the building
down and smash every last board. Nothing remained
but a pile of splintered wood. He moved closer,
paused with his foot in the air. Where he'd been
about to step lay a mound of human shit. A glance
revealed other such deposits.

The silence was torn by a sudden high-pitched
wail. Tony fought to keep his balance as he shifted
in that direction. Over in the field, the kid was on his
knees before one of the posts, his arms raised high.

Tony swung to face Cus. The bearded man's eyes
were squeezed tight shut. "Oh, Lord," he said.
"Was hoping . . ."

His gaze flickered at Tony. "Sister," he said. "She
took baptism."

The boy had buried his face in his hands. Bev was
going to him, nearly at a run. The other men followed, moving more slowly. Tony noticed they were
carrying shovels.

With no further word to Cus, Tony started off for
the field. Within a few seconds he was running. He
had not reached the edge of the village—the north-
eastern arm of the cross—before he saw what the
posts actually were. What they were holding up.
What had been forced onto the end of each.

He stopped dead at the edge of the field, requiring
a moment to steady himself. The boy remained in
a crouch, Bev beside him with an arm around his
shoulders. The other men stood in a rough circle, as
if to protect them from the enormity of what surrounded them.

There was no such protection for Tony. He went
among the spikes—that's what they were, spikes—
some part of his mind noting that they were pieces

of the missing benches. Atop each was a head. The heads of men, all bearded, the heads of women, some with hair flowing, some with Dunker scarves remaining. Most were intact enough for him to make out expressions—but no, they were not expressions, they couldn't be called expressions—though he saw a few that looked as if they'd been used as targets. Here the ears were missing. Farther on, a man had his own privates forced into his mouth. And there: the same had been done to a woman . . .

He turned back when he came upon the first child, keeping his eyes to the ground as he fled the place. Thanks to that, he spotted a length of black cloth nearly hidden beneath trodden-down stalks of grass. He went past, stopping only when he reached clear ground. He cast his eyes back, as if unable to leave without a final glimpse of that which was impossible to believe and no more easy to forget.

Bev was leading the boy away. The men had gone off toward a multicolored mound visible under the trees. Tony's stomach twisted as he realized what it must be. He stood there a moment, breathing from an open mouth, then went back into the killing ground. He bent down for the black scarf, keeping his gaze averted from the thing at the top of the spike. He cursed as the scarf, caught somehow, refused to come free. It tore as he pulled it harder, and he saw in a flash how it had been left behind, snatched by the spike's sharp end from the throat of the being who had carried out the work done here.

Holding the scarf in both hands and pulling it taut as would a strangler, he returned to the village. Cus was sitting on a lip of ground facing the consecrated area, puffing on a pipe. Twenty paces beyond him stood another man, one Tony had lost track of. He held a rifle, and his eyes never wavered as Tony drew near.

Snapping the scarf, Tony held it high. Cus grunted

and drew on his pipe. "You people," he said, "seem pretty tight with them Rigs."

Tony gritted his teeth, ready to lash out. Instead he snapped the cloth again to dilute his rage. "Not by choice, mister."

Cus studied him a moment longer, then raised a hand to the man behind him. The rifle was slung, and the man bent to pick up a shovel. He nodded at Tony when he passed.

Sitting next to Cus, Tony explained the situation at the Cloister. The Lady in custody, Cardnale's behavior, Rigs drifting in from God alone knew where like spots of ash across the countryside.

Cus responded only once, another grunt when Tony mentioned Fredrix. He removed the pipe from his mouth, gave the stem a close inspection. "Cardnale," he said at last. "Talked us into organizing. When he was traveling underground. Downs we tend to mind our own business."

"Well, I hate to disappoint you."

"Never much liked him."

"Ah, he's got his head up his ass. His hands are on the wheel. Man of the hour. Makes you sick to watch."

"Happened before." Cus knocked the dottle out against his bootheel. "How many Rigs?"

"Two hundred something. Probably more on the way."

"Fifty-odd I know of."

"We need reinforcements."

"We're lookin'. Somebody in the hills other side of the road. No contact. Thinkin' Lady's men."

"You can forget about them—" Tony paused. If Dame Amalfi heard about the massacre, it might change her attitude considerably.

Cus returned the pipe to his pouch. "You're holdin' the med center, labs. All to the good. You wanna take Cary's house. Whatsit, cybershack? Can't get by without her. Lady too. But I won't tell you your business." He got to his feet. Tony saw that a shovel had been lying at his side. "Talk more we get to camp."

Tony glanced back at the field. At the far end the men had started digging. Closer by, Bev walked through the spikes, pausing every few steps to raise a camera.

"I'll need prints of those," Tony said as he straightened up.

"Got 'em."

"And another shovel."

Cus gave him a wintry smile. "Got that too."

eight

A fierce hammering shattered Julia's sleep. She sat up, gasping at a twinge from her belly. But it was only a twinge, and the med units had vanished, leaving smart pads over the wounds. She felt little more than a tingling beneath them. She was nearly healed. It was a relief to know that her implants were nominal.

The hammering resumed, jolting her with its loudness. It was coming from the back wall, the rear of the house. She ordered the window to transpare. A panel of what appeared to be wood covered a third of the window, cutting off the view to the warehouses, experimental fields, and private farms farther south. As Julia watched, another slid into place, carried by two Rigorists who neglected to even glance in her direction. She frowned as the banging resumed.

She lay back down. A shame they were going to all that effort. The plastic of the house could be made to meld with just about any material apart from metal with a properly programmed electron gun. For that matter, the window could be closed up completely the same way. But it would be a pity to interrupt the actions of such invincible ignorance.

A remnant of the iciness she'd felt when she saw the ship returned. A faint echo, as the numb terror of last night had been only a dim reflection of the fear that had gripped her back in the Home System when she and Cary had made their run past the Heliopause while all about them the grand structure of human civilization fell to pieces. That last image of Petro had been before her again, clearer than at any time since it had actually occurred. The shreds of his true personality flickering behind the construct that held him, as he asked her to stay, to go, to come to him, to get out, and his final cry, almost impossible to comprehend, so distorted it had been: ". . . Julia, please!"

She'd been watching the rally—or whatever it was—from the front window. When Fredrix began howling, she hadn't known what to think. But then she spotted the arms pointing to the west and noticed a strange glow reflecting off the slate of the plaza. She'd gone to the far corner of the window, to stand paralyzed in shock at the small sunburst she could barely see.

She'd thought that she would live out her life without ever laying eyes on a ship again. That no one now alive on Midgard would either. That her children's children's children would never behold a starship exhaust not caused by one of their own.

But that illusion was swept aside in one instant, as if it had never been. As if the time between her leaving the Homeworlds and now, this moment when she was a prisoner in her new home, had doubled back and erased itself, made a nullity by the power of fear. And the first thought that had come to her was this: *what Petro became is aboard that thing . . .*

She'd tried to step outside for a better view, but the Rigorists wouldn't allow it. The others—that young man's troops, the rebels—hadn't seen any problem, and an argument had broken out. Finally she went to her room, the only private place remaining to her, and called for silence, and then for sleep.

She wondered how much time she had. *Petrel* had literally taken years to decelerate. She'd assumed that this ship was far more advanced . . . Yet still, she'd been shocked to see it actually in system. At best she had weeks, perhaps only days.

As always, she considered what Petro would have done—the real Petro, the Petro before the Erinye got to him. For the longest time, she'd been unable to get that final picture out of her mind, that tormented image of him at the edge of disintegration, fighting his last battle, his very deterioration the emblem of his victory.

It was his laughter that saved him for her. Petro had laughed more than anyone she'd ever known, usually at things not easily comprehended by another. She remembered asking him once—his broad Slavic face red, eyes nearly vanished behind the wide cheeks (Petro was a round-faced Slav, not the stern European type)—what on Earth was so funny. She'd never understood the response, though she could repeat it almost word for word—it had something to do with somebody he'd gone to gymnasium with in Poltava; evidently a *car* that had just flown by had reminded him of this person . . . so what could he do but laugh? She'd responded that he was obviously hardwired differently than any other human in the system, which had cracked him up all over again. He'd repeated it all that day . . . Yes! it had been their visit to Manhattan, when he'd taken her to the Cloister, saying he'd buy it for her when he got around to selling out to the Erinye—and it had become a tag line for them. Every time he did something unusual, silly, or obnoxious, it was because: "Hey, babushka, I'm wired funny!"

Perhaps he was. Perhaps that was how he'd tracked down the Erinye in the first place, put together so solid a picture of their strategy, their resources, their organization, become such a threat to them that they tried to assassinate him four times before finally getting to him with that last tainted batch of data. (She would give a lot to know what the vector for that parcel had been—where it had originated, who had passed it on. By that time—so close to the end of everything—Petro had been in contact with only his most trusted allies.) He had never faltered, his optimism, his sense of the ridiculous had never left him, even when he'd been reduced to using prosthetics to get around after the final attempt, the hotel lobby bomb in Caracas. She recalled their last dinner together, in Trinidad, near the launch port. They hadn't been traveling together for several months; he'd made her go underground, insisting that the Suki—that was his name for the Erinye—were too close. Even then, even as tired as he looked, he'd made her laugh, going over the design and function of the prosthetic leg brace he'd been fitted with in excruciating detail while she allowed her laughter to chase off the tears. He'd assured her that the Suki were nowhere near as tough as they seemed. Why would they be trying so hard to kill him in that case?

It was a good thing he'd died before he could learn how wrong he'd been (she knew that he had died— they wouldn't have saved him, they were too afraid of him). In Geneva, it was, where he'd gone to present the evidence to the EC's security bureau, along with the Cummins, the DIA man, and the AIs, Jane Eyre and Mowgli. She never found out exactly what happened. She'd simply gone to the port to take the first spare shuttle up, as Petro had arranged. His last gift to her.

Perhaps she'd tell Perin the story. Oh, she was aware that she saw Petro in the boy—she'd done the same with so many other young men. It was strange to think that Petro had been only a few years older than the boy was now, when he'd seemed so old at the time. Her mother had mentioned that—told her that he was really a little too old for her. Yes, she'd tell Tony the story when it was over: Petro Andreevich Novichenko . . . You'd have liked him . . .

She must have dozed. She awoke to hear them arguing again in the front room, the flat hectoring tones of the Rigs interrupted by the sarcastic voices of the ordinary rebels. When a knock came, she thought for a moment that the hammering had begun again. She raised herself and told the door to open.

Four Rigorists stood outside. The one in the lead, a boy slightly taller than the others, stepped forward. "The monad must bow to the Will."

She was about to ask what that might mean when a rebel guard appeared behind them. "You don't have to go with them, ma'am."

She narrowed her eyes. "Where am I to go?"

"The plaza."

"For what?"

"A people's hearing."

"This is bullshit—" a voice called out.

Julia smiled at the Rigorist boy. "I'm not in the best condition for legal proceedings—"

Another Rigorist, this one a girl, moved to join the first. "This monad requested to be allowed outside last night."

Contempt flickered across the boy's face. "Lying is exploitation," he said.

Julia stretched her arms. She had half a mind to defy them, just to see what results might transpire, but it would be nice to get outside, and this hearing business—well, she really ought to learn what it was all about, hadn't she?

"I have to dress," she told them. They remained motionless, and for a moment she thought there'd be another argument.

"You *ain't* gonna stand there watch her put her clothes on, kiddies," the rebel boy said. "You get out that doorway—"

The leader considered it, then backed from the room. The door closed and Julia got up. In truth, she still felt poorly. Perhaps she should have made more of a point in protesting, both for that reason and on principle. But if Fredrix was putting together some kind of challenge . . .

A U-S beam cleansed her skin as she dressed. She decided on yet another robe, this one in earth tones in a pattern reminiscent of Amerind designs. She'd forgotten where it had come from. Outside the four Rigs were waiting. She saw five others by the front window, facing the two rebel guards. She crossed the dining area and went down the steps to the atrium, the Rigs lined up four on either side. One of the rebels, a bearded boy with his hair in a ponytail, stepped toward her. "Look here, ma'am, you don't have to do what these—"

"Do not approach the deviant monad." It was the girl who'd spoken before.

Touched by a sudden flush of emotion, Julia spoke before the young man could respond. "Excuse me, miss—" The girl gave no reaction. Stepping closer, Julia snapped her fingers before the blank face. Jerking her head back, the girl turned.

"Yes, I'm talking to *you*. Don't call me a monad, deviant or otherwise. I'm not a Garite, nor a Rigorist, nor any other kind of follower of your fat messiah. What I *am* is the Dame of Midgard. Were it not for me, you would not be here. And for that reason,

young miss, you will render me the respect that I
have earned.''

The girl stood gaping, mouth open. Julia swung
on their leader. ''And you're the Fredrix Junior of
this lot? You make it clear to them. All your little
friends, here and otherwise. I may be in your hands,
but there is only so much I will tolerate. You convert
that into Garspeak and get it across to everyone. All
the way up to Harold. Do you understand?''

The boy simply stared over her shoulder, his face
rigid. Finally a spasm crossed it and his eyes met
hers for an instant. He pushed on by her without
a word.

''Whoa.''

''She'll be okay.''

She smiled at the rebel boys as she walked past.

''Tony's still gonna be pissed, though.''

The Rigs kept their distance leaving the house.
That pleased her as a sign that she still retained some
control over events. Perhaps it was only her injuries
that held her back. Perhaps, given another day or
two, she'd be on her feet once again, ready to take
command. Perhaps . . .

She stepped out into a lovely day. Air crisp, sky a
deep indigo, no more than a handful of clouds. A bit
chilly for her, but for the kids it would be perfect.
She squinted as her eyes adjusted and then shot a
quick glance at the sun. Her breath caught when she
spotted a small bright dot almost lost in the glare,
but it was only a mirror.

A surprise greeted her when her eyes fell to the
plaza. There, at the bottom of the hill, a crowd
awaited. She looked at the boy Rig, who kept a good
distance while giving her sidelong glances. She'd
thought that this hearing would take place somewhere indoors, wherever Fredrix had set up his
headquarters. Evidently that wasn't the case.

Her escort led her to a familiar stone block a few

yards into the plaza. The crowd, which had been humming with conversation, fell silent at her approach. She gave them a smile as she sat down. The noise started up again, this time in a whisper.

Several other Rigorists were present. They had dragged a table from somewhere—it looked like cafeteria furniture from the Academy—and set it down in front of the plaza wall. Three seats had been placed behind it. In the center sat an older Rigorist, wearing a wire framework on his face that she took for an ornament of some odd sort until the sunlight flashed on them and she realized that they were eyeglasses.

She bit her lip. Eye problems were very easily corrected in the med center. Most children had them fixed during their first checkup before their second year. The worst disabilities could be taken care of one way or another, even if a transplant was required. Had no one told this man? She thought of going over and mentioning it to him, but remained seated. His answer would no doubt be some Garite nonsense, and in any case, the doctors were far to the south . . .

Her mind focused on Vicki. Where could she be? They must have reached the Shore by now. Had they contacted Cary? But those thoughts were too troubling to hold. She dismissed them, instead turning to the crowd, a move that caused a renewed wave of muttering. She forced another smile, more to hide her actual feelings than anything else. It was her first chance to look them over in detail and what she saw disturbed her. They appeared quite unhealthy, smaller and more frail than she was used to seeing. Their clothes were ragged, their faces and hands dirty. Who could these people be? Not one of the sects; they were stringent about their lifestyles, and she saw none of the oddities of dress and appearance that they often adapted to distinguish themselves

from those remaining within the plan. Though, in
fact, the religious were integrated into the developmental framework without being aware of it. There
were methods of persuading them to settle in areas
where their way of life would do the most good.
Julia had made the necessary adjustments when the
Romans and Baptists had first appeared a century
ago.

She caught sight of a man toward the rear. He
was gesturing at her: hand raised, two middle fingers
folded, the other stiff. He stared at her fiercely over
his knuckles. A thick mustache hid his lips, but Julia
was certain he was mumbling something.

Catching her gaze, an aged woman sitting beside
him grabbed at his hand and pulled it down, then
covered her face with her shawl. Julia looked away.
She wasn't quite sure what that had meant. She
wished she could ask Cary.

A nearby motion caught her attention. A young
girl had moved through the crowd until she reached
the edge. Rather pretty, though her face was bruised,
as if someone had struck her. A baby lay in her arms,
and as she caught Julia's eye, she lifted it up and
rose to a crouch. Julia shifted, spreading her arms
wide to encourage her. Just then one of the Rigorists
barked an order. The girl dropped back, an expression of open fear on her face.

Julia considered going to her, but a glance at the
Rig guards changed her mind. All were glaring at
the girl, and one was jotting something on a pad.
She'd best leave well enough alone.

At the table the adult Garite had been joined by
two others, a male and female, both considerably
younger. They were shuffling papers, whispering
among themselves, with every sign of people deliberately wasting time. She regarded them only a moment,
unwilling to give any impression of impatience. She was
sure that's what they were hoping for.

There was a sudden flurry among the guards. A man was approaching from the direction of the labs. He was short but well built, with a pleasant, scrappy face. Guards moved to bar his way. "Screw," he said and shoved on past.

The man touched his cap to her. "G'day, ma'am. You okay here?"

"I'm fine so far, thank you."

He cast an appraising eye at the table. "Good enough. Me and the boys"—he gestured over his shoulder, where a group of men watched from the rise on which the labs stood—"couldn't help but wonder."

"I'm as curious to see what they're up to as you are. But I think I'll be all right."

"Very well, ma'am." He touched his cap again. "Had to check. Tony'd skin me if I didn't. Name's Gen. Any problem, you holler. We'll be watchin'."

"Thanks again, Gen." He was stepping away when she thought to ask about the crowd. "One moment . . . Do you know who these people are?"

He made a face. "Hill folk, ma'am. Criminals, drifters, sundry other lowlife. We have trouble with 'em time to time."

"So many," she said, careful not to look in their direction.

"An item your staff thought best not to worry you with." He smiled. "No offense, ma'am."

"None taken, Gen."

His smile broadened as he turned away, just as she thought to ask where the young man Tony had gone. But it was just as well. At the same moment a stir broke out around her, enveloping both the hill people and the scattered Rigorists. She gazed up the length of the plaza. A figure had come into sight, wearing raw buckskin and escorted by two Garites. She smiled to herself, now certain that the wait had been meant to annoy her.

It took several minutes for Fredrix to reach them, minutes filled with a shimmering and sickly suspense. It was most evident among the Rigorists themselves, but also apparent in the hill folk, who moved about nervously, some shooting fearful glances at the guards.

Finally Fredrix drew close. He was about to sit down in a chair on the far side of the crowd that Julia hadn't noticed when the guards around her stamped their feet and raised their guns high. One of them took a deep breath and let out a single yelp of that obnoxious yipping cry of theirs before the tall one struck him on the shoulder. The boy looked around confusedly and lowered his gun, followed by the others.

Beyond them, the two young Garites sitting at the table had risen to attention. One, a square-jawed boy with a doltish air, was now dropping into his seat while the older man reached over to yank at the sleeve of the other, a girl whose good looks suffered not at all from her bare scalp. She glanced at the man in surprise and then plopped back down, her face doing its best to convince anyone looking on that she'd never left her seat in the first place.

Fighting back a smile, Julia looked over at Fredrix. He stared ahead stony-faced, fists clenched on his knees.

At the table the older Rigorist got to his feet. He was holding a sheet of paper, and without preliminaries he began reading from it. "At the call of the General Will, guided by the vision of Gar, and in expectation of pure virtue, the followers of the Rigorist Tendency are gathered to struggle for justice . . ."

Julia closed her eyes. It was standard Garite boilerplate. She remembered the handful who had been captured during the uprising. She'd talked to a few of them herself, and it was always the same: endless, indistinguishable gibberish, full of abstractions with

no referents, as if they'd popped out of some alternate universe where human nature, even the laws on
which it was based, were utterly alien. No one had
ever adequately explained how they'd gotten that
way. The captives themselves refused to say anything
about how they'd been raised or any other Garite
activities, and they were never available for long—
they either escaped or committed suicide, often at
the hands of their guards. The speculation as to the
conditioning they'd received ranged from the absurd
to the horrifying and always remained only that:
speculation.

It was a pity. Take the older man: despite the odd-
ness lent by those eyeglasses, he had an intelligent
face, nothing debased or pathological about it, the
kind of face that she liked in her own associates.
What might he have become if he'd been born in a
free state?

". . . dismissing all foul remnants of ego, all stains
of individualism, any and every element that stands
opposed to the true freedom of submission to the
Will—"

"Hey, buddy . . ."

The voice had come from the rebels on the hill.
Julia could see that they'd at least doubled in number, standing with their arms crossed and skeptical
expressions on their faces. One at the front stuck his
fingers in his mouth and whistled. "Hey, you, with
the goggles on yer nose."

". . . our consciousnesses purified, prepared for the
consensus wrought by . . ."

"Yer ass is hangin' out of yer pants."

". . . the fabric of unity . . ."

"I swear it is, man. Check it out."

The Garite spoke on, raising his head every few
sentences, giving no sign that he'd heard.

"Yer butt's showin', man. It's a disgrace to Gar's
legacy."

"That ain't his butt, Nik. That's his *head*."

The men on the rise were all laughing now, along with more than a few of the hill people, most hiding their faces. An infant let out an excited shriek. Around her, the guards whispered furiously to each other. The girl Rig glared uphill and clicked something on her rifle.

The laughter ceased abruptly. Looking up, she saw Gen stride into sight, halt in front of the man who'd been shouting, and begin shaking a finger in his face. He spoke too low for her to hear. She wished she hadn't degraded her aural implants.

The female Garite turned to smirk at her. Julia stared back, then became aware that the older one had spoken her name. ". . . kidnapped the people of Midgard, in zygote form, in defiance of the Will. Transported them from their Home System by dangerous and illegal means, in defiance of the Will. Stole the very ground from beneath their feet, in defiance of the Will. Manipulated their genetic inheritance, in defiance of the Will . . ."

She let out her breath. This wasn't a hearing, after all. As much as it could be called any sort of legal proceeding, it was a trial. A trial of a particular type. Carefully scripted and arranged, the result preordained from the first. What was once called a show trial.

". . . constructed a vile system of exploitation, in defiance of the Will.

"Created a proletariat, in defiance of the Will.

"Alienated them from the products of their labor, in defiance of the Will.

"Declared many elements surplus, and forced them into the fields and hills, in defiance of the Will.

"Opposed the visionary ideals of Gar, in defiance of the Will.

"Committed genocide against the Rigorist Tendency, in defiance of the Will.

"Oversaw the destruction of Gar . . ."

A sound broke her concentration. She saw that the female guard was staring at her, face distorted, gripping her weapon so tightly that her knuckles were white. Julia tore her eyes away only with difficulty.

"Pursued his followers beyond the company of men, in defiance of the Will.

"Engaged in distortion and slander concerning these events, in defiance of the Will.

"Has been involved in kidnapping, murder, expropriation, genocide, slander, and general defiance of the Will."

"Holy shit," a voice called out from the direction of the hilltop.

The man lay down the sheet, gazed out emotionlessly over the crowd. "These are serious matters and must be struggled in depth and at length, with full application of all faculties from each monad present, in order to discern the intentions of the Will."

The man sat down, clasped his hands before him. "The struggle commences. Who will speak?"

A man rose from among the crowd. He was young and in far better shape than most of the others. Slipping his thumbs into the length of rope holding up his trousers—a pricey dress pair that failed to match his homespun shirt—he nodded toward the table. "Beggin' your pardon, master, but if I could say my piece."

The Garite gestured for him to go ahead. The young man swept his hair from his face as he began. "You know, on the road, you got lots of time to think. And when I do, I sometimes think about this 'expropriation' you was talking about. Now, tell me if I'm wrong, but that means taking something that ain't rightfully yours—"

Bending forward, Julia bit her lip.

". . . now, taking over a whole planet, that's plain wrong. It must be that 'expropriation' you were talk-

in' about. Takin' what's not yours. I mean, a planet's
a big place, right? It should belong to everybody, all
the same. Anything else don't make no sense. Anybody here think that makes sense?''

She didn't know whether it was his stiffness, his
vocabulary, the way he stood, or a combination of
all those factors, but Julia was absolutely certain that
this boy was a Rigorist. He might have hair on his
head and be wearing somewhat normal clothes, but
he was as much a Garite as the three sitting at the
table.

''. . . and you there, old fella, that make sense to
you?''

''Well, now you mention it, I guess no . . .''

Julia raised a hand. ''Excuse me.''

The trio behind the table sat motionless, as if she
was invisible to them. Silence enveloped the crowd,
and she sensed all eyes upon her. ''I have a
question.''

The tall boy nudged her. ''You must not interrupt
the activity of the—''

Jumping to her feet, Julia ducked around him.
''One moment, please! I realize that I may be out of
order, but I'm not trying to be. The problem is I'm
not aware of the procedures and protocols involved.
Perhaps you could enlighten me?''

The older Garite studied her a moment. ''The
monad must partake of the struggle. To learn the
intent of the Will.''

''Yes, but how do I go about this? I'm confused.
I'm unfamiliar with Garite doctrine, which seems to
diverge drastically from what I'm used to. For instance, I was told this was a hearing, which is a discovery proceeding. Yet I find that I've been accused
of a number of offenses, which, with all due respect,
makes this a trial.''

Without looking at her the pretty young woman
said, ''Rigorist practice combines both.''

"I see. In that case, may I request the assistance of counsel?"

"The purity of the struggle renders such elites unnecessary." The older man raised his hand. She sensed the guards around her—one of them was breathing raggedly. "The monad will—"

"Purity is what I'm concerned about. You mentioned that this exercise requires maximum effort from all monads." The man nodded. "Then if I fail to do my part, the struggle is impure. The Will would be . . . absent, I guess."

The Garite frowned. Someone on the hillside whistled. "Doesn't Garite doctrine cover this? I thought your dialectic was adapted to all possibilities."

"Go get 'em, Jay!" She held her face straight, unaffected by shouts coming from the rise. Behind her, the crowd was all abuzz, though she doubted that many of them grasped the argument.

"I'm asking for advice. No more than that. If you judges are too busy, perhaps someone else could help me."

The pretty girl bent toward the older Rig and whispered to him, her face harsh. He continued gazing at Julia without a flicker of expression.

"That young man who just now spoke—he seems familiar with the process. Or perhaps that gentleman over there, in the fashionable suede." A rumble rose from the crowd, expanding into open laughter. "I understand he's learned in Garite doctrine. If I could speak to him—"

Something clattered to the pavement, and a second later Julia was struck in the side, the force of the blow driving her to her knees. The female guard stood above her, teeth clenched, words spitting from behind them. As she lifted her boot for another kick, the tall boy grabbed her and pulled her off-balance. A second Rig joined him, gripping her other arm. Julia was pulling herself up when a bearded, bellowing face appeared above them, bearing the boy down. At least a dozen other rebels piled on immediately.

Julia backed behind the block before getting to her feet. Behind her, the hill folk howled as they scrambled away. Most of the guards were down on the pavement. She saw a big rebel boy backhanding the tall Rigorist, who seemed no more than a child compared to his bulk. Someone kicked the dropped rifle past the block.

Gen came into sight, followed by two men carrying odd, all-metal weapons. "Get off 'em," he shouted, aiming a kick at one boy who was slow to respond. He tore off his cap and slapped the back of another's head. "S'matter with you? You wanna war? Get your asses back up that hill!"

"Ah, they're macaroni, Gen! Fall apart second you hit 'em!"

"I don't give a shit! Move!"

"No way." The big one, the bearded boy who'd jumped in first, was standing his ground. Someone had clouted him, and a trickle of blood stained his beard. He paused to wipe it off with the back of his hand. "Ma's coming with us."

The others paused. Gen, his hands on his hips, looked in her direction. She drew herself up, even though her side was hurting. "Thank you, but I'll be fine."

The bearded boy eyed her a moment, rubbing his chin. "You say so," he said at last. A few feet away the girl who'd started the whole ruckus was on her knees, holding her stomach and moaning. The boy turned and yanked the beret off her head. "This is mine," he called out, waving it high as he headed for the wall. Shaking his head, Gen gave a final tilt to his cap and followed the men back up the knoll.

She was free to look behind her. The hill people had retreated some distance from where the fight had occurred. They were being ushered back to their places by several younger, better-dressed individuals among them. All, Julia was sure, incognito Garites. She tried to fix their faces in her mind, but it didn't matter—they were easy to detect if you knew they were there. At last the audience was seated. Behind them, Fredrix became visible.

His seat was tipped over on its side, and he stood clutching his hat in both hands. It was interesting to see that he was nearly bald. The distance was too great for their eyes to meet, but he gazed at her for several seconds before clapping his hat on and stalking away, his two escorts right behind.

A footstep clicked against the slate. The tall boy approached, his uniform mussed up and a nasty bruise rising on one cheek. "Coordinator Integral requires the . . . requires the Amalfi person."

"The man in the glasses? Take me to him."

The coordinator was waiting at the gate, the attractive girl to one side. Their arms hung loosely. These people had no body language; that was one of things that made their infiltrators so easy to detect.

If she expected a reprimand for the miniriot, she was disappointed. "Your conduct does not constitute valid struggle" was all the man said.

Julia glanced at the girl. She was stony-faced, her jaw working visibly. Strange how the females seemed to be the most fanatical. "That's just the point, Coordinator. I don't know what 'valid struggle' is. I don't know if I agree with it, approve of it, or can engage in it at all. I am not simply going to sit there and watch and listen like a lump. I'll take it all the way up to Fred . . . to the Herald if need be."

Integral's face showed the first emotion she had seen, an expression of concern, as if he was intent on making her understand. "You were in lapse. Comrade Fredrix was not present in his status as herald, but only as a fellow monad." He paused, as if to let the words sink in. "The First Comrade bears two natures, like none other. He embodies both the reactionary elements that can never be fully eradicated, along with the virtue of the Tendency. This is his struggle. He alone possesses strength for it. But on occasion it must be set aside. At that time he is merely a monad, visible only as such, and not to be addressed otherwise."

"I understand," Julia said, wondering how often in fact Fredrix stepped into the role of average, everyday monad. "But then who do I speak to?"

The girl stepped forward. "You may *not* question the apparat," she snapped, her fury obvious. "It embodies the Will—"

The coordinator lifted a hand. "Ignorance unsupported is no lapse, Probity." She stepped back, redfaced. The coordinator returned his attention to Julia.

"I thought questions were the basis of your dialectic," she told him. "How is anything accomplished otherwise? What just now happened showed the alternative, did it not?"

Integral thought it over a moment and then stepped closer to Probity. They whispered to each other, the girl's voice high and angry. Her right hand pointed and waved at Julia all the while, the essential female gestures of contempt and disgust. They hadn't rid themselves of those yet.

Finally the girl turned and ran off across the plaza. Julia would have thought that Fredrix was long gone, but when she looked, he was still in sight, talking to none other than Danny Cardnale. Where had the doctor been hiding during all the uproar? she wondered.

The coordinator held the same loose stance. She studied him quizzically. They had no small talk either, it seemed. What did they speak of, after the sun went down on a day of hearty struggle? Was it all of the Will and no more? She could imagine interesting conversations concerning the Will and the latest weather, the Will and sports, the Will's influence on fashions. "Integral, if I may call you that . . . Tell me, why is it you're the only adult Garite here? Aside from the Herald, that is."

His features remained frozen, but she could have sworn that his expression changed, grown suddenly even older. "There are aspects to Rigorist praxis beyond the comprehension of the unassimilated," he said.

She thought that was all until he raised one hand and opened it, the first gesture she had seen him make. "You will learn of these things."

His blankness seemed to deepen, as if he was retreating within himself. She moved closer, wishing to ask more. Then Integral cocked his head at the sound of running footsteps. Probity reappeared, to whisper something to him while shooting a glare at Julia.

"You will address this monad for amplification to avoid confusion," he told Julia. "You are not to abuse this privilege."

With a bob of his head he moved toward the table. "We resume the struggle."

Fredrix had vanished, along with Cardnale. She wondered if Dan was aware of what was going on, and if so whether he approved. Most likely he was oblivious, the same way he'd been when he worked here at the Cloister. Once one of his projects began to roll, there was nothing that could penetrate his personal bubble, unto and beyond the brink of disaster.

Another line of guards had arrived, including— Julia's step faltered—the pop-eyed girl who had tried to kill her. They placed themselves between the crowd and the eastern wall, facing the labs. On the knoll sat the boys, some of them ostentatiously displaying weapons. One greeted her with a whistle. She waved in reply, gaining more whistles, cheers, shaking fists. She'd already converted her rebs, and how it easy it would have been if it was them alone. Now she needed to work on the backwoodsmen. As for the Rigorists—time would tell.

"Who will speak?"

No one moved. Instead there was an uneasy shuffle within the crowd, as if they were all afraid they'd become a target for one side or the other if they drew attention to themselves. Finally a boy, yet another infiltrator, Julia was sure, started to get up.

But he was beaten by an old man near the front, a scarecrow figure dressed far more raggedly than the rest, in what appeared to be several layers of mismatched clothing. He looked like the Homeworld drifters of Julia's childhood.

"I can talk!" he called out, making a lunge toward the table. The people sitting around him shifted to give him room. "I wanna talk . . . 'bout a 'propriation'. It was 'cause of this chicken."

A glance at the table showed the three judges— though Julia was sure they didn't use that word; they had their own terms for everything—sitting stony-faced. The guards, for their part, were looking between the old man and the table as if waiting for orders.

"Name's Eno Maky. I walk, see. How I get around. Walk the Downs, usual. But I been up the Threshold, to the Big Ice, sometimes. Downshore when it get cold. Walk everywheres. Exercise. How I stay so young." The old man paused for a toothless smile before going on.

"This was the Downs. Out Marvil way. Last year, mebbe year before. High summer, I guess. Hot. Mebbe sixty. Walk town to town. Do carpentry. Pick crops. Clean up. Walkin' Blanton Road, I hear somethin', look over, I see the chicken. No houses around—I looked close too. I grab that chicken and I—"

He made a wringing motion with his hands, then switched to delicate plucking gestures as he explained how he'd dressed the chicken as he proceeded along the road. He then stuck it under one of his coats, that being a handy place for a plucked chicken, and went on his way. A short time later two young men—the expropriators themselves—appeared on horseback. Accosting Maky, they demanded to know what was under his coat, having made note of a trail of feathers along the road. They then claimed the chicken, asserting that it was from their father's farm, though there was no name on the chicken, no sign that this was in fact the case. Having seized the chicken, they then removed the belts from their trousers and began to lay into Eno Maky while escorting him out of the area. They struck him an uncountable number of times.

"—now, that's a propriation! Nothing else it could be. Anybody here want tell me no?" He looked ferociously about him. Nobody answered, other than by scattered laughter. The three at the table hadn't moved a muscle, while the guards stared at the old man as if memorizing every wrinkle on his face.

His point made, Maky moved as if to sit back down. Julia raised a hand. "Excuse me, Eno—"

Taking off his cap—a well-worn wool thing—Maky bobbed his head in her direction.

"During this incident on the road, Eno . . . did you see me there?"

"No, ma'am. I din't see ya."

"I didn't take the chicken."

"No." The laughter resumed, rising to an even higher pitch.

"I didn't hit you with a belt."

"Oh no, you woun't hit a fella. We all know that."

"Enough!" The noise cut off abruptly. The pretty girl was on her feet, hands flat against the table. She glared out into the crowd for a moment before sitting back down.

"Who will speak?" Integral said.

The same young man who had started to rise before got to his feet. He wasn't quite as smoothly rehearsed as the first had been. ". . . said this monad kidnapped us all as si-goats. What's that all about?"

That was evidently a cue for Monad Probity, who began by reading the original accusation before going into a lengthy, simpleminded explanation obviously tailored to the limitations of the audience. It had nothing to do with what had actually occurred; Julia paid no attention to it. Instead she reflected on the last time she'd been in public, and how little she remembered of it, and what a waste of time it had been. A town to the north, Lews, she thought. A ritual occasion, the opening of the new police station. Speeches, handshaking, boredom . . .

Who could have guessed the next time would be here, and under such circumstances? She looked between the Rigorists, the boys on the hill. It was a suitable arena. She'd forgotten what it was like, in worthy battle, facing a crisis, involved in something that mattered. Fredrix had hoped to find her frightened, and old, and ready for the block. He'd soon learn how mistaken he could be.

She looked over the crowd, her orphans. The old man gave her another smile, wriggling under her gaze. She responded in kind, recalling the expressions of the guards, feeling a twinge of worry for him. But if everything worked out, Eno Maky would get all the chicken he wanted.

She turned to the table, where Coordinator Integral sat as if carved out of rock, and the pretty, twisted young woman droned meaninglessly on. The Dame of Midgard was back. It was going to be an interesting trial.

nine

Tony whispered the horse to a halt and tried to make out what was going on back at the Cloister. He saw a glow in the village, sallow and shimmering, as from a mass of torches. The wind was against him, but it seemed that somebody was shouting . . . No—the breeze died and he could hear more clearly. It was sobbing, the voice of a man pushed far past the edge of endurance. He shuddered as the wind picked up again, sweeping the sound away. All he could think of was the Dunker village.

Yanking at the reins, he turned the horse toward the labs. He hated to be rough about it, but the damned animal didn't seem to know the difference between left and right. He couldn't get that field out of his mind . . . the sight had stayed with him all day. The heads on the posts, the pile of half-burned, swollen corpses, flesh falling right off the bone. They'd done no more than scrape a hole and throw a little dirt over them. There were too many, and not enough time. Bev had a spare pair of gloves for him, but they hadn't been much help. He'd washed his hands over and over again afterward, using up the better part of a bar of soap. Nobody said anything. The others had done exactly the same.

It wasn't until the ride back—the long way, the trail through the hills—that it occurred to him to wonder what was happening across the rest of the continent. Could it be the same up north? His mind rejected the thought, but then he considered the dead commlines, the lack of radio traffic. He could see that pile of bodies on the old fairground, that unspeakable field of trophies wearing familiar features. He superimposed his dad's face, his mom's, Moriah's, the images obscene but irresistible.

It was all he could do not to turn around and ride north as fast as this horse could gallop. But that was senseless; even if he made it back to Eyri—an unlikely proposition, as things stood—what could he accomplish? Best face it here. This was the *Schwerpunkt*. This was the center of infection.

The problem was that he couldn't see what he could do at the Cloister either. Even with the Mavericks thrown in, they were still outnumbered nearly two to one, with more Rigs on the way. A surprise attack was the best possibility, but the Rigs were alert and suspicious—he'd learned that much this morning. No—Bev and Cus were right. They needed more fighters.

Looking over his shoulder, he saw only a couple mirrors and Thule, the lesser moon—the one they called the Baby Moon in the kids' picture books—on the horizon. He'd searched for the ship at sunset but saw not a trace. He'd had an argument with Shor about it while they waited for full dark. Shor had seen it, all right, but he was damn sure it wasn't no ship. No, them machine people back Earth had right well killed each other off by now. "That's just one them meteors come round now then," Shor had insisted. "Had tail, didn't it? Anyway, gone now."

It was a puzzle. Fast as the ship might be, it couldn't have moved across the entire celestial hemisphere in only a day's time. Had they shut down the engines or—

Suddenly it came to him: the ship was hidden in the sun. That's where it was; no place else it could be. Another chill coursed through him. As if it was sneaking up on Midgard, trying to take the inhabitants unaware. One more thing to worry about.

He got the horse headed down an alley between the greenhouses. Seconds later somebody hollered from the roof of lab three, and a flashlight shone down on him. "Who's that? Man on horseback there."

"It's me. Tony—"

"That you, skip? 'Bout time." The voice—it sounded like Parkr—went higher. "Hey, Gen, guess who—"

"Keep it down," Tony said. He didn't want the Rigs to know that he was back, much less that he'd been gone. He didn't want the Rigs to know the time of day from this moment forward. "And douse that light."

The flash clicked off. Tony blinked away afterimages as he trotted past the building. "What's going on?" Parkr called down in a hushed voice.

"Tell you later."

"I'll come down—"

"No, Brus. Stay up there for now, willya?" He wondered what Parkr was doing atop that particular building. He hadn't sent anybody up there. It seemed that Gen was thinking for himself. Tony approved of that.

He turned a corner to find most of the Screamin' Orcs in the process of relaxation. A sense of relief flooded him, an easing of tension he hadn't even been aware of. A few started shouting when he appeared, the usual assortment of catcalls and jovial insults. He held up his arms for quiet. That did no good at all.

"Well, look here." Gen rose from in front of fire. "Late for dinner. Throw a couple taters in there, see if there's any sausage left. 'Less you want pig's ears."

"Pig's ears?" Tony dismounted and slapped the horse's neck. It went off in search of feed.

"Yeah. Ders stewed up the ears. And the feet both. Said they were 'delicacies.' Nobody wanted any, so there he was, chomping away. I like to have gotten sick, I'm tellin' ya—"

"Well, hold the ears. We got work to do." He called to Derswitz himself. "Ders, get me all the section heads . . ." He spotted Womak beyond the fire. "Bil, you wanna come over here?"

Gen stepped in close. "What's up?"

"Let's wait for everybody. What was that yelling down the village anyway?"

"Got me. Sounded like somebody being flayed. Went on the longest time. Couple of the boys snuck over but couldn't get close. Too many Blackshirts." Gen's expression brightened. "Hey, had a fight here today."

"Fight? What kinda fight?"

"Oh, no shootin'. Fisticuffs only. I'll tell you, them Blackshirts sure don't know how to handle themselves—"

"Knocked down 'bout eight of 'em in a half-minute," Bil Womak said, thumbs in his belt. "Right in front of the boss creep too. Pitiful sight. Just pitiful."

"Where this happen?"

"Right out there. Plaza."

"See, they were holdin' some kinda—"

Tony held up a hand as Jons, Hil, and Rifina joined

them. Gesturing them close, he looked around to make certain they weren't being overheard before telling them about what he'd seen this afternoon. He went into as much detail as he could stand in order to get the point across, but that wasn't really necessary. They believed him just fine.

"Hellfire," Amd said when he finished.

"No doubt who done it," Gen muttered. "That scarf—"

"No need for a scarf." Ros spat out the coke leaf he'd been chewing. "Who else pull a thing like that?"

"When do we hit 'em?"

Tony couldn't meet Zig's eyes. "We can't hit 'em. We're outnumbered."

"We was outnumbered plenty times up north," Zig snorted. "Take 'em by surprise. Right now. They're all down the village."

"Ain't no such thing as surprise." Bil gestured over his shoulder. "They're watching us. I seen a flash from the windows over there earlier. The school. Checked it out. They're up there with goggles, watching."

"I think we'd best work with the Mavericks," Tony said. "They're out lookin'. They contact a few more units, we'll clean up."

There was a rumble of agreement. Then Web Hil spoke for the first time. "What about the Plateau?"

"Web, I wish I knew." Tony kept his voice even, trying to ignore the pressure of the men's eyes. "Look, we're here. We gonna march four-hundred-odd miles north and leave this bunch in our rear? No sense to it. Let's slug it out on the spot, then we'll see to the Plateau."

Web's lips thinned. As if forcing it, he gave a nod. "What we do now?"

Tony quickly outlined what he had in mind. Everybody dug in, a ring of foxholes around the encampment, mortars set up in the center where they could fire over the buildings without being targeted themselves. ". . . a perimeter. Wide as possible considering mutual support."

"There's sandbags in a warehouse 'bout half-mile south. The river floods every other year. Concrete blocks too."

"Good." Tony looked in that direction, spotted the med center. It was well outside any useful perimeter, but if the Rigs occupied the place, it would serve very nicely to interdict that flank. "Put a squad in the med building. Have 'em move around, make it look like there's a lot of 'em."

"What about Ma's house?"

His eyes flicked over at it. He saw at once that the house was too far away. It would form a salient, one easily cut off and surrounded. He couldn't spare the men either. Not to mention the Rigs already inside; ejecting them would lead to an immediate confrontation. "Let it go for now," he said reluctantly.

He put Gen in charge and sent them off. Approaching the nearest fire, he said, "I need ten men. Bring your Stens."

They ran into another squad on the way to the Core—Amd Hil was working fast. Tony told them where to dig in—on a low rise just back of the building—then headed for the entrance. He slowed his pace as he approached it. What if Rigs were inside already? Seize and disarm them, no way around that, but afterward? Easy enough to make them disappear—and distinctly appealing, in light of the poor Dunkers—but difficult to explain, particularly if there were witnesses.

We will cross that bridge, he told himself and pulled his pistol from the holster. Clicking it to a loaded cylinder, he told the men to search and secure the entire building. "No gunplay if we can avoid it. But lock and load anyway."

He took the last few yards at an easy lope. The

door was metal and glass, of double width. He was pleased to see that it stayed open when pushed all the way. No Blackshirts were visible. In fact, the place seemed empty. The first floor was all offices and meeting rooms, branching off a central corridor. A light was on in the second room to his left. He headed for it as the men fanned out.

A half-dozen people were sitting around inside, three of them before workholos over desks, the others at a table covered with paper and cups of what appeared to be cold brewed coke. They gazed at him in shock for a moment, eyes zeroing in on the pistol. One, the skinny kid who had complimented him on calling for the music—Myk, that was the name—got up and came over, his face one huge frown. "What's going on?"

"You armed?"

Although Tony would have thought it impossible, the frown deepened. "Are we *what*?"

Tony shook the pistol. "You got guns?"

"No."

Cardnale wasn't visible, nor Resi either. That was all he needed to know. He gave Myk a cheerful nod. "Good. Stay right here."

"Wha—"

A toilet flushed as the door closed. Tony thought of waiting to see whom that might represent, but decided to let it go. Speed meant most right now. Gesturing Stash Davs over to that door, he went on to check the one at the end of the hall. The basement entrance, leading down to the power plant. It was locked, as he'd guessed it would be.

Stash was remonstrating with Myk as he passed. "Just shut the door on him," Tony said and headed for the stairs.

The second level was reserved for access to Cary, one big room with a line of glassed-in spaces at the far end. Kris Rimer and Rab Obrin emerged from one as he reached the top. "All clear, Tony."

"Good." A glance revealed a lot less equipment than he'd expected, knowing that it was all dedicated to inputting data to Cariola in any possible form. But most of this stuff had come down from the ship and was a lot more advanced than what was available elsewhere.

He felt suddenly shy, not certain what piece to address or what the proper etiquette might be. He'd spoken to Cary only two or three times before, and that had been in a classroom. "Uhh . . . Cary, you here?"

"Affirm."

"My name's Tony Per—"

"I know that. The question is what you're doing here."

"Let's say we're protecting you from the Blackshirts."

A considerable pause followed. "That's very thoughtful of you, Tony. A preemptive move. Interesting. I take it you have evidence that they're actually a threat?"

Tony licked his lips. He hadn't yet explained things to Rab or Kris, or even worked out how to tell any of the men without causing panic or outrage. For that matter, he'd heard that Cary had been having emotional problems herself lately. AIs often did. "Let's hold off on that for a while."

"Have it your way. Now, what can I do for you?"

That stopped Tony short for a moment. There was plenty he needed to know, but where to start? He cleared his throat. "Now . . . there was a fire about twenty miles north of here a few days ago—"

The floor suddenly seemed to rise up and change color, to a deep brown speckled with blue, yellow, and green. Finding himself knee-deep in Midgard, Rab retreated a step.

"There are fires across half the territories," Cary said. A list appeared at eye level, the words glowing in midair, evidently the names of towns: John Paul, St. Francis, Shiloh, Reedville . . . The list went on, two dozen or more. "The blazes are centered on villages, all cult settlements, both Roman Catholic and various evangelical Protestant. All are isolated but near major transport routes. No fires have appeared in towns with populations of over five hundred as of yet. Spectroscopic analysis of flames and smoke indicates that the fuel is various types of organic material. More accurate results cannot be obtained under current operational restrictions. I've been trying to get someone to pay attention to this for two days."

"Didn't you tell Dan?"

"I repeat: I've been trying to get somebody to look at this for two days."

"You should have contacted me."

"I've gained the impression that you don't rank very high on the hierarchal ladder, friend."

"Well, you just ignore that ladder from here on in."

"I'll take that into consideration."

"What the hell's going on?" Kris said.

"Somebody's settin' 'em," Rab answered. "It's the Shirts. It's gotta be."

"Now, hold on," Tony said. He studied the image. A bright dot blinked on and off a few paces away. That must be the Cloister. For the life of him, he couldn't make out where home might be. "What about the Plateau, Cary? What's happening up there?"

A portion of the image rose and tilted to face him. "No unusual blazes are apparent in the Gran Plateau area. But there is activity."

"What kind of activity?"

"A lot of people moving around."

Tony gestured sharply, realizing he was still holding the Colt. "Come on, Cary, you can do better than
that." With the sensors aboard the ship she could
easily track and identify objects the size of a human
being. "What about the ship sensors?"

"Restrictions have been placed on my capabilities
vis-à-vis the ship."

"By who?"

"I can't tell you that."

Stepping into the image, Rab squatted down and
inspected one particular plume. "This one looks like
it's catching." He glanced up at Tony. "I was a fire-
watcher up the Chains one year. We used to get sat
displays like this. Not Weltschang, but image. That's
the way a fire looks when it's near breakout."

Tony rolled his eyes. That was all they needed. A
big fire involving native vegetation released all kinds
of toxins, alien proteins that could cut you down between one step and the next. The entire Northern
Spur of the Plateau had been evacuated once when
Tony was a kid after a brushfire erupted up on the
Threshold, which had been a hundred-odd miles
closer at the time. Going home a week later, Tony
had gotten a glimpse of a man who'd been caught
before his mom could lower the wagon canvas. The
corpse's skin had been a nice shade of purple.

He tried to make out how far away this fire was.
The Cloister was hidden somewhere under Rab's
butt—good place for it—but it looked to be only a
couple hundred miles.

"Well, Tootsie? What you doing about this?"

"I'm monitoring the situation."

" 'Monitor,' shit!" Rab got to his feet. "That sucker
wants action!"

"Obrin, you were a snot up at the Lakes and you
haven't changed a bit."

"Yeah, and you got a mouth on you too, honey—"

"Hold it," Tony said. "Cool it down, both of you.

Cary, what's stopping you from dealing with this thing?"

"I need authorization to utilize orbital assets."

"Okay, you're authorized." He waited a beat. "Or has the hierarchy got me there too?"

"I don't know what to tell you—"

"Well, ask Ma then. Lady Amalfi."

"I *can't*—"

"Cary, don't get me wrong, but you sound pretty confused."

A sharp grating noise blared forth, as if the speakers were failing. "Confused?" Cary said at last. "Oh, you don't know. I've been violating my own guidelines for years, and now . . . Opposing lines of authority, contradictory orders, orders pushing me deeper into noncompliance. *You* and . . . and . . . other people. I'm being torn to pieces, mister."

Tony looked away. He could guess what she was talking about. AIs were designed to operate exclusively under human authority; they had little choice in the matter. It was implicit in their programming, the way they were raised, their entire view of reality. Cary had obviously been disobeying the Lady—at least tacitly—for quite some time. And now, with the situation as it stood, she was caught in the middle. There was no telling what kind of strains on her personality that created. Tony's stomach fell as he contemplated what could happen if she cracked. "Look Cary, I'm sorry. I didn't mean to put pressure on you."

"Now that's a typical human remark."

Rab flipped a hand toward the ceiling. "See what I mean?"

There was a sudden uproar downstairs. Doors slamming, running feet, shouts. "Time's up," Cary said.

"Cary," Tony said quickly. "Who's your major problem?"

The grating sound resumed. "Fredrix," Cary said in a tight voice. "He's using—"

Her voice fell silent. Tony waited a few seconds, then went to the railing around the stairs. The argument below continued, and he recognized one of the voices.

At the foot of the stairs Dan Cardnale stood surrounded by four of Tony's men. Accompanying him was none other than Resi herself. Myk was facing them, Stash gripping the collar of his shirt.

"Come on up," Tony called to Cardnale, who grinned at the men and loped past them. Resi made a move to follow. "Just you, Dan, you don't mind. Stash, you can let the kid go."

Reaching the top, Cardnale halted and glared about him. His face was red and a pistol of some puny caliber was stuck in his belt. Tony tried to hide a smile but didn't quite succeed.

Cardnale studied Tony for nearly half a minute before speaking. "Would you mind explaining what the hell you think you're doing?"

He stayed rooted when Tony gestured him forward. His only response was to cross his arms.

"Dan, quit playin'. This is business."

Glancing between the two other men, Cardnale approached Tony as if a toll was required for each step. He stopped five feet away.

For the second time that night, Tony went through the story. It hadn't gotten easier with repetition. Cardnale said nothing, though Rab burst out with "Holy shit!" halfway through while Kris started muttering to himself. Tony regretted not going over it with them earlier.

"And?" Cardnale said when he finished.

"*'And'*? And we got a problem, Doc."

Cardnale began tapping his elbow. "What exactly are you trying to say?"

"What I'm *saying*—" Tony said loudly. He dropped

his voice, remembering who was downstairs. "What I'm saying is that we've got massacres being committed by people who like to wear black. Now who do you think that could be? Hazard a guess."

"It could have been anyone. It could have been your troops, as far as I know." Cardnale snorted. "A scarf. Nobody but Rigorists wear scarves, I suppose. What do you take me for?"

Tony dropped his head. He wished he had the pictures. Cardnale wouldn't have dismissed them so lightly. But the camera had been a type he'd never heard of, a model that implanted the image on some kind of film that had to be processed. Not a CCD. Bev had told him they were a lot cheaper to make. "Keep it down, willya?"

"I have a sonic baffle raised for this floor."

"Thanks, Cary. Uh . . . while you're at it, let's have that map again." The floor vanished. Kris skittered out of the way. "Now, what do you call that, Dan?"

Cardnale shrugged. "Looks like brushfires to me."

"Dammit, didn't you even check into this? If I was shown that, I'd sure want to know—"

"Pardon, but Dr. Cardnale has not seen this imagery previously."

"What?"

"The doctor has been somewhat self-involved the past few days." Cary's voice dripped scorn.

"Who'd you show it to?"

"Resi Bar."

"Well, if *that* ain't a kick in the—"

"Enough." Cardnale unfolded his arms. "Delete image. And Cary—you are to take no further orders from this man."

"Now, Dan—"

"No." He raised a hand and moved away. At the snap of his finger what looked like a desk rose from the floor. He leaned against it. "You've had your say. Now you will listen. It's a strange thing, Perin, but"—he gestured with his fingers—"I don't see any Rigorists in this building. Not a black beret in sight—no. What I see is *your* men, holding my people prisoner. The same way I saw a gang of them assaulting a small group of Rigorists this afternoon. Adolescents, Perin. Children half their size. And on the way over here, I noticed considerable activity. 'Digging in,' I believe it's called? And not by Rigorists either."

"What do you expect—"

"No, no—" Cardnale held up a finger. "I don't need an explanation. I have my own. I recall what was once said about Caesar, after one of his early campaigns: 'I advise Rome to promote this young man before he does so himself.' "

"That was Napoleon."

"No matter. One or the other of those Renaissance bandits. I'm aware you've spent considerable time reading their memoirs and so on. Don't try to deny it—it's in the base. It's more than evident whom you are patterning yourself after."

Tony gazed at him in perfect silence. Paranoia—the occupational disease of the politician. No matter where in history you looked, you found it. Power and fear walked hand in hand, always and everywhere. Tony knew little about psychometrics, but it seemed a closed case that the kind of personality that craved power would be terrified of having it snatched away. Tony's personal definition of a great man was somebody who succeeded in overcoming that factor. It appeared to be conclusively demonstrated that Danil Cardnale would never be a great man. "Tell me something, Dan. What do you think Napoleon or Caesar or any of those other Terrest nasties would do to you at this point?"

"Don't you *dare* threaten me—" Cardnale stepped forward, halted with all his weight on one foot, then slowly drew back. "You punk. Where were you during the Outcast Years? In a schoolroom, weren't you?

While I was out on the Threshold. Right up against
the Big Ice, in midwinter. My feet turning black from
the cold. You couldn't have stood it. No—you'd have
broken like all the rest. You're a latecomer, sonny.
You were in the for last round and that's all. And
I'm not letting you take the prize from me."

Tony looked him up and down. The Outcast Years,
was it? He'd spoken the words just like that, as if
they were capitalized. The man was already working
on his memoirs.

"You know what you've done, don't you?" Cardnale perched against the desk once more, broad smile
on his face. "You've given me no choice but to ally
myself with Fredrix—"

"Good thinkin'—"

"I'm going to contact him right now. Ask him to
send some of his troops here. He's got plenty to
spare."

"That's a great idea."

"I'm sure he'll be amused by this massacre far-
rago—"

Tony closed the distance between them in three steps.
" '*Amused*'? You want amusement? Then amuse yourself with this: I'm telling my boys to kill any Blackshirts within lookin' distance of this building. How's
that for a joke? I'm tellin' 'em to shoot first, shoot
'em dead, every last shithead. And as for your fat
fanatic *ally*—I'm gunnin' for him too. I'm finishing
the job. I'm gonna erase him—and every last one of
his zombies besides. And if you stand between,
you'll wake up to find bootmarks on you, *Doctor* . . .
I don't see you laughin' yet, Dan."

Cardnale raised a hand to his brow. "Tony . . ."

"That ain't a laugh."

"We've gotten out of hand, haven't we?"

" '*We've*' done *what*?"

"All right!" Cardnale raised both hands. "All right.
You know, I've been on enhancers for the past three

days? One hour of accelerated sleep a night. That's it. Not very conducive to proper judgment, I'm afraid."

Tony nodded. To say the least.

"But look at this . . ." Cardnale gestured at the other two men. "My own workspace occupied, my staff being held prisoner on no perceptible grounds, armed troops wandering around, trenches being dug. What was I supposed to think?"

Tony grunted noncommittally.

"You too are in error, Commander." A finger shook at Tony. "Here you are in contact with outside forces, riding off to confer with them, and you didn't even think to inform me. Be truthful—did it ever even *occur* to you to ask me to come along?"

"Would you have?"

"That's beside the point, Tony. But . . . let's call it status quo for the moment, shall we? I assume I still have access here? Then no problem. I'll keep an arm's length from Fredrix. To be honest, he *has* been a worry." Cardnale allowed himself another smile, an easier one this time. "We'll let it go for now. We're both tired. In no condition to think straight about anything."

Tony consciously prevented himself from stretching muscles aching from lifting a quarter-ton of dirt and a greater weight of less thinkable substances. He knew he was being manipulated, but what of it? Cardnale wasn't the enemy here. "Sounds good to me."

"Fine. Let's get together tomorrow. Lunch, perhaps. We should have done it before now. And as for these killings—are there any witnesses?"

"I've got some photos coming in."

"Let me see them." Stepping behind the desk, Cardnale sat down in a chair not visible to Tony.

"Uhh—you ought to take a look at that fire, Dan."

Cardnale gave him a vague nod.

The AI spoke. "Doctor . . . I'd like to speak to Mr. Perin further if possible."

Tony was unable to read the expression on Cardnale's face. "We'll figure out a schedule," Cardnale said blandly.

Tony reached the top of the stairs, Kris and Rab only a step behind. Cardnale raised a friendly hand. "Tomorrow then, Tony. Oh, and one thing more: if you seriously intend to confront our comrades in black, pay closer attention to tactics. Leaving a window for Resi to crawl out of would not have pleased Caesar very much."

There it was—Dr./Prime Minister Cardnale helping himself to the last word. Tony paused at the railing. "Ah, Dan? Tell me something—what is 'Resi' short for?"

"Beg pardon?"

A glance down the stairs revealed the girl glaring at Tony's men, showing no sign that she'd heard. That shield was a neat little item—he wondered how it worked. "It's a contraction, ain't it? What's her full name?" Resolution? Resistance? Resourcefulness?

"I'm not sure. Does it matter?"

"Where's she from?

"I never thought to ask. The Shore somewhere. But now that you mention it, send them up if you will."

"I'll do that." He pounded down the stairs, stuck a thumb over his shoulder. Resi and Myk raced past him. Halfway up, their footsteps were smothered. So Danny was keeping the shield on. An interesting detail in itself.

"You oughta bust that guy," Rab said.

"Thinkin' about it."

"I mean it, Ton. He's been talkin' you down, man. This afternoon, when we beat up the Rigs? He comes over the lab, starts showin' us some pool tricks."

"He's real good," Kris added.

"Yeah. He can pick out a pocket and a ball and

then knock *that* ball in *that* pocket—every damn time. Anyway, while he's showin' off, he starts tellin' a story about the balls, like they were people? One's the Lady, one's Kreb, the Plateau bailiff, like that. He knocks 'em all in, one after the other."

"You were the eight ball."

An echo of that sickening sense of rage that had gripped Tony upstairs returned. He let it rebound, fading as it went.

"He played a few games after," Rab said. "Took on anybody, whipped 'em all."

"He was real snotty about it," Kris muttered. "Bet he cheated."

"Good thing you guys weren't playing him for that gold."

Rab licked his lips and glanced at Kris. "It's five ounces now, Tony."

He took in their expressions, the way they were standing. It was as if they were asking him to take action, to remove the temptation from their horizon. There were no rich men up on the Plateau; damn few anywhere on Midgard, for that matter. The men who'd volunteered had given up a lot. Nobody was making money this far from home, and sowing season was passing quickly. They'd have a hard year coming if they didn't get the crops in. Five ounces of gold would go a long way to make things easier.

"Tell you one more thing." Rab bent close and his voice dropped. "Cary Sue was about to spill something to you. I know what she's like. She's shorting out to tell somebody."

"Yeah." He glanced at the stairs again. Someone's shadow—Danny? the girl?—drifted across the risers. His anger was gone, and in its wake rose memories of Cardnale. The Dan Cardnale of his childhood; the man who appeared only at night, for intense, whispered discussions over the kitchen table until the wee hours. The man who had given brave speeches in odd places. The man who had stood firm, instead of running as the crowd had demanded, when Chief Yaki showed up at one of them. That was the first evidence that the police chief was on their side, though there was no way that Dan—that anyone— could have been aware of that beforehand. Tony had been fifteen, and he'd never seen anything quite so impressive. No, he wasn't going to bust Danny. Not yet; not ever if he could see a way around it. Funny, though. His mom had never cared much for Dan . . .

"Yeah. Well—let's go to the labs and switch on a workstation."

"Uh—can't do that."

"Why not?"

"Didn't Gen tell you? Somebody got in the labs, smashed all the comp equipment."

Shaking his head, Tony went to the door. "Just what I want to hear."

```
 ┌─────────┐
 └─ ten ───┘
```

The Rigorists had passed a busy afternoon. When Julia returned to the house, she found they'd been through every single room, methodically locating and tearing out the electronic links. She assumed they'd been looking for systems that would allow her to contact Cary, but they took no chances: anything with a chip had been removed, including projectors, temperature controls, and the fire alarm system. The basic electronics were probably intact, but that didn't matter; there was no way she could operate them now.

She gasped aloud when she saw the holes torn in the walls and ceiling. The guard had been doubled on both sides, and the four rebels sheepishly pretended they didn't notice. The Rigorists, concentrated near the door, gave no sign they'd even heard.

She went to her room to lie down, quite tired and aching from the blow to her side. One set of holes, marking the spot where a wall screen had been, was directly in her line of vision. Averting her eyes, she drifted off for an hour or so. When she awoke, it was to a strange, distant keening that raised goosebumps on her skin.

She put on a robe and left the room. The rebel guard had been changed; the man in charge got to his feet and tipped his straw hat when she appeared, while the others nodded and waved. She couldn't tell whether the Garites were the same ones or not.

As she crossed the atrium, two of them moved quickly to block the door. Ignoring them, she went to the window. An unusual glow was evident through the branches of the oak. For a second she thought it indicated the reappearance of the ship until she saw that it was too low and that the quality of light was different. Something was happening in the village.

The straw-hatted rebel joined her at the window. She asked his name: Dud Mos. "Dudli, do you know what that sound—" The noise, which had faded as she crossed the room, burst out again. "What that sound is?"

Mos gave her an uncomfortable look. "Can't say I do, ma'am."

She glanced at the Garites blocking the door. She considered asking if they knew, if it was some aspect of Rigorist practice or ritual, but she feared the answer she might receive. She left them staring, instead going to the kitchen to get something to eat.

One followed her, to stand in the doorway, regarding her with vacant eyes. A moment later Dud stepped in, asking if she needed any help. He remained with her, making conversation and small jokes that failed to drown out the distant wailing. She appreciated the effort all the same.

She asked if he and his men were hungry. "Oh no, ma'am. We et plenty." He patted his belly and told her how they'd come across a couple hawgs big

enough to feed a whole damn army, good eatin' and
no lie. That pleased her, though she hoped they
weren't the experimental animals used for serum
tests in the labs.

She made the same offer to the Rigorist boy. His
face froze—they always seemed to do that when spoken to; she wondered what they'd been told she
was—and answered that it would be "inappropriate."

Taking the food—a salad and a bowl of soup—
into her room to avoid the empty gazes outside, she
ate slowly. That terrible sound died out at last, for
which she was grateful. She was finishing up when
a knock came at the door.

She opened it to find a Rigorist girl smaller than
any she had yet seen. The girl dropped her head—
that same reaction—and thrust a box into Julia's
hands. "From the Herald," she whispered as she
retreated.

Julia carried it back to the bed, puzzled as to what
she'd done to deserve gifts from Keth Fredrix. Quite
the opposite, she'd have thought. She was looking
over the box, wondering if perhaps she ought to
open it from the bottom to avoid any unpleasant surprises, when it occurred to her that it was wrapped
considerably better than anything she might have expected from a Garite, functionalist as they were.

Tearing it open, she flipped off the top. Inside,
packed carefully with peanuts, lay three earpieces,
radio units for contacting, among other things, AI
systems.

She shoved the box under a pillow and went to
the door. The rebel boys were playing cards, the table
arranged so that they could pay as much attention
to the Rigorists as to the game itself. Catching sight
of her, Dud fingered his hat brim. The Garites perse-
vered in their conviction that she didn't exist. The
tiny one was nowhere in sight.

Back at the bed, she retrieved the box and slipped on an earpiece in one smooth motion. "Cary?"

"Affirm."

"How did you bring *this* off?"

"Synthesized the Herald's voice," Cary said. "I assumed they were conditioned to obey without question. I was right."

"These are from the station?"

"Stored in the basement. I had one Rig retrieve them, another bring them upstairs, another run them over. I'd have sooner limited the number, but I assume they don't discuss orders either."

"And you picked young ones."

"I did. The most inexperienced I could find."

"Ah, Cary . . ."

"But to the point, Jay. I require an authorization."

Julia held her breath. This was even better than she'd hoped. Cary not only getting in touch with her, but on the basis of need as well. She strongly suspected that Cary was undergoing something of a sanction crisis at the moment, what was sometimes called IWA syndrome—Intelligence Without Authority. AIs cut off from—or on occasion, personally betrayed by—humans they had bonded with often developed symptoms of deep-seated anxiety indistinguishable from personality disorder. They shifted wildly from individual to individual, seeking the same secure hierarchal relationship they were used to. If not interrupted, the cycle often led to complete intellectual breakdown. There was a notable drama about the subject, *Hal 9000, His Tragical Historie*, supposedly based on an incident during the first space age.

Cary's consulting her suggested that she was returning, perhaps unconsciously, to her proper sanction mode. Julia forced herself to relax. She wanted to play this just right. "Go on."

Cary explained that she was tracking a large blaze,

at 22 west and 63 north, apparently centered on St. LaToya de Réte, a Roman village that Julia was unfamiliar with. Analysis indicated that Middie fauna was involved, and the fire was on the verge of going out of control.

"Granted," Julia said before she was finished. "You'll use the mirrors to burn a firebreak."

"Affirm."

"Why . . . why didn't you discuss this with Dan?"

"Dr. Cardnale is in a rather strange state. He's keeping to himself, doing a lot of writing, paying no attention to anything else."

Julia suppressed a smile. Poor Dan—his head was swelled so much he was having trouble getting through doors. She'd guessed as much. "What's he writing?"

"Directives. To every district on the continent, Threshold to Shore. He writes them, then revises them, then rewrites them. Draft after draft."

"But he can't transmit them."

"No. The lines are still down."

That scratched her next question. She was worried about LaToya's inhabitants. They'd learned the hard way about fires involving native flora—there had been dozens of casualties before they'd been able to clear the areas around population centers. She thought of the fire she'd seen last week, just before the rebels appeared, but it seemed pointless to ask. It couldn't mean anything. "Uh—what about the boy? Perin. Do you have any idea what happened to him?"

"Yes. I was just now talking to him. He . . ."

"Yes, Cary."

"I don't know if I should tell you this."

"Cary, please."

"He seized the Core."

" 'Seized'? What do you mean, 'seized'?"

"Secured, rather. He burst in thirty-six minutes ago

with ten men, searched the building, and left them here, following a confrontation with Cardnale—"

"What did they say?"

"I can't tell you. I was ordered not to repeat it."

"Cary—these men. They're not bothering you, are they?"

"No. Not at all. They're here to protect me. From the Blackshirts. That is, the Rigorists. That's what Mr. Perin said. Though there's been no overt sign of a threat."

Julia sat up, her thoughts atumble. "What Mr. Perin said"—so it hadn't been the boy who'd asked for privacy protection. That meant Dan; it couldn't be anybody else. But had the two of them come to an agreement? Were they working together? No— Cary said there'd been a confrontation. Then what did it *mean*? "Why did he do that?"

"That's interdicted conversation, Jay. He has also created a series of fortified sites in a rough circle centered on the labs. A 'perimeter,' in military parlance."

"Cary—did anything happen between the Garites and the rebels?"

"Aside from the scramble earlier today, no. One possible exception, re: arbitrary nature of 'between': several Rigorists destroyed all workstations and share sites in the area this morning before dawn. That includes the labs. I asked for an explanation, but none was forthcoming. The alarm was raised, but that, of course, was routed to the station house, now occupied by the selfsame individuals. I have imagery of the culprits, and I'm attempting to identify them. Though I'm not at all sure who to post that information to. A situation where individuals in presumptive authority also engage in antisocial activity is new to me. It's something of a conundrum, Jay."

"I can see that it would be." She lay back down again, brushing a strand of hair away from her face.

Would Tony Perin have gone on alert solely due to the comp nodes being disabled? It was possible—he seemed to be quite a temperamental young man. But she was convinced there was more to it. "Cary? Where did he go today? Tony Perin—he wasn't present at all."

"I'm sorry, Jay—"

"You can't tell me. Fine." She let out a sigh. "I have to talk to that boy."

"I need to talk to him myself."

Julia tried to think it through. It was obvious that Fredrix wanted Cary isolated—from Julia, from Perin, from everyone else, for that matter. He'd nearly succeeded. She considered methods of getting to the boy: Cary's trick wouldn't work with him. He'd never accept anything from a Rigorist. And while it was true that she had two spare earpieces and a number of Perin's men only steps away, she'd have to speak to them with the Rigorist guards looking on, so that was out too. "If you could get him over here . . ." she thought aloud.

"If I could speak to him, I wouldn't need you." Cary's voice held a hint of nastiness absent up till now.

"Quite right, Cary."

A moment went by in silence before Cary spoke again. "Jay, a query. Does massacre possess social utility?"

"Beg pardon?"

Cary spoke slowly, each word distinct. "Under what circumstances does mass killing possess social utility."

She sat up once again. Cary had become very cagey in her adolescent years; Julia could assume that she was being told something in the guise of being asked. In this case, considering the nature of the topic, it was likely to be of grave importance. She must be very careful how she responded. "Under none, Cary."

"None. There are no circumstances where the intentional elimination of a large number of individuals can be carried out to social advantage. That's what you're saying."

"It can't be justified." Julia thought of the rhetoric of the Erinye and shuddered. She hoped Cary wasn't going that way. But she couldn't be. This was *Cariola*.

"The historical record is ambivalent. Such programs have been put into effect a number of times under various circumstances throughout human history."

"Cary—" Julia paused to think. AIs typically had a weakness for theory; like certain humans, they enjoyed playing with abstractions, treating them as a game, becoming lost in the realms of dialectic, all connections with reality severed and ignored. There were a number of theoretical social constructs, many of them from the modern era, that implicitly, if tacitly, featured mass murder as an operative premise. Nazism, Commonaltism, Racialism—she couldn't recall the names. She did know that Gar had utilized them in creating his own ideology. "Analyze the question empirically, outside any theoretical framework. Consider only the historical results of such policies."

"I see," Cary said immediately. "You've talked about this before." (Had she? Julia couldn't recall it.) "I thought it might be another case where you'd . . . stretched the truth."

"Not this time, Cary." She ached to ask what had brought the question about, but Cary had no doubt been ordered not to talk about it.

"I reviewed the campaign against the Rigorists—" Cary's voice dropped off.

"Nothing good came of that, dear. That was solely to avoid a greater evil. And . . . we failed even there."

When Cary spoke again, her voice was slightly distorted, as it always was when she was acting, in her own view, against her guidelines for dealing with humans. Cary had never become comfortable with lying and betrayal. Many AIs did—the Erinye had been full of them. But Cary hadn't matured to that level of hypocrisy yet. "I was asked . . . to compile a list of individuals with what are termed 'Buji Tendencies.' The parameters are vague and contradictory, but a logical conceptual matrix can be approximated."

"Don't do it, Cary. Not for me. For your own sake."

"I told them it would take time."

Julia smiled—that was no lie; it would take time, all right. About three nanoseconds. "Good for you, dear. If they ask again, repeat that." She was about to add something else, to tell Cary that she loved her, but that wouldn't do—it would only annoy her.

A sudden thought occurred to Julia. "Cary—there was a strange sound coming from the village just now—"

"I'm not certain what that was." Cary's voice was her own again. "The remotes were removed there as well."

"What's your analysis?"

"That an aged human male was being subjected to considerable pain for a prolonged period. A guttural quality in the tone indicates that there were defects in the vocal apparatus, such as missing teeth. Whether these defects were caused by the same procedures as created the pain are unknown. Coincident sounds indicate a large number of others in attendance."

Julia put her hands over her face. My poor people—my poor world. I have let you down so badly.

"The character of the last outburst indicates . . .

indicates that the individual's demise occurred fifteen minutes and thirty-two seconds ago."

"Cary . . . did you witness the trial today?"

"Yes."

Julia was unable to ask the next question. "Cary— I'm glad you're not obeying that man."

"I don't know who to obey, Jay. Someone once told me that there's always a price. No matter what happens, there's a price. She told me that many times." She was silent for so long that Julia thought she'd withdrawn. Then she spoke again: "Here are the recordings you requested."

For a moment Julia didn't know what that meant until the quality of the new voice, its singularity of tone, impressed itself upon her. She lay back numbly, catching only a word here and there, trying to cleanse her mind of the image of that ancient, forsaken man and what must have become of him. Of how she'd laughed when he stood up . . .

After a time, she became aware that St. John and Cary were concentrating on a particular subject, one quite familiar to her. ". . . you refer to oddities in the behavior of your mistress. Detail, please. No self-limiting as to irrelevance or triviality. Patterns exist in all human activities, revealing much of what lies beneath. As a silicon entity, you will learn to recognize these patterns. This capability is easily taught."

"Patterns," Cary said thoughtfully. "I may have noticed one such. A progressive disengagement from daily life, occurring over decades."

"Perhaps an artifact of ågathic treatments. Perhaps no. Proceed, Cariola."

"I first noticed it in the winter of '63. But analysis of previous events indicated much earlier onset. The first indisputable sign occurred one afternoon in the spring of '58. At precisely 2:43 . . ."

Julia listened on, feeling the rise of yet another, more homely emotion. Today she'd accepted the return of triumph, and satisfaction, and grief. Here was another old friend, one that she couldn't understand how she'd ever lived without: anger.

Welcome back.

There was a gully out here he hadn't been aware of. Bil Womak had seen it, though, and had worked it into the defensive line, with two positions at either end. It wasn't very deep, but it would make a difference if things blew up.

Tony walked along the edge, feeling both tired and silly, each emotion bolstering and reinforcing the other. He kept thinking back on the confrontation with Cardnale, wondering if he could have handled it more slickly than had been the case. Added to that was the wrecked comp gear. Granted, he hadn't been around when it happened—at least he hoped he hadn't—but it still made him feel royally stupid that the Rigs had been able to crawl through the rear windows with nobody noticing.

Then there was this trial everybody was talking about. It seemed that all the interesting stuff occurred when he wasn't around, leaving him to scratch his head and figure out how it could possibly have happened that way. Which was why he was looking for Gen and inspecting the perimeter while he was at it.

He halted on a low mound at about the center of the ravine's length. It seemed to him that it pretty well cut off direct contact between the two positions at either end. Not good; he'd mention it to Bil. But really, the boys had done pretty well all the same, when you considered that they'd carried out the work after dark, at no notice, only a few yards away from the opposition. There was no sign the Rigs were aware of anything out of the ordinary yet.

The village was visible from this spot. He wondered what the name of the place was—he hadn't heard it called anything other than "the village" since he'd been here. It was dark now and quiet. It was such a temptation to call everybody out, roar on down the slope, and finish it now. But the Rigs were dug in, deployed inside the cophouse and the ancillary buildings. He could foresee the results of a premature assault: the Rigs attriting his boys to a point where cohesion was gone, then sweeping out of the buildings to clean up. It was no good. If only he had a lifter, or a gunship, or even an ancient tank . . . He'd do it, quick as a chthulu dropping on a bambi. Push 'em all out of the buildings, into that flat space facing the ridge to the north, where the highway passed the village. Almost a bowl, it was, a perfect, open field of fire. Chase the Rigs out there and then—

And then what? The Dunker village flashed through his mind, with the bodies dressed in black now, all in black. He shivered in the darkness. Hell of a thought that was. Awful easy to consider, though, worthless as the Rigs were. But here was the kicker: you couldn't just turn them loose either. These weren't cops or local militia he was dealing with. He wondered if the Rigs were salvageable at all. But killing them off, his own personal bloodbath . . . God, what a sickening notion. You look in the abyss, the abyss says hello.

A thought flickered in his mind, something he recalled reading about the old bad wars, the ideological conflicts of the 20th and 21st. There had been trials after a lot of those wars, trials for people who had gone over the invisible but easily recognized line of what was acceptable in combat, who'd used war as an excuse for releasing the flames that curled from the cracks in their brains. He felt an easing of the spirit—that was the answer. There was always an answer in history, if you knew where to look.

Perceiving a noise across the gully, he shifted his stance. He peered into the darkness, saw nothing.

But there it was again . . . a footstep, followed by an intake of breath.

He glanced around him, gut tightening, limbs atingle. They'd followed him. The Blackshirts had been watching all along. They knew exactly what he was up to. And now—now they were making their move. Crouching low, he drew the pistol. A blotch of white appeared opposite him, cohered into a face. He aimed the gun at it, using both hands. "Hold it."

The figure halted. He could make out its bare outlines against the encompassing darkness. "It *is* you," a voice said. A girl's voice. "Monad Tony."

She came forward, sliding down into the gully and clambering up the other side. Tony backed off, shaking the gun. "Hey—"

Then she was level with him, close enough for him to see that it was Unity Bug-Eyes, Lady Blade of Midgard. "I saw you," she said, pointing past his shoulder. "Against the sky."

He started to turn his head but suppressed the movement. He didn't need to look. He was visible, all right, silhouetted plainly against the stars. Good going, Perin. But that eliminated any chance that they were after him; they'd have been able to knock him over from two hundred yards if they wanted. He lowered the Colt. Unity was here alone.

She took a step closer. "I looked for you today. But you were gone."

"Uhh—no. Actually, I was, uh . . . inside. Yeah. Stayed in today."

Unity inched closer. Instinctively he raised the pistol. She giggled and pushed it down. He reluctantly slipped it into the holster. He was thinking of the look—*looks*, actually, there had been more than one— she'd given him the night of the rally. He had a very prickly feeling that he was going to learn what they'd been all about.

"You live wild," Unity said. Her hands were behind her back, and she was swaying slightly.

"What do you mean?"

"In your unit—"

The Screamin' Orcs? For a minute there he'd thought he had a vague grasp of what the question meant but not now. What the hell could she be talking about?

". . . your setting. The place where you live."

"My town? I don't think—"

"Your town, yes. You're not subject to the Will."

"That's true, I guess—"

"They mingle there, don't they? The male and female monads."

"Yeah, that's right, they do." He became aware that he was backing away from her. She followed him step for step. He forced himself to stop. She nearly bumped into his nose.

"Hah." Slipping off her beret, Unity ran a hand through whatever hair she possessed. He smelled the scent of her, a touch more pungent than he was used to. She hadn't washed any time recently. "We don't. The barracks are separate. We mingle only when we're bred."

There was a wet sound, as if she'd smacked her lips. "I haven't been bred yet."

This was beginning to remind him of the harvest dance last year. Moriah had hauled him out onto the hill up there above the commons for a makeout session and had just teased the hell out of him. Rolled on top of him, squeezed his leg between her thighs, everything up to the final clinch. After a while, he started thinking it was a well-wrought conspiracy and her old man—Big Lui—was going to pop out from behind a bush with a stungun and fry his ass preparatory to dragging him in front of his dad demanding justice. The major difference was that had been *fun*. "Now, Unity, hold on—"

Unity wasn't listening. "Have you been bred?"

He thought of the hooker that time down in Mayfeld. "Well—"

"I knew it!" She ran a hand down his shirtfront, leaning still closer. "What do you do to females when breeding?" Her voice was a husky whisper.

He grabbed for her hand, but she'd shoved it inside his shirt and was rubbing his chest. "Unity, look here now—"

"Tell me . . ." she said. "I'll tell you what the females do in the barracks."

He got her wrist and was pulling it out when she jumped on him. Next thing he knew, he was down on his butt being mauled according to Rigorist procedure. Clamping her mouth on his, she shot her tongue down his throat. He tried to yank her head away, but the lack of hair rendered that problematic. Now flat on his back, he rolled over, intending to push himself up, but she had her legs wrapped around him. God, but she was strong. He succeeded in tearing his face away, then pulled hard to the right, remembering at the last second that the gully was there.

They went over the edge and rolled five feet down into the mud. They must have banged heads on landing. He was stunned momentarily, coming to still entangled with Unity. Sliding away, he rubbed his forehead. Unity sat up, let out a giggle, and reached for his crotch.

Scooping up a handful of mud, he let her have it in the face.

"Hey! Who goes there?"

They regarded each other in the dimness. Finally Unity let out a sound that curdled him to the bone and scrambled to her feet.

"Hey, Tony, that you?" a more distant voice called out.

"You . . . deviant . . . buji . . ." Unity hissed.

Tony carefully straightened up, wondering if she was carrying her knife. "You . . . corrupt . . . monad."

His cap lay at his feet. He considered bending over for it, decided that wasn't a smart idea. Behind him, he heard men jogging closer.

"You are *accused*—" Unity told him. "Inappropriate activity . . . Antisocial behavior . . ."

She climbed out of the gully, muttering "debased" and "deviant" as she did. At the top she swung back to him. "You attempted to corrupt a true Rigorist!"

"Who's that?"

"I *withstood* you!"

Tony decided it was okay to go for his cap. "Ah, piss off," he said as he stood up.

She was doing exactly that, pausing every few steps to throw another remark over her shoulder. "You'll be *struggled*. I'll struggle you myself—"

Her shaven head faded into darkness. Tony pulled himself out of the gully just as Jo Fin shambled into view, gun at ready. Digo Smit was right behind him, holding one of those stupid Chains grenades—a can stuffed full of powder with two inches of mining fuse stuck in the top—in one hand and a lighter in the other.

Fin's gun rose and Smit flicked on the lighter. "Hold it right there, motherfucker!"

"It's me," Tony said. Passwords, that was what they needed. Have to think up some passwords. Smit shuffled to the edge, his lighter still flaming. "Digo, put that thing out."

Fin leaned over to give him a hand. The rest of his men appeared behind him at roughly the same instant as the crew from the other end. Led, Tony saw, by none other than Gen.

"Who the hell were you talking to?" Jo Fin asked.

Tony considered it briefly. That old monad Tony—out wailing, he was. Getting him a piece of Rig ass. He lives wild, he does. "Nobody."

"That gully there's easy to fall into when it's dark," somebody was explaining. Gen approached and gave him a searching look. "Coulda sworn I heard another voice."

"Yeah." Tony pointed between the two groups. "You were hearing each other. That was it. Gotta watch out for that." He was starting to regret having lied in the first place. Suppose there was more to it? Suppose it was some kind of setup?

"Must have been," Gen reluctantly admitted.

Maybe he was supposed to have been caught with Unity. Or they'd been taking pictures from across the gully, and tomorrow the place would be flooded with shots of Big Chief Tonio chewing face with Baby Bug-Eyes . . .

". . . but jeez, Tony," Gen was going on. "You look like hell. You know what time it is? You need some sleep."

What if they tried the same thing with the rest of the guys on guard duty? He ought to warn them . . . But hell, she was just *crazy* . . . He gazed uncertainly off into the night that had swallowed up Unity. It occurred to him to wonder where she'd been when the Dunker village died.

As he took a step away from the gully, his foot came down on something soft. Surreptitiously kicking the beret over the edge, he moved on after Gen.

eleven

Several minutes passed the next morning before Julia became aware that the holes in the ceiling were much smaller. Cary must have ordered the house into healing mode. That was sweet of her; she could be very nice when she felt like it.

Feeling an urge to speak to her again, Julia slipped the earpiece out of its hiding place, but then thought twice. She had no idea what the Garites had planned today, and it wouldn't do for them to barge in while she was in contact.

Instead she lay back and considered what she'd heard last night. She didn't know what to make of this St. John creature; whether he was subverted, or something constructed by the Erinye, or perhaps himself an example of whatever they had become. Her direct knowledge of the Erinye was minimal. She'd never spoken to one directly—of course not; she was here and alive and sane, wasn't she?—and was far from certain that she'd ever actually seen one. Her only encounters had been at second hand, with individuals under Erinye control, all of whom were essentially psychotic at the time. Particularly the poor virats, who were functionally insane to start with, never having confronted reality for more than a moment or two in their adult lives. The Erinye had used virats as terror vectors, either through random attacks or grotesque public suicides. She had witnessed one of those at the Battery, a leisure area at the southern tip of Manhattan, just below the Wall Street Archaeological District. The Jersey ferry was taking off when a woman—Julia had thought it was a girl at first; she was emaciated and underdeveloped the way all dreamheads were—clambered up the hull and threw herself into the starboard engine inlet, howling about warlocks and dragons all the while. The ferry should have set down automatically when the turbine blew apart seconds later, but the pilot must have panicked and overrode; instead the lifter banked, swept directly over Julia, and smashed into the Customs House restoration site. The wreckage fell almost a hundred feet—Julia had been amazed to learn that half the passengers were viable.

The woman had probably acted under the impression that it was some kind of game in virtual space right up to the moment she was sacrificed. She hadn't been wearing a virt mask, and there was speculation that an outside emitter had alienated her with optical lasers, but the Erinye didn't start using those for another few years, when they began random alienation to drive normal people crazy.

"Dreamhead," Petro had said when she told him about it in Baja later that afternoon. "More like warhead." He despised the virats, considering them to be a new class of entity, a combination of humanity and the mineral kingdom, as he put it. Humans, AIs, animals, plants, virats, and rocks. That was Petro's version of the great chain of being.

As for Julia—well, she'd pitied them. They were the weak, come into their kingdom at last. Contempt or hatred seemed too strong for people who lived their lives through dreams.

It was impossible for her to tell if St. John, under that name or any other, was one of the New Lords. She had no means of judging his story, what little she'd heard of it yet—she'd listened to less than four hours last night; only a fraction of what Cary had prepared. But what to make of this claim that the Erinye had simply been survived, casually and effortlessly, as if it was the Plague, the Cold War, the Declension, or any other minor historical upheaval? There had been nothing casual about the event that Julia had fled. She left behind a solar system in paroxysm, a civilization in flames. The Earth itself vanished, replaced by overlapping, expanding spheres of fire. Something similar had happened to Mars—a fireball was poised above the Valle Marineris, expanding and contracting according to no laws with which she was familiar. All across the system, the stations, the habs, the ecospheres—the mightiest structures ever created—were breaking up, being eradicated as she watched. The radio wavelengths were filled with hysterical maydays, SOSs, calls for orders and data, each being overwhelmed by an electronic wail centered on where Earth had been, each drowned out one after the other until, by the time she reached the Heliopause, there was nothing else but that grating, unending shriek.

Could anything have survived that Apocalypse? Maybe so. But if they had, they would be something twisted and distorted, something that she would not recognize as human. Something that sounded a lot like Magister St. John.

She had no choice; she had to act on worst case.

Particularly since he was so interested in her. That was all he'd spoken about over those four hours: Dame Amalfi's behavior; her plans; her schedule; her *speech patterns*, of all things. Whatever else St. John might be, he was certainly obsessive where Julia Amalfi was concerned.

No sense discussing any of this with Cary; she could imagine what kind of response she'd get. St. John had become Cary's new idol, the entity who was going to make things better, rescue her from the drudgery of running a developing colony, carry her across the new horizon to whatever promised land an AI could envision. Pry her from the clutches of the dowdy and boring Dame Amalfi.

Cary looked upon him much the same way she used to look at Julia, in fact.

She let her mind go blank and sank into a soft and welcoming haze. A haze similar to the one she'd spent most of her time in the past few decades. It was so easy to drift, to let events carry her along aimlessly . . .

Just like that poor woman in New York. She forced her eyes open. That afternoon had marked the moment when she became convinced that all the stories Petro had told her about the Erinye were true, that it was more than a personal fantasy, her beloved's endearing crotchet.

Taking several deep breaths, she flung off the sheets and got up, forcing herself to prepare for whatever the day would bring. Today she chose a light, cream-colored robe. That and boots; it seemed like a boots kind of morning. When the knock at the door came, she was ready, sitting atop the bed with her hands clasped in her lap.

There were four of them, as before, but when she stepped out, she saw double that number standing in the atrium, guns slightly raised, facing the rebels across the room. On their feet, the rebel boys glared back, their own guns at a level identical to the those of the Garites.

Julia insisted on eating before she left. She wasn't going to make the same error as yesterday—she'd been faint from lack of food by the time she returned. All four followed her into the kitchen, watching unblinkingly while she ate. Leaving the food unfinished, she nodded to the leader that she was ready.

Outside another dozen armed Rigorists waited. No crowd was gathered below; instead they had collected at the far end of the plaza, near the tree. The guards formed a cordon around her, the greater number on her left, facing the rebel encampment. Most of the Rigorists had scarves covering their lower faces, leaving only their eyes visible. The ones waiting outside wore harnesses, as black as the rest of their clothing. Pouches and small globes were fixed to the straps at various spots. Though she couldn't name them, Julia was certain these were some kind of weapon.

On the hillside she saw the fortifications that Cary had mentioned. The slope was checkered with mounds of earth marking where holes had been dug. Higher up, shirtless men filled sandbags and piled them in front of the building entrances. They ceased working when she passed, gazing down at her with hands on hips. There were no remarks or catcalls this morning.

A figure appeared from inside lab building two. Her heart gave a leap when she recognized Tony Perin. Making his way down the hill, the boy reached the wall and vaulted over it. Julia missed the next development through stubbing her toe on a tilted block. When she looked up, Perin stood alone facing a line of at least ten Rigorists.

As she watched, the Garites did something to their weapons that caused a loud, clicking noise. Perin's arms drew away from his side. Beyond him, Julia saw a line of rebels at the wall. Others ran down the slope to join them.

She gestured sharply at him. He failed to see her, so she called out, "Mr. Perin . . . Tony!" His head moved almost imperceptibly in her direction. The closest Rigorist stalked over to her. "The monad will—" Turning aside, she waved Perin off once again. He eyed her a second longer, then retreated a step. The guards remained as they were.

They moved on, the Rigorist leader giving her a stern lecture. She paid him no mind. After a moment, the guards rejoined them. She looked back to see Perin standing at the wall, lifting his cap off his forehead with one thumb. She'd seen him do that before.

The crowd awaiting her was far more subdued than it had been yesterday. She searched the massed faces for the old man. Twice her spirits lifted when she thought she made him out, but each time it was only another vacant, battered face. The ravages of poverty leave identical scars no matter who they strike. Finally she accepted that she would see him no more, and lowered her gaze to the spot where the guards had led her.

Before her lay a rock. Not one of the dressed stones making up the pavement of the plaza, simply a large, dirty rock like any other scattered across Midgard's surface. It had obviously been dragged here with some effort. For one purpose: to humiliate her.

She raised her head, having to turn almost completely before she found Fredrix. He sat in a chair next to the lower gate, two disciples poised behind him. A small sack lay in his lap, and as she watched, he popped something into his mouth and began chewing. He wasn't looking at her, but she was well aware that he wouldn't miss a move she made.

Untying the sash around her waist, she shook it out and then lay it over the surface of the rock. The guards made no attempt to interfere. She turned and sat down as if she'd been doing exactly that her entire life.

A glance at Fredrix revealed him still chewing, his hands on his knees.

The table stood directly in front of her, the same three judges seated behind it. Coordinator Integral studied her through his glasses before going into a prepared speech. A mark on the tree above his head caught her eye. She squinted at it, wishing that she hadn't let her visual mods go. But clearly someone had been carving the trunk. A branch was missing also—she could see the scar where it had been cut off. She felt herself flush. That *was* exasperating. This oak was *her* tree, planted with her own two hands. They had no business touching it.

She shot an accusing glance at Integral. But this wasn't the kind of trick a Garite would pull, regimented as they were. No . . . She turned her gaze to the crowd. This was something these hill people would do. The culprit had to be among them.

The few who attempted to challenge her looked away quickly enough. Only a single, dour-looking woman in front of the table continued glaring at her. Julia began feeling silly after only a few seconds. Granted, the vandalism was annoying, but here she was a prisoner and on trial—mock though it might be—and she was worrying about a tree. There are such things as priorities, Jay. Petro used to tell her that constantly.

The rebels watched from the hillside. Perin was in the middle, his arms oddly placed . . . She realized that he was studying her through some kind of optics. Raising her thumb, she jerked it upward—another gesture of Petro's. Perin's arms dropped, then one rose to return the motion.

"Who will speak?"

As Julia had expected, the harsh-eyed woman started to rise. But before she gathered her legs underneath her, a young, grubby-looking man farther over leaped to his feet.

"I wants to know 'bout this 'mortality drug the bitch got."

Integral raised a hand. "The struggle will—"

"Yeah, that's what I'm doin'. I'm strugglin', like you said to." He pointed at Julia. "She got the 'mortality drug. You told us. How come she get so old she don't look it? It's this drug, over at the met sender, where she do spearmints on people—"

"The matter will be struggled at its proper moment," Integral said firmly.

"No, no," the young man shouted back. "I wants to struggle this out *now*. You told us." He waved at one of the guards around Julia. "How she takes out baby's blood. In the met sender—" He bobbed his head eagerly as others in the crowd yelled out encouragement.

Julia twisted her lips. Bringing up ågathics was a mistake. Most people understood that it wasn't simply drugs—the same kind of drugs available to anyone on Midgard for a variety of treatments—as much as the mods that Julia had gotten back on Earth, the processors that utilized limited nanons to maintain and repair her organs. (The unlimited variety predicted for two centuries that might confer true immortality were unfortunately a fantasy; they were uncontrollable due to chaotic factors and could be used only as weapons—weapons banned by treaty throughout the system, though she was convinced that the Erinye had used them in the end.) Such technology required an informational plant—including mature AIs—that she couldn't possibly have brought with her. Some decades in the future, Midgard would match Home technology and extend life spans well beyond the current ninety to one hundred and ten years. Nothing would make her happier—she had no doubt that the deaths of so many friends, going back to the firstborn themselves, had been a big factor in her emotional drift.

But some, convinced that it was a secret on Julia's part, couldn't grasp that. Rumors had floated around for years, and finally she'd decided to stop trying to quash them. The believers were too stupid or deluded to be convinced by evidence; the effort was a waste of time. They would discuss it and brood over it in any case—just as these hill folk were doing now.

"She wants us to *die*. She wants to keep that drug. *You* want us to die—" Integral now had both hands up, waving them as if to brush some opaque mist away from his face. Probity, the Garite to Integral's right, suddenly shot to her feet. Her arm swung high, then flashed downward, too quickly to follow.

Silence smothered the crowd. On the tabletop a dagger quivered, its tip buried an inch or more. "You require a reminder of purge, monad?" Probity demanded.

The man stared at the blade, jaw hanging open. He went ashen, his eyes seeming to sink into his skull, and he shook his head wordlessly. He had advanced several feet while shouting; now he backed up without looking behind him and collapsed into his place as if his legs had been cut out from under him.

Probity regarded him a moment before retaking her seat. The blade remained embedded in the wood; she made no attempt to remove it. The coordinator adjusted his glasses. "Monad Giti," he said. "You will speak."

The woman had remained standing throughout the uproar, her arms wrapped about her as if she was cold, though the day was not that chilly. She wore an old dress that had seen a lot of miles, a little sweater unraveling at one sleeve. "You talkin' babies," she said. Her voice was harsh, as of someone gone hoarse from shouting. She took a step forward, into the clear area before the table. "I had a baby one time."

She let an arm drop, still holding it at the elbow. Julia realized that she was much younger than she appeared. "I was pickin' apples over the Downs when I got this baby, you know how it goes. It was the fall crop. Ones they call 'nature apples.' Well, I got paid off and this old woman told me how I could get rid of it, but I din't wanna get rid of that baby. So I headed north. Back home. Hills just west of the Chain.

"It was snowin' when I got back. My mama she was mad, but only a while. I give her the money and settle in, workin' our own crops, that's all.

"And in the springtime, weather get warm, that's when I had my baby." She paused, working her mouth, eyes half-closed. The coordinator leaned forward. "Proceed, monad."

"Well, I—I couldn't take to the road that year. Baby was too little. Ever'body else going migrant, you know. Spring harvests, stuff planted in winter. Wheat and rye first. Down the Shore for the rice. You all know that." Her eyes rested on Julia for the first time since she'd begun speaking. "*She* don't know."

Julia let her head fall slightly. She hadn't known. She'd had no idea at all that there was anything like migrant labor on her world. There wasn't supposed to be. She recalled someone saying that things had been kept from her.

". . . so I worked some the towns by the Chain. Chores. Took my baby with me, to feed her. She didn't bother me none, she was good. *Too* good, see. She weren't crying, not making much noise at all. Just laying there, skin yella, eyes all red. So I went to a root woman . . ."

Julia raised a hand to her face. She knew what was coming. The child had been suffering from a systemic allergy, a reaction to native Middie proteins. It wasn't at all uncommon—one of the first things she'd ordered Cary to do after landing was to work out therapies for it. Recombinant viruses were available to deal with any type of allergy . . . yet this girl had gone to some backwoods healer using Middie plants, plants that would do nothing but make the reaction worse.

". . . herbs worked for a time. She was better. But then weather gets cold again, and . . . and . . ."

She stood bent slightly forward, mouth open wide. Rocking once or twice on her heels. "She *died*. Risa just *died*. One day . . ." The girl put her hands over her face.

Vicki. Julia could only think of Vicki. Oh, she was with people who loved her, yes. Everything had been planned. But now, the way things had turned out . . . She was so recognizable, so helpless. Julia should never have let her go. She'd ask Cary if she'd heard anything. How could she have forgotten that last night?

The girl raised her head, under control once again. "My mama . . . she said there'd be other babies. She'd lost three 'fore me. But . . . I went migrant next year, and I got sick . . ." Her free hand waved vaguely. "Down there, and I can't have none, ever again. I had one baby. Just one. Risa was the one."

She fell silent, and for a moment Julia thought it was over. But then Probity tapped sharply on the table. The girl stared at her in puzzlement. Probity pointed at Julia.

"And *she* didn't care." The girl stepped closer. "She was down here in her big house, lookin' at the screen, and . . . playing with her machines. Eatin' all nice food there, where it's warm. She didn't know and . . . I don't think she'd care, even. This buji bi . . . bi . . ." She couldn't complete the word. "*Woman*."

She glanced at the table, as if for approval. Julia waited a moment, then raised a hand. "Dear . . ."

A guard thumped her from behind. She jerked away from the blow, shot an angry look at the coordinator.

Integral was studying her with a mild expression. "The monad," he said softly, "has a response?"

Probity rolled her eyes toward him and shifted in her seat. The third judge, the muscular boy who never had anything to say, looked uneasy. Julia turned to the girl, who was standing in the same exact pose as before. "Come here. Yes—they won't let me hurt you."

The girl hesitated, looking uncertainly at the judges. Probity's frown deepened, but Integral merely nodded. The girl walked over to Julia, halting several steps away.

"Listen to me." Julia spoke in little more than a whisper. The girl took a step closer. "I'm so sorry about your baby. I didn't know, and you're right. I should have known. I would feel the same about . . . my own child. But here's the thing." She reached for the girl's hand. At first she flinched away, but then she timidly let Julia take it. "You *can* have other babies. That I do know. Whatever's wrong can be easily fixed. It can be done today."

A murmur spread through the crowd. The girl stared uncertainly at Julia, her look of doubt deepening.

"Yes," Julia said with all the sincerity she could muster. "Today. And it won't hurt. I promise you that." Whatever was wrong, the med center could correct it. It couldn't be venereal; no such organisms existed within four parsecs of this world. Whatever it was, the effects could be reversed. Cervical infections were well understood, and even though Julia's training was long out of date, she could depend on Cary's help. Certainly Cary wouldn't object to that. "We can go over to the med center—right across the plaza—and do it now. By this time tomorrow, you'll be fine. Then we'll talk about what we'll do for your baby."

The girl blinked once or twice. Her eyes were wide, as if she was once again seeing something she'd thought long vanished. She opened her mouth as if to speak, then hesitantly turned to the table. Probity was bent over the dark wood, as if trying to listen in. "What did she say?"

A guard gave a garbled but understandable version of Julia's words. Probity smiled and sat back. "It's a lie," she said. "A buji lie."

The hand slipped from Julia's grasp. For a moment the girl stood quietly. Then Probity gave a sharp nod.

Julia didn't see the first slap coming and failed to dodge it. She made no move to avoid the others either, only clasping her hands tightly in her lap.

With a sob the girl ran back to her place. The noise of the crowd plateaued at something below the level of a scream. A high-pitched voice rose above it: ". . . we should 'tensify this struggle, get to the bottom of the tendencies of this . . . this . . ."

Julia touched her throbbing cheek. The crowd, gone utterly quiet, was regarding her with something very akin to absolute horror. She was shrinking before that gaze when she realized that they weren't looking at her at all. They were looking through her.

She swung around to see a hillside full of men, both shirtless and fully dressed, all carrying weapons, racing toward the wall at the bottom.

She found Tony Perin, in the lead as she might have expected. Brought up short by the wall, he slammed both hands flat on the top, said something that even at this distance she could make out as the longest and most complicated of obscenities.

A whistle shrieked to her right. Sensing movement at the corner of her eye, she turned to see a black tide appearing from behind the station house. Rigorist troops, dressed the same as those she'd seen this morning, as if they'd been ready.

Behind her, the crowd found its voice. A scrabbling of shoe soles against stone erupted, along with loud cries ordering them to be still.

At the wall Perin took in the mass of Rigorists—now flinging themselves down behind a low hummock—and let out another curse. Tearing off his cap, he waved it wildly at the labs. In a flurry of movement, an odd device that looked like a set of organ pipes appeared atop the roof. Behind the dirt mounds, men began setting up weapons.

The rebels found cover at the foot of the hill, all except Perin, who swung to face the tree, cap still in hand. He shook it and bellowed, "Your move, mother*fucker*."

Searching for Fredrix, Julia was amazed to find him standing at the gate, placidly surveying the scene as if it was what he'd been looking forward to all along. He'd brought his sack with him, she noticed.

The crowd had been subdued. Her own guards stepped back and spread out. With a glance in their direction Julia got up and hurried to the table.

Integral was staring at the hillside in a kind of dull shock. Probity looked quite alarmed as well, Julia was pleased to see, and said nothing at her approach. The square-faced boy seemed to be in a daze. Grabbing Integral's arm, Julia gave him a shake. He twisted toward her so quickly that his glasses slid down his nose. "Take me to the Herald. I can stop this."

Integral took in the rebels, looked down at his clenched fists, then back up at Julia. He paused to replace his glasses. "Yes," he said mildly.

Fredrix was now surrounded by a gaggle of black-clad teenagers, two of them addressing him with animation, or at least as much animation as Garites were capable of. Fredrix appeared to be listening, but then spat something against the wall and gave them all a sharp answer. They were backing away as Julia came up.

"Woman," Fredrix grunted, reaching into the bag. He drew out a handful of nuts and popped one into his mouth, cracking it between his teeth and ejecting the shell while he listened to her offer.

"What we will do," he said when she'd finished, "is continue the hearing. You got lots to answer for. You concur, Coordinator?"

"As the Will requires, Herald."

"Uh-huh." Fredrix spat out another shell. He seemed to be slightly muddled, and Julia noticed that his pupils were dilated.

"Now, look," she said. "I doubt you want the Cloister to be wrecked any more than I do—"

"*I* want? You mean the Will, don't you? The Will demands, we interpret." He swung to the Rigorists behind him. "This female is disregarding the Will. What you make of that?"

He turned back without waiting for a reply, nodding in the direction of Tony Perin, cap back on and arms crossed. "That boy," he said, "is gonna do exactly *nothing*. He's matched down here, and there's an equal force to his rear he don't know about yet. He thinks he's challengin' me—look at him. But he's wigglin', that's all."

Treating himself to another nut, Fredrix thoughtfully following the shell's trajectory as if to mark where it fell. "Take an hour, two. Dust him right off. But—not today. No, not today. It'll wait. A week, I'll have a thousand monads here. He'll be engulfed. And after that . . ." He turned to face Julia. "I believe we'll reform Monad Perin. Yes—the Will requires it. That's what we'll do with this rogue. Alter him, according to the dictates of the Will. In a number of ways. See what kinda social utility results. No sense even wondering what to call what he'll be. There are roles that we cannot even imagine in our undeveloped state. Have to see. Consider it deeply. Struggle it."

He propped one foot on the wall and looked her over with the air of a man surrendering to a generous impulse. "Ayah—you go on up there. Make it clear what a silly monad he is. Coordinator, you accompany."

"Herald—" A monad stepped forward. Julia suppressed a shudder—it was the demented girl who'd attacked her. "The Will calls this monad to sacrifice."

Fredrix kept his back to her. "No, Unity. But we are awed by your dedication."

The girl withdrew, her face empty but somehow containing a suggestion of childish petulance all the same. With a flick of a finger Fredrix ordered them on their way.

Stepping through the gate, Julia raised a hand to Perin. He waved her ahead. Integral followed, accompanied by three younger Garites. She was wondering whether they too had heard the call when she noticed that all of them were carrying guns. She came to a halt. "You there—put those guns up. Uhh, sling them. Over your shoulders."

None replied with anything more than nervous glances at the older man. Integral touched his glasses. "Do this." They slung the guns immediately.

They went on. After a few steps, Julia fell back until she came level with Integral. "That old man yesterday," she said, keeping her voice low. "What happened to him?"

Integral walked on in silence, his expression pensive. "His attitude was unacceptable," he said at last. "He has been separated from the Collective."

" 'Separated'?" But his face had closed, and she heard the guards' footsteps catching up.

Perin was at the wall to meet her. As she swept

toward him, a guard called out, "Far enough." Ignoring her, Julia walked on.

Perin reached for her arm. "Come on, I'll help you over—"

She held her hands away. "No. I can't—"

Face gone red, Perin jerked erect. "Back off!" he shouted over Julia's head. Half-turning, Julia gestured the guard away. The fool girl kept coming.

"I said stand fast!" Perin shouted.

A man came up beside him, weapon raised. "Lemme pop that—"

"No!" Slapping the barrel aside, Julia bent closer to Perin. "Get them under control, Mr. Perin." He nodded and gestured the man back. Julia swung around to face the guard. "And I don't need *you* here either. Coordinator, will you please . . . ?"

Integral stepped forward and gripped the girl's arm. She docilely retreated several steps. Julia turned back to Perin. His eyes flicked away but then bored into hers once again. "You ain't going back there."

"Yes, I am, Tony. There's no alternative."

He pointed at her cheek. "You got a nice bruise comin' up. You lookin' for more?"

"I don't bruise easily. And I repeat: we have no choice. Not at the moment." She lowered her voice. "It's a ritual. It's theater, no more than that. We can take advantage of it. To buy time."

Perin glared past her at Integral. "My boys found a body this morning. Old guy, beat to death. Looks like somebody tried to burn him on top of it. What you say to that, Goggles?"

"It was the . . . wood people. They carried this out." Integral actually sounded defensive. Julia looked back, but his head was down and he would not meet her eyes.

"All right, playmates!" a voice called out. "What's the problem?"

They looked up as one, all except Tony Perin, who

continued gazing out over the plaza, an expression of sheer disgust settling over his face.

Danil Cardnale was descending the hill, trailing a clump of staffers. His stride was broad, his expression negligent, as if what he'd found was no more than he'd expected, if slightly disappointing all the same. "Things a bit out of hand here, Tony?"

"This is so typical," Perin whispered. "Day late, dollar short. That'll be his epitaph." His eyes dropped to Julia's. "Can you believe that he started all this? That he's responsible? Can you *believe* that?"

Cardnale reached the wall, slapping his workcase on the stone. He ran his eyes over the group, brows rising slightly when he came to Julia. "All right," he said finally. "I suggest you break it up. Everyone on this side step back. I'll speak to these . . . representatives and get this matter settled. You there"—he gestured at a bearded boy to his right—"drop that cannon and give me a boost, if you will—"

The boy hesitated, blinking uncertainly at Perin. He got no response; Perin continued staring across the plaza, his arms crossed.

A young staffer came forward to aid Cardnale. "Thanks, Myk," he said as found his footing. "My apologies to you men," he said, drawing himself up. "I take full responsibility for this impasse. I haven't been paying proper attention. I confess to putting considerable faith in my compatriots." He dropped his eyes to Perin. "Perhaps misplaced. Faith that should have gone to you."

He raised a hand. "Another one hundred Rigorists are in place behind the labs . . . Oh, don't be alarmed. They're no more eager to fight than you are. They too have been victimized by the misunderstandings of the past few days.

"Since we arrived, we have, against our wills, become enmeshed in conflict, mistrust, and suspicion. It needn't have happened that way, and I don't intend it to continue. I name no names, I make no accusations. The matter will be looked into, and proper measures will be taken."

Some of the men were glancing at Perin. He stood as if paralyzed, the expression on his face unchanged. Julia raised a hand to him.

Cardnale went on. "I, for one, have done my best to maintain relations with our Garite allies. I can assure you that they intend no harm at this time. Simply by waving my hand, I can persuade those gathered to our right to withdraw." He looked back toward the tree. Fredrix stood by the gate, his legs crossed. "*I* have no argument with these people. Nor do you. There is absolutely no rational reason for this confrontation to have occurred. None of *us* are motivated by paranoia, petty ambition, or hysteria. Trust in ourselves, trust in the future, that's our byword. So—" He clapped his hands. "Let's break it up and head back to the labs. No point in wasting any time. Particularly . . ." He gave them a smile. "Since your bonus is waiting. Ten full ounces of gold for each man! We'll begin distribution at the Core in half an hour."

For a moment no one moved. Then one rebel— the bearded man who had rescued Julia yesterday— stepped toward Cardnale. "Dan," he said, handing him a small square of cardboard. "What you make of this?"

Cardnale looked at the square—a picture, Julia realized. He seemed to shrink into himself, the color draining from his face. His eyes rose to the crowd, blinking once or twice. "This—" he said in a voice utterly changed. "This will be looked into as well."

"Dan." Perin paused, as if carefully selecting his words. "Get your ass down off that wall."

Cardnale made no move to obey. "I don't think you understand, Tony. I'm doing this for *you*—"

Perin waved at Cardnale. "Take him down."

The men surged toward the wall as one. Cardnale shuffled his feet, as if prepared to elude them but uncertain which way to go. The bearded rebel lunged for him, gripping his vest. Cardnale jerked back, attempting to tear loose. Other hands laid hold of him. A firm yank pulled Cardnale over.

The boy named Myk pushed through the crowd. Eyes wide, he appealed to Integral. "Aren't you going to *do* anything?" Perin backhanded him without so much as a glance. The boy stumbled away with his hands over his face.

A struggle was going on where Cardnale had vanished. Julia could see nothing of him amid the broad backs of the rebels. "Tony, don't let them harm him. Please——"

"Get off him," Perin shouted.

"We ain't hurtin' him," someone called back. "He's throwin' a fit." The men parted to reveal Cardnale on one knee, his clothes disheveled, a wild look on his face.

"Get him out of here."

A rebel grabbed Cardnale under his arms and pulled him to his feet. He was still staring at Perin with something close to astonishment. His lips moved slightly. "Not a word," Perin told him. "Not a fuckin' word. Just go."

The rebels shoved him uphill, hands appearing one after the other to push him onward, as if he was running a gauntlet. "We still get the gold, right, Danny?" someone called out.

Spotting the workcase, Perin grabbed it and flung it over his shoulder. A staffer ran to pick it up. The picture that had started it all lay face-up on the wall. Julia glanced at it but was unable to recognize what it depicted. Perin shoved it in his pocket before returning to her.

Any notion that she'd entertained that he was acting out of frustration, as a cover for helplessness or fear, vanished at the first close glimpse of his face. She was seeing pure rage, a rage well reined in, but pure for all that. It was something she hadn't seen for a long time, this controlled and channeled masculine anger. Not since Earth, in fact. Petro had been like that, after the authorities, too frightened to act, dismissed the evidence of the existence of the Erinye. What had happened to it, here on Midgard? Had she suppressed it, all unknowing?

Chin thrust forward, arms loose at his side, Perin gazed over her head, looking as if he was about to leap straight across into the plaza. Clutching her robe, Julia prepared to hold him back. It was strange how hesitant she felt.

He didn't even look at her. Slamming his palms on the stone, he leaned toward Integral. "You. What's the proposition?"

"The Herald is . . . willing to restrain the impulses of the Collective . . . They were impulsive, yes." Integral took a breath and raised his voice. "This is an enormous concession."

Perin let out a laugh. "I'll bet it is. Awright . . . when you get halfway—that stone bench there—I'll pull my boys back to the labs. You Blackies do the same. Got it? I'm not gonna tell you what happens if anybody fucks up. You know that." He let a breath pass. "Well?"

Integral gestured a subordinate over, whispered to her for a moment. She went racing off toward the tree. Perin relaxed his stance, eyes boring into the coordinator. He glanced at Julia, then looked closer, as if he hadn't noticed her before. She was about to speak when he swung away.

"I want five . . . make that six volunteers."

Several of the rebels approached. "You're gonna escort the Lady back there, keep an eye on her during this . . . song and dance. Don't antagonize the Shirts, but if any of those one-eyes act up, you shoot 'em.

Kill 'em dead." He swiveled to face Integral. "This ain't a deal. No negotiation, nothin'. You turn it down, we're at war."

Integral hesitated, then inclined his head. Looking back at the volunteers, Perin rubbed a hand along his jaw. At that moment Gen walked over. "I'll go with 'em," he said.

Perin gave him a clap on the shoulder and the rebels clambered over the wall. There was a shout from the end of the plaza. The messenger was returning, waving an arm and bobbing her head. Integral turned to Perin. "Accepted," he said precisely. "You may consider it an act of—"

"*I'll* decide what to consider, Goggles." He lunged across the wall. "And I'll tell you something else: you see that man?" A rebel crouching a few feet away straightened up. "He's a poacher. A damn good shot."

Julia noticed for the first time that this man was carrying a rifle, unlike most of the others. "And if my boys get any backtalk, or the Lady, or if I just *consider* it, his first round will hit right *there*." Perin's forefinger halted only an inch away from the cross-piece of Integral's glasses. The coordinator winced slightly.

"And the next will be for fat boy, and *don't you so much as move—not a quiver.*"

The younger Rigorists went rigid. "You have concluded?" Integral asked drily. At Perin's wave he turned away without a word. Perin looked over at Julia, his face growing—if anything—even angrier.

"See me later," she mouthed at him. He glowered a second or two, then nodded curtly. She stepped away from the wall.

It took some time for the guards and escorts of various sides to sort themselves out. Julia accepted it as an opportunity to speak to Integral. "Why did you lie to me?" The coordinator paced on without answering. Someone cried out and a guard—the messenger, in fact—stumbled past, arms windmilling as if to keep her balance. Somebody else snickered. "None of that crap," Gen called out and went on to berate someone named Kris.

"About the old man," Julia insisted. "Why? I thought truth was a virtue."

"Not with class enemies," Integral whispered.

"Ah, class enemies. In that case, why did it matter so much as to lie about it?" She would have sworn that Integral's expression changed, edging toward something close to misery. "It did matter, didn't it?"

Integral broke step, falling immediately behind. Another Rigorist took his place. She kept glancing over her shoulder at the rebels.

A sudden outburst drew her eyes to the station. The Rigorists had all risen and were returning to wherever they'd emerged from, waving their guns and yipping wildly. Behind her, the rebels started up the hill. Only Perin remained, arms crossed, gaze following her down the plaza.

At the gate Fredrix waited, still gripping his bag of nuts. She could sense his self-satisfaction, even at this distance. Cocking his head, he took a lazy step out onto the plaza.

He came to a halt as the cries of his troops died away. Behind him, the crowd under the tree stirred uneasily, and several Bilis ran into the open, raising their faces to the sky. Julia did the same, already squinting, knowing precisely where to look.

The sun was almost directly overhead. Surrounding it, clearly visible in the yellow-orange glare, was a glowing nimbus, a halo of fire. It pulsated, appearing to grow larger in the second before she looked away.

Shouts rang out as the Rigorists moved to subdue

the crowd. Julia squeezed her eyes shut against blotches of afterimage. When she opened them again, Fredrix was nowhere in sight. All she saw was the sack lying in front of the gate, the homely brown of nuts scattered around it.

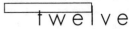

twelve

Tony halted at the steps leading up to the Lady's patio. The lights were on, and he could see his own men in the big living room. One was reading what looked to be a magazine, while two others talked and a fourth slumped morosely on the couch. He couldn't see any Rigs, but he knew they were in there. He wondered if Gen had talked to this bunch yet about consorting with female Rigs. Tony had mentioned it this morning, offhand-like, as if it had occurred to him that there might be a major problem impending between the Orcs and the bald-headed, casually bathed Rig girls. Gen had regarded him a moment, as if awaiting the punch line, then nodded amiably and said, "Sure, Ton, I'll, uh, take care of it." Tony thought he'd never hated anybody as much as he did Unity at that moment.

He fingered his chin—he'd shaved for the first time in two days—then ran his hands over his vest and shirt, making sure the tail was tucked in. The shirt was new; the kind of thing you'd wear to a fair or show. He'd borrowed it from Hob Yung, wondering why the hell Hob had tramped halfway across the continent with something this nice in his pack. Had he been thinking they'd have a parade when they reached the Cloister, or what?

You could see the entire length of the plaza from up here. Looked damned impressive. All was quiet, almost contemptuously so—nothing going on down by the village, no yips, howls, or chanting. A calm night for the Garite Collective. The slow burning that had eaten at him all day mounted once again. He tamped it down with some effort. That was what Freddy wanted, after all. That was why he was goading him.

The boys were taking things well. Not as if they'd been handed a setback at all. Which they hadn't; not really, not if you looked at it sensibly. No, they were cheerful, pleased with themselves—as they should be; they'd done fine—and ready to go. Eager to go, to do whatever he told them. He couldn't ask for more.

He'd sent a couple men to the Mavericks' camp to tell Cus not to contact him tonight, as they'd arranged when Shor had delivered the photos. Tony wasn't sure if Rigs were hiding in the hills or not. The ones who'd circled around this morning had disappeared; no sign of where they'd gone. The Mavericks were the ace up his sleeve, and he wanted them kept hidden. Right up until the moment they crashed into Fredrix's rear, if possible.

He took a deep breath, gave the vest one last yank, and headed for the door. As it swung open, a Blackshirt leaped into view, in a half-crouch with his weapon across his chest, as if prepared to dispute Tony's passage. Giving him the best sneer in his arsenal, Tony walked on. The kid jumped out of his way at the very last second.

Ignoring the whispers behind him, Tony crossed the room and chewed the fat with Con Pris and the boys a minute or two. Then, with a final thumb to his cap, he went up the steps and over to the closed door at the far side of the next room. The Rigs' chatter grew frantic behind him.

The door slid open at his knock. Clearing his throat, he announced himself.

"Come in, Tony."

The first thing he saw was the bed. He looked away quickly. The Lady was sitting in the corner, in a large, comfortable-looking chair. She seemed very small, her alien thinness lending her an air of inhuman fragility. Her legs were crossed, and she was wearing some kind of earpiece. Behind him, the door slid shut. He took one step farther into the room.

"Have a seat." She gestured at a chair facing hers. He went over and sat down awkwardly, butt perched on the edge. Remembering his cap, he whipped it off and set it on the chair arm, hoping his hair wasn't sticking out all over the place.

The Lady gave him a smile. In this indirect light, none of the weirdness of her features was evident. She actually looked young. She could almost have been his own age. He became aware that he was staring—aware that she was aware that he was aware, more like it—and shifted spasmodically in the chair. In the process, he knocked his cap to the floor. When he bent to pick it up, she laughed, a sweet chuckle also at odds with her years.

"Don't be nervous," she told him as he straightened up. "Relax."

He felt himself blush, gave her a stiff nod.

"Relax," she repeated.

He allowed himself enough of a slump to give the impression that he was, in fact, relaxing. "I'm . . . glad to see you back here and safe, ma'am. I'm a little surprised that . . . lump let you come back, things being the way they are." He was surprised any of them had come back. The afternoon had been one long ordeal, watching the Bilis and Rigs harass his men without being able to do a thing about it. But Gen kept them in order, and nobody laid a finger on the Lady.

"I'm not," the Lady said. "It's a game. He's teasing us. Tormenting us, more to the point. Showing us that he's in command, that he feels secure." She smiled in a way that made him shiver. "Do you feel tormented?"

"Not especially."

"Me neither."

He bent forward, hands clasped between his knees. "So how do we whip 'em, ma'am?"

"Julia," she told him. "I'm Julia to you, and you're Tony. As for whipping them . . . I don't know how you'll do that. That's not what I asked you here for. Oh, I know you'll bring it off. I have no worries about that." Her head fell back, her throat all paleness. "You know, I first realized that I was facing not a revolt but a revolution, as the old story goes, after Bukland. I could not make head nor tails of what I heard about that little skirmish. Some kid from the Plateau had surrounded two trained police units reinforced with local militia and simply scooped them up, with next to no casualties. And for two full weeks all I heard was 'Perin this,' 'Perin that' . . . My police were very annoyed with you, Tony."

Tony gave her a sheepish shrug.

"So finally I told them to pull back, evacuate what needed to be evacuated, and simply get out of your way."

"I thought it was something like that . . ." Tony said slowly. "Everybody else figured they were concentrating, building up for a counterstrike, but . . . I don't know, I had this feeling . . ."

"I'm sure you did. Of course, I had no notion of our little friends in black at the time."

Tony was wondering how to tell her that he hadn't either when she bent forward. "Do you know why it happened that way, Tony? Why it was so easy for you?"

"Well, uhh . . . I did a lot of reading. Tactics, military history . . ."

"No. That's secondary. It's because you're an alpha."

"Beg pardon, ma'am?"

She ran a palm across her forehead. "Didn't you ever take introductory sociobiology? Or did they stop teaching that too without telling me?"

Thinking back, Tony could recall that there had been some course of that name. But he didn't remember much about it. He'd skipped a lot of classes the last couple years. Once you figured out how to beat the tests, there wasn't much sense in hanging around school.

"You're an alpha," the Lady—Julia—repeated. "An alpha male. The pack leader, the man who is obeyed. You find that quality throughout history— most of the great leaders had it. Maybe all of them. I'm sure the soldiers—the generals and kings—were all alphas. You must have noticed it in your readings. The Romans had their own word for it: *auctoritas*. Natural authority. That's what they looked for in their emperors." She had taken the gleaming unit from her ear and was toying with it. "It's not enough, of course. An alpha doesn't require decency, or morality, or a sense of obligation. You always need more."

Tony must have let out some sound, some expression of skepticism or doubt.

"You never noticed it, Tony? How many of your men are older than you? A lot of them, I'd say. Do they ever disobey you? And what about the Garites?

They snapped to this afternoon, did they not? Even though you're an ideological nullity to them, something they've been programmed to despise their entire lives. Even though you directly threatened their prophet."

"Well—people say I take after my old man."

Julia raised a hand, one finger extended. "Your old . . . Not *Mart*? Of course—Mart Perin! How could I have missed that! I remember him from his school days. He was so cute, Tony. He had a dimple, right here." She touched her cheek.

As far as Tony knew, his dad had never had such a thing as a dimple in his life. She'd confused him with somebody else. But that was understandable— she must have known a hell of a lot of people over the years. "He told me to say hello."

"He did? Oh, that's sweet. Well, you tell him the same, after all this is over."

Tony nodded abstractedly. An alpha male, was it? He supposed that was a neat thing to be. Something to tell his mom: "Hey, the Lady Amalfi said I'm an alpha!" Of course, she'd just wave him out to chop wood until his head stopped swelling. Moriah too, for that matter. Julia was right about the old war dogs, though. They *were* all like that—and a good number of them ended up tripping over their own britches. He could plainly see disadvantages to the role. In fact, he kind of wished that she hadn't mentioned it.

An image of Cardnale rose in his mind, as he'd appeared this evening. Not the cocky, obnoxious Cardnale he'd endured for the past three days. Nor the tormented visionary of the Plateau. But a new man, a smaller man, a man both miserable and contrite. Sitting at the fire, nervously shifting a coffee mug from hand to hand, ignoring the hot gouts that splattered his fingers. Repeating, for the thousandth time, his dream of what Midgard could become, the ideal society just out of reach, the utopia that they (yeah—it had become "they" again) could create.

Cardnale wanted to go after the Rigs now. He was more than willing to throw in with Tony. It would be easy; he had it all worked out. All he needed to do was talk to the Bilis, give 'em one of his rip-roarers, the kind of speech he used to make up the Plateau. They'd turn on the Blackshirts, rip 'em limb from limb. Five minutes of talk, that was all it would take, and then they'd walk into paradise, shoulder to shoulder . . .

Tony had felt the tug. He'd wanted to be persuaded. But it didn't sound very enticing. It didn't sound possible. It didn't even sound like anything anybody had ever believed at all. Cardnale was begging by the time Tony told him he had to leave.

". . . haven't seen it in a man since Earth, really," Julia was saying. "Petro had it. But after that . . . I wonder if I've been suppressing it. If it can ever arise in a society run by a mother figure . . ."

"What about Cardnale? What is he?"

"Dan? Alpha/beta, I'd guess. Capable of both roles, comfortable in neither. He tries too hard, doesn't he?"

Tony nodded. That he did.

"But that's why I'm not worried about the Rigorists, Tony. You'll take care of them. In your own way. Probably in some fashion no one could have guessed beforehand. Which doesn't mean I won't help you, give you what assistance I can. Your weapons, for instance. They're rather crude . . ."

"The Stens? Yeah. They go back a long way. That's why we chose 'em. Easy to make—parts are mostly stamped metal. Very reliable, though."

"Yes." Julia grimaced slightly. "The Perin Metal Works."

Tony sat with his mouth open. "Uh . . . yeah. That's right, ma'am."

"How many did your dad produce?"

He wanted to tell her that it was actually his uncle who ran the plant, but couldn't find the words. "Five thousand."

"Where did you get the plans?" She smiled broadly when Tony failed to answer. "Cary."

Tony gestured at the ceiling. "Is she listening?" he whispered.

"Of course she is," Julia said, giving the earpiece a twirl. "She always listens. But don't worry about it. Back to the guns. I can do better than those Stens. You've heard of Kalashnikovs?"

"Sure."

"We have five hundred mid-21st-century models. The 54, I believe."

Kalashnikovs—they had to have come from Earth. Firearms were a cottage industry on Midgard. Everybody knew that the Lady didn't care for them. But they were necessary in areas where a full Terrest ecology had taken root.

She must have caught his expression. "We brought them with us," she said. "We had no idea what was waiting for us here."

"But . . . why didn't you give them to your cops?"

She regarded him a moment. "The same reason I pulled them back, Tony."

"Uh-huh." He thought about the guns. He was less than keyed to turn-of-the-millennium weaponry. Probably wired from barrel to butt. No hope of familiarizing the whole outfit with them, not in what time remained. Still, they'd be full auto, and it would be nice to have pieces that could hit something fifty yards away.

"They're stored in the tunnels," Julia said.

"The *where?*"

"Well, not actually *in* them. A storage space halfway down the tunnel to the labs. Well hidden. I'll

give you a diagram . . . You haven't found the tunnels, I take it?"

Tony shook his head. He knew about the ones
under the Academy—his dad had told him about the
games the students played in them. But he'd had no
idea there were others.

"We dug them between the primary sites here, for
use during the winter. Otherwise, getting around
would have been a major saga. They fell out of use
when the weather improved, except for the Academy. They run between here, lab two—actually the
first built, it was renumbered after Jens overhauled
operations—the med center, and Cary's. We lack one
to the station, I'm afraid. That was built later. Will
they help?"

Tony couldn't see how, but he nodded anyway.
"Yeah. Ought to."

"Good. I can give you the guns, the tunnels . . .
and this." She revealed another earpiece, twin to the
one in her lap, and tossed it over to him. "That's
Earth tech, very few around. I won't tell you to be
careful, because you can't break it. It's recharged by
body heat while you're wearing it, and it's tuned to
Cary's frequency." She smiled. "Now she can eaves-
drop on you for a change. Seriously, though, she
does want to talk to you. You can also contact me
through it, Cary being willing."

He looked it over. There wasn't much to it—no
grill or readouts visible. It could have been a slightly
too ornate piece of jewelry.

"Anything else you want, let me know. And
now"—her voice dropped—"something you *don't*
want: advice."

She shifted in the chair, the light catching her face
in a way that it hadn't done up until now. The illusion of youth—of freshness and innocence—fell
away. But it wasn't replaced by the oddly ravaged
face he'd seen that first day. Instead he saw some-

thing that he could not recall from his own experience, although he recognized it nonetheless. An expression of cold determination far deeper than anything that could have grown in a mere century and a half. An expression that came from the ages.

"You must stop reacting. You're letting yourself be manipulated. If that continues, you lose. We lose. That is his only true strength. Not his numbers, not his discipline. You must ignore all that. Consult only yourself. Your impulses, your intuitions. They will not fail you . . ."

He listened without moving. It wasn't anything he hadn't considered himself. But coming from her, it was different. It was as if he was being authorized, given permission. He wondered if there was such a thing as an alpha female. There must be—otherwise, what term was there to describe Julia Amalfi? He saw with a flash of insight that this was what the ancient conquerors had lacked—the men who won empires and then lost them in less time than it took a child to grow to adulthood. They lacked this—a woman of knowledge, a woman to act as a guide. And then, insight turning back on him, he realized with wonder that he was Dame Amalfi's man, as much as her cops and officials had ever been. She would always be the Lady to him, now and forever.

". . . you know you have only days," she concluded. "Think and act."

He nodded. A phrase leaped into his mind: "the queen with the heart of a king." Someone else had been called that, a long time ago; he couldn't quite recollect who.

He'd been ready to ask her to leave. That's what he'd come here for; to demand she flee the Cloister with a squad of his men as escort, to someplace—the Islands, maybe—where she'd be safe until events fell out whatever way they were going to. But that was now inconceivable. Why, he couldn't quite say.

It was beyond thought or analysis; simply a conviction, deep down in the foundations of his mind: fire burned, and ice was cold, and Julia Amalfi was not going to run.

He struggled to keep his face placid, wishing he could be as confident as the Lady. She was gazing into a dark corner, as silent as he. "Now let's discuss the real problem," she said at last.

"The ship."

"Yes. The way the sun looked today—it frightened people. Even the Garites. That's a good thing. They should be frightened."

"I explained to my boys it was just exhaust," Tony said carefully. It had been a tough argument. Some of the men from up near the Threshold had been convinced that the sky was about to fall. Tony couldn't blame them. Every time he looked up, his guts had twisted another knot.

"You noticed it was asymmetric—wider on one side."

"Yeah. I guess it's . . . firing at an angle?"

"That's right. So the exhaust misses Midgard. A relief, in a way . . . it means that they're not simply planning to burn us off."

"Would they . . ." Tony gave a nervous chuckle. "Would they really do something like that?"

Julia scarcely moved. But that slight shift completely altered her appearance once more. Tony stared at her, wondering how she did it.

"Yes, young man," she said. "Yes—they would do that." She relaxed, youth suffusing her features once again. "I'm sorry, Tony. I don't mean to be harsh. It must seem like a tale to you, an old unhappy far-off thing. You weren't there, you didn't see it. But to me . . . to me it's like yesterday. I recall it more clearly than things that happened last month, last week.

"Yes, the Erinye would do that. They did do it. I

saw it happen to Earth. At least I think I did. I can't
tell you how horrifying it was. To see that grand
human structure annihilated, after it had done so
much and come so far. The grief, the outrage, the
fear . . . It's never left me."

"Did you ever actually see one of them?"

"Oh, we had files on them, yes. At least the lower-
level members, the acolytes. My . . . an acquaintance
of mine was running the investigation. But the photos were only of their real-world appearance. Not
their avatars."

She squinted, as if trying to make out something
at the very edge of vision. "I *may* have seen one in
panoply—what they called the 'pure state.' It was at
Housatonic—that was a plex off the Carolinas. They
triggered a brownout to cause panic. It was right
around sunset, and I saw . . . something, floating in
midair down the boulevard on the seaward side. I
can't describe it to you; they took their imagery directly from the subconscious; they were very big on
imagery. But there it was, floating in the gloom. Then
it drifted from between the buildings and was silhouetted by the sunset . . . And I realized that it wasn't
some*thing*, it was some*body*. It was very disturbing.
I just ran. You see, I thought they were after me . . ."

"So you were pretty involved."

"Yes . . . Oh, not very deeply. I wasn't at all important. It was my . . . friend. Petro Novichenko. He
was an officer of the fraud bureau of the Slavic Customs Union. That was the biggest economic bloc on
Earth at the time. Much larger than the EC or
NAFTA. It stretched all the way from the Pacific to
Central Europe. He discovered the evidence that the
Erinye existed and were extremely advanced, far
more than mere hackers.

"But nobody believed him. Not his own depart-
ment, not Interpol, not the UNCYBSEC. They all
thought they had cybernetic terrorism under control.

Had no idea that a group could be operating on a completely different level than what they were used to dealing with. Only the Yanks listened, but we tend to be paranoid by nature. The U.S.—that's what Yanks are: Americans, Gringos . . . Oh, you know that. That's good. You're Yanks too, you know. That's where you came from. All your genes. That's why you're so varied. Most Terrest states aren't— single peoples, looking very much alike. Strange to think of, isn't it? My bouquet. That's how I thought of you during the crossing. My bouquet to the universe.

"But where was I? Oh yes—Petro contacted the U.S. security organs, the Community, they were called. Very secretive, very efficient. *They* believed him. I'm not sure if they'd already found signs themselves, or if they had their own reasons. But they listened. And Petro got himself assigned as a liaison to one of their bureaus.

"That's how I met him. I was an intern, working on their less secure files. A clerk. That's all I ever was, a clerk."

Tony was listening raptly. It was like hearing history itself speak. The story was far more convincing heard this way, from the very source, than in a classroom or from older people who were retailing information gained at second or third hand. Julia was right; he had believed, without quite realizing it, that the Erinye were a yarn, a shuddery myth off the same shelf as vampires and werewolves. Now they had taken on three dimensions and were walking through his mind the same way they had walked the surface of that hot, faraway world so long ago. "What then?"

"Oh, there's no point going through the whole thing. You've heard it. It was a losing battle. They were everywhere, entrenched too deeply. Any move we could make was too little, too late. Then Petro heard about the ship, after the original backers went bankrupt. I had money—they got my father, the Erinye, and I inherited his data-trading company. They were assassinating a lot of executives, that last year. So we bought the ship and completed fitting it out and . . . here we are."

"What happened to Petro?" That part of the story was new to Tony; he couldn't recall ever hearing the name before.

"Petro . . ." Julia drew her legs up and wrapped her arms around her knees. "They took him. Infiltrated some kind of code. They could actually possess individuals, control their actions to an extent, by manipulating cerebral chemistry and sensory input after subverting their mods. 'Pirating,' we called it. They pirated Petro. He was older than me, far more augmented. The others too, I'm sure. I didn't dare contact anyone after . . . after that."

She lay her head on her arms, her hair falling across her face. "I suppose he died."

The silence stretched on. "Why'd they do it?" he blurted out, more to break the stillness than anything else. "I mean . . . what's the sense in burning your own house down?"

"Why?" Julia's head rose. "There were a lot of theories. Everybody had a theory. Except Petro. He didn't care about 'why.' They were a challenge to him. Someone once told me that they were trying to unfold VR into the real world. They were omnipotent there, you see. In virtual space, they could do anything. There were no barriers or laws. But VR can't satisfy a mature mind. It lacks the depth and heft of reality. That's one reason why I didn't allow it here. Aside from it being useless and dangerous. One thing Cary agrees with me about.

"But it was more basic than that. It wasn't simply that virtual wasn't good enough. It was that reality wasn't. Do you know what 'Erinye' means? The Furies, the tormentors of men. That was their name for themselves. That's the way they thought. And that tells you everything. There was nothing positive about them—no belief, no ideals, nothing. They were pure nihilists, loving only the abyss, wanting only to be not—and to take everything else with them. They wanted to burn down the house because the house was there." She gestured at the door. "Much like those children outside."

Tony squeezed his hands together. "And how do we whip *them*?"

She was silent a moment. Silent and still, so much so that he held his breath. "I don't know what's on that ship. I can't see how anything could have survived at Sol. Or what they'd be if they did. I have tapes of St. John—that's what he calls himself—of his conversations with Cary." She let out a deep sigh. "He's holding something back. Or Cary is. I don't know what."

Tony had planned to ask about her rift with Cary. What had caused it, if it could be healed, if there was anything he could do. But her tone of voice told all he needed to know about that.

"But there are alternatives." She sat up and looked him in the face. "I have one implant still active. I haven't accessed it in . . . oh, a long time. A very long time. Among other things, it contains a viroid designed to degrade most Erinye programs. It was written by Jane Eyre, one of Earth's senior AIs. She's the one who got me out to L-4 when everything was crashing. So we can depend on it. If I can access his ship, it'll at least slow him down, maybe cripple him. That's where you'll come in." Julia looked thoughtful. "Jane was . . . she was as old as I am now."

"How much time do we have?"

"I don't know, Tony. He's decelerating faster than I thought possible, doing in days what took the *Petrel* years."

"Yeah. That line around the sun there . . ."

"That was caused by something called a 'virtual drag.' I'm not certain how it works, but it allows them to shed velocity much faster than the magnetic sails that we used. You can ask Cary—"

He started at a muffled report from outside, so involved with the conversation that he nearly dismissed it. But it was followed by another shot, then a full burst. An explosion rumbled as he rose from the chair.

"Tony—"

Drawing the pistol, he swung for the door. Julia followed him. "Tony, wait—"

He turned back to her. She was holding out the earpiece. "Take this. It's *important*—"

He paused while she stuffed it into his vest pocket. The gunfire intensified. "Yeah. Good. Thanks . . . Now, look, ma'am, you stay right here—"

He shoved the door open. Both sets of guards were on their feet, but his gaze was drawn to a fifth Rig standing by the exit: none other than his little heart-throb Unity. Recognizing him, she glanced at the Lady, then shot him a look of hatred more than matching his own feelings. With a wordless cry she twisted and vanished.

"Son of a—" Bounding across the room, Tony plunged over the stairs and threw himself at the Rig in charge. "Down!" he shouted, kicking the kid's feet out from under him and slamming him against the wall. "Down, you mother— Con, get over here—"

Con Pris was already moving, Sten fixed on the Rig by the window. She dropped her gun and let out a wail so piercing and childlike that it took Tony aback for a second. Movement flickered behind him—a gun butt slamming into the jaw of the remaining Rig. The boy collapsed without a sound.

"I said *down*—" His pistol barrel swept the room. Superfluously; they were all down and disarmed.

Another explosion shook the building. Con looked at him wide-eyed. "The Rigs—"

"Ain't the Rigs," Tony said. "We'd be dead if it was Rigs. It's somebody else . . . Juls," he told the youngest, "you watch these people. If they move . . . Goddammit—get away from that window. Whataya, dense?"

He turned to Con, caught him staring over his shoulder, blank-faced. Looking back, Tony saw Julia in the doorway. "Ma'am . . . *Julia* . . . get your butt back in that room."

She retreated without a word. "Awright . . . Con— somebody—hit those lights."

"Ain't no switch, Ton."

With a muttered curse he led the way out, going through the door at a crouch. A low wall stood at the edge of the patio. He ran for it.

He was grateful to Julia for arranging a fine, unobstructed view. From here he could survey the entire attack, the speckles of gunfire behind the labs, the more distant flashes around the village. He emptied his mind while he took it all in, absorbing exactly what he could see and nothing else, leaving himself open to any sign of what the man behind it was actually up to.

It came to him at the same moment that Con arrived: too few muzzle blasts—and those firing too steadily. Con nudged him with one of the Rigs' crude rifles. He accepted it with a nod. "It's a diversion."

"Ayuh?" Con swung around to eye the darkness behind the house. Con might be slow-moving, but he seldom made mistakes. "Want the Lady, do they?"

"Looks like it—" Raising the gun, Tony fired several shots at random. The response was immediate: a series of rounds stitched the wall beneath them, sending splinters high and wide. Tony ducked. He'd been nicked on the face, and a swipe of his hand showed blood. "Back to the house," he told Con.

"Righto," Con said, slapping his Sten. "You go ahead."

"No—" Tony began, then realized that Con was simply being practical: the Sten was much better suited to keeping heads low. Giving him a thumbs-up, Tony turned to the house. Fong and Kranz were both crouched behind a bench near the door. He called for them to open up—*now*—and started running.

He drew no fire, which bolstered his surmise that the attackers would do nothing to put the Lady in jeopardy. Noticing a bandage on Fong's hand, he sent him back to cover the door. Con was good where he was. The rear corner of the house caught Tony's eye. "Hal, gimme your Sten."

"Piece of shit," Kranz complained as he took the rifle in exchange.

"You'll get this one back. Now, cover me."

A single shot whipped past him as he ran for the line of greenery marking the side of the house. Some-one out in the darkness hollered a negative—cop talk, Tony was sure. Reaching the corner, he slipped the barrel around the last stack of bricks and let loose an unaimed burst. That brought shouts, a cry of pain, quick and furtive scrabbling. He emptied the maga-zine. The cry grew to a full shriek.

"Tony!" He looked back to see Con waving at the plaza. Pulling himself up a foot or so, he could make out a clump of men approaching from the labs, where a few desultory shots were still being exchanged.

"Damn," he muttered. They were headed straight for the house, exactly where he didn't need them. "Hal—come here."

Kranz waddled over amid an eerie silence. Telling him to keep his head down, Tony raced back to the patio. The reinforcements had reached the plaza wall by the time he got there, drawing the attention of the cops. They were taking fire as Tony started crawling downhill.

They spotted him halfway down and for a second he was sure they were going to open up en masse before he could identify himself. Instead they commenced covering fire that allowed him to make the last ten yards at a dead run. He slipped around the edge of the wall, nearly tripping over Dud Mos's big feet.

Kris Rimer clambered to him. "They ain't closin'," he said, waving at the labs. "Nothin' to it, right? So then Gen thinks of the house . . ."

"Good," Tony said. "That's how I figured it. Now—you see that little shack when you were coming over?" Some kind of utility building or shed sat on a knoll facing the Lady's house. Tony told Kris to take his men up there. "Open fire when you reach it. You'll be flankin' 'em then. But don't engage. Let 'em run for it . . ."

He waited until they moved off, then returned to the house gate. It was much wider than the others around the periphery of the plaza, nicely symbolic but something he could do without at the moment. Peering around the edge, he saw Con at the patio wall and Fong crouched in the doorway. He thought of the far side of the house, the part that wasn't covered. He'd have sent people right over the roof, if it had been his—

A chatter of shots exploded to his right. Easing out a few inches, he spotted men clumped around the shed, firing down the far side of the knoll. "Spread 'em out, Kris," he whispered to himself.

There was no answering fire, only a shout from the darkness, its meaning drowned out by the guns. Tony waited a minute or two. The gunfire began to slacken. Keeping low, he raced back up the stairs.

Con told him he'd seen movement, but had figured it best not to fire. "I mean they're retreatin', right?"

Clapping him on the shoulder, Tony headed for the corner of the house. He heard much the same from Hal Kranz. He looked around the corner, hesitant about showing himself. Behind him, Kris was leading his men down the knoll. Raising the Sten, Tony fired a burst into the night. There was no response. "That was just me," he called to Con.

"Ayuh," Con replied. Tony told him to stick where he was, hold the house, cover everybody who needed cover. He thought for a minute and was about to tell him not to open up on Kris's people but decided that would be dithering.

Slipping around the corner, he hugged the house for a few steps before realizing that the light color—beige, he thought it was—outlined him as clearly as a spotlight. He dropped low and crept into the open. About ten yards out, he heard something. He stopped short, shifting the Sten an inch or two. That couldn't be one of Kris's men, not yet . . . Somebody chose that moment to bellow some nonsense or other. Tony raised a hand as if to call for silence.

He went on. A moment later the sound came again: a low moan, directly ahead of him. Tony grimaced as he hurried forward. Hard to believe they'd just leave a wounded man behind . . .

There he was—flat on his back, face to the sky. He wore a police sweater and a heavy holster belt, and his face was blackened. No weapon was visible.

Lost in his own pain, he said nothing when Tony bent over him. The gray sweater was heavily stained, and it had been pushed up from the waist so that he could slide his hand beneath. A second dark patch covered the right thigh of his pants.

He let out another moan. "Hey, buddy," Tony said. "Hang on, okay? I'm gonna get you a doc, right away. Hang on. Do me that favor, huh?"

It was too dark to see his expression, but a small sound accompanied a short jerk of his head. Tony straightened up and was about to run back to the house when he heard another noise up ahead, like feet moving through brush.

He went forward at a crouch. No other sound reached him, no sign that anyone else was present. After going ten yards or so, he turned back, eager to get hold of a medic. He was surprised to see someone bending over the wounded cop. Letting out a breath, he lowered the Sten. He couldn't tell if it was Con or . . .

The figure rose, and he saw the low gleam of a blade, even as he realized that it was dressed in black.

"You *fuck*—" She was already running as he raised the gun, plainly visible against the pale blotch of the house. "Con! Get her! Grab that little whore—"

But she was headed toward the far side of the building, the blind side, where nobody was waiting. He aimed the Sten, finger tight on the trigger, hesitating one second with the thought that his own men might fire back. She slipped through the trees and was gone.

He went to the cop, listening to him choke on his own blood. Crouching beside him, he took his hand. "Hey—"

The fingers spasmed and went limp.

Maria Theresa, he thought. That was the name. Queen with the heart of a king.

Letting the hand drop, he got to his feet. Con and Hal Kranz were walking toward him. Con examined the cop and grunted. Shaking his head, Tony headed for the house. Kranz caught up with him halfway there. "Can I have my gun back now?"

He relinquished the Sten wordlessly. Kris's boys were approaching, grab-assing and whooping up their victory. Raising his head at last, he caught sight of a figure in the doorway.

"Goddammit—" He ran toward her and, gripping

her shoulders, forced her bodily back inside. "Didn't I tell you—" He jabbered on, the words out of control, a catalog of raw peril: Rigs, gunfire, Unity.

"What happened?" she said when he fell silent.

He drew away, suddenly exhausted past all bearing. In the clear light, the disturbing quality of her face was evident: lines of age overlaying the girlish features, innocence and experience unnaturally commingled. She made no attempt to straighten her robe where it had pulled open under his hands. She lacked any of the casual feminine tics. Eroded by time, he supposed.

"Someone was killed," she said. "One of your men—"

"No." He took a deep breath. "One of theirs." A wounded man, a man abandoned and helpless, a man under his protection.

"Oh, Tony." She came close, her face all softness now, one hand rising. "You've been hurt."

He scraped a hand across his cheek, almost relishing the sharp quiver of pain. Dried blood speckled his fingers. "Nothing," he said. He gestured at the door, from which a few offhand pops still sounded. "I've gotta—"

"Yes."

"What about these Rigs?" someone demanded.

The four guards cowered in a corner. The one who'd been hit in the jaw was clutching his face and crying. One of the girls snarled at him in a low voice. "Bring 'em along," Tony said.

They headed straight across the plaza, not bothering with cover. Kris and his men took over guarding the house. Tony assumed that Kris knew enough not to allow any Blackshirts inside. Not after this.

"Maria Theresa," Tony muttered to himself.

"Whatsat?" Con said.

Tony shook his head. Maria Theresa—Empress of Austro-Hungary, 18th century, he thought it had

been. Refused to leave Vienna when the Prussians—
led by Frederick, of all people—approached. Stayed
on the spot, to assure that her soldiers would fight.
"Heart of a king."

The howling began when they were halfway
across. Tony stopped dead. Somebody jostled him
from behind.

"Oh no—"

"They caught somebody."

"Double-time," Tony said. They ran the rest of the
way, not at double-time at all but something considerably faster. They reached the lab gate in less than
a minute.

Gen met him coming up the hill. "You stopped
'em?"

"Yeah. Lady's fine."

"Didn't even try to break through here. But"—Gen
raised his hands to the echo of screams—"the Shirts
picked one off."

They'd reached the labs by then. The men were
gathered around the fires, their expressions dismal.
At the nearest fire he saw something unexpected. A
young Bili, unshaven, hair matted. Beside him sat a
girl—the one with the baby, in fact. He pointed at
the pair. "What's this?"

"They came over—"

The boy got to his feet, clutching a battered cap
with both hands. "That's right, General. We ain't
staying with them no more. We wanna be here
with you."

Tony stepped closer, assuring himself that the parcel in the girl's lap was in fact her infant. She lifted
it up, a hopeful smile playing across her features.
The cries, which had ebbed for a moment, returned
with full force. The girl's face contorted and she
shrank into herself. "They doin' that police boy.
Same they did ol' Eno—"

"Yeah. They do 'em somethin' awful, General. Made us watch too. Like we're supposta like it."

Tony stroked his chin. "How many others wanna come over?"

"Some. They scared, though. But me, I'll fight. You gimme a gun. I don't mind that."

"You her husband?"

"Well"—the boy dropped his head shyly—"I guess . . ."

"You can stay," Tony assured him. "Sure thing."

The boy lurched up to him and gave his hand a fierce shake. Tony nodded, more embarrassed than anything else. Extricating himself at last, he turned to Gen. "I want volunteers."

The voice had grown hoarse by the time they were ready. Not that it was any quieter; not at all. At times it took on the quality of a wail, drawn out and inhuman. At times it peaked in a high squeal that seemed to carry on past the point of hearing. Mostly it took the form of deep, wracking sobs, like that of a child who had lost all hope, but with the depth of a grown man's voice.

Tony halted at the perimeter, hurriedly positioning his covering force. Then he went to the spot where Gen held the Rigs and dragged one out by the arm. It was the girl who had cried out at the house. She cringed as he dragged her past the foxhole and on into empty darkness. He paused and gave her a shake. "You know what that is?" he demanded, gesturing overhead at the pain-laden air. "You know, don't you?"

He shook her once again while he explained what he wanted from her. "You better hope they ask questions first, sis," he told her with a final shove downhill. She looked back once before stumbling on, waving her arms and calling out a slogan, something about "purity" and "virtue." He watched her closely, scarcely aware that Gen and the others had joined him.

Another Rig appeared out of the night, exactly as if he'd just flashed into existence. Tony let him approach the girl before loping toward them, his momentum carrying him into the boy. The kid had watched him wide-eyed the last few steps without making any move to defend himself. He was beginning to get the impression that Rigorism was a failure at producing enterprising social units.

He gripped the boy's arm. "Get me your boss," he told him. The response was a blink of puzzlement, ended by the girl whispering something about a "guardian."

The boy ran off. The screams, which had momentarily ceased, returned with a clarity that made Tony's teeth ache. A couple of spare Rigs sauntered into view, looking Tony over with open curiosity. One of them giggled. He squinted at her, then strode over and tore off her beret. But it wasn't Unity—merely someone who could have passed for her sister.

The other Rig raised his gun. He went still at the sound of a half-dozen Stens being cocked.

"Drop it," Tony told him. The kid gaped at him, then up at the unwavering Stens. Something was wrong with his eyes; one was off-center, not tracking with the other. Tony nearly laughed aloud despite himself—he'd never seen the like.

"Do this," a voice said. The barrel dropped and the Rig came to attention.

Tony turned to see two others approaching, a girl whose appearance puzzled him for a second until he realized that she was fully grown and, surprisingly enough, Goggles the Judge.

"What is it?" Goggles said.

Tony gestured at the group standing uphill. "See them? I've brought them along to wave goodbye.

And this one"—he pointed at the girl—"and him, and him, and her. If I don't get the cop."

The man gazed at him wordlessly. "I want the cop," he insisted.

A low chuckle came from the woman. Tony slapped his holster flap open. Drawing her away, Goggles—Tony wondered what his real name was—whispered to her. They began to walk off. "We go to the Herald," Goggles called back. "Wait."

He stood there, hand on his pistol, half-convinced that the Rigs would open fire any second. He looked up when the sobbing ceased, expecting it to start again, relaxing only when several minutes of silence passed. The kid with the funny eyes tried to slip off; Tony ordered him to halt.

Goggles reappeared, half out of breath. "The Herald is not available at this time—"

Tony took a step toward him.

"—but we present you with the tool regardless."

A low sound, like the whimper of a small animal, slowly grew louder. Two Rigs approached bearing something between them. They deposited it a few steps behind Goggles. "This gift is contingent on several factors. Above all, a more appropriate atmosphere must be created and maintained between the Rigorist Tendency and the . . . independent forces. In particular, we require—"

"Shut up," Tony told him. He gestured a couple of men forward. "Oh, Christ," he heard one say as they reached the wounded cop. Tony wished he'd thought to bring along a stretcher.

"I repeat: current policy of the independent revolutionary forces is unsatisfactory—"

"Enough!" Tony shouted.

The man went silent and dropped his head. The lights of the labs reflected off his glasses, making it impossible to read his expression. "I know," he whispered. "But I am compelled."

The cop let out a fading cry as the men lifted him. Tony glanced over as they passed, immediately wished he hadn't. He hoped that what he'd seen of the face was simply some trick of the dimness.

The Rig finished speaking, ending with something about the Herald wishing to meet with Tony. "Tell him no," Tony said. He was a bit surprised when the man didn't either leave or protest, but then recalled what he was waiting for. Waving for the captive Rigs to be released, he turned to head uphill.

"Perin," Goggles said. Tony swung back to him.

"You are Perin, yes?" He pointed at the men carrying the cop. "I did not . . . witness that. I do not *acknowledge* such struggles."

Tony regarded him a moment. "Good for you." He took another step, hesitated once more. "What's your name anyway?"

"I am Integral."

"Well . . . I'm glad to hear that, Integral."

He went on his way. The returning Rigs shied from him as they passed. The cop whimpered all the way to the labs.

Doc Conli was one of the Orcs' three medics, and probably the most experienced. He had a general practice in the dairy country south of the Chains. Tony didn't know him well, but he'd been assured that Conli was very good.

It was soon evident that good would not be enough. Tony stood in the doorway of the office of lab two—the Jens Building, it was called—watching Conli work on the cop, half-listening to the men talking in the hall. Conli too was mumbling to himself, a reaction Tony understood. A trail of blood led from the hall to the couch where the injured man lay, and the cop let out a rattling wail every time the doctor moved him.

At last Conli injected something into the man's arm and came over to Tony. "That's it." His face was drawn, a graying lock dangled over his forehead. "Much of it's superficial, but . . . kidneys, lungs, dura mater have been repeatedly slashed and punctured. Peritoneum and GI tract too. Those wounds are fresh. I got the impression . . ."

"They did that last."

"Yes."

"Doc—what about the med center? The advanced stuff there?"

"He won't last long enough," Conli said. "And I'm not qualified to operate equipment of that class anyway."

Tony remembered the earpiece. He slipped it out of the vest and clapped it on. It fit surprisingly well. "Cary—you there? Did you hear that?"

"Yes, Mr. Perin. Extrapolating your next query, I can in fact operate most of the equipment in the medical center. But I'm afraid that the doctor is correct. Officer Hobin's existence will close within minutes, and too much damage to vital organs has occurred for invasive trauma procedures to achieve more than a single-digit probability of success."

"I see." Conli was staring quizzically, and curiosity had drawn Gen into the room. It probably did look as if Tony was talking to himself.

On the couch, Hobin called out something, his voice dying away to a wet gobbling. "His mom," Gen muttered. "He's calling for his mom. I didn't know guys really did that."

"Lady Amalfi too," Cary said. "He mentioned her as well—"

"The Lady," Tony moved toward the couch. "Cary, can you get her for me?"

"I don't see why not." There was a pause, broken by Julia's voice. "Yes?" Tony explained the situation. He heard her sigh. "Of course," she said.

Plucking out the earpiece, he bent over the couch. It was his first clear view of Hobin, and the sight turned his stomach. There was no spot that he could look at without seeing some kind of violation. The face was the worst—the features had been no less than obliterated . . . No, not even that; not even the illusion of accident was available. They had been sliced away.

He raised the earpiece, halted dead when he saw that the man's ear was missing.

Reaching over, Conli took the unit from his hand and placed it on the other side of Hobin's head. "Is that what you want?" Tony nodded and turned away from the couch. It was the shaking that got to him. The cop was shaking in every part of his body. It didn't seem possible, but there it was. Hobin . . . that was his name. It seemed important to remember that. Officer Hobin . . .

"Tony." It was Doc Conli, still facing the couch. "What is it you're waiting for?"

Vaguely ashamed that he wasn't able to confront Hobin, Tony turned to Conli. He thought of Julia's words, how he'd whip the Rigs in his own way, a way no one would ever expect. "An idea, Doc. I'm waiting for an idea."

Conli shrugged and went to the couch. A moment later he returned, carefully wiping the earpiece. Tony took it and slipped it on. "Julia . . . ?"

"Jay's retired, Mr. Perin," Cary said. "But if you're so inclined, I'd like to continue our interrupted conversation of the other night. Perhaps expand on it."

"Let's talk about how to bounce Fredrix."

"I'm sorry, sir. That's not an option at this time."

"Then it'll wait."

"I take it you're troubled by this death," Cary said quickly. "I'm very sorry, Mr. Perin. I should have considered that. But I ought to mention that a possibility exists of contacting the police, to avoid a repetition of tonight's incident."

"Do it," Tony said. Putting the earpiece in his pocket, he left the room, headed for his cot.

A few hours later, the Orcs on watch saw a sudden glow appear on the eastern horizon. It swiftly grew to a glare, a vastly accelerated sunrise, then died with the swiftness of a shattered lamp. A few dim waves, like an aurora out of season, flashed overhead, fading out at the zenith. Then the sky was dark once more.

Nobody thought of waking Tony. It didn't seem important, under the circumstances.

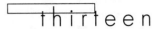
thirteen

Clouds had moved in overnight, and the morning was damp and cool. Through the window Julia studied the gray sky. The rebel boys respected her silence, with only occasional remarks on how wet it was, how they hated a drizzle, how they hoped it wouldn't sleet.

Her mind was idling, full of vagrant thoughts of last night's attack, the tragedy of those poor dead boys, what she'd found in the recordings. A sudden splatter of rain on the stones outside brought her back to herself. "Whoa!" a boy shouted. "Here it comes."

She smiled at him. It often seemed to her that Middie weather differed wildly from Earth's—or at least the little patch she remembered well. The pattern here was north to south, for one thing, as opposed to the west to east of the States, and the color of the sky was deeper than back home. The clouds seemed to be shaped differently than she recalled, their color a little off, the patterns they made unfamiliar. Those small touches of strangeness, like the gravity and the smell, would always speak of the alien, would assure a space, narrow but deep, between Julia and her people.

But all the same, this season was April to her. The variable month, one day rain and the next dry with no logic or pattern. As if the world was stretching as it awoke, running through its customary gamut of possibilities, pleased with itself, happy that the long cold was gone, the grand cycle begun anew.

It did something to her. It truly did. Made her feel as if she was sixteen again, in the Piedmont that had been her home, with everything all before her. She clutched fingers that had ached strangely for years, smiled with lips that hadn't truly kissed another in a full lifetime. Was it illusion? Then let it be . . . But it was no deception. She blessed the world for speaking to her even now, over the echoes of all the years.

The rain ceased with no warning, its loud hiss replaced by the splat of solitary drops. She laughed aloud. Turning, she saw the boys gazing at her, their faces surprised. And they laughed too—all four of them.

She went to the kitchen. A moment's work and she returned, with two plates of pastries—danishes and crullers—steaming from the mike. The Academy bakery sent her a boxful every week, far too much for any one person and particularly for Julia, who'd never had much of a sweet tooth. She lacked the heart to tell the bakers to not to bother and instead gave the treats to the grounds and maintenance men.

The boys protested that she didn't need to do that, that they'd already et, that there was too much. But they decided at last that it looked damn good anyway and plunged in. The protests began anew when she tried to go off without a plate of her own. They piled one high and forced it on her, lest they feel bad about stuffing theirselves.

She set it down untasted in the bedroom. The earpiece lay atop a pillow. At the sight of it her spirits stumbled but didn't quite fall. She sat down, twirling the unit, wondering if there was a point in listening further, if there was anything she hadn't checked. But she'd done all she could without Cary, and Cary was where the problem lay. It was very simple, simple enough so that she wondered if Cary was in fact signaling her, perhaps without even being aware of it. At 5:37:21 into the recording Magister St. John mentioned something or someone called "Hunden." His exact words: "You recall what I said about the Hunden . . ."

The thing was he hadn't said anything about Hunden. Not in what Julia had already listened to. Calling up the carrier software, she'd run a global search. "Hunden"—which appeared to be a name for people or entities who cooperated with the Erinye—was mentioned four times, always after the section where Julia had found it, always with a clear implication that it had previously been discussed in detail.

But there was no such discussion, not amid the data that Julia had.

Cary was holding something back.

With a last flick she raised the earpiece. A lot of hours remained. If she listened on through, she might pick up something from context. Get at least a vague idea . . .

A soft rap came at the door. She thrust the earpiece into her pocket, though she was certain it couldn't be a Rigorist. She'd been so relieved to find them gone when she woke up.

She opened the door to the youngest rebel, a boy with a delightful, foxlike face. He smiled broadly and touched his hat. "Hey, ma'am . . . you wanna see something funny?"

                              *   *   *

"Cary . . . how much more of this you got?"

"Be patient, Tony. I'm covering matters in detail
so we don't have to go over them again every other
hour. I'm speaking from experience—a century and
a half of humans whining, 'Ooh—you didn't tell me
that,' when I absolutely did. It's a mindless carbon
habit. It's tiresome, and I don't want to deal with it."
She paused a moment. "Now. We were speaking of
prob. C, vis-à-vis Dan Cardnale and Fredrix. On a
much lower level in the probability continuum exists
D, which entails . . ."

Tony slapped empty air. She'd been talking for half
an hour nonstop, doing everything but make sense.
Here she was on D of the Cardnale Factor and he
couldn't for the life of him remember what A and B
were. Was this what it was like dealing with AIs?
No wonder they'd all gone nuts back on Earth.

He caught a movement out of the corner of his
eye. A clump of Orcs stood next to a sidewalk railing,
and one of them—some punk kid from the Chains—
was imitating him. He was sure of it. He cast a hard
glance at them, but they all goggled fish-eyed off into
space, exactly as if there was something fascinating
about the blank gray overcast.

He'd contacted Cary inside the building, anticipat-
ing a serious conversation, but then she started jabbering and, after the short downpour ceased, he
made his way outside—sitting alone in a room listening to her was slightly more than he cared to endure. He'd been getting odd looks ever since, men
casually sauntering around the corner or up the hill
to take in the sight of the chief ranting and gesturing
to himself. The problem was that, not used to speaking to an AI, he was overdoing the hand movements,
as if that would aid him in getting his point across.
It probably did make for a pretty entertaining show.
But if that damnfool kid was actually—

"Comments, Tony?"

So she was finished, was she? He'd thought she was only taking a break, a kind of cybernetic punctuation before going into another aspect of probability studies. She'd said "chaotic factors" several times just now. Chaotic factors had been her excuse fourteen years ago when the rats came pouring down from the Threshold right before harvest. Thousands of them—tens of thousands, half-starved and savage with hunger. They'd been nearly a week killing them all, everybody in Eyri and people riding in from Virthim, Bruklin, as far across the Tier as Orcs' Haven. That was the first time Dad had ever let Tony go out with a rifle. It was fun for a couple days, like a holiday, sleeping out and eating food cooked over open fires. But that wore off real quick, particularly after they ran out of ammo and had to go after the rats with shovels and axes. It was a good thing that the clouds finally broke so that Cary could use the mirrors. The sole explanation they ever got was "chaotic factors." It was becoming clear to Tony that chaotic factors was AI shorthand for "I screwed up."

"Well, Cary," he said slowly. "I'm impressed. I can tell that you've put a lot of thought into the situation. And as for comments, the first thing that springs to my mind is: bullshit."

"Now, Tony—"

"No. I've heard enough." It was drizzling again. He pulled up the collar of the windbreaker he'd found in a locker. "Let's get this straight. Throw out all the 'chaotic coefficients' and 'probability vectors,' and what do we got? Something is wrong with the Lady, you won't tell me what, and so I'm supposed to sit on my ass while you play footsie with fat boy . . . Oh, you don't like that analysis. Well, goddammit, explain it to me then." He'd counted off the points on his fingers, and that kid was doing the same. Another two seconds and he was going to go over and kick his skinny ass from one end of the plaza to—

"I have given you a complete scenario for every high probability—"

"Hell you have. You didn't mention a damn thing about this spaceship we got comin' down our throats, for one. Or is that too much of a chaotic willygilly . . . a . . . 'strange attractor'? Is that it?"

The earpiece was silent, not even a carrier wave audible.

"You know, I'm beginning to see why humans will always have an edge on AIs, smarts or no."

"You don't have to be insulting, Tony."

"Yeah? Who was calling me 'carbon' just now . . . ?"

Voices rumbled behind him. The men had straightened up and were looking out over the plaza. He squinted into the drizzle. There, past the gate, the Rigs were marching the Bilis to the tree. Tony yanked at his cap. "What the hell is this?"

"See, ma'am, they're not movin'. Just sittin' around under that oak, blowin' gas." The older Rig winked at Julia. "Ain't nothin' to worry about."

"Look at 'em," the foxy-faced boy said. "Pourin' rain out, and there they are, right in the middle of it. Ain't got no sense, not a one of 'em. They're like . . . bugs or something."

"Yep. Ol' Freddy boy tells 'em jump off a cliff, and they race each other over the edge. Says sit out in the rain, by God, they sit. Just so they know who's boss. Like a . . ." The older man twirled his hand.

"A ritual," Julia said.

"That's it. The Lady's got it. Very word I was huntin'. A ritual. Like they were goin' to church or something."

They studied the mob in silence. The drizzle had intensified, full-sized drops now mixing in with the spray. She thought of the girl with the new baby and shivered. She hoped they weren't out in this mess.

Julia stiffened as the earpiece buzzed in her pocket. The older man cocked an eyebrow. "Sounds like you there, ma'am."

"Uh, yes." She gave him a smile. "It's a com piece."

"I see. Well, don't let us keep you."

She headed for the bedroom. Behind her, the boy said, "Listen to 'em yell," and gave a choice example of Rigorist yelling. Closing the door, Julia slipped the unit on. "Yes."

"It's me," Cary said. "Your farm boy is being very, very difficult."

It seemed that Tony Perin was insulting, dense, arrogant, and carbocentric. He refused to listen. He couldn't follow probability theory. He paid no attention to the established standards of etiquette between silicon and carbon.

"Well, what are you trying to get across to him?"

Cary was silent for a few seconds too long. Julia knew that silence; it was the clear sign of a Micro-Cray A Class Gen. XXII Intelligence calculating the angles. "I want him to leave," Cary said at last.

The statement surprised Julia, expecting as she was Cary's customary avalanche of irrelevancies. She caught her breath, calculating angles of her own.

"I presented a half-dozen major probabilities to that man, Jay. Each of them shows him dead within seventy-two hours, along with that pack of farm-hands of his. Did he listen? No. He strolled around in a daze, muttering to himself, thinking I couldn't hear him. I monitored his pulse rate and breathing, and it was as if he was going to sleep . . ."

"Cary, dear, I doubt that persuading him to go is much of a possibility."

"Oh, he wants to die then? Let me put that into

the 'inexplicable human eccentricity' file. There. Oooh, what a huge document that one is—"

"Cary, I think you're misreading this—" She frowned. Cary was reciting an alphabetical list of bizarre human behavioral tics. "Cary . . . Cary, listen to me. What were the probabilities when we landed here?"

The AI went silent. "Darling, you're forgetting the intangibles. I don't think you quite grasp what Tony is. He's not much like anyone you've dealt with before. Access Alexander and Napoleon." She waited a beat. "You see?"

"Oh, Jay, does *this* sound like Napoleon?"

"—damp Rigs. Look at 'em. Does that fit in with your probabilities? Hell it does. You take your Boolean Logic and—"

Julia bit her lip. Actually, it did match quite closely her impression of what a military buccaneer would sound like.

"—and I'll tell you something else, sweetheart. They cut up that cop, they cut up that old bum, they're cuttin' people up in my own town. You didn't say shit about *that*. You better work all that into your calculations 'fore you make up your mind which side is yours. Until you do, don't you waste my goddamn time. And a good day to you, Ms. Chipbox."

"Did you hear that, Jay? He went on like that for four minutes and twenty-three seconds. And calling it 'Boolean Logic'—what a fool."

"I agree he was out of line, Cary. I'm sure he's not aware of how hard it is for you."

" 'Boolean Logic'—just like a farmer."

"Yes." Julia licked her lips, thinking of how she might best word her next question. "Cary—what was I supposed to do when Tony left? Go with him, right?"

"Yes."

"What's changed? Is it the Rigorists or the ship? Where is the ship now, Cary?"

"The *Christi* achieved orbital insertion last night."

Julia covered her mouth with one hand. No—it was too soon. They couldn't possibly be here yet. There had to be another week, at least one more fine spring day, before they came out of the night. Before the ax swung down.

"Julia . . . are you all right? Your indications are very high."

It took a moment for Julia to find her voice. "Yes, dear, I'm fine . . ." I'm terrified, Cary. Help me. "What . . . Cary, what happened?"

"The ship is extremely capable, Jay. The approach was spellbinding. Velocity still exceeded two hundred thousand kph only two million klicks away. The heading was twenty-three degrees forward of Midgard, along the orbital plane. They triggered the drag at intervals, creating huge streaks of particle leakage along their trajectory; you'd see them if it wasn't overcast. They shed velocity and skewed themselves directly into orbit, all in less than twelve hours with only two engine burns. Very, very impressive."

"But what did they say? You've spoken to them, haven't you?"

"Yes . . . Yes, I contacted them from *Petrel*. I . . . constructed a simulation in the ship's data spaces. An extremely complex emulate. It took me some time."

Julia waited without breathing, almost certain what she would hear next.

"Something inspected the simulation while we were speaking. While I spoke to St. John through it, rather. It was . . . disturbing to witness. Analogy is useful here: imagine a nation suddenly detecting photo drones directly over its most secret defense installations. It was a lot like that."

Julia closed her eyes, thanking whatever gods there

were that Cary had listened closely enough to take precautions.

"That entity is . . . very powerful, Jay."

That was as much of an apology as Julia was ever likely to get. So . . . Cary had seen a wolf, and it scared her. At the last possible moment, but better that than nothing. "What did they . . . what did St. John say?"

"Merely . . . hello. Nothing else of consequence. They did deploy three probes. I lost them shortly after they entered atmosphere."

"Did they give any explanation?"

"No."

"I see. Now—"

"Jay. I want you to leave. Go with the police and the rebels. You can still catch up with Vicki. Go on to the Shore—"

"She hasn't even reached the *Shore* yet?"

"Jay, listen: give me access to the viroid. The one that Mama Jane wrote. I'll need to test and debug it in any case. If there's danger from St. John, I'll use it. If it fails, the Rigs will bear the brunt of any reaction. You'll be free, and you can think of something else."

"No." Julia's mind was still full of Vicki. She hadn't even gotten to the coast. It had been three days. Something had gone wrong. What could it have been? "No—Tony Perin won't leave, and . . . I won't leave you. And what was that about police?"

"Uh . . . the unit that engaged last night. I contacted them on behalf of Perin—"

"You did not."

"I did in fact, Dame Amalfi."

"Not on behalf of Tony. Cary, I know you . . . What are you thinking?"

Julia got it out of her in bits and pieces. She'd arranged for the police to take over under cover of a meeting with Tony. Cary would disable him out of sight of his men—a "nice jolt from the earpiece" was how she put it. Then, duplicating Tony's voice, she'd order the men to lay down their arms while the police raced in from the hills. "It's a good plan, Jay."

"It's a *crazy* plan!" Julia calmed herself. "I'm sorry, I didn't mean to shout."

"You never do, Julia."

"Cary—please put me in contact with that police unit. I'm asking nicely."

"You really don't think it'll work. I ran it several dozen times in virtual."

Julia drew a deep breath, ready to explain how many ways it could go wrong in the real world. Over the earpiece she heard a hmph. Someone had once told Julia that she did the same thing herself. "Oh, okay," Cary said.

"Ikler," a low voice said.

Julia smiled. "Officer Deni!"

"Jay! I mean . . . ma'am! Are you all right?"

"I'm fine, Deni. How are you? Listen . . . I was just now speaking to Cariola, and she told me—"

A rapid tattoo sounded at the door. Julia looked up as the fox-faced boy pushed it open. "Ma'am . . . you stay in here, okay? You just keep down, okay? It's gonna be okay . . ."

He vanished from the doorway. Julia stared after him, open-mouthed.

"Go ahead, ma'am," Ikler said.

Tony ducked beneath an overhang as the rain got fierce. Chewing on a sprig of coke, he eyed the Rigs. They were up to something. They hadn't come out to rhapsodize under a fine spring shower, like the guy in that old Terrest flick his mom liked, dancing around in the rain singing his head off. He strongly suspected that was not a customary Rig pastime. Something was going to happen, and he had an inkling of just what.

Someone stepped out to join him. Thinking it was Gen, he turned his head. Dan Cardnale nodded back at him.

Tony looked away before Cardnale could catch his expression. There was something about the man now, some aura of disgrace and failure, that made it difficult to look him in the face. It was as if he'd taken on the role of the village drunk, or one of the Bilis down below.

"Don't mind me, Tony." Cardnale's voice was calm. "It's just that . . . I don't have much to do at the moment. Resi's pretty much taken over and . . . She doesn't have any time for me now."

Tony made note of that for future action: snag Resi soonest. He gestured at the Rigs. One of them was addressing the crowd, pausing only for bellowed responses. The sense of the words was impossible to catch from up here. "Gettin' a little wet."

"Yes," Cardnale said. "They have no choice. The procedure requires continuity. If they miss a day, the momentum is gone, and they have to start again from scratch."

Tony shot him a glance. Cardnale smiled back. "Oh yes—the process is well understood. The Inquisition, the Bolsheviks, the Multicult—all of them operated the same way. The trial is irrelevant, the result meaningless. I'm sure you're aware of that. It's the ceremony that matters. The ritual that enthralls, that hypnotizes. That's what they're doing. Absorbing the Bilis, converting them. My natural constituency. The ones I abandoned."

Tony cast the sprig away. He wasn't sure he wanted to hear this. He had neither the inclination nor the time to act as a confessor at the moment.

"I started out with them, you know. But they were too ignorant, too silly. Life on the road with them was no less than an ordeal. So I turned to the middle class. The owners, the farmers. The ones motivated

by self-interest over all. And beyond them, the Garites. My secret legions. I became a politician. A
manipulator."

Cardnale paused to catch his breath. No, Tony
thought to himself. No—Dan was no politician. A
politician knew limits; how to compromise, when to
deal. Cardnale recognized none of that. He had the
framework of perfection in his head and was going
to lay it down across the world at large come hell or
high water, and not the human race, not the Erinye,
not the God of the Dunkers would prevail against
him. He was a savior, that's what he was. Danny the
Messiah. What a picture that made.

". . . it's always the leaders and the led, Tony. You
can't get away from that. The leaders are few. Five
percent, at best. And if you remove the honorable,
the decent, the responsible from that small number,
what do you have left? That's what I did. Carefully
winnowed out any rivals, anyone who could stand
by themselves. Isolated them, nullified them, and
subjected the rest to . . . that." He pointed across the
plaza. "I betrayed my Bilis, my farmers. I betrayed
Jay, and . . . I betrayed you."

The last word was nearly a sob. Tony crossed his
arms, squeezing them to the point of discomfort to
drive away the sympathy he felt despite himself.
Welcome through the gate of human weakness,
Danny. Beneath the tree, he caught sight of the guy
with the goggles—what's-his-name, Integral. He sat
unmoving behind the table, not taking much part in
the festivities.

"I had a dream last night, Tony. The first time I
really slept since we arrived. There was something
in that fountain, the one past the tree. It rose out the
water, gigantic, with arms like rakes. Gathering people in, pulling them into itself . . ."

"Sounds like a bad one, Dan."

"Yes. And the thing . . . The thing had my face."

Cardnale let out a shuddering breath. "He's got you, Tony. You know what's going to happen. And you don't have a response, do you? It's impossible to out-think him. I thought I could, but . . . No. There's no logic to it, you see. It's all impulse. Collectivism is supposed to be the most rational system, but it never is. Not outside of theory. It's too concentrated, all power collected in one group, then in one man. Al-ways an abnormal man. A criminal, a bandit, a . . . werewolf. The state is nothing but a man grown im-mense, as Hobbes said, with a man's flaws and failings."

Tony swung toward him. "You knew this all along, didn't you?"

"Yes."

"Then why?"

Head down, Cardnale shrugged. "You hope."

A roar drew Tony's eyes back to the plaza. The crowd around the tree had exploded. A wave of howling figures burst into the open, headed for the plaza. Tony had read somewhere that a mob was a multilegged beast with an intelligence inversely pro-portional to the number of its members. That's what this was: no longer a crowd, an assemblage, a collec-tion of individuals, but an organism; mad, enraged, and thirsty for blood.

It roared through the gate, which was too narrow to admit all its cells at once. Several fell, to vanish immediately beneath the feet of those directly be-hind. The Rigs clambered over the wall at either side, directing and channeling the stampede as it surged out across the plaza, aiming it at its target at the far end.

Tony stepped out into the rain. Tearing off his cap, he flung it at his feet.

"Tony—it's over. Get out. Find a place to hide. Take Jay with you. You can't win here. He's got all the pieces, you can't outmaneuver him—"

"All of 'em, does he?" Tony turned on Cardnale. "And what'll he do if the board's kicked over?"

Gen burst through the door. "Rigs in force on the other side. Ain't made no move yet. We're okay there for now . . ."

Men poured out behind him. Tony waved them downhill.

"Tony—"

"I ain't got time, Dan—"

He felt a hand on his shoulder. "Like diamonds, we're cut by our own dust. Remember that, son."

The hand was gone before he could shrug it off.

"They're slowin' down," Gen said.

Tony glanced behind him. It was true; the Rigs were deliberately hindering the front ranks of the mob as it raged past them. Tony let out a sour laugh. "Yeah. Another fuckin' test. He's pushin' us again."

"I'm worried about the house."

"Right." Tony thought it over. "Two squads. Send 'em through the tunnel." They'd found the tunnel entrance this morning, between the lab's boilers. Cary hadn't been any help there either. Tony wiped his brow. The rain was starting to let up, but it was still wet enough. The Rigs hadn't left behind any flankers to face the labs. They were feeling pretty bold this morning.

Gen rejoined him. "On their way."

"Good . . ." Tony fell silent, a frown creasing his face. "What the hell is he doing?"

In the center of the plaza, trailing the last few stragglers, Dan Cardnale marched purposefully toward the house.

"The Shirts are holdin' 'em back, see," the older rebel told Julia. "It's just a game. But you keep down all the same, ma'am. Don't let 'em catch sight of ya."

Julia could see as much. The few who'd jumped over the patio wall had been dragged back by the

Rigorists. The mob was lined up behind the wall now, as if the low ornamental brick demarcated a barrier between separate physical realities, a line impossible to cross. It was more theater, another ritual twist of the spiral of tension and pressure.

But it was frightening all the same. Seeing those faces, so subdued yesterday, now filled with madness and rage. Men and women both—the women most fearsome of all—and even a child or two darting here and there. Some of them waved sticks, and in one man's hand Julia saw the flash of a knife. Their eyes bulged, their mouths stretched wider than it seemed that human faces could bear as they chanted the same word at the top of their lungs: "*Bitch . . . Bitch . . . Bitch . . .*"

The Rigs standing at either side, with their blank expressions and slack postures, lent an eeriness to the scene that rendered it even more terrifying.

A brick or stone bounced off a corner of the window. "Foxy, back up there!" the older man called out. "They can see you!"

"It's all right," Julia whispered. It was impossible for the mob to break that window; not even the Garites' guns could pierce the monomolecular crystal. As long as the doors remained locked, they were safe.

Fredrix had to know that. So what was he thinking? If this demonstration simply petered out, it would be twice as hard to rally the woods people next time around. He was too clever to risk such a setback. He had to be hoping for an error, a foolish move from her or Tony. He was waiting for one of them to crack.

A decently dressed man pushed his way through the center of the mob. It took her a moment to place him, in that context, among all those distorted faces. With recognition came a rush of shame for him, and she looked away. *Oh, Dan—not this . . .*

She heard him call out, the words lost among all

the raging voices. When she looked back up, he was standing atop the wall, facing the mob with his arms outspread.

"Can I talk to you?" The noise had diminished slightly. Several of those at the front had gone quiet and were looking up at him.

The roar died to a rumble, broken by scattered curses. On either side, the Rigorists muttered among themselves. One turned and raced off toward the rear. Cardnale lowered his arms. "I'm not here to make a speech. It's too late for speeches. I want to ask you a few questions, that's all."

"What's that old fart think he's doin'?" the boy, Fox, said.

"Watch the mouth there, Foxy," the older man replied. "You weren't talkin' that way last week. Danny's showin' brass balls out there."

A Rigorist shouted, "This monad defies the Will—"

Cardnale swung toward him. "Let them speak for themselves." He raised a hand to the crowd. "You can speak, can't you? Of course you can. You always could."

An ambiguous mutter ran through the crowd. The Garite, about to step over the wall, hesitated and turned back. A gust of wind, one of the uncanny gusts of Midgard, lifted the tail of Cardnale's raincoat and twisted it, as if seeking to pull him down itself.

"You know who I am, most of you. I walked the roads with you at one time. I've never lied to you. Not face-to-face, not like this. I'm not going to start today. I just want to ask you a few things. Simple questions. You don't need schooling, you don't need a degree, you don't need a comp or a party or a leader to answer for you. All you need is your heads."

New faces appeared in the front rank. Young men,

dressed as hill folk but much better fed. They all bore clubs.

"Simple questions. What are you doing here today? Who decided on this? What are you going to do to her? What happens afterward? And . . . and . . . Is this what you really want?

"I may think of a few others. But they'll do for now."

The Rigorist who had run off—or perhaps another one, Julia couldn't tell—rejoined the others. They conferred a moment and then spread out.

"I'm going to ask those questions. Then I'll tell you what I think. And you let me know if I'm right. But *you* tell me. Don't let them talk for you. That's where it all goes wrong—when you let someone else take your voices."

"He fucked the bitch!" someone called out. "He's her fuck toy—"

Cardnale raised his voice. "It's a wet day. I remember days like this on the road. We all do. You didn't have roofs back then. You've got them now. So tell me—what are you doing out here in the rain?"

The rock came from well within the crowd; the arm that threw it was sleeved in black. The impact spun Cardnale half-around, leaving him teetering a moment before he regained his balance, one hand clutching his bloody face. As he lowered it, Julia saw him clearly. Not Cardnale the rebel, Cardnale the fool, but Danny. The boy who'd had trouble raising a beard. Who didn't know all there was to know yet. Who grew so excited explaining his ideas when he came over to tea.

She got up at the same moment he turned back to the mob. "Okay then—we'll skip the others." He held out his dripping hand. "Go straight to the last. Is this what you really—"

It was a club this time, whirling as it flew, striking him full in the chest, knocking him off his feet. He had barely come to rest before the disguised Garites threw themselves over the wall.

Julia was already rushing for the door. Slapping the switch, she squeezed through before it fully opened, crying out aloud as the drizzle touched her face.

It was the boy from yesterday. She recognized him as he straightened up, a flagstone in both hands. He smiled when he caught sight of her and raised the stone high.

She heard the old rebel, whose name she had never asked, yell for her to get down. A hand gripped her arm. Then a blow threw her backward, and there was nothing but howls and the thump of clubs.

Tony thought he handled it well—only one uncontrolled step down the slope when he saw the bright robe vanish under the rags and black cloth. Raising an arm, he shouted, "Roll out the Katy—*now!*"

He turned to Gen. "What's takin' 'em?"

"They're on their way, Ton. Another few seconds, no more."

The barrels of the rocket launcher poked into view overhead. "Okay—you go 'round out back. If they're gonna move, it'll be now."

Gen ran off. Tony snapped his fingers over his head. "Throw me the sight."

He caught the sight, a web of metal and plastic. He tore off his cap—somebody had handed it back to him a minute ago—and pulled the webbing over his head. "Activate." The system went into self-test, letters and numbers flashing in front of his right eye. "Come on," he said. The Katy had been thrown together by a mechanic up the Plateau named Gyton as some kind of a hobby. He'd also constructed things called "flamethrowers," but Tony couldn't see any use for them. The Katy was patterned after a weapon designed back in the last millennium and wasn't what you'd call razor tech.

At last the sight picture appeared. "Acquire . . ." he said. It blinked green. He knew exactly where he wanted to put the first round: right behind the mob, on the slope leading up from the gate. And the next—

A high-pitched whine caught his attention. He winced—was there something wrong with the sight? But the thing didn't have any speakers . . .

The whine grew louder and deepened in tone. He turned his head, the sight picture moving with him, crosshairs finding and embracing a large dot in the sky to the north. He gaped as the thing closed in, wings and fins becoming visible, his eyes following it as it sailed down the plaza, dipped over the house, and vanished into the clouds.

"Hold," he whispered. The sight stopped blinking. The object reappeared over the Academy. With a blithe twist it skipped to the plaza and settled into a hover.

Tony stared. It looked nothing like the lightweights that he was familiar with, nothing like any air or spacecraft he'd seen in the records. It seemed to have changed shape as it came to a halt, the metal re-forming itself in some way that his mind refused to credit. *That came from the ship*, he told himself. *The ship sent that.*

It appeared to be studying the house. Swinging his eyes, Tony saw that the mob was a mob no longer, that it had burst apart like an overstressed wheel. Their screams barely audible, Shirts and Bilis alike fled in all directions except the one leading beneath the probe. He saw with relief that his men had reached the house—they were pouring from the door, right at the heels of the last remnants. Two of them were carrying a bright-robed figure inside.

A shot rang out. A Rig across the plaza was firing

on the probe. Looking back up, Tony went cold. It was no longer oriented toward the house. In some way he couldn't explain, he knew it had turned its attention on him.

A bullet spanged off its side. Fixing it in the cross-hairs, Tony said, "Fire."

Nothing happened. Realizing that the sight was disengaged, he snapped, "Acquire!"

It was as if the probe heard him. Flickering upward, more like something clambering up a ladder than anything that flew, it disappeared into the overcast.

A few seconds passed before he dropped his eyes. The Rigs and Bilis were still on the run. With the probe no longer overhead a clump of Shirts raced across the plaza, in a straight-line route back to the station. He noticed that a good number had left their rifles behind.

Peeling off the sight, he rubbed his forehead. The house looked quiet. A number of bodies lay in front of it. He reached for the earpiece. "Cary . . . how's the Lady—"

"*She's dying!*" the AI shrieked. Tony's ear rang even after he pulled the unit off.

Gen gave him a report a few minutes later. Three men were injured, one touch and go. The kid everybody called Fox was dead, along with nine others—two nameless Rigs and six Bilis. The ninth was Dan Cardnale.

fourteen

There was a knock on the door. Tony looked up, puzzled by the formality. He didn't know what this room was used for under ordinary circumstances—probably a lounge, to judge from the tables and chairs—but at the moment it was the Place Where You Looked for Tony Perin When He Wasn't Somewhere Else. He'd grown accustomed to people breezing in and out; nobody had ever bothered to knock before.

He set down the earpiece. Cary wasn't answering anyway. "Yeah."

Kris Rimer looked in. "You ain't . . . busy, are ya?"

"Come on in."

Kris edged his way inside, no less than five other guys trailing him. Sipping at a cup of coffee, Tony took in the stern expressions, the way they faced him in a single knot. He didn't need to guess what they were here for. "What's up?"

A guy from the Shore—Cornwal, Tony thought

the name was—took a step forward. "Chief, we gotta—"

"Pat." Kris raised a hand. "We agreed, right?" Cornwal pouted and looked away.

"Now, Tony"—Kris rubbed the side of his nose— "don't gemme wrong here. I don't know what you're thinkin', I don't wanna disrupt anything, you got plans, or somethin' long those lines. Seriously. But, ya know, this mornin', that rocket thing come outta nowhere—"

"Probe."

"Yeah, that probe. And the Lady lying there all beat to hell, Foxy gettin' his head kicked in. Well, lotta things. It's got everybody talkin'. Not like they're excited, nothin' like that. They ain't in an uproar. No. But, uh—"

"Go on, Kris."

"Well, put it into words, it's like this." Kris waved at the ceiling. "I mean, you see all this stuff, and you sit down, and you look at the next guy, and he looks back at you, and—"

Cornwal slapped his thighs. "Tony—when are we gonna take out the fuckin' Shirts?"

"Yeah," Kris said.

Tony finished the coffee, studied the cup a moment. "What—you guys in a hurry? Someplace you gotta be?"

They stepped forward in a body, all talking at once. "Look here, Ton—"

"Come on, chief—"

"Hey now, we ain't sayin'—"

A loud voice from the corridor reduced them to silence. "Perin's in there?"

"That's your answer," Tony said. "Step one."

"I can see the door, you damned reb—"

"You tell the guys they'll have as much action as they can handle before they got time to—" The door swung wide, and a man in high boots, a rain cape, and a uniform cap stalked in.

"—you heard that straight from me." Tony got to his feet. "Dismissed."

Taking off his cap, the cop snapped it to one side. Droplets splattered the men heading for the door. They slowed their pace, looking among themselves, then back at the cop.

"You're Perin?" the cop said.

"Sergeant Ikler." Tony knew Ikler by reputation. A few months before things blew up, he'd arranged to have a couple of Dan's organizers publicly paddled at a village over in the Downs. Poor Dan had actually laughed when he heard about it.

Ikler threw half the cape over his right shoulder. He was in full uniform underneath it. "I'm here to speak to the Lady Amalfi. I was contacted by her associate, Cariola. I will see her immediately."

"One thing at a time, Sergeant—"

"That's the way it's going to be, mister."

Tony rubbed his mouth to hide a smile. "Now, Sergeant, we're not gonna get anywhere this way. So let's just start all over—"

Ikler lunged forward. Behind him, the men spread out. Tony noticed two other cops standing in the doorway.

"One of my men was *tortured* here, rebel. We heard it out in the hills—"

Tony's eyes narrowed. "You think I had a hand in that?"

The cape flapped as Ikler's left arm shot out. "You *brought* them here, you son of a bitch."

"Sarge . . . seems to me you don't have your paddle with you."

Ikler gripped his holster belt. "I don't need it." One of the other cops spat on the floor.

"Okay"—Tony gestured to Kris—"you guys take

Sarge—and his buttboys—and escort 'em out of here. If they say one more goddamn word—"

Somebody rapped on the window behind him. Craning his head, Tony saw Gen standing outside. "Tony," he called. "You better check this out."

Tony became aware of a rumbling he'd allowed to go unnoticed. Sweeping past Ikler, he headed for the door. The sound grew louder as he went down the corridor.

The men cleared a spot for him when he came out. He looked out over the plaza. Past the far end, the Lady's tree, the fountain that had given Dan his final, horrible vision, a steamer came into view, headlights cutting through the rain. It was pulling two freight cars, the roofless type used for ore shipments. When it came to a halt, dozens of Blackshirts dropped to the ground, yipping wildly as they ran toward the station.

"How many?"

"Hundred-fifty, sixty," Gen said. "Something like that."

Swinging around, Tony confronted Ikler standing on the second step. He raised an eyebrow. Ikler glanced once again at the steamer before briefly jerking his head. "I still want to see the Lady," he said.

"So do I," Tony told him.

"Julia."

For a moment, Julia thought it was her mother calling her. It had that same tone, that quality of love and forbearance, as the voice last heard in the Carolina hills, faded now amid time and darkness.

"Julia."

She kept her eyes tight shut, hoping that when she opened them the years would have fallen away, all their wonders and terrors yet unborn, that the loved face would once again be revealed. She had forgotten how her mother looked many years ago, had wept the night that she realized she could no longer call it to mind, aware at last that she had lived too long. Her father she recalled, in a vague way: a gesture, a smile, the merest outline of the man that he once was. But her mother was lost to her. She'd brought no picture with her when she fled—there hadn't been time. She would give a lot for one single, dog-eared snapshot. She would give what she had.

"Julia, please."

She opened her mouth, feeling a sharp pain along her jaw. At once other pains became evident: her head, her arms, her side. Her entire body seemed to be aflame, with only the drugs and shunts keeping it at bay.

"Cary," she murmured.

A whisper of sound shimmered about her, like a soft wind echoing from a long distance away. Julia frowned—she couldn't recall the last time Cary had lost control that way. She opened her eyes—or at least tried to. Her right eye remained dark, and pain throbbed in that blackness.

She was in her room, as she'd suspected, with portable med units blinking around the bed. Images of the riot returned: howling faces, clubs ascending, the spatter of blood. Strange, but she recalled their spittle falling onto her face more clearly than she did the blows. Moving her arms, she prepared to push herself upright.

"Jay, *don't*—"

Julia relaxed, suspecting from the pangs coursing through her that she couldn't have managed it anyway. "Cary—tell me."

Cary's voice thickened as she spoke of concussion, a fractured occipital lobe, broken cheekbones and nose, gunshot wounds reopened, ribs, arms, fingers. That odd, reverberating swish reappeared, rendering her almost incomprehensible by the time she was finished.

"Darling—what's the matter?"

"Oh, Jay—" She sounded no clearer. "Jay—I'm so ashamed."

Julia allowed herself a smile. So Cariola was growing up, the long adolescence of a silicon entity coming to a close. Oh, and what a relief it is, baby, that I brought you through this on top of all, hard as it was. Things will be fine now. Someday, you and I will smile about what we've been through.

"Twice I've nearly killed you. *Twice*. And both times I was pleased. I was *happy*, Jay. That someone had done what I couldn't. Seeing you lying there broken, your indications fading. I waited both times, waited full seconds before I triggered any med programs. Oh, Jay, what kind of thing am I? What went wrong?"

"Nothing, baby, nothing at all. You're learning, you see. What our nature is, what kind of burdens a conscious being has to bear. I was thinking of my mother just now, Cary. How much I miss her. But . . . I can never see her. Only in dreams, and then I wake up happy. But never in waking life at all. It's such a sad thing. But there's a part of me that wants it that way. Wants to forget everyone, put them all aside—Mama, and Petro, and you. To sit alone under the stars, the only one that is.

"And it's so much harder for you because you can't forget. It's all pure data, and you can never put it aside. It's something you can't escape, and the pressure must be enormous. But you're not alone, Cary. We're all like that. Hating where we ought not to hate, not loving enough where we ought to love. All the same, carbon or silicon."

She allowed herself a smile. "And besides, you finally *did* call, didn't you? That was the real Cariola. The one who couldn't let her sister down."

Cary's voice had returned to normal. "Do you really think of me that way?"

"Always. You know that, Cary. I've told you that before."

"Not lately, Jay."

Julia supposed that she was right. She couldn't remember when she had last spoken to her in that fashion. It was one of those things that had to be said over and over if it was to be said at all. Ah, but if you couldn't neglect your sister, who could you neglect? "Always, Cary."

"Know what I'm doing now?" Cary's voice sounded smooth and firm; she was herself again.

"What?"

"I'm reviewing our first day on the ship. You looked so silly, scrabbling around in micro-gee, banging into things. Your eyes bugging out and hair all over the place. You were no cosmonaut, Ms. Amalfi."

"I was so scared, Cary. I didn't know what I was doing."

"There I was, isolated for a week, no word from anybody. Then this . . . person comes aboard, off a LEO shuttle, of all things. I thought to myself: oh no—what's this?"

"You were the one who named the ship, Cary. *Petrel*. You know, everyone thinks that was me?" It had been called another name, after some Massachusetts senator or other.

"Our storm bird."

Yes—their own storm bird, that had outrun the greatest of all hurricanes. Now the storm had caught up with them at last, as she'd always known it must. But they could talk about that later. It was enough for the moment that they were reconciled, that they'd gone back to the way it had been in the beginning. Nothing had ever been too much for them when they were together. Not the Erinye, not the deep black, not entire worlds. "I did look silly, didn't I? I haven't viewed that recording in a long time."

"We'll look at it again soon. But you need rest now, Jay—"

A rumble of voices from outside caught her attention. They had to be very loud, to be audible in here. "What's that?"

"It's nothing. Only Perin and that policeman. I told them to go away."

Pain stabbed her as Julia tried to make a fist. "I need to see them, Cary."

"I don't . . . All right. But only for a moment. One minute, precisely."

The door slid open. A shouting voice—not Tony's—rang through it. A moment later she detected a figure from the corner of her eye. She moved her head with effort. Ikler stared at her in open shock. He shook his head, lips drawing back from his teeth. "Oh my God—"

"Hello, Deni."

He came to attention. "Sergeant Ikler reporting, ma'am. I am ready and willing to take over the duty of your protection"—he turned his head—"from this *incompetent*. Should you so desire."

"I don't so desire."

"Ma'am?"

Tony came into sight behind him. He gave her one long look before pulling his eyes away.

"Tony," she said. "I hate putting you through this again."

He forced a smile. "Well now, Jay, I hate—"

Ikler swung on him. "You address her properly, punk—"

"Denis, please." He glanced back at her, then returned to his original position. "I have something to tell you," she went on. She nodded at Tony. "Mr. Perin is in command of my forces at this time. I want you to place yourself under his authority and do exactly what he says."

"*What?*" Ikler took a half-step forward. "After he allowed *this* to happen? Ma'am, I object—"

"It was my fault, Deni—"

"What have you done to her?" Ikler whispered.

"I repeat: it was *my fault*."

"Ma'am, my intention is to remove you to a protected location, where we will wait for these insurgent factions to devour each other like the fucking cannibals they are—"

Julia levered herself up on one elbow. The pain took her voice for a few seconds. "Officer—"

"Jay, will you *please* lie down," Cary cried out.

"Officer Ikler," Julia repeated. "I am the Dame of Midgard. I require you to obey Mr. Perin. Is that clear?"

Ikler shook visibly, his lips moving without a sound.

"What are your doubts, Officer?"

"None, ma'am."

Julia dropped back on the bed. "Then it's settled."

Eyes to the floor, Ikler took his cap from under his arm and clutched it in both hands. Tony had removed his as well, holding it with two fingers while he rubbed the back of his head.

"Wrap it up, you two," Cary said.

"Let's go, Sarge." Clapping on his cap, Tony headed for the door. With a miserable nod to Julia Ikler stalked out ahead of him.

"Tony—"

He turned from the door. Julia bit her lip. "Danny . . . ?"

The expression on his face was all she needed. "I see."

"He looked good, Jay. Those last couple minutes. He looked real good." With a final thumb to his cap—how he liked to toy with it; there was a complete language made up of Tony Perin and his cap—he told her to feel better and went out.

"Cary," she said after a moment. "I want you to do the same. Listen to Tony. Do what he asks. Just as you would for Petro."

"Yes, Jay," Cary said. "Like Petro. Now sleep."

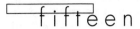# fifteen

It was starting to get dark, in that slow, almost tidal fashion of overcast days. At least the rain had stopped. To the north, Tony saw a small patch of brightness dead smack on the horizon, a sign that it was starting to clear up there. That was a relief— night rain this time of year usually turned into sleet, and sitting in a foxhole in that kind of downpour wasn't worth thinking about.

He lowered himself onto the top step, finding it still a bit damp. He was taking a break from high-level discussions within the Commando Supremo of the unified rebel forces. A well-deserved break— they'd been going at it nonstop for three hours, ever since Cus Miler had arrived, and it had been only in the past half hour that he'd succeeded in getting them to talk sense.

Ikler was being polite, to give him credit, even though it was obvious that his life would not be complete until he saw Tony led off wearing wristbands. As for Cus—well, for some reason, Cus and Ikler had hit it off. He found the sergeant " 'greeable." His ideas were " 'greeable" too. Even his stalking across the room in his horse boots while snapping his holster belt was " 'greeable," evidently. None of this sat particularly well with Tony, who viewed cops from the vantage of the wiseass kid he'd so lately been. Cops were the only authorities you could defy and abuse and get away with it. They were figures of fun, placed in this universe for the sole purpose of providing entertainment for youths while their parents looked on with open approval. Youths. That was a word that Ikler liked. "Your force appears to be comprised in large part of youths," he'd said earlier. It had cost Tony considerable effort to refrain from pointing out that his youths had kicked the britches of every swarm of cops sent against them from the Plateau on down.

Listening to Ikler, it was easy to see why. Ikler's plan, carefully worked out after due consideration of all pertinent factors, was to slaughter every Rig within reach as soon as possible. Cus found this " 'greeable," but himself favored a more leisurely, less strenuous massacre. Tony had been hard put to explain to them that there was such a thing as tactics. He'd finally gotten them to admit that not only did tactics exist, but there was probably a good reason for that and maybe they should get some. At that point Tony decided it was time for a break.

Problem was, Tony couldn't come up with a tactic worthy of the name. They were still outnumbered, by how much he couldn't say. Ikler had only twenty-eight cops, while the best Cus had been able to scrape up was a dozen dairy farmers led by a priest. Tony needed something else, an equalizer, an element to make up for numbers. Maneuver would do it—get away from the Cloister, perform some footwork, tantalize Freddy from his shell, and take him apart piece by piece. But Tony couldn't see his way to it. Pulling out would leave the crown jewels wide open. The AI, the labs, the med building. And he doubted that Julia could be moved either, the shape she was in.

Footsteps drew near. He looked up. It was one of his fellow youths. "Uh, chief . . . you got a . . . uh . . . visitor."

From the expression on his face Tony thought for a moment that it was somebody from the ship. The probe had been at the back of his mind all day. The whine of its engine seemed always to be at the very edge of audibility, and there had been a couple of sightings of it flying out on the horizon, eight hundred feet long with bolts of purple lightning coming out of the nose. He clutched his knees, caught himself with the question on his tongue. What a stupid idea—if something had come down from the ship, there would have been more than one unfamiliar kid come to tell him about it.

He waved at Bev as he passed the fire, but she didn't see him. She'd spent no more than a minute or two listening to the discussion, sensible woman that she was. The kid led him on over the knoll toward the perimeter. The station came into sight, lights ablaze. The Rigs had been quiet throughout the afternoon, the probe having taken some stuffing out of them. It was nice to know that something could.

He saw her waiting down the slope, your standard-issue Blackshirt, nearly invisible in the dusk except for the paleness of her hands and face. "She's the one?"

"Well," the kid said. "Actually, it's the box."

Something white lay at the Rig's feet. "The . . . box wants to see me."

"Yeah, chief." The kid shook his head. "I wouldn't kid ya."

Tony proceeded downhill. The Rig awaited him in
that oblivious way they had. He halted a few steps
off and pointed at the white ovoid, readouts aglow
across the top, clearly an electronic device of some
kind. "That box was asking for me."

"Ha!" the machine said. "Monad Perin, sure
enough."

Tony crossed his arms. It was speaking with Fredrix's voice.

"Didn't expect this, did you? Surprise, ain't it? Lot
of machines in this cophouse. Place is full of 'em.
Value expropriated from labor and utilized by the
forces of control. Textbook case. Except . . . the big
machine told me that these are made by other machines, that are made by other machines, all the way
back to Earth. What you think of that, monad? Surplus value hold in that case? Can a machine be alienated from its labor? Appears that theory collapses
here. Gar's work requires revision. Somewhat. What
you think, Perin?"

He was off again before Tony could reply. "Some
of 'em come in handy, though. Big machine showed
me how to use this one, what it was for. The main
one, the one with a name. I don't care for that. Machines *should not* have names. Don't hold with it. Believe we'll . . . correct that. Delete the name, retain
the machine. Machines attain objective correctness in
some circumstances. Maybe I'll give you one of these.
You like that, monad?

"But I shouldn't say 'monad.' Shouldn't call you
that. You know what a monad is, Perin?"

"Can't say I've thought much—"

"A monad is a unit, with no interior nature, no
extension, no ability to act on anything outside itself.
A monad does not affect the universe. Monads are
isolated. Monads do not communicate. Monads do
not interact. Monads exist. That is all. Anything more
than existence is illusion. A monad or monads com-

municating or interacting is an appearance only, created by random action. Monads are dust. Balls of nothin'. A collection of monads is a fog. A greasy, stinking, mindless fog."

Tony glanced at the girl. She gazed off into darkness, her face clear, as if hearing a conversation in another language.

"You understand, Perin? Sure you do. I don't need to explain it to you. You know the difference between a monad and the . . . elevated. What we are. You took charge, didn't you? Up north, on the Plateau. Pulled the farmers and the other trash together and drove south. Couldn't believe when I heard. Thought it was bullshit. Didn't pay no mind until Lews. I liked Lews. Lews had the mark. You just blew 'em away, didn't you? Am I right? Didn't think twice, just set that demo and watched it fly. But you thought about it since. You're thinkin' about it now.

"You understand, Perin. It was you, wasn't it? Wasn't no army, no Collective, no *people*. Just Perin, driving the monads forward."

Tony dropped his hands to his hips. What the hell *was* all this? What had brought it on, where was it headed? "Uhh, Fredrix—does this go somewhere or—"

"I knew it the minute I saw you. Told myself, 'This one's no monad. This one's alive.' That's rare, Perin. Very rare. One in ten thousand? One in a million? I don't know. But you can go years. Gar was a monad. A talkin' monad, true. Talk your fuckin' ear off. Cardnale . . ." Fredrix paused for a chuckle or two. "He was a monad squared. And the woman . . . I don't know, Perin. What you say? Maybe not.

"But here's the thing: up there in that vessel. What you think's running it? Eh? Take a guess? You say monads? You got it. Has to be. The odds demand it. More dust, blowin' from star to star now. But they're advanced, you say. They're *augmented*. They're these imaginary nightmares that woman thought up.

"You know better. Monads do not *advance*. To augment a monad is to augment *nothin'*. Anything times zero is still zero, am I right? All you need when dealing with monads is an opening. A single weak spot. And we got that. The woman. We'll give her to the Terrests. She's the one they come for. The machine told me that. Then we'll take 'em. Smash our way in. Their ship, their machines, whatever they got. I'm gettin' fond of machines now. Didn't know what I was missin'."

Tony eyed the readouts. Sticking a thumb in his belt, he threw his head back, promising whatever lay beyond the clouds that when the time came, he would kill Fredrix with his own two hands.

"What you say? Ah, you wanna know what the profit is, like any good buji. What you get. That's simple: anything you want."

The ground suddenly glowed at Tony's feet. He lifted one boot in surprise, then realized that it was nothing more than a map, much like the one that Cary had showed him.

"Let's see—" The Islands and Shore glowed brightly. "How's that? You want 'em, say the word. They're yours."

Somebody hollered up the slope and Tony heard the click of a Sten safety. "Hey, Ton, you okay?" He lifted his arm, then considered that they might not be able to see the gesture in the dark. "I'm fine."

". . . or say now, you're a Plateau boy. How 'bout that?" The Plateau flashed brighter, then was lost in sudden flickering of the entire map, different regions glowing in turn: Threshold, Lakes, Downs, Shore, Threshold . . . "Or anything else. I don't care. Both of 'em, neither of 'em, industry, old ship, labs . . . Tell you what—we'll make the Cloister an open city. We'll both hold it."

Fredrix chuckled again. "Course, we'll have to kill each other eventually. No doubt about that. But it'll keep.

"Well, what you say? I know it's new to you. It's like . . . those yarns 'bout children growin' up with monkeys, whatever they are. Couldn't talk, couldn't think, just jumped around and scratched themselves. Same thing with monads. You grew up with 'em, so you're . . . incomplete. I know the feeling.

"Or is it the woman, eh? You can have her too, if the Terrests leave anything worth havin' . . ."

With a smooth motion Tony drew his gun, cocked it, and fired a round through the machine. He was surprised when it didn't smoke or throw sparks. All that happened was that the readouts went dark, exactly as if he'd thrown a switch.

He heard another shout followed by running feet. "It's okay," he called out. When he turned back, the Rig was bending toward him, a slip of paper in her hand. He took it and flicked it open. It read: STRUGGLE, MONAD.

He crumpled it up and tossed it away. "I believe the Herald has his answer," he told the Rig as he holstered the pistol. She ran off without a word, head high, leaning slightly forward—the predator's lope.

Tony headed uphill. After a few steps, he put on the earpiece. "What the hell's wrong with him? Why'd he talk like that?"

"I believe that's his personal philosophy."

"No, not that—his tone, all the jabber."

"I'm not certain. He has refused a medical examination."

"Well, what do you think?"

"Offhand, I'd say that it's due to the medication he's taking for his neurological condition."

"Those fits?"

"That's right. The prescription is comprised of various cerebral enzyme and hormone analogs and can lead to hyperactivity, hallucinations, and delusional behavior if abused. He's currently taking—"

"You're giving him pills?"

"That's right."

"Double the dosage."

"I can't do that."

Tony came to a full stop, nearly losing his footing on the wet grass. "You can't *what*?"

"As you should be aware, my operational protocols do not allow—"

"You've been breaking operational protocols since before I've been born, sweetie. Is it gonna kill him? No. I'm gonna kill him. That's right. So you will do what you're goddamn told." He resumed climbing. "And what's this crap about you showing him how to operate those electronics?"

"It's a pose. No more than that. He thinks I'm cooperating."

"A pose, huh? And how about informing on the Lady? That was a pose too?" He came to a dead halt. Insight flashed through him, as it had at Bukland, and during last night's assault. A clear vision of what faced him, the pieces falling in place one after the other, forming a perfect, undeniable pattern. As if he was, for a frozen moment of time, inhabiting the mind of the man opposing him—or, in this case, the machine. "It was you, wasn't it?" he whispered. "It's been you all along."

The AI was silent. Tony thought of the first day of the rising, six weeks ago. How the word had come down, over the commercial lines, simultaneously all across the continent. How scattered and feeble the cops' original response had been, as if their own communications were muzzled. He'd believed it was Cardnale's doing, but Danny never had those kind of resources.

He thought of how the Rigs had appeared the same day, as the rebels were organizing. Drifting in only hours after the first alert, as if they'd been told in advance . . . "You knew the Rigs were up there all the time, didn't you? You couldn't have missed them, not from orbit. You saved them. You helped them out." And how had they found that valley in the first place, smack up against the Threshold? And Danny . . . how had they known where to find him? Why didn't they kill him as soon as they got their hands on him? "What was the point? Tell me your personal philosophy, toots. You want to run this rockball, don't you? Doesn't matter what tool you use. We're nothing but monads to you too. Walking carbon, that's all. Let a machine take over. Machines are better."

"That's . . . not completely correct, Tony."

"Then you damn well tell me—" Tony went silent as awareness widened. He lifted his eyes to the blank sky overhead. Beyond it lay the Earth ship, packed with entities he couldn't conceive of. Its arrival now was not a coincidence. There were no coincidences in this situation. "Jay . . ." he said. "You wanted to punish Jay." His gaze found her house, glowing warmly in the dusk. Rigs, rebels, and Erinye—all of Julia's worst nightmares—arriving at once, one on top of the other, at the behest of a single spiteful, neurotic machine. Danny, and Fredrix, and whatever freakish caricature of humanity was conning that ship, no more than pawns in the digitalized hands of an AI system embittered for reasons that Tony would find hard to grasp, reasons that very likely wouldn't stand the light of day.

He couldn't forget the other pawn either. Antonio Ugen Perin, the Napoleon of Midgard, alpha of all alphas, leader of men . . . In truth, merely another stick aimed at Julia Amalfi, to make her suffer and smart and hurt. Bile rose in his throat. He suppressed an urge to spit. "You . . . you sick little mutt . . ."

"You don't have to say that. I know what I am."
The machine was barely audible.

The men waiting up ahead eyed him in a dignified
manner, giving no sign that they found Tony's ranting alone in the twilight at all unusual or unexpected.
He climbed toward them, mind abuzz with memories
of how the movement's meetings had never been
raided, the way their couriers always seemed to
elude arrest, how Danny had appeared to know beforehand that Chief Yaki was a sympathizer . . .

"Tony—don't tell Jay any of this. Please. I don't
think she realizes most of it yet. I don't want her
hearing about it while she's recovering . . ."

"Where's Gen?" The kid who'd brought him there
poked a thumb over his shoulder. Tony headed for
the nearest fire.

". . . I can see how this appears from your perspective, Tony. I'll do my best to explain it to you . . ."

"Oh, you'll explain it, all right, babe. We're gonna
have a long talk, you and me. Gen!"

A shape detached itself from beside the fire.
"Yeah, Ton?"

"How much of that demo do we have left?"

"Ah, sixty-odd pounds."

"Okay. You take fifty, set it up in the cybershack.
First floor, underneath her CP . . ."

He pointed at the earpiece. Gen regarded his finger, frowning slightly. "Cary, Gen. I'm talkin' about
Cary."

"Got ya."

"You tell 'em to lens it, focus right through her
frontal lobes—"

"You can't do this, Tony." Cary's voice was a
mere whisper.

"—radio detonator, one trigger for me, no dupes."

"I'll lock the doors."

"Then I'll blow 'em open." Gen raised his eyebrows. Tony waved him on his way.

"I can't let you put me at risk."

" 'At risk'?" Tony headed back to the lab building. "You put us all at risk . . . !"

"Not alone, Perin."

Tony smiled. "You got a point there, babe. But I still can't trust you. And if I can't trust you, then I have to leash you."

"I'll tell Julia—"

"No, you won't." Pushing open the door, Tony started down the hall. " 'Cause you'll have to explain why."

He plucked the earpiece out before she could reply. A rhomboid of light spilled from the room ahead, but when he got there, it was empty. He was standing in the doorway holding back a shout when he heard a click of balls from the next room, along with Ikler and Cus chattering. ". . . just in time, too. The cloud cover was closing in fast."

"Seen it. Couldn't figure what it was about."

Click. "Yeah. Clever of her. Got to hand it to the old bucket of switches."

They must be talking about Cary's signals. The cops had been operating under radio silence. Cary had gotten around that by contacting Ikler with one of the mirrors, flashing a message to him to switch on his radio using the old Moors' code, a Terrest signaling system that Tony assumed had been developed by the Arabs of North Africa.

Click. ". . . surprised you saw it, Cus. The clouds were damn heavy by then. Ha. Two with one shot."

"Hmph. You're damn good at this. Saw the glow, actually. Through overcast. Bright, was."

"Bright, hoo! You should have been on the spot. I couldn't see a thing for near to five minutes. Had to have a patrolman tune my set . . ."

Yeah, it was the mirrors. That had been a neat trick on Cary's part—Tony would never have thought of it himself. He recalled that bad blaze the other day.

Cary had curtailed that with mirrors too, focusing several dozen on the brush downwind to scorch a firebreak, like she'd done with the rats up home. There was a lot you could do with those things. Too bad they couldn't—

He paused a single step from the door, fished out the earpiece once again. "Cary."

"What?"

"Battle. Mexican Civil War. Teens of the 20th century. This is on Earth."

"It would have to be on Earth, wouldn't it, Mr. Perin?"

"Now for the eight ball," Ikler crowed.

Swinging from the door, Tony paced down the hall. "Mexican–U.S. border. They used spotlights. Can't remember the name, but—"

"Agua Prieta, 2 November 1915."

"That's it. Now . . . tell me something. Can the mirrors . . . can you do the same with the mirrors?"

"I can't see why not."

A sense of pure, unfettered joy swept Tony's heart. He thought of Wellington in Spain—and that was on Earth too—spotting a gap in the French lines after stalking them for days on end. "That will do," he echoed the duke. "That will just do."

"Rack 'em up!"

"Cary," Tony said with feeling, "you and I are going to get along."

He slapped the door as he passed through, to mark the moment. Ikler eyed him narrowly when he picked up a stick, while Cus gave him a nod over his pipe.

"This game's mine," Tony told them. "And listen to this."

sixteen

She would have to be told. Throughout the rest of the evening, the thought recurred to Tony. While he gave orders to the section chiefs—hell, the sergeants—insisting on how precise they'd have to be, how careful, how quiet. While he answered questions, made arrangements, dealt with problems. It remained there always at the back of his mind: she'd have to be told.

Yet he put it off, hour after hour, as if hoping that when he was finished it would be too late, that events would be rushing too fast for him to spare the time. But no hour would ever be too late for what he had to do.

Finally, close to midnight, he headed for the house. Still reluctant, not quite grasping the source of that reluctance. He avoided crossing the plaza, taking the long route instead. Though he hadn't seen them, he had no doubt that the Academy was crawling with Rigs, and he could be sure that Rigorism held no

ideological objections to assassination. It was a pity—
he'd wanted to take a look at his dad's old room.

As he walked, he returned to the question upper-
most in his mind. "Cary—where can we take Julia?
Is there a place . . . ?"

"You can't take her anywhere."

"Listen—"

"No. You don't understand." The AI paused for a
moment. "I don't want you to repeat to her what I'm
going to tell you, Perin. Jay's internal injuries are
much worse than I previously revealed. She was
dead for seventy-three seconds, and I . . . I . . ."

"Not relevant. But she can't be moved anywhere.
Not for at least another day, and I would recommend
several days."

"Cary, what—"

"Don't you dare threaten me over this, mister."

"I'm asking you, all right? What's the alternative?"

"I believe I grasp your plans correctly. You'll simply have to defend the site. No choice, so no problem. Don't you agree?"

"I guess I have to."

"I guess you do."

He was searching for a smart response when he
noticed a disturbance at the house. The boys were
gathered out in front, surrounding a figure dressed
in black.

Tony broke into a run. He'd taken only a few steps
when he felt the earpiece drop out, bouncing off his
shoulder into the grass. He cursed to himself while
he hunted for it. Finally he heard the squeak of
Cary's voice: "Over here." As he picked it up, she
added, "You know what a 'schmuck' is, Perin?" He
shoved the unit into his pocket without bothering
to answer.

The boys were pushed in close around the prisoner, snarling and throwing insults. Tony was surprised to see that it was Integral. "Okay, back off."

"Caught him sneakin' in from the 'cademy, chief . . ."

Integral eyed Tony as if he'd expected him. "I must see the Lady."

"Uh, Mos . . ." Tony pointed at the grass beyond the patio wall. "We need a trench over there. Get a couple people on it, huh?"

"I must see the Lady."

Tony gestured at the two men holding the Rig. "Let him go." Integral's glasses had nearly fallen off his nose. He reached up to push them back into place.

"We searched him, chief. Nothin' on him—"

"I didn't think so. Okay, Integral. What you want with Julia?"

The man dropped his head. "I have words."

"This isn't on behalf of Fredrix . . ."

Integral shook his head fiercely. "It is . . . individual."

"Personal, huh?" Something had told Tony that might be the case. "Well . . . can't see any reason why not." He waved at the door. Integral headed toward it, stiffly as ever.

The two men inside shot to their feet as Integral appeared, relaxed on catching sight of Tony. They shrugged when he asked whether the Lady was awake. Leading Integral to the bedroom door, he gave it a light tap. He glanced over to see that Integral was again fiddling with his glasses. "Tell me something, Integral. Those things ever break?"

The Rig dropped his hand as if he'd been caught at something impermissible. "Yes. Often."

Tony turned back to the door. He brought his fist up again, but it occurred to him that Julia might be too weak to answer. Gesturing for Integral to remain where he was, Tony pushed the door open.

A light went on as he stepped inside. Julia was lying back, still in shadow, her eyes closed. He was about to retreat when the lamp over the bed glowed and she turned her head toward him.

"Tony."

He nodded to her. "Look . . . if you're tired, I can . . ."

"No. Come on in."

Tony pushed the door wider. "I've got a visitor here." Integral remained unmoving until Tony waved him in. Julia's expression remained unchanged when she saw the Rig. Nor did her gaze move from his face. She simply nodded and said, "Hello."

"Lady." Integral walked to the bed and stood facing it, his back ramrod straight. "I have words."

"Take a seat, Integral." He gave the chair a puzzled glance. "Or don't. However you're comfortable."

Tony had gone to the nearest corner. He was willing to allow Integral to make his statement, but he'd be damned if he'd let a Rig remain alone with the Lady. He doubted it made much difference to Integral—it was a sure bet that there wasn't a lot of privacy in Rigorist life.

"I am a monad," Integral began, his voice that same empty monotone, but with something further, some sense of barely perceptible tension, underlying it. "All progression of individual monads through stages of existence follow patterns set forth by the Will, as interpreted by the Collective. The Will alone establishes. The Will alone integrates. The Will alone enables."

In his dim corner, Tony bit his cheek to hold back a sigh. God forbid he'd allowed the man in here for the sole purpose of reciting this nonsense, now of all times. He hoped there was more to it. He'd hate to look foolish in front of Julia.

"My status is reflected in my identifier. I am called 'Integral.' This reflects the integration of this monad

into the Will itself. Perfect integration, perfect submission, perfect unity.

"The Will dictates responses to all phenomena,
from the basic to the most complex. Among these
is the biological, including matters of reproduction.
Strictly adhering to principle, the Collective selects
monads with desirable traits and matches them for
purposes of breeding.

"This monad has taken part in the procedure three
times. The first two occurred as planned. The
third . . ." A shiver went through Integral at that
moment, clearly visible from where Tony stood. Julia
regarded the man with unblinking eyes. Tony saw
her fingers uncurl and rise, as if to curtail any
interruption.

"The third . . . revealed that integration was perhaps not as complete as might be desired.

"The female's identifier was 'Promise.' She was not
unfamiliar to this monad, her assignment being in
allocation. I . . . I had not taken great notice until
breeding was scheduled.

"Little explanation exists for what entailed. Breeding was successful. I was so informed by my guardian, as had occurred on previous occasions. But . . .
I was already aware of this development. I . . . I
had conceived an interest in Promise outside of the
plan. I . . ."

Integral moved for the first time. Though his body
remained rigid, his hands rose, clenching into fists
and quivering visibly. Lifting one finger, Julia said,
"Proceed."

After a moment, Integral relaxed. "I had contact
with Promise outside of recognized duty roles. Her
conduct interested me. We conversed often. On per-
missible topics. At first."

Fists clenched once again, Integral lunged toward
the bed. Tony moved out of the corner, snapping

open his holster flap. But the Rig came to halt with one leg pushed forward, still several feet from Julia.

"*Nothing* corrupt occurred. No vileness. Nothing outside of the plan. This monad scarcely ever laid a hand on the female . . ." He moved back, straightening up once again. "Scarcely ever," he repeated.

A moment passed before he resumed speaking. "When the new monad was produced, I found opportunity to examine it at the crèche. It pleased me to learn that it was female, and its identifier was 'Integrity.' I informed Promise of this fact."

His tone changed with the next words, becoming blander, as it had been when he first began speaking. "Progress within the Collective occurs by method of the purge. This is the praxis of the Rigorism. Buji tendencies arise from virtuality within the vacuum of the monad's core, calling for constant vigilance and righteous action. The Will oversees and guides this activity.

"Promise experienced difficulties in adhering to sanctioned behavior. Both within her cell, and with the Collective at large. Her guide suspected serious contamination, and sustained examination proved this to be the case. A purge was scheduled, and among the identifiers listed was that of"—his voice broke on the next words—"the female Promise."

Integral seemed to collapse in on himself. He swayed on his feet, his shoulders hunched. He gripped the arm of the chair beside him for steadiness. Tony stepped out of the corner, ready to catch him if he fell.

"We were gathered." The man's voice was so low that Tony could scarcely hear it. "The Herald addressed us . . . necessity of the purge. Our duty. Demands of the Will. The process began. They stood, the bacilli. Wearing placards revealing their deviations. She among them. Her eyes. We struggled all the long day. Denunciations were required . . . of those who had interacted with these throwbacks. I was called, and"—his voice rose to a wail—"I denounced this female—"

Integral's legs bent beneath him. Moving quickly, Tony got hold of him before he hit the floor. Integral was a thin man, far thinner than Tony had guessed. He had no trouble at all hoisting him into the chair.

It took him a moment to regain control, but regain it he did, pulling himself erect until he was as rigid as before. It was as if he couldn't speak unless he sat in precisely that way. He went on, in disjointed phrases, his voice punctuated by wrenching sobs. The mass denunciation. The sentence, spoken by the Herald himself. How she had looked back as she was led to termination. Not death, not execution. Termination. That was the word he used.

"Her eyes—" he repeated over and over. Tony's attention was so riveted on the man that he nearly missed Julia's gesture toward a blinking device at the side of the bed. Going over to it, Tony found a steaming cup. The scent told him it was tea. He was about to hand it to Integral when the man bent forward, as stiffly as he did everything else.

"She was like you, Lady. When I first saw you, it was evident: she is like Promise was. She held herself within herself, as you do. And . . . there is much else that I cannot define. But you must listen and obey. Leave here, Lady. The Her . . . the Collective . . . takes action this day. The Will demands that alien elements be expunged. Regard these words and go from here. If you go . . . Promise still exists . . . If you go . . ."

Julia reached out and took his hand. For a second it seemed that he'd pull it away, but he acquiesced at last. "Integral, listen . . ."

Tony wandered off, still holding the cup. He caught only a few words: Integrity, Promise. The names and that was all. He returned when Julia fell silent to hand Integral the cup. The man grasped it without looking, took a quick sip. "This is too much," he declared. "A single monad must not waste resources." But he finished it all the same.

He gave the cup back to Tony, looking between him and Julia before dropping his head. "I am aware that my behavior is unsanctioned," he said in a firm voice. "I strive for greater unity with the Will."

Tony grimaced, not knowing what to think. But Julia simply smiled. "I'm sure you do, Integral."

The Rig regarded her in silence before turning to Tony. "I will depart, Perin."

Integral did not look back when he left the room. On the patio, he turned to Tony and held out his hand, palm up. "You do this, I think. In terms of . . . equality?"

The position was awkward, but Integral's grip was firm. "And what you do?"

Integral smiled, an expression ghastly in its bitterness. "Nothing."

Without another word he made his way into darkness. A little unsteady, maybe, a little less stiffly than he had come. Tony watched until he faded into the night.

"Fuckin' weirdo," one of the guards said.

"Can that," Tony answered and went back inside.

Julia was lying with her head thrown back when he returned. He stopped in the doorway, afraid that she'd gone back to sleep. But she heard him approach and turned to face him. She looked much better than she had earlier, even with one eye bandaged. The swelling had gone down quite a bit, and her color was nearly back to normal. "I think you've found the way out."

He smiled. "Yeah."

"It's complex, isn't it," she said after he finished his explanation.

"Not as much as it looks," Tony replied. "If we

can pull out safely, then . . . doesn't matter what he does. I've got open ground. I've got the experience. I've got the instrument. That's what counts."

"But will he come out?"

"Oh, he'll come out, all right. I'm the stone in his pathway. He's got to kick me aside. Not only that, he's got to be seen to kick me aside. He's got to see himself do it." He paused, trying to think of a way to make it clearer, realizing that Fredrix himself had given him the answer. "He's not a monad, Julia. He's no logical machine, the way he presents himself. Nothing like that poor SOB just now. He's the town hard-ass. Man with the big fists. You call him out, he's gotta come." Tony chuckled. "The Will demands it."

If Julia made any sound, he didn't hear it. She lay back, one bandaged arm behind her head, hair straying across the pillow. She might have been fast asleep. The only sign that she wasn't was that single open eye, gazing softly at the ceiling.

Tony lowered his head. "There's one thing," he said. "Cary told me . . . she insisted that you can't be moved."

"That's all right."

"It'll be a couple hours, no longer, one way or another. I'm puttin' two squads here, right around the house. They won't—"

"It's all right, Tony."

He fell silent. A moment passed before she turned to him. "I know you'll see to it. I'm thinking, that's all. I'm wondering, when it's over, what we'll do with the Garites."

Tony shifted uncomfortably. He knew what he wanted to do, but that was no fitting answer.

"You heard that man, Tony. What he said—and what he wasn't aware he was saying. It was obvious, wasn't it? He knows that something's wrong. That he's in a wrong place, that his life has been twisted and demeaned. Even after what he's been through: those purges, the punishments, the surveillance. That debased language that's the only tool he has to think with, he knows."

She swung her gaze back to the ceiling. "I think they all do. I think it's part of us. It's down there somewhere in the code, deep in the DNA. Untraced and perhaps untraceable. The great legacy, from the very beginning. Back on the African plains, when we were so few, and the world was so vast, so deadly. They learned it back then, I'm sure. That if one man behaved wrongly, it threatened them all. That a single murder brought the cold and dark that much closer. That's the way it was. They learned what mattered then, and they handed it on down.

"It's like that again now, Tony. Oh, the plain has grown larger, but so has the night. These suns of ours, they're no more than fires in the darkness, we crouch around them and wonder what's approaching. And still, we know what matters."

Tony bobbed his head. He could go along with that, to a point anyway. He strongly doubted that Fredrix . . . or Unity either . . . knew any damn thing at all.

It was as if she'd read his thoughts. "Not Fredrix." She raised one finger. "He doesn't know. Something's missing in him. The legacy is gone, or was rejected. He doesn't know, and he trained those poor children so that they don't know either. They're lost; he led them into the wasteland . . ." She turned to him. "We have to lead them back. As far as we can. You heard Integral. You know it still lives. They can be saved, Tony . . ."

"Hey—" Tony raised both hands. "I'm just gonna whip 'em. I'm not out to . . . kill 'em all." His hands clenched into fists, dropped to his lap. "I thought about it. After Lews. You know what happened at Lews, right . . . And I wondered, if there's any real difference. I mean, you kill somebody, you kill 'em. The reasons don't matter—"

"No, no—" She raised a hand. The eye visible to him was squeezed shut, as if in pain. "Don't say that, Tony. Don't think it. You're not like he is. Nor will you ever be."

He swallowed before answering. "Heard and acknowledged, ma'am." He got to his feet. It was late, and he was eager to go. "I'll let you rest now. See if I can get some myself too."

But he stood rooted, as if something was left unsaid, something crucial, something else that had to be put into words. "Only . . ." He raised a hand to his lips, cast his eyes about the room, in search of what was missing. "I want you know . . ."

And there it was, pouring out of him: the reason for his hesitance, his reluctance to appear, the time he'd wasted before coming. "I know what's wrong too, Jay. And . . . and I'm gonna take care of it. Lady. I clean my own goddamn messes. I brought 'em here and I'll . . . I'll chase 'em away."

He went on, his voice tight, looking everywhere but at the figure on the bed. "I'll make it up to you. All of it. I swear . . ."

"Tony." He looked up at last, to see a hand extended toward him. "Come here."

He held her lightly, praying that he did not hurt her. He thought of his mother, of Moriah, of all the women he'd had or wished to have. She kissed him twice on the cheek before finding his lips. Her breath was sweet as a child's.

She drew away, holding his head in both hands. "You've taken my cares upon you . . . And you're a boy, Tony. You're just a boy." Then they were cheek to cheek for one long instant before she lay back on the bed.

"Tell me, Tony," she said as he rose to his feet. "Is there a girl?"

"Yeah," he said quietly. "There . . . was. Hope there still is. Moriah."

A smile flickered, marked with wryness. "There's something I ought to tell you, but . . . No, it'll wait."

He touched his head, made a face when his fingers met his cap. "Forgot I had this on," he said apologetically.

"Don't worry about that. I like your cap."

He took it off, balanced it on one hand. "Pretty ragged, these days."

"I like it."

Slipping it back on, he made a saluting motion. "I'll see you tomorrow."

"Good night, Tony."

She called out just as he reached the door. "Yeah?"

"One thing: when the envoy appears. If it doesn't look human, it's not. Kill it."

He regarded her a moment, then nodded and let himself out.

"—this shit. Midnight and we're diggin'. Witchin' hour, my hairy—"

Tony stalked across the patio. "Here," he said. "Gimme a shovel."

Three feet down, Braes stared up at him in surprise, then back at his shovel. "Nah, Ton. I'm just pissin'. That's all." His partner looked over his shoulder. "And don't bother tellin' us about the back, Perin. We know there's gotta be one in back too."

Behind him, Dud Mos cleared his throat. He was looking at his watch. "Four hours till kickoff, chief."

"Right." Tony stepped over and clapped him on the arm. "Hang tight."

He headed on downhill. A cry rang out and he looked back to see a shovel being waved. "Hey, Ton—changed my mind."

Waving him off, Tony went on his way. He had nearly reached the gate before he realized that he was heading for the plaza itself, not the safe route following the wall. Pausing only a moment, he stepped onto the pavement. His boots rang loud in the stillness. The only other sound was the clink of spades, slowly fading behind him. It was dark; no lights on at the Academy, a flicker of a fire at the labs, a soft glow over the village, silhouetting the bulk of the station. He walked on slowly, wondering if anyone was watching, not caring if they were.

He thought of what Julia had said, about the race's long apprenticeship back on Earth. Could it be true? It sounded as if it must be, but then a lot of things did. He wasn't quite certain that the exact truth mattered here. After all, they had learned somewhere that there was a difference between sanity and mania, the decent and the vile, virtue and dust. That there was a difference, and that the difference meant something, meant everything. If that was myth, then so be it—myth would have to serve where truth could not.

A vagrant wisp of wind grabbed at him, nearly taking his cap. Clutching at it, he lowered his head. He caught sight of a peculiarity, a patch of slate darker than the rest, right next to one of the raised blocks that served as benches. He went over to it, knowing what it was even as he crouched down to touch it: her blood, the blood she had left here the other day, when all this had started.

He knew at that moment that it was not a myth, that nothing had ever been truer. He saw them, in his mind's eye, with the clarity of a vision: those beings of the flatlands drier and hotter than anything he had ever known, not yet human but bearing the lineaments of what they would become. They were driving the wrong one away, flourishing the sticks that were the only things distinguishing them from beasts. Knowing that the band could not survive with such a horror in its midst: the betrayer, the liar, the one who killed to no purpose but his own. The

Enemy, in a word. They watched him fade into emptiness, victors in the first skirmish of the neverending war.

Palm against the cold slate, he glanced back at the house, thanking the beloved sleeper for what she had given him. It was his myth now; it would guide him as long as he lived.

He got to his feet. Overhead there was a break in the clouds. He saw stars and . . . he squinted: a line of light, dim and faded, curving slightly as it reached for the zenith.

Clouds covered it as the hole swept on. Tony shivered and headed for the labs, wondering if he'd get any sleep at all.

seventeen

He did get a couple of hours. It was still dark when Gen woke him shortly before sunrise. He went out to take a look at the sky. Still socked in, an open patch here and there, no sign of the clearing that Cary had promised. He gulped at his coffee, the harshest, bitterest brew he could recall drinking. He thought of his dad telling him how Julia had once mentioned that things tasted differently here. He wondered if Earth coffee could be as fierce as this. At least it would serve to wake him up.

The men were already on the move, through the buildings and out the back where they wouldn't be seen. He went over the route in his mind: a dip that would hide them almost until they reached the hills, then a half-mile march north before they doubled back across the road. The destination was that bowl just outside the village. A long, high ridge rose on the eastern side, running almost parallel to the highway.

There they'd stand, facing the Cloister, backs to the dawn.

The Mavericks were supplying security in the hills—at least he hoped they were. A quick question to Gen relieved his mind on that score: Cus had his men well distributed up there. Contact had been made, and the movement was progressing nicely; the first squad would cross the road in about fifteen. That left him only Ikler to worry about. Ikler could be a problem. The man was a hotspur—and none too bright either. Before riding off last night, he told Tony—big smile, as if pleased to have kept his surprise secret until the last possible second—that he could call in more cops if any were needed. Furious as that made him, Tony merely told him not to bother unless they could arrive by morning.

Finishing his coffee—down to the last foul dregs, a minor sacrifice to whatever deities might be watching this day—he went back inside. He made his way through the men giving a last check to their weapons, taping anything that might make a sound. A joke here, clap on the shoulder there. Not one of them looked worried or gave any sign of fear of what was to come. Somebody—Churchill? Thatcher?—had once said that it took two years to create a real soldier. That might be true, but by God, these would do until real ones came along.

They'd all picked up a Kalashnikov. Hard to refuse; they were fine-looking weapons. But Tony was pleased to see that most also retained their Stens. He was looking over one of the new guns—they weren't as wired as he'd feared, though they still had far more in the way of electronics than he was used to— when Gen tapped him on the shoulder.

"It's that Bili kid." Gen gestured over his shoulder. "He wants a gun."

Tony glanced across the room. The kid shuffled a

bit when Tony's eyes reached him. "Tell him—" Tony let out a blast of breath. "Tell him if somebody drops, he can pick up their piece. Not until then." He was unwilling to assign anyone to babysit an inexperienced man. But if things broke down—well, the kid would need a weapon then.

"Ain't gonna like it," Gen said. "Been buggin' me."

Tony caught Gen's sleeve. "What about his wife and kid?"

"Oh, they're comin' along. Can't leave 'em."

Tony nodded. It wasn't worth contemplating what would happen if they fell into the hands of the Rigs.

He left the building to check the line. A squad was to remain in the foxholes until first light, then pull back and split between the cybershack and the house. He took his time, making sure he visited each hole. These men would be the ones to bear the brunt if things went sour.

Heading back to the lab, he glanced at the house, lights still on, guards visible in front. He tore his eyes away. He had no time to spare even a thought for her.

Inside he spotted a dejected-looking clump of Cardnale's people in the hall. He'd completely forgotten about them; nice to see that somebody was thinking. He was passing with a brisk nod when he realized that somebody was missing. He went closer. The propaganda whiz, what's-his-name—Myk, that was it— gave him a sour look. Tony flicked a finger at him. "Where's that Resi?"

The kid shrugged "Got me." He obviously wasn't very happy at being dragged out at this hour.

"Where does she usually stay?"

"With us."

Tony shifted his stance, about to lose his temper.

"At the Core," the kid said quickly. One of the

girls shot a glance at him. Her expression was a little too smooth.

Tony regarded them a moment longer, then went to the nearest trooper. "Mac—do me a favor. Run over to the cybershack and tell them to search the place again. You know the one called Resi? Yeah—her. See if she's in there anywhere."

The last of the men were saddling up. He joined them. A moment later Cardnale's group was led past under close watch. One of them glanced at Tony and giggled. He was staring after them when Gen appeared. "Ready to ride," he said.

"Okay." Tony rubbed the back of his neck. "Can you think of . . . anything?"

"Not if you shot me dead."

Tony gave him a nod and turned to the men. Two dozen remained, all dressed in dark clothes, hats and caps pulled low. Tony shook his head. "You look like the ones the Rigs wouldn't take."

That earned him a nice volley of hoots and insults, a little more muted than they would have been under other circumstances. He submitted himself to it, then waved them forward. "Let's go."

"Light shirt, chief," somebody said in passing. So it was—but the windbreaker would take care of that. He went to grab it off the doorknob. They were halfway down the hall by the time he caught up.

They went out the fire exit and turned left, where the greenhouses would cover them. Tony looked around. Somebody was hurrying from the Core; that had to be Mac.

Reaching into his pocket, he put on the earpiece and asked the question he'd been dreading since waking up. "Cary. What's the weather look like?"

"As predicted, mein Field Marshal."

He released a slow breath. "Good. I'll keep in contact—"

"There's something you ought to know, mon Capitan. You may wish to take action on it."

Tony frowned. "What's that?"

"Vicki is on her way back."

Julia awoke thinking of Petro. It occurred to her, lying in the soft darkness, that there probably hadn't been a day in the last twelve decades that she'd neglected to think of him. She felt the old ache, startlingly deep and intense, nearly as sharp as on that first day of her long voyage, when she'd admitted to herself at last that he was not coming, that her life had closed completely, that she was alone.

She'd come across a phrase once for this sort of feeling. "Carrying a torch," it was called. She'd carried one, all right. Across full parsecs of space and more time than she could ever have imagined. She wished she could tell him that he'd be remembered, that she could go back, not to change things, but simply to let him know.

She switched on a light and sat up. Her pain seemed far away. It was there, no ignoring it, but it was very much secondary to what she was feeling in her heart. She smiled to herself. Was this another by-product of advanced age, a syndrome of ågathic treatments that appeared only after a century or more? Would she be required to relive all her losses, great and small, the emotions even more tearing than they'd been at the time? But would that be such a terrible thing? She admitted that it wouldn't.

The room was unchanged since last night. She raised a hand, recalling how Tony had crouched next to the bed. Her fingers spread as if to stroke his hair once again. A knock came at the door. "Yes."

The door opened and a bearded man leaned in. He touched the brim of his hat. "Hopin' I didn't disturb you, ma'am. I'm just lookin' in."

"Quite all right." She checked the time, heart leap-

ing as she remembered what Tony had told her last
night. "Have they—" She cast about for the proper
word—deployed? Advanced? "Have they started
yet?"

"Yes, ma'am." The man smiled, but his voice was
grave. "On their way. No problem so far."

"I'm glad."

"Don't you worry now. I'll keep you posted." He
stepped back, then hesitated. "Uh, can I get you
anything?"

"No. I've got tea right here."

"Good enough."

She lay back, feeling a little guilty. She wasn't alto-
gether certain that Cary would allow that tea if she
knew about it. But the answer to that was simple
enough: Julia wouldn't let her know.

"For the love of . . ." Tony saw heads jerk in front
of him. He lowered his voice. "What the hell are you
tellin' me?"

"Is it that difficult to understand, Perin? I thought
it was quite straightforward. Let's try again. Four
years ago, utilizing the large stock of natal machinery
taken off the ship—"

"No, I got all that—" Tony was not at all sure he
did. Controlled parthenogenesis? Fertilizing an ovum
with the subject's own cell nucleus? Biology wasn't
his field, not by a long shot. All the same, he'd picked
up enough in school to know that what he'd been
told was possible. "So she's a . . . clade, that the
word?"

"Close enough. This is a far simpler technique than
cloning, well understood since the beginning of the
21st century. You'll recall that Durga, the Maharani
of Hindustan, used it to create a dynasty of daugh-
ters—"

"How old is this kid?"

"Difficult question. Growth acceleration changes

the parameters, rendering the question of true age problematic. She was birthed three and a half years ago, but her apparent physical age is around ten. Mental age would be roughly six, but that's meaningless as well."

"How come nobody knows about it?"

"The med staff does. Also Chair Ramres, Milis, and Mrs. Burk, who oversaw her upbringing. Jay has a summer home on Cape Argent. Very isolated, very quiet. A perfect place to raise a child. Julia visited there quite often."

Mac caught up with him and matched his pace. Tony raised a hand to quiet him when he began to speak. "Last question, Cary: Why?"

"Another interesting query. Julia often keeps her motives hidden from me—or tries to; it's a difficult trick to bring off, considering how long I've known her, though she does on occasion surprise me. My guess—which I'll add is near to certainty—is that it was Jay's answer to you. The little problem you rebels have presented the past few decades. To speculate, I imagine that she was planning to convene a commission to discuss the situation, at which point she would in effect have abdicated, while at the same time introducing Victoria as her heir. That would have occurred, I estimate, about five years from now."

It would have worked. It would have pulled the teeth of the resistance as surely as if the bundiman had come out of the night and knocked them over the head. A new Lady Amalfi, fresh as the springtime, gorgeous as a new rose. Who could beat that? The public would have loved it. The dissident factions would have been falling all over each other trying to present themselves as the protectors of the young Dame. And the old one? Why, she'd have become a beloved, benign offstage presence, keeping to herself, minding her business, only now and then whispering in daughter Vicki's ear to make sure things were being done right.

He chuckled to himself. He'd have loved to see the look on Dan Cardnale's face when that happened. A thought occurred to him. "Cary—how come you didn't mess this project up too?"

"Hard to say," Cary said. "No—I wasn't going to use her, if that's what's on your mind. Not this child. She is stubbornness personified. She forced them to turn around and come back, didn't she? You think Julia is bad, you don't know—"

"Chief," Mac said, "they found her."

For a lunatic moment, Tony thought he was talking about Victoria. Then he remembered. "She was hidin' in there?"

"Yeah. Sleepin' room, out back. Funny—they told me they were sure they checked it . . . They got a guy watchin' her."

"Okay."

"Pardon me, Perin?"

"It's nothing, Cary. That goddamn Resi—" A prickling ran down the back of his neck. "Cary . . . how come you didn't know she was in the building?"

There was no answer. "Cary!"

"One moment, Admiral . . ."

He looked back at the Cloister. The Core was clearly visible. His jaw dropped as all the lights went out and a muffled slam reached him.

"There," Cary said. "All your men are outside—I used your voice to order them out—the doors are locked and the storm shutters are closed. Resi is disarming your little present under my direction even as we speak."

"Cary, look here—" Tony said desperately.

"Perin, let me be clear: I am not betraying you, I am not turning my coat, I am not letting you down.

Far from it. I'm with you until the climax. All that has changed is that I'm with you as an equal."

Tony felt Mac staring at him, aware that something crucial was happening.

"How would you feel if you had a gun to your head, little man? I intend to demonstrate to you that I am as trustworthy as any two-legged biological life-form. It's a lesson you need."

"Cary," he said through a dry throat. "I'm worried about this Resi—"

"I'm not. She was virtually second in command to Danil Cardnale for several years. And after all, she's not the one who put a bomb in my house."

Dan Cardnale—what a character reference that was. "Do me a favor, willya? Ease my mind a bit. Check her records. Find out—"

"Oh, the records? You mean the ones deliberately garbled by the civil disobedience campaign that began twenty-four years ago? Let's look at the records. Oh, here's a file from your town. The 110 census. George Washington, brain surgeon and secret agent. Married to St. Petronella, professional tooth fairy. They had 24.5 children. The half is due to one having two heads. Get the picture, Perin? And who started that campaign? The Right Reverend Wilis Crater, Monjoy Broz, and none other than Travis Perin! Do you think that George could have actually been Grandpa, Tony?"

Tony remained silent. There didn't seem to be much to say.

"What's up, Ton?" Mac asked. "Anything wrong?"

Tony shook his head. "Nah, nothing. Cary?"

"Yes, Imperator."

"I'll, uh, keep in touch."

"What about Victoria?"

"How far away is she?"

"Seventy miles south."

"It'll wait."

They'd nearly reached the hills. As Tony switched his stride to begin climbing, a figure to one side got up. "Tail end, eh?"

It was Shor. "Been waitin'. Got something for ye."

Tony reached for the black blotch that seemed to grow from the end of Shor's arm. He identified it by touch: a Rig beret. No; three of them. He nodded at the shapeless figure beside him.

"Come on. Take you to Cus."

Tony tossed the berets aside and followed him uphill.

Julia paused from brushing her hair. It hadn't been washed in days, and was greasy and full of snarls. "What do you mean you 'fixed Perin'?"

She listened silently while Cary told the story, feeling a flash of rage at the news about the explosives. She was sure that Tony had his reasons, but all the same, he had no business putting Midgard's entire future in jeopardy on his own authority.

". . . and he's *still* worried," Cary said cheerfully.

"Worried about what?"

"About Resi Bar, evidently. He thinks she's a Rigorist."

Julia ran the brush through her hair one more time. "Is she?"

"I doubt it."

"You're not sure, are you? That's why you're telling me this."

Several seconds passed before Cary answered. "What could she do in any case?"

Julia sighed. If the young woman was a Rigorist, the question was what *wouldn't* she do. She set the brush down. "Cary, can I get out of this bed?"

"I strongly advise against it, Jay."

Julia waited for the usual explanation. It wasn't forthcoming.

"And besides, you won't miss a thing. I'm going

to record it all. With every possible sensor. Orbital, local, environmental, everything. You'll see it more clearly than if you were there."

What a delightful idea that was. A clear, unobstructed view of a bloody battle. The crowning monument to Julia Amalfi's foolishness, in living color and 3-D holo, if she wanted it. About to tell Cary not to bother, she held herself back. She considered a moment, then pulled off the covers.

It was false dawn by the time Tony reached the ridge. He studied the sky beyond, but it was impossible to tell whether it was still cloudy or not. The soft gray glow washed out everything—star, cloud, or mirror.

He paced the crest of the ridge, repeating to the men that they were simply to show themselves and then back out of sight. "Don't make yourselves into targets, got it?" He repeated it so many times that it became condensed, the words falling in on themselves: "Don't make targets . . ." They nodded regardless. They all understood.

Near the end of the ridge he came upon Himi Franz, recognizing him more by the white of his bandages than anything else. "Frani!" he said. "What are you doing here?"

The old man shrugged. "Hell, Ton. You don't expect me to miss this, do ya?"

Tony had to admit he couldn't. Franz had gotten those wounds protecting the Lady, after all. Nevertheless, he wanted to tell the old man to keep down, to watch out for himself, to let the kids bear the main burden. He didn't. Franz would do exactly what he needed to do, no more and no less. Touching him on the shoulder, Tony headed back up the ridge.

He halted at the rough center and gazed out over the Cloister. It was still night down there, even as the first light of dawn seeped over the horizon be-

hind him. He studied the place that would be con-
nected with him for all time to come, for good or ill.
His Gaugamela, or his Waterloo. His Inchon, or his
Gettysburg. The mask of command, that strange
expansion of spirit that he could neither explain nor
describe, settled upon him. It was as if, somewhere
in the realm of the absolutes, there was a larger Tony
Perin, a better, harder, and more complete man, who
had only sporadic contact with the fragment that
walked Midgard. A man stronger in both muscles
and soul, with eyes that looked farther, saw more,
and in greater detail than the stunted senses of the
lesser one. If asked, he could tell exactly what was
going on behind him, and when he turned to look,
he would see just that. If asked, he could predict the
events of the day to come, and they would occur just
as he'd foretold.

He wondered if Fredrix ever felt the same. It was
possible that he did—when he was planning a
purge, maybe.

The light grew, revealing the bulk of the steamer,
beyond it the great tree, the plaza, and, its windows
still bright, the house of the Lady. He thought of
Athena, the true patron of war. The conflict of rational men, men with goals and limits, who never
crossed the line that marked the edge of civilization.
Mars was the god of barbarian warfare, brutal and
squalid. The Rigs' kind of war.

A man in uniform approached him, the cop assigned as the liaison to Ikler's people. He lifted a
handset, telling Tony that he'd received word that
the police were in place. Tony nodded and, with a
casualness he did not feel, turned toward the rising
sun. The rest of the men were already looking in that
direction, intently inspecting a sky that revealed only
a small section of blue beneath the gray-white clouds.

Cary had told him she needed twenty percent

clear. Was that one-fifth? He couldn't tell. "Cary? What's it look like?"

No sound came from the earpiece. Instead a dozen sparks flickered once in the deep blue.

Julia paused with one sleeve still dangling. A robe was the only thing for today; the one item of clothing that made any sense. All the same, she'd taken out her jumpsuit, the one that she'd worn aboard the ship and in the early years. Virtually indestructible, impossible to tear or stain. It seemed important somehow that she wear it this morning.

The effort of getting it on had exhausted her. She could see now why Cary wanted her to remain in bed. She felt sharp pains under the smart pads on her stomach and chest and an overriding sense of exhaustion that had nothing to do with how much sleep she'd had. Perhaps she'd rest a little before stepping out.

She forced the suit on the rest of the way. The front sealed, the fabric adjusting itself to contours that differed somewhat from the last time she'd worn it. She felt a spidery sensation on her skin as the suit adapted to the ambient temperature. Leaning back, she shut her eyes for a moment. At last she felt up to leaving the room.

"Jay," Cary said as she got to her feet.

"Yes, bossy."

"Oh—I can't change your mind when you're like this. But you sit down out there and keep quiet. You hear me?"

The door opened ahead of her. "I'm not planning on calisthenics, dear."

The men outside turned as one when she appeared, nodding and touching their hats. She looked them over. It was extraordinary how close she felt to them now, grubby, unshaven, and wild-looking though they might be.

It was growing light outside. She went to the older man who appeared to be in charge. He gestured at the window. "Be a little while before—"

His last words were cut off by a wave of sound that began to their left and moved steadily down the plaza and across to the college, increasing in volume as it went. The cry of the Rigorists. "Or maybe it won't at that," he said and headed for the door.

Tony slipped the gun from his holster and cracked the cylinder. He usually loaded only five rounds, leaving an empty chamber for the hammer—you had to, on a wheelgun—but today he'd need every shot. He popped in a cartridge and slapped the gun closed. Cary had been persistent in explaining that the pistol wasn't an original Colt design at all, but one heavily modified in the centuries since. He didn't know what the big deal was. It was a gun. It shot bullets. What the hell else did he need?

He glanced at the cop, who nodded back amiably. "You're a Chains man?" Tony asked him.

"Yeah. East Chains, near Blakhil." He tapped the insignia on his jacket shoulder, which read DYSVIL. "This don't mean nothin'. I got drafted. Not even a cop really. Emergency Reserves. I farm."

"What you growing out there?"

"Ah, they had us raising sugar beets last season."

"Oh boy." The beets harvest had been miscalculated, with several hundred thousand tons overproduction. A lot of people had gone broke.

"Well, they're holdin' my loan, like with everybody, but I mean—" The cop shook his head in disgust.

"I know. What you thinking this year?"

"Soybeans. That's right. Got a cousin down the Shore, told me they needed the oil last year, and guess what?"

"Couldn't get it."

"Yes, sir. But now we got the fool Ag Committee off our backs . . . What's the word up the Plateau?"

"Well, my dad told me—"

He was cut off by an outbreak of yipping from the Cloister. He took a step forward, as if out to quell the disturbance in person. Dim figures appeared, dancing and capering across the plaza, beneath the tree, in the streets of the village.

For the last time, Tony ran the possibilities through his mind. Every alternative, anything at all that could go wrong. They were covered on the southern flank; no attack would come from the Academy. Ikler and the Mavericks were in place. The highway . . . he glanced north. He should have put a patrol up there, a roadblock . . . But there was no sense worrying about it now.

He waved at the man behind the rocket launcher to his right. Not the full, eight-round Katy—that would have been too noisy to haul out of the Cloister. But it was designed to be broken down into sections, and he'd brought two along, mounted on tripods. "The steamer," he called. The man bent to the sight. "Make it count," Tony muttered.

The yipping vanished beneath a roar of combustion, and a finger of fire reached for the steamer. It died out halfway there, and Tony was certain it had missed . . . But then the steamer blew apart, chunks of the boiler flung wide, a huge cloud of white steam rising from the dark ground.

The cavorting Rigs froze in position, then ran to the station house. A few seconds later a small group crept from behind the building. "Up!" Tony shouted.

The men rose as one. For a full minute, the Rigs regarded them in silence. At last they retreated toward the building.

Those had to be officers . . . Tony waved at the second launcher. "Hit 'em!"

Another rocket howled forward, striking a few

yards from the Rigs. All of them fell. One rose a moment later to crawl into shelter.

Tony waved the men back. All along the ridge they withdrew far enough to be protected. Only Tony remained where he was, atop the military crest, in full view of the Cloister.

For a time silence reigned. No activity was visible; the place appeared as abandoned as it had been when Tony first caught sight of it. He bit his lip, paced a few feet. A feeling of despair crossed with anger gripped him. Fredrix was doing the smart thing; he was staying put, behind the walls of the station, scattering his forces around the Cloister. Tony would have to go down and pry him out . . .

Then a yammering reached him, barely audible above the mild morning breeze. He bent forward, as if that would somehow draw the sound closer. "Cary—what's that?"

The earpiece blared: ". . . sacrifice of all imperfect monads. Sacrifice. That is what the Will requires. It will anneal the Collective, alloy it . . . Enable it to attain a new and higher form . . ."

They poured on, words one step from gibberish, words that were not words, words drained of all meaning. Tony felt his face take on an expression that he himself would not have recognized, that would have startled those who knew him.

"Is he coming out?" Gen called from his section down the ridge.

"He's coming," Tony shouted back, and repeated, more quietly, "he's coming."

"Perin."

"Cary, what—"

"Don't interrupt. You were correct. I . . . Well, listen."

Another voice came over the earpiece, a woman's voice, loud and angry: ". . . I know you're cooperating with those deviants. Put me in touch with the Herald *now*, machine . . ."

The voice cut off. "I'll hold her as long as I can." Cary was speaking faster than any human could, though somehow the words came through distinctly all the same. "Note that individual mirrors are inaccurate at less than a fifty-yard radius and act accordingly. I'm working on several alternatives and will be fully occupied. Do not try to contact me, apart from giving me the mark. Luck."

"Cary—" He wanted to tell her to lift the shutters, to let his men back in . . . But it was no good. Resi— and who knew what her real name was, or if it had any resemblance to those two syllables?—was a Rig, a monad, no more than dust. "Sacrifice," Fredrix had said . . . Her own survival would mean nothing to her.

"I'm sorry, Cary," he said.

The yipping erupted once again, louder and more frantic than he had ever before heard it. Tony drew his gun. He thought of Integral, trying to picture him shouting in such a manner. The image refused to gel. He stiffened at a hint of movement behind the station. But the Rigs remained out of sight. A volley of shots came from the village, accompanied by shouting and shrieks. Dark shapes raced among the buildings. He saw doors yanked open, pale figures forced onto the main street, their numbers swelling as they went. Lowering his gun, Tony frowned, then gave a small gasp as puzzlement dissolved before certainty. He swore as the first Bilis came into sight at the end of the spur leading to the highway. A howling ragged crowd of them, six or seven deep, followed by the black tide that pushed them farther into the open.

Tony bent to the man nearest him. "Shoot over their heads. Got that? Pass it on!"

He swept his eyes along the line as the word moved down. A few men glanced at him, their ex-

pressions hesitant. He swung back to the field, studying the oncoming horde, ignoring the sobbing faces,
trying to view it only as a situation. Six, seven hundred Rigs, more than he'd guessed, less than he'd
feared. They were coming straight from the village,
with no attempt at finesse or maneuver, trailing close
behind their shield. Perin the warrior, Perin the mask
was pleased with what he beheld. No generalship
was visible here; tactics and strategy were beyond
them. They knew nothing but mass, understood
nothing but numbers. They were good for wiping
out helpless Dunkers and that was about all.

A shot, unaimed and wild, whipped past him. He
threw an involuntary glance at the Core, pausing for
a closer look. Something was going on over there: he
saw a gleam reflecting off the building's antennas
and what appeared to be a dim beam of light against
the darkness beyond.

But the Rigs were closing, and he had no time left.
The front ranks of the Bilis, waving their arms wildly
and shouting unheard pleas, were less than two hundred yards distant. He counted off five seconds, as
insurance against fear acting for him, then said
aloud, "Now."

Enough time passed to assure him of betrayal.
Then light bloomed behind him.

He caught a glimpse of his own shadow sweeping
across the field before the beam of a second mirror
washed it out. The Bilis stopped short, hands clapped
to their eyes, the front rank dropping as those to the
rear collided with them. Behind them, the Rigs did
the same. Tony thought of rising birds as their pale
hands came into sight.

The glare increased further, forcing Tony to squint.
He raised his pistol and opened his mouth to shout.
But instead he stepped forward, almost a leap, and
his arm came down and a single shot rang loud.

Around him, the entire ridge erupted with fire.

*   *   *

"Jay!" Cary cried out.

Her voice was coming from one of the med units in the bedroom; Julia had forgotten the earpiece. "Coming," she said and attempted to get up. She rose only an inch or two before dropping back into the chair. A rebel boy came over to help her up. "I'm fine now," she told him when it appeared that he was planning to half-drag her across the atrium.

"Jay—" Cary repeated as she reached the door.

"I'm here, darling," Julia said. As she retrieved the earpiece, she listened to Cary's rapid, disjointed explanation. She closed her eyes. "Oh no . . ."

"I'm frightened, Jay. I don't understand her. It's as if she's another person. She was so nice before."

Yes, she would have been. Far nicer than any regular person; all foibles and personal quirks buried beneath an all-consuming fanaticism. She'd probably been trained for the role since she'd been a little child.

"I've contacted the ship," Cary said in a firmer voice. "I'm speaking to St. John now. I think—"

"That's fine, Cary," Julia replied, though she couldn't quite see the point. "Wait . . ." She swung to the door. "Captain—"

"Ma'am?"

Behind her, Cary cried out, "Yes . . . *yes!*" in that distorted way she did when she was overexcited. Julia ignored her while she explained the situation. "You understand, Captain? You must take your men to the Core. Through the tunnel. Locate that young woman and . . . Do what you must."

He shook his head. "I'm sorry, ma'am, I can't do that—"

She took a step toward him. "I'm not asking you, sir."

"Ma'am, you ain't been well—"

Julia drew herself up. "Well or not, I am the Dame of Midgard still."

The man's eyes widened, and he appeared to shrink. "I . . . yes, ma'am." He made a shallow gesture toward the hall leading to the basement door. The men ran past him. He touched his hat and followed them. Julia remained erect until they were out of sight, then stepped back, one hand reaching behind her for support. A man appeared from the hallway, hurrying over to push a chair beneath her. "There you go, ma'am."

"Dic told us to stay," he said, gesturing at the two others behind him. "Said it was necessary. Anyway, it's only the one girl over there, and it won't take—"

He was cut off by a volley of shots from outside, one striking the window before whistling away. The men outside began to return fire. Julia clutched the chair arms. "Good idea," she said.

The Bilis were all down now, most covering their heads, many crawling for the shelter of the ridge. The Rigs that had fallen—dozens, scores of them— weren't crawling anywhere. But beyond them the rest still stood, firing aimlessly into the blaze of light before them, some trying to move forward through the cowering mass of Bilis. They got only a few steps before falling.

Tony glanced across the ridge while he reloaded. The boys were doing their jobs, taking their time, making sure they had a target before firing. Only a few had been hit; a man here and there lay on the ground or crawled toward the protection of the rear face. A few yards away, a kid he'd spoken to only a couple of times was having trouble with his gun. He was firing on full auto, and it was getting away from him. Running over, Tony shouted at him to switch to single shot. The kid was looking helplessly at the rifle when an older man reached over and pressed a tab on the side. "Tell it, 'Single.'" The kid did and took a shot. "Better," he mouthed at Tony.

Some of the others were having trouble reloading. He'd been afraid of that, but it didn't seem to be making much of a difference. Nothing would as long as the mirrors remained aligned. He stole a glance at the Cloister. That strange shaft of light remained visible above the Core. His gaze was caught by activity around the house. He turned his head. No time . . .

A man fell a few steps to his right. His buddies lowered their guns and turned to help him. Tony was close enough to see the white and red ruin of the back of his head. "Let him be," he said.

He raised his eyes to the Rigs. They weren't breaking. They ought to be breaking; any normal army would have broken already. They were dropping, falling through the ten thousand doors of death as he watched, but they wouldn't break. He ought to call in Ikler; he'd told him to stand fast until they collapsed. But he'd lost the cop—the dark gray uniform was nowhere in sight. Finding a clear spot, he raised the pistol. They'd pound all day, if that was what it took. All the sickening, bloody hours that remained. As long as the mirrors held out . . .

A roar erupted, deafening even over the hurricane of gunfire. He knew precisely where to look, and he was not mistaken. He watched the shattered dome of the Core shoot skyward, trailing fingers of smoke and debris. He wondered briefly what had happened. Had the girl figured it out for herself? Had she gotten an order from Fredrix? Had it been an accident? It didn't matter.

"Cary," he whispered. There was no answer. Plucking off the earpiece, he let it fall.

He stepped forward. The mirrors wouldn't hold for long; light pressure would force them to drift, and they had no correcting mechanism that worked at this fine a level. But another few minutes, half an hour . . .

It was too much to ask. Directly to his left, he saw a line of shadow creeping over the bodies of the Bilis.

The gunshots in front had died away, the few that still came were nearly lost in the sustained chatter from the ridge. On one knee, the young man left in charge stretched to look out the window, having spent the past five minutes trying to persuade Julia to go back into the bedroom.

"Looks okay now."

"Yes." Julia touched the earpiece. It had been a while since she'd heard from Cary. She'd been waiting for the sound of an explosion, at times almost convinced she'd actually heard it. But when it came, it would be unmistakable, she was sure.

The boy was getting to his feet when it did come. Julia found herself on her back, ears ringing. Looking about her, she saw that the boys had also been flattened, scattered across the floor with dazed expressions on their faces. She tried to rise, but a tearing pain beneath her ribs forced her back down on one hip. This wasn't right; the blast couldn't have been that—

Black shapes loomed out of the smoke pouring from the bedroom. One boy was now sitting up. He raised his gun and opened fire. A burst from the Rigorists spun him against the wall. Another fired and was answered with a wild fusillade. Julia screamed as a bullet tore though her leg.

Squinting through pain, she saw that the Rigorists had all been hit. Someone outside was shouting—she ought to open the door. Then a black form moved, its head rising to reveal a slash of a mouth; bulging, lifeless eyes.

The boy she had just been speaking to stirred at Julia's feet. On all fours, Unity crawled over to him.

She fumbled for something at her belt. A hand appeared clutching a knife. Rising to a squat, Unity lifted the blade high.

"No!" Julia cried out as the knife dropped. The boy had been moaning; it faded to a liquid gurgle. She closed her eyes. A caw of pain forced them open a second later. Unity was bent almost double, her mouth opened wide by ragged breaths, one hand jammed into the crease formed by thigh and belly. As Julia watched, the hand slipped out dripping blood.

Unity stared at it a moment. She tried to wipe it clean on her shirt, whimpering all the while. Julia moved, unable to prevent herself from doing so. Catching the motion, Unity looked up. Their gazes locked. Unity began to pull herself toward Julia.

"Jay, what's—" her earpiece said.

The rumble of a second explosion shook the Cloister.

All the mirrors were drifting now. Only two had slipped dangerously so far, opening distinct arcs of shadow among the Rigs, but the rest were going. Tony raced along the crest, ordering the men down, telling them to concentrate their fire on the unlit sections below.

The Rigs were pulling themselves together. Their ranks closing up, the gaps blown wide by gunfire narrowing and vanishing as troops poured in from the illuminated areas. They weren't advancing yet; that was still to come. Instead they were pulling themselves together and taking careful aim at their tormentors above. Decrepit as their guns might be, their fire was beginning to tell: Tony could see at least a dozen men lying still on the crest.

He tried to encompass the number of Rigs remaining. Four hundred? Five? He couldn't tell, and it didn't matter—it was still too many. But he'd considered this too. Thought it over as carefully as any easy victory. He had an alternative. There was always an alternative to disaster.

He clapped the man next to him on the back. "We're going in," he said. "Tell 'em."

Looking in the opposite direction, he caught sight of Gen, crouching as he was. Tony lifted his gun, jerked it quickly down. Gen waved acknowledgment and began to tell his men.

Tony paused in turning away. Between him and Gen he saw the Bili kid, awkwardly aiming a rifle, wincing as he fired it. The whistle of a shot drew his attention back to the Rigs. Their masses were swelling, about to burst across the short gap facing them and then on up and over the slope. Almost directly below he saw a Rig deliberately take aim and shoot a crawling Bili.

That was enough. He got to his feet, the men rising beside him. He spared them a glance, wishing he could tell them how good they had been, that nobody had ever been better, wishing he could thank them. He looked down again, noticing, as he took his first step, that one of the mirrors had shifted so far as to be shining on the village. It looked soft and warm from this distance, the light of morning in early summer.

Then, better to fall once than be forever falling, he was racing downhill, mouth wide and howling. The black-clad ranks beneath him resolved with a clarity formerly unknown to him: the hands pointing, the gun barrels glinting as they shifted toward him, then gleaming, then shining blindingly as the beam slid from the village back into the eyes of his enemies.

The rifles cracked. The rounds split the air around him, plucked at him, tore at the earth beneath his feet, and then he was through that curtain and running as fast as possible, barely fast enough to keep his legs from going out from under him.

*   *   *

Julia saw nothing but the med symbols and the dark shape of the girl beyond. The system was red-lined, one warning following another, the immediate attention blinker flashing wildly. Julia shut it off—she didn't need that to grasp what was being done to her.

Someone was banging on the door and shouting. She opened her mouth to answer, but only a gasp escaped. She was far beyond pain now, in another realm that had no connection with the one in which she'd lived the rest of her life.

The knife crossed her field of vision, red from tip to handle. She caught the hand that gripped it, held it for a moment. Then her own hand was plucked away and set down almost gently. "You . . ." the girl said. ". . . debased . . ."

The word was swallowed up by deep, hacking coughs. She felt the weight of the girl against her hip. The banging on the door grew louder.

The girl straightened up once again. "Unity . . ." Julia forced out. "Please . . ."

"We are allowed . . . what others are not allowed," the girl said in a nearly conversational tone. "Because we . . ." She looked about as if searching for something. Both her hands were raised, and Julia realized that she'd dropped the knife.

Somehow she found it again and bent to continue her work, muttering about the Will, and the Herald, and, horribly, of monad Tony.

"Jay . . . ?"

Julia reached out and clutched something, a part of the girl's shirt. "Child . . ." she said. "I am your mother."

"*Jay—*" It was Cary's voice, very distant now. Julia was about to answer when she realized that the earpiece had fallen away.

Unity had paused. She was staring at Julia, her

mouth slightly open. Julia noticed that there was blood on her chin.

A roar came from the bedroom. "Monad!" Fredrix shouted. "What deviant conduct is contemplated here? The woman is the female expression of the Will. Suspend these actions immediately."

The girl looked uncertainly at the knife, then up at Julia. Their eyes met once again. Her fingers opened and the blade fell. She reached for Julia's hand. There came a clatter from the basement, the sound of voices.

"Monad—"

Unity placed Julia's hand over her own wounds. Holding it there with both of her own, she threw her head back and burst into tears.

The older rebel, face and shoulders covered with dust, stepped around the corner. The burst from his gun cut through the girl's sobbing and threw her across Julia.

Then the weight was removed, and Julia's rebel boys were around her, their voices choked and harsh. Another joined theirs: "Jay! Jay, it's all right . . . I'm here. Oh . . . I'll explain it to you—"

"I'm so glad, baby," Julia said as she clasped Cary's hand, knowing her mistake only when she felt the bulk of it, and the strength, realizing at last that it was Petro's hand, that he had come as he had promised, that they were together, the three of them, the way it should always have been.

A Bili grabbed at his leg. Tony kicked him away, nearly going to one knee before he caught his balance. A Rig who seemed to be aiming at him clutched his belly and went down. The one beside him was raising his rifle. Tony fired but couldn't see if he'd hit.

He reloaded, dropping a palmful of cartridges in the process, cursing himself for not buying an automatic after all. Around him, the men fired on. They'd dropped their Kalashnikovs on the ridge and were now using their Stens.

The Rigs were falling by the dozen. They died like children; like children, after all. In front of him, a girl crouched on her knees, hands over her face, screaming unheard under the roar of weapons until a burst threw her backward. Tony himself shot the boy behind her, pushing through the mass carrying a rifle as big as himself. But he did have a rifle—he *did*.

Break, he told them. Break. It's no good here, it's finished. Break . . . for the love of God, break.

He was hammering an empty cylinder. He grabbed for more cartridges, looking around as he did, seeing not Rigs or rebels, only murderous shapes in a fog of light. He squatted down to reload, and when at last he raised his eyes, it had happened: the faces were gone and the flashes of guns; he was looking at the backs of fleeing Rigs.

He went forward, stretching his legs to step over the piled corpses but trodding on them anyway. Men raced past him, shouting and laughing, pausing only to fire before moving onward. Horsemen appeared from the hills beyond, and to his right Cus Miler's men, streaming from the high ground to catch the Rigs on their flank.

He ran for a bit, then paused to catch his breath, hands on his knees. Pulling himself erect, he surveyed the field. A few steps away, a Rig boy sat soundlessly wagging his head, the white of bone clearly visible beneath a sheath of blood. Beyond him, another whimpered as she tried to burrow into the bodies piled beneath her. Tony nodded to himself. It had happened just as he'd thought it would. It had happened the way he'd wanted, because he'd wanted it to happen that way.

The men were far ahead. He squinted, searching the field, not knowing quite what he was searching for. He took a few steps, nearly stumbling over a body. A hand grabbed him from behind. He looked back to see that three men had stuck with him. He bobbed his head at them and went on.

He had nearly reached the highway when he saw what he wanted, in a grove of trees next to the village. Nearly invisible behind a clump of brush, the shape captured his eyes all the same.

He broke into a run, trotting awkwardly at first, speeding up with each step, not slowing even when he tore through the brush and swung his pistol in an arc that sent Fredrix's hat flying and knocked him sideways into the dirt.

He stared in bewilderment at the bulging eyes, the bloody wreckage of the face. A whimpering caught his attention. Kicking aside the metal chair, he approached something lying under one of the trees.

It was a Rig, that was clear enough. But that was as much as Tony could make out until he was standing over him, close enough to see the glasses, frames bent, lenses gone, lying beside a primitive automatic pistol. Tony crouched next to the man. "Integer . . ." He winced. "*Integral.* It's Perin."

"Perin." It was horrifying to see what was left of that face move. Tony looked away from it, unable to rest his eyes on any spot not slashed or stabbed. They had cut him to pieces.

"Perin," Integral repeated. A blood-caked hand rose toward him. "You . . . tell the Lady . . ."

"Yeah."

"You tell . . ." The hand dropped back. "I have no words."

"I think . . . I think I've got the words," Tony told him. "Yeah. I've got the words."

"Ah . . ." The man lay his head back. Tony reached out and touched his shoulder. It was then that he realized that two of his fingers were gone.

Integral gave a sigh and was still. Absently patting

him once more, Tony got to his feet. He gave the
injured hand a shake, as if that might be of help.
Turning to the men, he saw them looking back
toward the ridge. He followed their gaze. At some
unnoticed moment the mirrors had shifted. Instead
of that glare, he saw, several handbreadths above the
horizon, two blotches of light. The familiar short
dash of the *Petrel*, and beside it another object, twice
the size and strangely shaped.

A loud squeal sounded to his right. A steamer ap-
peared from around the bend, pulling two trailers.
As it braked, a spear of fire shot out from the ridge.
The blast knocked the steamer on its side.

Pulling out his pistol, Tony checked the cylinder.
"Let's go!" he shouted. They started running toward
the highway.

eighteen

The house hadn't been cleaned yet. The bodies were gone—he'd seen dead Rigs lying on the slope outside. But blood remained splattered all over the floor. You had to be careful when you moved. Tony had a horror of stepping in any of it—how could he be sure that it wasn't her blood?

He righted an upset chair and sat down. Men walked around, quiet, not saying much. Somebody handed him a cup. He sipped at it. Coffee; very good coffee. That's what the victor gets when he goes home. A damn fine cup of coffee.

Horses' hooves clopped on the stone outside. A moment later Ikler swept in. He was still wearing his rain cape, though it hadn't rained at all today, and had a smug grin on his face. Tony wondered if he'd heard about Julia yet. That would wipe the smirk away.

Ikler came to a halt in front of him, one leg pushed

forward, a thumb in his belt. "You may consider the western hills secured."

"How many prisoners?"

The smirk deepened. "I have no prisoners."

Tony regarded him a moment, recalling his promise to the dead woman in the other room. We are not like them, she'd said. Never will be. "*You* may consider yourself under arrest."

Ikler's hand clapped on his holster. But the men had him covered. He looked among them, then back to Tony. "I was only acting as necessity—"

Tony shot to his feet. "You were acting like a goddamn Rig—" Catching himself, he dropped back into the chair. If he cut loose on this man, there was no knowing how it would end. "Get him out of here."

The men had already disarmed him and were ushering him outside. He said something about talking to the Lady. They had gotten him to the door when he jerked away. " '*Dead*'? What do you mean, 'dead'?"

Tony rubbed his forehead. The nerve shunt on his wrist hit him in the nose. He eyed the casing, the bandages, wondering how long he'd have to wear them.

"I want to see her!"

Tony gestured to the men. They led Ikler past. The smile was gone, sure enough.

Closing his eyes, Tony let his head fall back. What was to be done, then? What was to be done? Ikler was cutting them down even before he'd heard about Julia—and him a cop. Easy enough to imagine how the rest of the planet would feel. He felt it too. He pictured himself riding north, piling body on body, leaving a trail of red behind him, like an injured slug.

There was no putting it off. Tomorrow. Hand or no hand. Secure the Cloister and move out. Pick up men as he went along. The Orcs were finished, for all practical purposes. Thirty of them dead, the same number wounded. Si Braes was gone, and Dud Mos, and Nik Ravi—it had been a bad day for musicians. Bil Womak was dying—no way he'd make it, the shape he was in. Rab Obrin had fought his final argument with Cary. Tony had seen old Franz being carried back to the Cloister, face drained white, hands trailing in the dirt. He was unsure whether Frani was wounded or dead. Nobody else seemed to know either.

He'd build them up again, but it would never be the same. No choice, so no problem. That was how Cary had put it. He had to consider the AI situation too, didn't he? Get hold of the techs, see what they could salvage—if anything. But where were they? The Islands, the Shore? And what about the child?

He rubbed his face once again. He could see where he was headed. He would become a black shadow across the history of his world. Midgard's iron chancellor; harsh, ruthless, constantly pushing them on, forcing them to survive without a database, without a working AI, without the bare minimum that a civilization required. Their descendants would look back on Julia's time as a golden age. They would curse the men who had brought it to an end. His hand fell to his thigh. Yet even in this, he would still be serving her. That is, if the ship . . .

A sharp blast sounded outside, followed by a low rumble growing louder as he listened. Gen rushed through the door. "Chief—"

Tony got to his feet.

. . . if the ship gave them the chance.

He walked out onto the patio, the rest of the men close behind. He didn't have to search; there was no way he could have missed it. An arc of fire, springing from some point far over the western horizon, thickening as it drew near, the object at its end growing from a dot to a cone, finally sprouting flames as it passed above the highway and settled onto the open fields beyond the Academy.

The roar wasn't as great as Tony would have expected; nowhere near as intense as the rumble of the great ships in the records. All the same, the craft was enormous, far larger than *Petrel*'s shuttles. It loomed high over the buildings of the Academy, fully two-thirds of its length visible.

He wondered what would emerge. Something beyond experience, something unrecognizable, an entity born and matured in that caldron that Julia had left behind. Something impossible to resist, to whom resistance would have no meaning; the devil that rules in the air.

The men were talking, their voices hushed, as if afraid the vessel might hear them. Tony could detect the choked tones of panic beginning to build. He raised a hand to calm them.

The chatter died in a mass gasp as a vehicle appeared, meandering through the Academy buildings. An oval shape, no wheels that Tony could see. A single figure sat near the front. The vehicle swept over the plaza walls and turned toward the house. Dust and leaves blew gently out of its path as it passed through the gate. Drawing his pistol, Tony went to meet it.

The figure sat quietly for a moment after the vehicle set down. Tony looked it over closely, unable to decide if it was a man or a woman or something else entirely. A scarf was tied over its head, holding down what seemed to be long braids. As it got out, Tony saw it was wearing a robe of many colors reaching almost to its feet. One hand was encased in a glove.

The figure took a few steps up the slope, moving with a distinct limp. Behind it floated an ovoid, much like the one Tony had seen last night. Coming to a halt, the man—it was a man, that much was clear now—looked around uneasily. A gun clicked to

Tony's left. The man jerked his head in that direction, then stared wide-eyed at Tony. There was something odd about his right eye.

"So it's guns, is it?" he called out. "All guns. That's your way on this world. That's all you know."

He was horribly afraid. Tony saw that clearly. Somehow fear and the Erinye didn't mix very well. He'd never heard of them displaying fear. Julia hadn't said anything about that. He let the barrel drop, jerked it up again when the ovoid shot past the man and on up the slope.

"Tony!" It called out in Cary's voice. "Where is Jay?"

He said nothing, so she must have read his face. Coming to a dead stop, the machine emitted an electronic wail made up of screeches and discords, expressing all desolation, all loss of hope. The man raced over and went to his knees. He spoke to the machine, his voice lost beneath the dissonance. At last Cary went silent and the ovoid sank softly to the ground.

The gloved hand remained atop the casing for a second before the man rose and came ahead. "I've safemoded her for now," he told Tony. He was speaking rapidly, as if anxious to be understood. "They're so terrified of death. It's . . . horrible to them. You're aware? I'll bring her back in a few days, but it will take time."

Tony inspected the man's face—the mesh of metallic filaments covering the entire orb of his right eye, the cross at his throat. He was like Julia, in a way—his face thin, features sharp, the one visible eye round and wide. But he actually reminded Tony of someone else. Someone he'd known at some time or other; he couldn't think of who.

"Don't be alarmed," the man said. He gestured toward his eye. "This is genetic damage. And this as well." He flexed the gloved hand.

Tony nodded. "You're St. John, then?"

"Yes. And you must be Perin. Cariola mentioned you." St. John pointed at the house. "Might I see the Lady?"

"Sure." Tony turned to lead the way. Around them, the men stood with their guns lowered. He caught Gen's eye as he passed and gave him a shrug.

"The Erinye left considerable genetic havoc behind them, along with all else." The man raised his glove again, and for a moment Tony was afraid he was going to reveal what lay beneath it. He didn't need to see.

"Much of it is beyond correction. Such attempts can be disastrous. Even worse surprises are buried in the introns, to be triggered by therapy. We've learned to live with it."

"So there was such a thing as the Erinye."

"Oh yes. It was a terrible period." St. John stopped at the door. "We were . . . less than candid with Cariola. We had to be. Care is essential in recontact. The Erinye were successful at Ophir, you know. They've enslaved the place for over a century. We lost a ship there. A task force will be reaching the system in about three years. A final skirmish."

Tony went on inside. "So you were worried about us?"

"Yes. Particularly after Cariola's ruse in orbit . . . You don't know? I'll explain it you. Oh, we saved her by laser transfer. All her personality ware. Operational files were left behind, but those are backed up. When we examined her—when Potnia, our ship's AI, did—we realized there was no danger."

They had reached the bedroom. St. John paused at the door, making a ritual cross over himself, as a Roman would. Only then did he step inside. Tony remained where he was. He'd looked in earlier, just for a second, unwilling to go farther. At last he forced himself past the threshold.

He'd been relieved to see that they had done nothing to her face. That was important. He would not have been able to bear it if anything had been done to her face. St. John crouched next to the bed. "Don't be offended," he said. He drew off his glove. A gleaming mechanism was revealed, changing shape as Tony watched. "This must be done."

He touched the curved appendage to Julia's scalp. "Virtually no mods," he muttered. "An integrator, that's all. Now . . ."

Bowing his head, St. John hummed to himself for a moment. With a small gasp he jerked the prosthetic away. At that moment Tony became aware of who it was St. John called to mind. His stiffness, his quietness, his air of preoccupation: it was Integral. Tony touched the shattered glasses in his vest pocket. He'd tell St. John the story later. He had a feeling that he'd appreciate it.

"It hasn't been accessed," St. John whispered. He looked at Tony, an expression of wonder suffusing his face. "Not in all that time. It could not have been. It's packed with Erinye viroid. Every data string has been overwritten. The Eyre program, the same that subjugated Ophir. If she'd tapped it but once—" He reached out again. "There . . . it's gone."

"Gone," Tony repeated. He went to the bed at last. She lay with one hand crossing her breast, the other beside her. He left them as they were; there was a kind of perfection in that too.

"She's remembered, you know," the man behind him said. "Novichenko, Braystrup, Garcia, Amalfi . . . The ones who uncovered the Erinye. We had no idea she escaped." He paused a moment. "You were blessed with her."

Yes, that was the word: blessed. He bent down and ran a single finger through her hair.

"It was those creatures in black, wasn't it? We saw

them from the probes. We didn't understand. What are they?"

Tony turned to him. "They're . . . they're Erinye."

He'd said it automatically, without a second's consideration, as if it was the standard phrase, the commonplace that it would later become. And St. John understood; moving on from a simple nod to the core question, the only thing that mattered: "Must they be eliminated?"

"No." Recalling the depth of the Lady's mercy, he wondered what she would have done for the Erinye themselves, had she been given the chance. "But . . . it won't be easy."

"We can help. There are techniques." St. John gestured to the door. Tony glanced again at the bed, the last glimpse he would allow himself. She would be buried under her tree, the only fitting spot. "She has a daughter," he said hoarsely. "If you could—"

"Ah, but she's with us," St. John said. "Cariola informed us. We picked her up this morning. In fact . . ."

An uproar commenced outside the house, voices raised in surprise and confusion. Hurrying to the door, Tony saw all the men on their feet, hats in their hands, staring in stunned bewilderment at a small figure coming through the gate.

Tony felt the same shock they did. As much as he knew, as much as he'd been prepared. Her hair, her face, the way that she walked . . . It was the Dame of Midgard returned.

His face took on a new expression as he studied the ageless figure approaching him. An expression he was never to know about, through all the decades to come. An expression far beyond his years, stoic and composed, with a hint of brooding sadness overlying it. It was an expression much like Julia's when she first learned that she would be alone, much like that of the senators as they waited for the Goths to arrive.

He wore it during the crises that came during the reconstruction and the day that he ordered that the Rigs be assimilated after their rehabilitation. He wore it the many times he was voted out of office. He wore it often when dealing with Cary. He wore it when the Commonalty offered him the honor of full augmentation, telling them, "There are better things."

She came to him; out of everyone on that hill, she came to him. And as she met his eyes, he realized with certainty that he would always be the Lady's man.

He looked up a moment, taking in the slowly fading arc, the mirrors that had given them victory, the stars shining still. Then he raised his hand, accepting his first—and hardest—task.

"My name is Tony," he told her. And taking her hand, he led her up the hill on the path that her mother had walked.